BRUNO'S SECRET

A Novel of Intrigue

BY
ANDREW PARKIN

 FriesenPress

Suite 300 - 990 Fort St
Victoria, BC, V8V 3K2
Canada

www.friesenpress.com

Copyright © 2020 by Andrew Parkin
First Edition — 2020

All characters and events in this book are fictional, even though they could have existed.

All rights reserved.

No part of this publication may be reproduced in any form, or by any means, electronic or mechanical, including photocopying, recording, or any information browsing, storage, or retrieval system, without permission in writing from FriesenPress.

ISBN
978-1-5255-6165-8 (Hardcover)
978-1-5255-6166-5 (Paperback)
978-1-5255-6167-2 (eBook)

1. FICTION, THRILLERS

Distributed to the trade by The Ingram Book Company

> *O my small bark, your freight is wickedness!*
> Dante, *Purgatorio*, XXIII

> *I raised my own drink towards the sun,*
> *but it was opaque like many questions and let no light through.*
> Dick Francis, *Second Wind*

> *Wearing lip gloss and shooting enemies are not mutually exclusive.*
> Amber Smith, *Danger Close*

1

WORKING on his last job in Birmingham before moving into anonymity elsewhere, Agent Momo had entered the butcher's shop by a rear door. Satisfied he was alone on the premises, he glanced at the glowing dial of his Rolex watch. It was 3:15 a.m.

He grasped the heavy steel door handle of the big walk-in refrigerator. He was wearing thin gloves, the fingers and thumbs finished with a non-slip roughness inside and out, making it impossible for any trace of fingerprints to remain, even inside the gloves. He was pleased that another hefty handle on the door's inside surface suggested that nobody could get locked in the fridge by mistake.

Automatic lighting came on inside when the door opened. Cold air smelled of meat and fat.

Three sides of beef hung in the central aisle. Steaks hung above shelves to one side, and lambs' carcasses were stacked on shelves. Next to the door near his right hand was a brine barrel. He looked along the shelves and hooks. Dead meat!

He decided to see what was in the blood-and-water mixture of the brine barrel. Stooping, he felt around in it with one hand, shifting two ox tongues near the surface. He put in his other hand and grasped what felt like an ear. He put his other hand into the brine. Two ears. Human ears.

Next he grasped both ears. The back of the head seemed to float. A couple of ox tongues concealed most of it, but Momo saw the face, eyelids shut, mouth agape. The skin was puffy, pink, and seemed to be a plastic or rubber mask. It was not; Doctor Westlake had been dead for maybe a week.

Momo pulled out Westlake's head and almost dropped it, stifling an involuntary cry of horror. Blood and saltwater gushed from the open mouth, and more dropped from the ragged neck like red mucous, splashing back into the barrel.

Gripping the hair with one hand, Momo plunged his other hand back into the barrel. He felt the long curved tongues; they had rough skin, like his gloves. There was nothing else.

Momo's orders had been to search the shop and then plant some electronic bugs. Finding nothing unusual in the shop, he had hidden the bugs. After examining the fridge, he planned to leave. He thought it unlikely that anyone would find the bugs, at least for a few days, maybe longer. Nobody would know he had been there and that conversations were being monitored. But if they discovered the severed head was missing, they would know someone had entered the shop. Nevertheless, he decided to take it with him. Solihull would soon be reading the shop's babble and telephone chatter, recorded for analysis.

Momo preferred to be in the field, on the ground, in the action. Survival depended on careful planning based on knowing what was real. Clever guesswork and sound instinct were also essential, as were quick reflexes and a reasonable quota of luck. Analysis seemed crucial but remote. It could reveal unexpected connections but could also be entangled in faulty intelligence and disinformation from hostile sources. Sometimes major politicians relied on faulty or incomplete intel. People lied, and people died. Street smarts counted for a lot. Facts and tangible evidence were Momo's speciality. Yet he had read with great interest Professor Moghaddam's book about understanding the terrorists' point of view. He realized instinctively the importance of context in their motivation. The Muslim world's identity crisis was another factor.

As a schoolboy, Momo had suffered from taunts and bullying in Pakistani areas of Leeds and later in the Midlands. But he had understood the British context in which he, in an immigrant family, was growing to maturity. He had seen that the greatest good came from defending common humanity, decency, democratic politics, and toleration of lawful differences while others worked on the endemic social and economic problems as well as the tensions arising from waves of immigrants from different cultures. His anger at the wanton destruction of decency was a valuable asset in making him an effective agent and field operative. He knew the rule of British democratic law must be respected by all immigrant cultures and their offspring. His Anglo-Afghani mentor had picked up an Australian instructor's phrase: "Don't sweat the small stuff, but never ignore it." He had pointed out the necessity for directing controlled anger at those who deserved it, those who perverted Islam in order to gain money, power, and freedom to maim and kill in the name of Allah. Muhammed was not their real prophet, and Allah was not their real god. Their god had been reduced to a cowardly excuse for evil that was all too human.

Agent Momo realized what he must do. He was strong and wily and determined to bring down extremists. As a member of the British Special Forces, he had survived their extremely gruelling, rigorous training. Later he had gone under cover. His loyalty to the Crown was part of his life as an officer of the Crown. His admiration of Churchill, as champion of freedom and democracy, was part of his entire being. He also had a fierce loyalty to his British Muslim family and the moderate version of religion they practised. At the same time, he was a modern man, in some moods even agnostic. However, he would defend the monarch with his life. In every operation he felt he was using his life and his special skills to defend democracy—and what remained of British decency.

He was prepared to die, if it came to that, under Solihull's command. He had the deepest personal regard for Solihull. The man was a patriot of an England in which he and Momo had been born. As officers, both were defenders of the monarch, and as members of a secret unit, both had signed the Official Secrets Act. Their work was to defend a society that had its faults but was at least—usually—a tolerant democracy, leagues, even centuries, ahead of many other countries. Neither of them was sentimental about India and Pakistan. Both were appalled by what was transpiring every day in the Middle East and some African countries. Momo loved working with Solihull, and he hated what might be going on secretly in this suburban butcher's shop.

What had Dr. Westlake thought, if he had been capable of thought in his last moments of life? Had he blamed himself for betraying his country to those cruel power addicts in the Middle East? Momo assumed the terrorists had made a video of the beheading. They clearly had some further use for Westlake's head. Momo was not going to allow Muslim extremists to make another hideous video propaganda from the head of this man he had known as a dedicated scholar of Arabic. In fact, Westlake had been close to a deadly Muslim group for a few weeks in Birmingham. Then it was discovered that he was a double agent, working for the British as well as the terrorist cell. Momo reasoned that as soon as the head was missed, the terrorists would know they had to vanish. Solihull would just have to scoop them up or track them before they dispersed to become normal citizens again or perhaps leave the country for another haven, maybe even using British passports to go to any other haven they might have. After all, the shop would not be open until early Monday morning. Momo felt that despite alarm bells going off sooner or later for the terrorists, the proof of Westlake's fate was worth more to Solihull. And any further use of the head by the propagandists would be stopped. These butchers should know they were not in charge!

He glanced through the fridge doorway into the shop. A pile of plastic bags was on a counter nearby. He placed Westlake's head on the bags, closed the fridge door, and then put the head into a bag, opening another bag to contain the first one with its grisly burden. Double bagging would be safer.

He took an absorbent cloth from his pocket, wiped the door handle, and mopped up any traces of watery blood. Then he looked for a sawdust bin he had noticed earlier in a corner near a chopping block. Pocketing the cloth, he put some handfuls of sawdust into another plastic bag. Retracing his steps to the back door, he scattered sawdust to obliterate his footprints. No noise. Nobody was outside. He pulled the door closed behind him.

As if he were a man getting home from a long late-night shift, he walked back to the quiet side street. Then he turned a corner onto another street. A dog barked in the distance. Animals were relatively harmless. Humans were the problem.

A delivery van was parked farther along the street in the darker stretch between streetlamps. Momo tapped on the side of the vehicle once, then twice. A side door slid open. Agent Pike grinned, showing his sharp little teeth, and put away his squat automatic pistol. His lightweight headset was around his neck and unplugged, while his bald patch gleamed faintly in the van's lighted interior.

"Hop in, Sunshine. You were quick." Pike closed the side door again. They both slid into the front seats. Pike would drive.

"I was inside for less than eight minutes."

"Good one. Hey, what's in that bag? Don't tell me you've brought a sirloin roast back for the weekend!"

"Let's move. We need to get back to the nest. I have a present for Solihull."

The van moved slowly away, gathering speed when it joined a main road going toward a northern suburb called Great Barr.

Momo and Pike had worked together for well over a year. They had been particularly impressed by a French agent who had joined them in a major operation. She had posed as Momo's wife. Both men had wanted to get her into bed. Neither had been successful. She had saved Westlake's life. Momo thought it ironic that now, a few weeks later, he was carrying proof of Westlake's death.

They drove for ten minutes along streets wet from a recent shower and then turned into an underground car park beneath what appeared to be a modest low-rise apartment block. The four storeys of red-brick walls were like many others in Birmingham. There was nothing to indicate that behind the bricks were reinforced concrete walls.

Pike pushed a button on a key fob, and an iron gate went up. He drove into the underground parking area, waited for the gate to close fully, turned a corner, and waved at a sentry, who saluted him, then made a note in his book. The sentry worked in a bulletproof machine-gun post. Pike looked in the convex mirror high on the corner wall. It showed the gate and nobody loitering near it. Only then did he continue to the van's parking space near an elevator. They were inside Solihull's Birmingham headquarters.

2

BRIAN Atkins noticed a young woman silhouetted against the skyline. She was on a Roman road that the locals called the Ridgeway. He waved to her, and she returned the gesture. A hiker? She climbed over a dry-stone wall near the road and started across the sloping moorland toward his cottage. It had to be Alissa, whom he had heard about in the village. Now he saw her clearly as she approached. He was astonished by the rare physical beauty of her face. Her dark eyes were alert. Her nose straight and just the right size above her mouth and determined jaw. She was tall, lithe, and fit. Brian had been standing outside thinking about his work. Now he watched this lovely athletic woman moving fluidly toward him. She was inspiration itself.

Alissa Partridge noticed the isolated cottage of local stone had a slate roof that looked new. The window sills and squat front door gleamed with glossy white paint. A narrow, rutted track led from the cottage in a broad curve and vanished behind some wind-bent bushes. The morning sun shimmered behind a thin veil of cloud. The new warmth of June prompted her to unzip her dark-green jacket. On her hike across the moor up to the road, she had passed a stream near which a dead sheep was lying. She had not bothered to inspect it but would report it on her return to the village. A farmer might be missing it.

The man standing by the cottage smiled. She smiled back and, as she walked, took in more of the stone cottage. Beside it was a shed, perhaps a garage. Her path was just a narrow track. A wider one led to the Ridgeway from behind the buildings. She had tried to think about her real identity during her hike as she walked across the springy grass.

Some years before she'd come to be known as Alissa Partridge, when she was a Cambridge undergraduate. But her favourite name was one she rarely used: Kalitza. It recalled her Mediterranean family origins in Greece and Egypt rather than France or England. Her identity, however, had become international. She was the opposite of some tribal women, who were kept under tight control by customs and primeval thinking. Her code name in France as Agent Kim was now second nature. But would she ever go back to that world, now that she was Alissa once more?

A shadow from a cloud swept across the grass. Alissa heard the repeated cry of a seagull again. *The piercing mournful cry*, she thought, *probably gave Chekhov his idea for the tragicomedy of a young woman.*

"Hello there! Glorious day for a hike."

"Hello. You live here?"

The man had a lean, lightly tanned face, grey-blue eyes, and bright even teeth, his upper gums just showing when he smiled. His fair hair, brushed forward and cropped fairly short, had a few waves. *Handsome,* she thought. *Well, fairly handsome. Fit. Strong. Not a killer, but one never knows.*

"Yes," he said, "and it looks as though the weather will hold. I'm the art teacher, and I bet you're the new French teacher."

"How did you know that?"

"You're the woman who has made a buzz in the village. I visit the village shop, wait in a queue, and discover what's new! So, you see, you're the new teacher!"

"Where do I teach then?"

"Tomkyn Bridge."

"Yes, I do, as a matter of fact. Who runs the village shop? Mr. Parker?"

He smiled. "Nosey Parker, you mean? Oh, news travels fast around here, and you're the only coloured person I've seen recently, so I put two and two together."

"And scored four."

They grinned at each other. He held out his hand. "I'm Brian, Brian Atkins." His eyes looked at her as if he were wondering how to sketch her face.

Alissa shook his hand. He had strong hands. No wedding ring. No signet ring. She had once read that some British nobility did not wear such rings. Perhaps they considered it a bit vulgar, a bit "continental," or even just bad taste, like gold necklaces or bracelets on American men. She noted splashes of paint among the blond hairs on the backs of his hands.

"Alissa Partridge," she said. "So, you teach art. Where?"

"Where did you hear that?"

"You mentioned it a few seconds ago. Or did I hear it in the village shop, or was it elsewhere?" They shared another smile.

"Well, I paint up here, but I teach art parttime at a local grammar school. Keeps me off the streets."

"So, you're the painter who lives up in this cottage? Portraits, landscapes, still life?"

"May I divert you a little by showing you my studio? Well, my sheep farmer's hideaway converted. I have a few beers in the fridge."

"Well . . . I was about to knock to see if you were in. Actually, I heard in our dining hall about a painter living somewhere up here."

"You're really interested in paintings?"

"Certainly. I'm not guaranteeing I'll buy anything. Just interested to see them first."

"Okay. Where are you going next?"

"To the village shop to buy one of your works! No, actually I'm off to Ennerdale Water—and for a spot of lunch at the pub in Ritherdon." She smiled. "I'll probably discover a lot more about myself in the pub."

"You can bank on that." He laughed. "The pub isn't all that far from the lake. Or from here. Oh, I'd like ...to show you an idea. I'd like your spontaneous reaction. Immediate response. It might help. I . . . er . . . thought I knew where I was going with it, but I got stuck yesterday. Then a flash of luck—and it's finished."

"Sounds intriguing, Mr. At—"

"Call me Brian. It seems odd using family names up here in the wilds."

"Okay. Call me Alissa. Let's go into the studio, then?"

"Be my guest."

"What do you paint?"

"Anything I'm curious about. Do come in and have a look."

"Okay, but I don't want to be late for that pub lunch."

"You won't be. I promise." He opened the front door with a Yale key.

Alissa was surprised when they went inside. The interior was full of light instead of the gloom she had expected. The air was heavy with the smell of oil paints. A large portion of the side wall had been made into a great studio window, from which she could see a slope of the hill with its green expanse sprawling down to the gleam of a distant lake. There was a large wooden trestle table, burdened with papers, pots, and some small rocks heavy enough to use as paperweights. Nearby was an easel, cupboards, brushes in pots, and all the paraphernalia one would expect in a painter's studio.

"We can get to the road in just a few minutes from here," Brian said as she rested her hand on the large wooden table. "There's a stink of oil. Hope you don't mind."

"It's what I'd expect."

"I also use acrylic, ripolin, house paint, water colours, charcoal, pastels . . .but I'll get you a beer."

Ducking his head, he went through a doorway from which the door had been removed and into a scullery, where she saw the cooker, fridge, and a small counter. A frosted glass door at the far end led into a pantry or maybe a toilet. He reached into the fridge.

She called after him, saying she just wanted a glass of water. Then she turned away to look out the large window again, drawn by the peaceful feeling of space, liberty, and natural beauty. Behind the studio and to one side was a paddock with a few sheep munching at the grass, oblivious of the fact that their fleeces were red, blue, green, and yellow. Then she saw a ram painted gold. The golden fleece!

3

A British agent known as Carpenter had heard from an Irish agent. The big boys wanted him on the west coast of Ireland. London had sent him in a small jet. Some kind of flap was on, he guessed. *Well, ours but to do and die*, he thought—but on a need-to-know basis.

Carpenter always enjoyed his brief exchanges with the Irishman. The authorities in Britain and the Irish Republic acknowledged their cooperation by Dublin's naming the Irish agent Walrus. They were in a great tradition. After all, a senior Royal Air Force Officer had once been known as White Rabbit.

The Walrus and the Carpenter were sitting on a deserted headland that overlooked the sea stretching toward the Aran Islands.

"Is it a good day for oysters?" the Carpenter asked, smiling.

"It's a grand day for oysters!" the Walrus replied, stroking his handlebar moustache. "Our friends, the coastguard fellas, fished up a parcel or two from the Atlantic after a storm."

"Oysters in a parcel?"

"Body parts, alas. Dismembered." The Walrus shook his head and grimaced.

"Do I have access to see?" the Carpenter asked, suddenly serious.

"I can arrange that. It's no trouble at all. Fancy a Guinness?"

"You bet. I'll draw a smile in the foam's head. Solihull will know some key facts already, I expect."

"Ah, I wouldn't bank on it."

They exchanged the raised eyebrows that people often do when thinking of their seniors. Nonetheless, both men respected Solihull. He had directed security operations in the British Midlands with considerable skill and had dismantled many plots against innocent civilians. He was generally acknowledged as a tower of strength.

"Solihull's a force of nature," the Carpenter said, lying back on the short grass of the headland to contemplate a large white cloud.

"He is that," the Walrus agreed. "Talking of nature's forces, have you ever seen that calm blue water out there get into a bad mood?"

"Can't say I have. I seem to bring good weather with me whenever I visit. But I've had some choppy crossings on the ferry from Fishguard."

"Well, it's a good job you won't be crossing the choppy Irish Sea on a ferry when you see what's in those parcels."

"Human nature, still red in tooth and claw."

"Yeah. Let's push off. You want to consult with the coast guard, the medical people, and that Dublin analyst, I expect. Correct me if I'm wrong."

"You're never wrong, Walrus. But we must share a dish of oysters before I go back. When I'm on my way, I'll read the latest gen you might have on suspected Islamic terrorists over here."

***

Solihull was pleased with his operation on the Birmingham canal. A French agent, supposedly the Moroccan wife of his local agent, Momo, had been key. Solihull glanced at the papers on his desk and then sighed. *Never get romantically involved with agents, especially foreign ones.* Then he smiled. He had been using Special Branch to supply the details and the local police to mop up the minor players in that particular Birmingham terrorist network. *Doctor Westlake made a right fool of himself,* he thought, *and compromised the Brummie team.*

He looked at a message from Carpenter: "Westlake assassinated. Body parts found in Irish waters have been identified by DNA samples."

He realized at once why he had been informed of the discovery even while Carpenter was on his way to Ireland. His team had interrogated Westlake. That silly intellectual, however brilliant an Arabist, had been a double agent. The star woman agent from Paris he thought of as the "frog lady" had saved the turncoat when she found him drugged, pinioned, and fitted with an explosive waistcoat. He had been interrogated and then released with travel paid to Tasmania, where he had hoped to lie low. The British knew he had been abducted en route and had disappeared. The silly man had not followed their instructions to the letter. He had ducked out of his safe hotel and vanished. Westlake had known some few details and two or three agents' code names. These scraps of information had been quickly rendered harmless, code names having been changed even before Westlake was released. Nonetheless, photographs he *might* have taken with his missing cell phone could now be in dangerous hands.

Solihull did not feel sorry for Westlake; he was more worried about the damage the traitor had possibly caused. He'd advised Momo to avoid his usual mosque by changing his supposed workplace and job. It was more practical to attend a mosque in another town.

Momo would change his hairstyle and appearance as much as possible before going to another mosque. He would also change his name and address. Identities came and went, as did agents' code names, and the agents themselves. Momo had worked once more under his old code name. Now he was Agent Ali. However, Solihull had ensured his star agent had a discreet backup on the lookout for shadows and trouble. The retrieval of the severed head meant he had put Momo/Ali in charge of the interception of the Halal butcher ring and its contacts. It had been a brilliant success. His promotion was on the cards. Solihull clicked his thumbnail against his front teeth. He decided to contact his French and American friends to compare notes on the Westlake damage fallout.

***

In one of his secure rooms in Paris headquarters, Control, known to his closest colleagues as Monsieur Martin or even Hervé, his Christian name, was listening to Solihull, his British colleague, on a scrambled line.

"So, how was it identified?" Control asked, pursing his lips. "Ah, yes . . . but flayed? Not half-eaten by fish? Oh, wrapped in parcels. Hmm . . ."

Control listened, and then, after Solihull's warning that Kim could be badly compromised, the line went dead.

Flayed! Bruno's work? Possibly. Probably. Given the current suspicions, likely or highly likely. Control was tense and thinking hard. He envisaged Westlake's horrific death. He shivered. Were they sending a message? No. It was sadistic madness. Why dump the body in the Irish Sea? Solihull's interrogators might have some new information for him in due course. Were some terrorists on their way to the United States by sea? A small craft? Easy to get a body on board.

He got up from his antique desk and walked over to a bookcase. He'd contact

Harry at the US embassy and warn him of a possible new batch of terrorists heading for the North American coast.

He turned and looked at his desk. It was not museum quality, but he loved it. His father had used it from before the war until his death. He had unrolled maps on it and planned Resistance operations against the Nazi occupiers. Yes, Hervé knew Bruno had to be trapped, if he was, in fact, a traitor, and he had to be brought in alive, if possible. It was a matter of softly, softly... But Bruno had done impeccable work to date. All the same, there were some strange factors. Bruno had been in London at the time of the grenade attack in a London hotel from which Kim had narrowly escaped. And he had been unable to shadow Westlake consistently when that English traitor had appeared in France. Oh yes, Bruno had recently been in the United States. And now Westlake was dead. And a small boat might already be beached somewhere along the Canadian or American coastline. They had to figure out a way to limit the damage, and quickly. Security? *There is no security,* Control thought. Bruno was one of his most effective agents, and it was difficult to admit he had been turned.

However, Control knew it was a risk to be confronted. It was a hunch picked up from little coincidences. He had no conclusive proof. Was Bruno a latter-day Philby? If so, how to trap him? The lovely Kim could do it. But Control had given her a summer leave as a reward for her success in Birmingham. And where was she? Control didn't know. He'd have to find her

He would start with Bruno. Yes. He could—would—ask Bruno to find Kim and bring her back to Paris. He would leave France if the trail led that way. If she disappeared before Bruno could get her to Paris, it might mean Kim was lost, probably dead, perhaps kidnapped or killed by Bruno, if he was, in fact, a double agent. Oh God, she mustn't come to any harm!

He took off his jacket and put it over the back of his chair, then sat at his desk again. He ran his hands through his short hair and then sat with his elbows on the desk, his knuckles on pressing against his temples. *I must not let Kim be harmed. I'm afraid for her.* He resolved once more to get Kim to join him in Planning.

If Bruno killed Kim and then vanished into the sandy wastes of North Africa, Control would have lost two of his best agents. Bruno would have to be stopped before he could disappear to Syria, Iraq, or wherever. But if Kim killed Bruno, it would mean Kim had won, his best agent was still operational, and a double agent was defunct. Control knew he was playing a dangerous game, using agents who could be useful elsewhere. The more senior one was, the more one had to play with lives and maybe sacrifice. But doubts about Bruno justified it all. Bruno's contacts could be brought in for interrogation too if he proved to be a traitor. It was a risky affair, but Control's business was risky by definition. The best scenario was for Bruno to prove loyal, the next best if Kim brought in Bruno alive, especially if he was proven to be treacherous. But he had to let Kim know what she must do. Bruno had to be tracked and watched closely.

Control got up and poured himself some coffee. If Bruno had killed Westlake, he might be feeling so invincible and clever that he could slip up. Who could neutralize Bruno? Who could he count on for that? Bruno was difficult to read, for he was by turns passionate or cold as a snake. He seemed always to know a little more than he was saying. But as Control looked into the dark gleaming surface of his coffee, he had an idea.

4

"**WELL,** what do you think?" Brian asked, holding out a bottle of beer. "What do you think about these coloured sheep?"

"Cheers!" Alissa clinked his bottle with her glass of water. "Amazing. Unexpected. Great! Why? I mean, why did you do it?"

Brian thought for a second or two. "I was reading about a sheep, its wool dyed with henna, in a book about Egypt. It was sort of an advertisement for a locally famous courtesan. I simply extended the idea to make a kind of art effect."

"Do you keep a few sheep then?"

"No. I borrowed them from Barney, a local farmer. We're having an arts festival in St. Bees and trying to involve as many sections of the community as possible. I'm trying to do something with the sheep farmers."

"What are you going to do with these sheep of many colours?"

"We thought we'd have a whole flock of them, different colours, herded by a green shepherd, made up totally green in green clothes, and two black-and-white sheepdogs. Do you think it'll work?"

"Well, visually I think it's a wonderful idea. It depends on what they do, of course. Do people come up here to see it all?"

He took a swig of beer. "I thought I'd have the sheep all hidden behind a ridge on a slope above the arts festival space. At an appointed moment, with a boy in blue blowing a cow's horn, a shepherd in white trousers, shirt, and hat with a huge orange cloak will appear on the skyline and blow a horn in answer. It will be theatrical and medieval yet modern. And then the green man and his black-and-white border collies with the multi-coloured flock will appear, and the dogs will herd the sheep down the slope in great moving splashes of colour."

"Hmm . . . Action painting with a dramatic difference? It's all done with living creatures too. Painting in motion! It should be a great spectacle. When will it happen? Will it be part of next weekend's activities?"

"Yes, if the sheep farmers agree to give me enough sheep."

"I'm sure they will, Brian. This could make national headlines—if those fat cats in London have any sense."

"Hope so. If I were known to them already, they would make a big song and dance of it. But I'm obscure. Anyway, we make final plans on Tuesday."

"That's cutting it a bit fine, isn't it?"

"We can do what we need to do in the time available. It's a matter of confidentiality too because some of the effect is in the surprise." He took another swig of beer.

"Then why are you telling me?" She always valued the element of surprise.

"I'm excited by it, and I think I can trust you. Don't ask me why. I just do."

"I'll keep mum. You can trust me. Lips sealed." Alissa smiled, keeping her lips close together.

"If the local paper were to describe in detail what I'm planning, people would be expecting too much," he concluded.

"What about animal rights protestors? Will they be outraged by it?"

"If they are, they'll be wrong. This is all washable colour. It's no more than a bit of mud, if you like. I just hope it doesn't rain! The organizers say the weekend of the festival should be fine according to the long-range forecast."

"I'll keep my fingers crossed. Now, are you going to show me some of your pictures?"

"Absolutely. Follow me." He walked to a large cupboard across the room and then handed her an art folder of thick green-and-black marbled card tied at the top by a ribbon. "Here. Look through this, and I'll bring out some more things I have in the cupboard."

Alissa walked over to the table, took a drink of water, and then put her glass down on the paint-splashed wood. She took the folder to the big window and untied the ribbon. Leafing through a series of watercolours, all of them moody landscapes peopled by men and women riding naked on horseback, she stopped suddenly. One image struck her as something she could live with and always find fascinating. It was a moorland scene vibrating with different shades of green with a splash of purple to one side toward which three horses galloped, their bodies fashioned from planes of black, warm brown tones, and vivid yellow stripes. Their knees were exaggeratedly knobbly, their tails curved upright like broad mirror images of "s" shapes of intense orange and brown, and their riders were naked, two men and a woman, cubist in technique but with faces flattened and effaced as if by centuries of inclement weather.

They are at one, she thought, *with the old, weathered headstones and crosses in the local graveyards.* The picture was signed with one word, "Quint." It was undated.

"I like this one best," she murmured.

Brian looked over her shoulder. She smelled the beer on his breath. "It's the best one," he said."My favourite."

"Is it called 'Quint'?"

"It isn't. I haven't put the title there, but it's on the back.'Point to Point.' 'Quint' is my nom de brush, if you can call it that."

"Why 'Quint'? Henry James's ghost story, 'The Turn of the Screw'?"

"No. I never thought of that. It's my mother's maiden name—Quincy, actually. Brian Atkins seems too long, and B. Atkins reminds me of my schoolboy nickname, 'Batkins,' if the other boys were being polite, 'Battykins' if they were teasing. And Quincy is a bit too familiar for me. See what I mean?"

"Yes. I'll drink to Quint. It's more memorable than Atkins, I think. How much do you want "You can have it for fifty pounds. Unframed." He looked at her as if he had said something terrible.

"Done. Don't look so surprised, or I'll have to start bargaining with you to beat your prices down!"

"I'm just pleased."

"Will you write your name and date and give it a title on a proper bill, so I have a good provenance for it?"

"Of course."

Brian took the piece of artist's paper from her, inspecting his picture as if seeing it for the first time. "God, it's good!" he said. "How about 'Hide on Hide' as a title rather than 'Point to Point'? After all, the riders and horses are naked."

"Brilliant! I like it." *How long must I hide?* Alissa wondered. *I should contact Control. Oh, he can sweat a bit.*

Brian put her newly acquired painting into a large paper carrier bag while Alissa gave him two twenties and a ten-pound note. Brian was watching her closely, even minutely inspecting her. She looked up and caught his moment of intense vision.

"Seen enough?" she demanded in a Yorkshire accent.

He laughed. "I'd like to draw you. Charcoal."

"Nude?"

"You said it, not me! If you'd allow it, yes. If not, clothed."

"I'll allow it, but only if you leave out my face. I don't want nudes of me identified by girls, parents, or head teachers, if you see what I mean."

"Absolutely."

"And I don't want the lines filled in to make it obvious that I'm coloured. Just a nude, as if it's any white model."

"OK."

"Can I trust you, Brian?"

"Yes, of course. I'm professional, and I teach too, remember, for bread and butter. I wouldn't want any disputes, lawsuits or anything like that. No monkey tricks. Too much trouble. Not worth it. I'm a painter, not a lecherous politician."

"Let's do it."

"Now?"

"Yes, I'm willing. Wait for another day, and it will be different."

"You're right. You can undress behind that screen. Then you can make yourself comfortable on the armchair. I'll adjust the light."

She went behind the screen while Brian lowered some venetian blinds at the big window. He adjusted the slats so they tilted upward. Anyone looking in would see nothing of the room but the ceiling. He turned up his recently installed heating. Alissa emerged from behind the screen and sat on a dining table chair, one of her arms resting along its high back, one foot on the floor and one leg bent, her foot resting on the other knee.

"Marvellous. God, Alissa, you're... lovely. Now turn your head slightly away from me to look at the picture on the wall behind the couch. That way I get the curve of your neck and not your face. I'll also change your hairstyle. People certainly won't know it's you."

She did as he said and then heard the charcoal scratching on his block of paper.

"Perfect," he murmured. "You're a goddess, Alissa, do you know that?"

"I'm handsome, yes. Bloody lovely yes. Goddess, no."

She liked the sound of the charcoal as he worked. *He's been married, of course. It's remarkable that such an artist should be hidden away in this bit of Cumberland.*

"Do you have an agent?" she asked, thinking he might have an agent of a different kind without knowing it.

"Not yet, but I think I may have just managed to get one. She's excited about the acrylics she's seen in the few exhibitions where I've placed work. Thinks I can sell in the US and Japan. Oh, and Germany."

"Really? That's wonderful. You don't sound super excited though. It could be a breakthrough."

"Yeah, but I have a funny feeling she wants me as her next husband!"

"And you're married?"

"No. She is though, and she's, as she put it, 'pissed off' by her present hubby."

"And you take it you're in a kind of danger zone?"

"I think so."

"Tricky."

Alissa wanted to scratch the back of her head. She decided to obey the urge.

"Hold it right there, Alissa!"

"You want my arm up there?"

"Yes. It lifts your breast and makes it more . . . lovely."

"Is this going to be an erotic picture, Brian?"

"It is. In fact it's almost . . . finished. If you like it, I hope we can do a series."

"I can move?"

"Of course you can. Now I'm just dotting an 'I'. Come and take a look."

She moved onto the sofa as he held out the sketching block. She was so physically perfect that he was breathless with longing for her. He turned away to drop the charcoal into an old shoebox on the table, then went into the kitchen to wash his hands.

Alissa debated with herself: should she go to him now and take him, make love right there straight away? No, it could wait. She wanted lunch. She could tell he wanted her badly. Brian was not thinking of lunch! The atmosphere of unspoken desire was unmistakable. Was it wise to have a fling? No! She had some feeling for him as a person, not some male hunk. If she had to vanish, it would be tough for both of them. Keep him on hold! It wasn't a case of a desperate professional need, like that time in Hong Kong.

She put the drawing on the table and got dressed. The sketch was several lines fashioned into a stunning knot of desire and curving physical beauty. She turned, and he was looking at her through the doorway as he dried his hands.

"It's lovely, Brian. And the message is clear. But lunch! I don't want to miss it."

"And what's the message, Alissa?"

"It says: I want this. I want it badly." She smiled.

There was a sudden banging on the front door.

"Brian? It's Barney!"

Brian went outside. After a few minutes, he came back in.

"That was my farmer friend. One of his sheep is dead. He's lending me quite a number for the festival."

She met Brian's eyes. *They seem to look through me into some depth I cannot myself see,* she thought. In this he seemed as cold and penetrating as Control. *Is a dead sheep a warning?*

"I want to paint you," he said. "Oils."

"I'm flattered. But I really do have to go. I want my lunch!"

Brian laughed. He glanced at his watch. "May we have lunch together then? I can walk with you, or we could take my car."

"Let's walk, if we have time," Alissa said.

They set out together after Brian locked the door.

"Do you always lock the door, Brian?"

"Usually. There's nothing much that would interest any thieves. But mindless vandals could have fun with expensive paint."

"What about non-local yobbos killing sheep for fun?"

"You're probably right. But it's not usual. Stealing sheep would be more likely."

They soon reached the pub in Ritherdon, eliciting a few surreptitious looks from the regulars. Brian had shepherd's pie, and Alissa chose sausage and mash. They had rhubarb crumble for dessert. Alissa had a glass of Paul Autard's Côtes-du-Rhône Villages red with her main dish. She remembered drinking Autard's excellent Chateauneuf-du-Pape at his *domaine* in France. She was surprised that the landlord of acountry pub in Cumbria knew about Autard's wine. Brian had a pint of bitter. They both had coffee with fresh cream to finish.

They talked about their work as teachers. Brian seemed more interested in studying Alissa's face than in details such as where she grew up and the kind of background "facts" she would have trotted out to be in line with her Alissa Partridge role.

Alissa discovered that Brian was an only child. His widowed mother lived in St. Bees. Brian's father had died of a heart attack five years earlier. And Brian, unmarried, had gone out with only a couple of girlfriends before he started work as a teacher. Art college entanglements had not been something he wanted, nor had his sexual experiences turned into anything lasting.

Local teachers, Brian told her, were conspicuous targets for gossip. It made for celibacy until the right partner appeared. As they chatted, Brian wondered, was Alissa the answer, the right partner?

By the time they had walked back to the cottage it was just after 2:30 p.m. Alissa had not insisted on following her plan to go as far as the lake. She could do it later, on the following weekend. They had talked naturally, as if they had been friends for some time. She knew quite a lot now about Brian, but he knew little about her. It would have to stay that way.

They went back into the cottage. Brian insisted that he make them a cup of tea or another coffee. Alissa looked again at the charcoal sketch.

"Brian, it's very, very good. You have a girl sitting on a chair looking away from the viewer, yet her body seems to convey a moment of intimacy and calm, tinged with sadness. And desire."

He smiled and took her hand, then led her to what appeared to be a floor-to-ceiling door of a pine corner cupboard. He opened the door to reveal a small flight of steps curving up. Brian released her hand. She followed him up the stairs. They emerged into a loft with beams and a large double bed. A spotless white duvet was spread over it. Beyond the bed was a door. He turned to her. "The door over there opens into a bathroom with a walk-in shower."

"This is a calm and beautiful little room, and I bet your bed is comfy."

He grinned and kissed her briefly on the lips.

"No. Not now. Maybe another time."

"Soon? Something I can look forward to?" he queried, a hint of suspicion in his voice.

"I don't know. I don't make promises, but I feel we are friends already. We can keep business and pleasure separate, surely?" She smiled, her face alight with the pleasure of being there with him.

"You're right. When shall we meet again?"

"Can't say. What time do you wake up in the morning?"

"I always get up at about seven or thereabouts to get to the school when I'm teaching. Then I get home at about five. Other days I just have breakfast and then work."

"How many days a week do you teach?"

"Sometimes three, sometimes two. Depends on the timetable."

"Lucky man. I teach every day, Monday to Friday, and I have pistol shooting most Saturday mornings."

"Pistol shooting! But you can learn that in a morning. Why every Saturday?"

Alissa smiled. "If I trudge up here when I have some free time, you wouldn't mind? If you were working on a picture, I'd sit and look through a portfolio or an art book."

"Mind?" He laughed. "Will you, Alissa, really?"

"I might. Really. I'll climb up here when I can get away. Can't say exactly which day or evening."

"I'll never be able to sleep wondering if you're coming!"

"Don't worry. All this fresh air makes one sleep, I'd think."

Alissa turned and glanced from the large window at the deserted hillside. Not a sheep in sight. She remembered the dead sheep.

"Well, I'd better get going. I have things I must do. I'll be back."

They kissed. He held her close. It seemed to Brian that she melted into him so naturally. He did not want to let her go. But he had to do so. *Yes, she would be back.*

She waved as she walked away with her newly acquired picture, "Hide on Hide," then wended her way down the hill towards the school.

On that bright, clear day it felt good to be alive up in the Cumberland hills. Gazing down at Tomkyn Bridge School, Alissa realized she had taken her leave from France and that secret world behind the cyclorama of business and international affairs, and she had found an interesting man whose work she admired. She saw his friendly, open manner and his determined pursuit of beauty in his drawings and paintings. Well, she reasoned, she had an effective cover—so far. But the village gossip was a decided nuisance.

The dead sheep was also disturbing. She smiled as she had a mental image of Monsieur Martin, her elegant boss in the Paris headquarters. He of course wanted her to be his mistress. Dear Hervé! He called it "joining me in Planning." Did he already have a wife and family? Did he practise family planning? She laughed. Maybe. His agents certainly didn't know anything of him outside work. Had he sent someone to find her? Or was she a target for an Islamic terrorist? Perhaps. A dead sheep could be nothing or everything. She was due back towards the end of July. Decisions could wait a few days.

Alissa had almost reached the school. Brian, she allowed, was an unexpected advantage, but was he a potential husband? Maybe. Maybe not. In any event, a husband only if she could sever herself permanently from her secret world. She would find out within a week or so. Meanwhile, she had to be careful. The shouts of girls on a hockey field at Tomkyn Bridge School were strangely comforting.

5

HERVÉ Martin and Agent Miranda returned to his secure sitting room cum office in Paris headquarters after dinner for two in the vast halls of Le Train Bleu restaurant at the Gare de Lyon. They had looked like a fond elder brother with a favourite sister. He offered her a good cognac, but she declined. Control swirled his Chateau de Montifaud gently in a balloon brandy glass. He switched his probing blue-grey eyes toward the young blond agent.

"Miranda, I want you to find Agent Kim for me. Look at this photo of her. She has gone to ground somewhere unknown to me while taking a long-deserved leave. But she has not made contact recently. I don't worry about her but...well, yes, frankly, I am worried. Slightly. Most likely she is in England, though our friends over there have no info."

He put down his glass and tapped a pencil on the desktop.

"I'll do my best, Control. Kim is becoming a bit of a legend." Miranda was ready for the assignment. She took another mouthful of water. She looked at Kim's photograph and memorized Kim's face. Easy. Kim was a "bomb" all right.

He resumed the tapping of his pencil. *He's afraid of losing Kim,* Miranda thought.

"She's very, very clever. But that doesn't mean she's bulletproof. Well, I'm sure you'll find her. Contact me, but please don't contact her unless you need to or she's clearly in danger. You'll know when to consult with her. If anyone else seems to be looking for her, make sure you watch her back as well as your own. And let me know. I'd hate her to be harmed. If she's *in extremis,* be sure to bring her back alive. If necessary, eliminate any threat to her."

Miranda was eager to take on this impossible job. *Would he hate me to be harmed? Yes, I think so.*

She smiled at Control. He was rather "dishy" as bosses go. "Depend on me."

"I think an agent called Bruno will also be tracking Kim. Here's a recent photo of him. I want you to keep after him and let him lead you to Kim. If or when he finds her, you must be ready to help Kim bring Bruno back. If possible, I want Bruno back here alive. He may be playing a double game. If so he'll try to kill Kim and you. He's unpredictable. You must deal with him as best you can. If you must, be merciless towards him." Control was unsmiling, his voice betraying an inner tension. He swirled the brandy in his glass but did not sip.

"Understood."

Miranda felt suddenly cold. She studied the picture of a gaunt man with a skull-like face. His eyes looked straight at the camera, as if wanting to destroy it. How could she forget this face? Control was worried. She had to be extra careful. Bruno looked ruthless. If he proved to be a traitor, she could count on his ruthlessness to be directed at anyone getting in his way.

Control showed her a street map on the wall. He prodded the relevant point on the map, and a three-dimensional image of Bruno's building and the bistro at ground level appeared.

"That's where Bruno lives. It's a place to start, but don't go inside the building. Visit the bistro if it's worthwhile. You might see Bruno there. Who knows? Well, I must do a few things, so I'll wish you luck."

"Thanks, Control. I'll be careful."

"Oh, call me, Martin, or Hervé. Good luck."

"Thanks, Monsieur Martin."

Miranda and Control both stood up. She offered her face to be kissed, and then Control held her in his arms for a moment.

"Take great care, my dear. And keep in touch."

She looked back at him from the doorway and then closed the door behind her.

Miranda has great charm and excellent potential in this trade or metier, Control thought as the young agent left. He finished his brandy. Its subtle presence remained after he had swallowed the last drop. He closed his eyes and thought about his little plan. He had given Miranda a difficult agenda to accomplish. The difficulties would appear as she improvised, searching for Kim and trying to unlock Bruno's mystery. He hoped she would be as unpredictable as Bruno himself. Whatever extra resources she might call for, he would provide, whatever the cost.

6

FROM her family's background as Russian *émigrés*, Miranda spoke Russian like a native with a St. Petersburg accent. Her French was that of a smart parisienne. Her new mission pleased and intrigued her. As a child, she'd loved puzzles and had played chess with her uncle, Dmitri Aleksandrovich. She remembered her elation when, at age twelve, she had beaten him. It had been a long and complex match. She still had a chess player's mind. Now that her uncle was dead, she played a rather different game as an agent, yet still specializing in unexpected knight's moves and disguised mates.

Oh, Bruno, what's your secret? She imagined he was going to be a real problem. Monsieur Martin had advised her to follow him. He would, in theory, lead her to Kim. But Miranda thought of a different opening to the match. If she could locate Kim quickly, it would be better than waiting perhaps a week or more for Bruno to find her and then follow him. The Americans might know where Kim had gone. She might be able to pull in a favour from them. Then she would lead Bruno some of the way until, using a knight's move, she would evade him and his pawns or stooges. And when she moved Bruno would be exposed to her queen, Kim. As Bruno paused and then carried on, she would observe, report on any accomplices, and then follow Bruno distancing himself from Kim. Then she would make a few more knight's moves. Perhaps she would castle and be ready for a discovered check!

It would be a great advantage to this "now you see me now you don't" routine if she could flush out Bruno's contacts, topple some pieces one by one, and pluck them off the board before the calculated checkmate. Above all, she valued sudden changes in her plan. Bruno might be unpredictable. Well, so was she. "Unpredictable, that's what you are . . ." she hummed to herself.

Miranda's next thought was to meet an American she had worked with once before. He was close to early retirement. Was he her king? No, that was Control. Her American seemed to know everything that was worth knowing and had contacts with many agents, both American and foreign. Miranda knew him as Harry. He was her "castle." She found him attractive, a *dishy* man, even though he was in his mid-forties. He was a good defence. At the moment he was in Paris at the American embassy. She left him a message.

***

When Miranda arrived, Harry was already at their rendezvous, sitting at a small round table for two on the sidewalk terrace and studying a plasticized drinks menu with garish illustrations of popular cocktails. He glanced along the street both ways as Miranda walked out of a side street and reached the Brasserie Berthelot. She wore a fawn overcoat with gilt buttons. Her crimson neck scarf was fun, and the finely layered cut of her hair was neat and perky. Her hair glistened slightly. It had just started to rain.

Harry stood up and kissed her on each cheek. Her skin was pleasantly cool from the late-afternoon air. He looked over her shoulders as he kissed her. Nobody had followed her. Nothing but passers-by outside. But Bruno's flat was in the building above the brasserie, according to a friend in the US embassy. Was that why she had chosen it? Maybe. Bruno kept an eye on the comings and goings when he had nothing better to do. And she would keep an eye on Bruno, if her boss asked her to do that. She sat down opposite Harry. He held her hand on the tabletop.

"It's wonderful to see you again, Harry!" She was slightly breathless, and her eyes met his as she pursed her lips in a kissing gesture and blew a kiss towards him.

"I always enjoy meeting you, Miranda. That's three *bisous* in all. What'll you have, besides my admiration and total attention?"

"Well, after that, how could I not, so to speak, couple my drink with yours? Have you decided? I like your lightweight suit. Dashing!"

"Why thanks, Miranda. It's light but strong. A Langley special. I thought we could have Sex on the Beach."

"A bit cold for that, even at the end of May, but why not?"

"Why not indeed. Let's do it."

As if by remote control, a waiter appeared. His black trousers and waistcoat went well with his spotless white shirt.

"Would you like drinks, sir?"

"Yes, we'll both have Sex on the Beach."

"Yes, Sex on the Beach twice," Miranda added, keeping a straight face.

The three of them laughed.

"Sorry," Miranda continued. "I expect you've heard that a thousand times already."

"Eh oui, madame," the waiter said. He winked and then walked with a sprightly tread to the bar to place their order.

Harry and Miranda continued holding hands across the table, chatting about the next French Open at the Roland Garros tennis centre. When their drinks arrived, Miranda waited, musing over her glass before saying anything or drinking.

The two of us, when we reach for the concertina-bent plastic straws to sip cocktails bartenders have named Sex on the Beach, and glance into each other's eyes, it's then that I see the white sands of his retirement dream. Dreams leave trails like footprints broken by shallow ridges carved by restless seas, those salty tides we call desire.

"Penny for them," Harry said, looking at her intently with his light-grey eyes. Miranda shrugged and smiled. Her cornflower-blue eyes shone as she shook her head.

"Oh, nothing."

"Come on, you can tell me."

"I was just remembering when I last had sex on the beach!"

"The drink?"

"The real thing. It was in Goa, last November."

"Wow. Holiday, I suppose. You must be happy."

"No. Sad. My friend has died since."

"Oh, I'm so sorry. Sorry I intruded on your thoughts."

"Don't be. It's no good brooding. I was also thinking you must be planning your retirement."

"Dead right. I'm allowed early retirement. In fact, I want to retire to a quiet, sandy beachside village, do some fishing, restore a vintage car or two, keep a boat. That kinda stuff. But I still have a while to go. I'm no spring chicken, but I'm not that old, am I?"

She grinned. "Are you married?"

"Not yet. Difficult in our job. We agents don't *know* each other. We work together. We look out for each other. We try not to die, even if others have to. And we don't get personal, unless..."

"Unless?" She raised her eyebrows. Harry blew her a kiss and waggled his ears. They laughed.

Miranda nodded. "I know. It's best. I want to survive and retire too."

"Well, young lady, you have long days ahead of you. You're smart. Just try to be smarter than the opposition."

"In fact, I was wondering if you could help me."

"Oh boy! What now?"

"I need to find one of our agents who has gone on leave and also gone to ground."

"What makes you think I can help?"

"I thought your people kept at least one eye on all of us, allies or not." Harry looked at her, unsmiling. She was serious. "Sorry if that seemed too 'leftie'—or personal," she added. "You might have heard something. Little birds tweeting away?"

Harry thought for a moment. The Brits had contacted him asking for cooperation just the other day. He had also heard of an Agent Kim that Paris seemed to have lost.

His train of thought was interrupted when he saw someone across the street. He blinked his right eye, the lens of which was, in fact, a tiny camera. It photographed an immaculately dressed Middle Eastern man, who emerged from a Lamborghini convertible. It looked custom made. Harry had not seen this exact model before.

"Okay," Harry said, "I'll help all I can. But you'll have to think seriously about joining us. Langley calling, Miranda!"

"Not that again!" She smiled at him, then sampled her cocktail. It was refreshing.

"Look, meet me tomorrow by the rowing boats in the Bois de Vincennes. For lunch, say at noon, and we'll maybe have a bite to eat in a rowing boat. Tell me more about this absent agent."

"Late May in the Bois de Vincennes? Row boats, picnic? You're on."

They finished their drinks. Miranda and Harry got up, kissed twice on each cheek, and Miranda left.

Harry paid their bill and then strolled outside. The immaculate man was talking to a white woman. Harry photographed the car's licence plate and the woman. He stopped to look in the window of a toy shop. Then he turned to look at a bus that passed by, his eye recording the conversation between the man and the woman. They both got into the expensive car. A moment later, it sidled out into the passing traffic.

Harry realized the car's lack of diplomatic plates meant it could well have been rented from a specialty car agency. It was worth checking out. He did not recognize the ritzy guy, but his face had sent signals. *Might have seen him in Baghdad*, Harry thought.

He hailed a passing cab and went to the Hotel de Crillon at the edge of the Place de la Concorde. Then he walked along a side street. It was deserted except for policemen on duty at each end. Harry tapped a code at one of the doors in the street. It opened. He entered a small courtyard, turned at the caretaker's office, showed a pass to a black woman on duty, and descended a stone staircase. He was soon at the door of a secure laboratory with armed guards outside. He showed his pass, and they let him in.

A stocky man with cropped short black hair stood up and held out his hand. He wore a white lab coat. It was clean but had seen better days.

"Hey, how's it going?"

Harry returned the "Hey" and shook the man's outstretched hand. "I'm good, Stan. It's all my eye again!" Harry was ready for the machine he had to stare into while Stan extracted the information from his right eye. Within a few seconds, the photos and the conversation were copied and then deleted from the lens's memory. Stan held out a beaker of fluid and a small eyedropper. Harry tilted back his head and applied the eyedrops. Stan gave him a tissue and held up a mirror. Harry observed himself in it.

"Gee, I'm one helluva guy, Stan!"

"Jeepers, creepers," Stan said. "Where d'you get—"

"Yeah, yeah, yeah," Harry said and then left.

7

ALISSA had found in the St. Bees area an interesting man whose work she admired. She smiled as she thought again of Hervé, the elegant man with an intricate mind and penetrating gaze. Would she go back to join him in Planning? Did he have a wife and family? She had often wondered, and she was wondering again. Maybe. But she loved his elegance and his dedication to France. His agents certainly didn't know anything of his private life. Had he sent someone to find her? Or was she the target of an Islamic terrorist from Birmingham or London? Perhaps. A dead sheep could be nothing. Then she smiled as she remembered Solihull, the attractive British chief of operations for whom she had worked. He was interesting. Would she ever see him again? She was due back in Paris toward the end of July. The French would still be making for the holiday resorts and camping out en route in the traffic jams. She smiled. Decisions could wait a while. But she knew she should contact Control.

Alissa had to read some more Molière before she went to bed. Was Brian a man who could be a real husband? Maybe. Hervé, if that was his real name, would make a husband, wouldn't he? Maybe not. In any event, she came back to the knowledge that Brian could be a husband only if she could sever herself from the world of national and international secrets. She would find out within a week or so. She had to be careful though. The calm evenings in the school would bore her eventually, but for the moment they were restful, and rest, a genuine respite from her real job, was what she needed.

***

The brasserie at the Porte Dorée was already crowded. Harry preferred San Francisco's Golden Gate. He glanced at the luncheon crowd and walked on by, following the path to the lake. The man he had photographed the day before was, he'd been told, a Libyan money man. He also aided the smugglers sending refugees into Europe as illegal immigrants. Big tax-free profits were available for the *passeurs*, as his French friends called them.

Harry walked into the park area with its lake. Early June in Paris was wonderful. The Floral Park area of the Bois would be worth a visit and ideal for exchanges of intelligence. Harry's bag from Dalloyau held a bottle of Badoit water and a selection of savoury goodies for the picnic.

Miranda appeared from behind a small hut used by the man who rented out the long, elegant rowboats. Nothing leaky about those.

"Okay, Harry, what's the angle? You have a treat for me?"

"I'll pay, we go, I row, and then we talk. Just a loving picnic for a while. A man deserves to have a lunchtime chat with an elegant mistress."

She smiled to herself. *Will I be his queen tomorrow?*

As they clambered into a boat held steady by the rental man, Miranda smiled again and planted a kiss on top of Harry's head. The boat man chuckled. *Mistresses! Youth! Oh well, that's life if you're a boss, an executive type. Middle-aged men! Can they be trusted? It's life. Life's like that!* The boatman waved them off and, still chuckling, went back to his newspaper.

A swan kept its distance, the eternal question mark of its neck showing white against the dark glint of the water. Harry made for the far bank of an island where there was a little building. Eighteenth or nineteenth century or post-war copy? In any case it was a folly, there to give atmosphere. He'd check it out in his well-worn guide to Paris. The oarlocks squeaked slightly as he rowed. Then he stopped. They were far enough from the people walking along the paths near the lakeside.

"I know where Agent Kim is. In a manner of speaking."

Miranda leaned forward from her seat at the rear of the boat. She kissed the backs of his hands as they held the oars out of the water. Harry loved the glimpse of her cleavage as her blouse fell away a little. She settled back in her seat.

"You're a brick!" she said.

"And you're a gem. Did you know that?"

"Where is she, in a manner of speaking?"

"Go to Cumberland. She's in that neighbourhood."

"In the UK?"

"Cumberland, UK, sweetie." Harry grinned. His teeth were even and white. American dentistry had done a great job.

"Come on, Harry, row us back." She hummed the "Song of the Volga Boatmen."

"Hey, not so fast. We have a picnic here. We can chew over your plans while munching our goodies. Look in the bag while I hum the song about Stenkha Razin."

She opened the bag, wondering how much Russian he knew. "Smoked salmon. Tapenade. Ham-and-salad sandwiches. Do I see cheesecake?"

"Yes, you do."

"American army iron rations." They laughed.

"Well, Uncle Sam's paying. And don't forget this is standard fare at Langley, give or take a burger or three."

"And after this mission is over, how do I get to Langley?"

"Easy. Go to the US embassy, and ask for Uncle Sam."

Miranda put a smoked salmon canapé in Harry's mouth. Some ducks were squabbling over something in the water. The sun emerged suddenly from behind a big white cloud. Such moments should last for hours. But they had soon finished Dalloyau's dainties and shared the water, using plastic beakers supplied with it. When they left, they arranged to meet a little later in the Luxembourg Gardens. Harry had to confirm something at the embassy.

***

Miranda was sitting on a bench in the Luxembourg Gardens. Not far away was the Medici Fountain, where a few pigeons nodded and strutted around the water. She was not looking at the Medici grotto with Ottin's menacing statue of the gigantic Polyphemus looking down at the sensuous nakedness of the lovers Acis and Galatea. She was watching every person wandering by. Harry approached and sat next to her. He put one arm over her shoulder. She turned her head, and he kissed her cheek.

"I know where she is!"

"Hey, thanks, Harry. You're quick off the mark."

"It keeps me alive. Now you owe me."

"Deal. Let's go."

They got up and walked hand in hand, noticing and saluting Bartholdi's statue of Liberty before leaving the park. Harry murmured that Kim was in a small coastal town. In the busy street near the wall that bore a metal rod exactly one metre long, they found taxis. They travelled in separate cabs to the same place. A few minutes elapsed between their arrivals.

Harry looked around as he got out and then walked into the hotel and to a room on the second floor. When Miranda knocked at the door, Harry opened it to let her in. No one else was in the corridor. He locked the door. Miranda took off her coat and threw it on a chair.

"Where is she?"

Harry took off his jacket and threw it on Miranda's coat.

"Cumberland."

Miranda slipped out of her dress. Then she unbuttoned Harry's shirt and unbuckled his belt.

"That's a big place, Harry. You mentioned a little town."

"She's not far from St. Bees"

Miranda led him to the king-size bed.

"She teaches in a girls' private school."

"No kidding!"

They collapsed onto the bed, laughing.

"I used to be a schoolgirl," Miranda said as she took the initiative. They were both good at giving pleasure. After they had lain quiet, lost in their own thoughts, they took a shower together.

As they dried themselves and dressed, a plan began to form. Miranda talked about going to St. Bees via the Eurostar and then by rail again or else flying to somewhere near the little town and renting a car. She made no mention of Bruno. Harry advised her to go as a holiday maker. She should read the local press for the last two weeks, so she would know something of local life, personalities, and events. Miranda knew this meant going to London via Eurostar and spending a day in the British Newspaper Archive. Then she'd arrive by train in St. Bees. It would take longer, but the newspapers could be useful. Yes, she would have to be a woman on holiday, going where she could observe crowds. She would also visit local villages and beauty spots.

Miranda had to leave so as to lose no more time. Harry understood.

"Take care, sweetie," he said.

She smiled. "I will. See you when I get back—I hope."

"I wish you'd join us in the US of A. I mean it."

"I've just had a thought. Why don't we go to a bistro I know for a farewell drink? I'd feel better."

Harry agreed. She didn't tell him that she was hoping she might spot Bruno on the off chance. And Bruno might spot her.

She left after reminding Harry of the bistro's address. At the door she blew him a kiss.

8

AFTER his meeting with Miranda, Control sent for Bruno. It was urgent business.

"Ah Bruno, jeune homme, have a seat. Drink?"

"Oh, thank you, sir. A Perrier, please."

"Bruno, Kim is on leave, but she has not kept in touch. I'm a little disappointed."

Bruno smiled wryly but said nothing.

"She could be anywhere in France or Europe, for that matter. Yet I suspect she's in England. I want you to find her. See if she's alright. You've worked together, at least in training exercises. If she's in some kind of trouble, go in and get her back to Paris. Be discreet. It may be nothing. But we can't afford to lose her. If our enemies were to get her, it would be a terrible loss."

"Have you no idea where in Europe or England she could be?"

"Not a clue."

"Will I have some backup?"

"Difficult. We are short-handed as it is. If or when you follow a clue to England, phone in before you leave."

"And I'll keep you informed of progress, as usual?"

"Yes, absolutely. I think people are trying to find Kim and will try to interrogate her before killing her."

"That's worrying, monsieur."

Control was fairly confident that Kim and Miranda could deal with the situation. They would have a good chance of unmasking Bruno. Control chose his players carefully, trusting their skill and flexibility. That had been part of his success. He was delighted when Bruno suddenly broke the little silence between them.

"You are devious, Monsieur, and we shall, I know, bring Kim back home."
Ah, Bruno, you are beginning to disappoint me, Monsieur Martin thought.

**

As he sharpened his favourite knife, Bruno remembered a summer camp he went to with other teenagers. A camp leader, a man in his fifties with a small greying moustache, was surrounded by a group of adolescent boys as he held a frog in one hand.

"You see?" the man said.

He cut a circle in the frog's skin around its tiny neck. He put his knife down. Then he stripped the skin down from the frog's neck until it hung around its legs. He walked over to the edge of the lake and threw the frog into the shallow water. It attempted to hop to land in the shallows. One of the boys shouted at the man. The man shrugged and smiled.

Bruno frowned as he drew the blade across the whetstone. The knife had saved his life three, no, four times now. He would certainly find Kim. His subordinate in London had almost killed her in the grenade attack. He could pick up another man from his London safe house. Was Kim wounded? How badly? Or not at all? Was she tracking down those responsible for the attack on her?

Bruno had heard nothing from his usual sources. Maybe she had decided to leave damage control to the British authorities. London and Birmingham would be possible places to start the hunt. Bruno had people in both cities. He thought of his safe house in London. It would be worth a few sousnow, even in Brixton. It could be useful.

He looked through his Parisian window with its net curtain. In the street below, a girl wearing a black-and-white houndstooth tweed cap stuck at a jaunty angle over her blond shoulder-length hair kissed her older man with a friendly peck on the lips. They were at a table on the little sidewalk terrace. She turned away to scan people walking toward the small group of tables. She and her male friend were laughing with the conspiratorial joy of lovers.

The nineteenth-century apartments above the bistro reached up to attic windows on the eighth floor. Once maids' rooms, they were now studios or two-room apartments. Bruno's studio had access to a roof-top terrace via a spiral metal staircase. He had an escape route across the rooftops to another terrace with a metal door and another staircase leading down to a studio with a landing. A fire exit led down concrete stairs to street level. On the landing was a door into another apartment. An elevator from the floor below down to street level was of the old-fashioned type with a metal concertina door. Bruno owned his apartment and both studios, each unoccupied but ready for his use. He also owned the London safe house. His Muslim paymasters gave him plenty of money, but he lived on his official French salary, keeping his properties under other names. He did not use a car in Paris. There was no point in joining that infernal hubbub.

The blonde and her companion stood up, kissed four times on the cheek, and then walked off in opposite directions, waving to each other. A waiter immediately pocketed the change they left in a saucer on their table and stuffed their bill into his apron pocket. Inside, near the bar, the waiter went to a telephone and dialled. "Today. 18:03 Gare du Nord." He put the receiver back.

Replacing his own receiver, Bruno mused. The waiter's call had relieved his boredom. The American he recognized, but the blonde was an unknown quantity. Bruno would be at the station, but at 17:00, maybe earlier, to check out the scene before the American and perhaps the woman were due to arrive for the train at 18:03. He sharpened his knife yet again before packing a bag he could sling over his shoulder, if necessary. He took no knife or any other weapon except cunning and malice.

9

GRAHAM Curtis, a Canadian professor of English, was in bed in a hotel in London. He anticipated with much pleasure his lunch date with his new friend, Anne de Crevennes. They were both going to fly to Canada but on different days. Graham disliked the long haul to the west coast. Now he was asleep and moving his legs, so one foot stuck out from under the duvet. In his sleep he mumbled something to his wife's killers, two men who had shot and kicked her as they ran from the supermarket they had robbed. He knew what they looked like. The police had arrested them soon after the senseless murder. Several months had passed. Graham's words, though spoken aloud, were slurred, his voice drowsy. His dream's images, on the other hand, moved through his mind rapidly and repetitively.

Lift the axe again, and sever the gunman's wrist. The severed hand, still clutching a pistol, falls onto grass. The only sound is my voice. That foot you used to kick my wife's head could be varnished and made into an ornament on the fireplace mantel. Lift the axe again.

A door appears near a tree. I see myself open the door and walk onto a stage in front of an auditorium full of academics attending a conference. I have to present some ideas about crazy theories at a conference in New York. But where are my damned papers? This isn't the right room! Ah, there's the audience. I try to remember what I had so carefully written. First, thank the conference organizers. Panic! What do I say? I must be inventive

"Colleagues, many thanks. Yes, thanks. Thanks. I shall offer a few thoughts about my latest discovery, a collection of short prose pieces difficult to date. Oh, and I must thank the organizers for inviting me. I cannot prove it, but I can guess who wrote these short squibs. Were they the work of one or several hands? One of the pieces, no longer than a paragraph, deals with a severed hand. Furthermore,

I cannot even tell you the identity of the editor or publisher who collected these pieces and had them printed together in one slim volume. I can, however, offer a few speculations, useful perhaps for further inquiry and indeed criticism.

"Were these pieces the work of just one or of several hands? Were they the work of the unknown editor who published them? Can we date the pieces from internal evidence and their styles? My new edition will have copious footnotes where necessary for each short piece. I shall also supply a detailed introduction identifying the writer or writers, the original printer and/or publisher, and the place of first publication."

"How do you know it is a first edition?" a male voice shouts from the back of the hall.

"Good question, sir. In a word, I don't know if it's a first edition, but I shall find out! I shall also discuss the subjects treated and the style of each text, paying particular attention to what is left unsaid in each case. I shall assess the overall importance of the book, whose entire front matter is missing. This should have given details such as author or authors, publisher, printer, place and date of publication, and so on."

"Whose hand? Whose foot?" The cry is taken up by many voices.

I take a blue handkerchief out of my jacket's top pocket, wipe my forehead with it, and tuck it back into my pocket. I look around for more questions in the hall.

"How did you obtain this rare volume?"

"I found it, madam, on an empty seat on a bus." Loud laughter from the hall.

From the gallery at the back of the hall another woman, identifying herself as a post-doctoral researcher, asks if the quality of the prose warrants such an edition and a publisher.

"I honestly don't know," I hear myself say, "but I have a respectable university press that will publish it when my edition is finished. In fact, they are swayed, I imagine, by the fact that one of the pieces was probably written by a friend of Kafka."

An old man with grey hair swept back and secured with an elastic band to make a ponytail, stands up in the front row, his nose twitching like a rabbit's. "What do you like most about the book? Have you a favourite piece?"

"I don't know, sir. I haven't even read the book."

Graham heard himself saying this several times just before waking. Then he thought he was in Anne de Crevenne's house at Eden Roc in the South of France. Sweating and thrashing about, and suddenly wide awake, he recognized the hotel room. It was certainly not Anne's mansion. In the half light of the bedroom, he saw the flat-screen television positioned on a wall near the foot of the queen-size bed. The desk andchair were there, where they had always been. On the night table next to him, a clock radio stated it was 6:25 a.m.

Dreams were a mode of thought, weren't they? Did they tell us who we were? The real person inside our skins? Graham didn't know. He looked at the hotel booklet to see when breakfast was served. That was more pressing a concern than Dr. Freud on dreams.

Lying on his back, he remembered his recent visit to Anne's place in France and then his brief stay with his friend, Paul Wills, and his new wife, Mary Rao. Would she remain Doctor Rao or become Doctor Wills? Their wedding had been good for him, Graham acknowledged. He had started a friendship with the sophisticated and elegant French noblewoman, now known to him simply as Anne. He was looking forwarded to seeing her again soon. They had arranged to meet for lunch the day before he flew back to Canada.

***

Anne, the Marquise de Crevennes, was in London yet again that June. She wore a light suit, a chic raincoat, comfortable flat walking shoes, and carried a folding umbrella small enough to go in her capacious Lanvin shoulder bag. She was trailing a suitcase on wheels as she headed for the taxis outside St. Pancras. Her hotel room was a taxi ride away in Mayfair. She planned to visit the British Library the next day, have lunch with Graham, her Canadian admirer, take in a comedy at the Haymarket Theatre, and on the morrow take a train to Gatwick and then fly to Canada. But today she would have lunch with an old friend from Normandy who now worked at the University of London. Already Anne was absorbing the energy that seemed to be plentiful in London at the moment.

She was looking forward to exploring Canada, wherever her research led her, and to seeing a little more of Graham, whom she had met through Paul Wills, a journalist and now a friend. Paul had interviewed her for an article he was doing about violence againstwomen. Graham's wife had been brutally murdered in Vancouver. It was a senseless killing. Anne, Graham, and other friends had all been at the wedding when Pauland Mary "tied the knot," to use a curious expression favoured by those Anglo-Saxons.

Anne was going to Canada for reasons other than seeing Graham though. As an historian with a good readership in France, she wanted to research early female French settlers in Canada outside of Quebec and the rest of Francophone

Canada. She figured female settlers in Quebec had already received a good deal of attention. Others must have travelled farther, perhaps with newly arrived husbandsor in search of husbands. Her plan was to see Graham in Vancouver, look at the archives in Victoria, and cover the main university libraries and the archives in British Columbia. Then she would work back east across the country, province by province, looking for where the evidence might be and talking to people who might give her useful leads. Plenty of French women were living in the Anglophone provinces,but what was the history, if any, of those who had moved for whatever reasons to live outside the French communities since the seventeenth century? These thoughts occupied her in the taxi queue.

In the taxi she felt a sudden excitement at seeing London again with its famous higgledy-piggledy streets, eccentric, individualistic architecture, and the wonderful little red-brick St. James's Palace. Compared to French fortresses, it seemed like a toy palace.

Her taxi turned into the familiar street and stopped. She alighted at the bijou hotel she liked that was a stone's throw from where King Billy had once lived as well as a house that strange English novelist Somerset Maugham had occupied. Her parents had met him at least once in the south of France, where Maugham had bought a villa.

Anne didn't know if Paul and Mary were in London at the moment. She had seen them briefly after their wedding. Perhaps she would visit them on her return to London before returning home. That would depend on how tired she was after her journey across Canada. And, of course, whether they were free. She would telephone them in any case.

She settled into her hotel suite and then phoned her friend, Sophie. The phone rang a couple of times.

"Hello . . . Anne! Welcome back to London. How was the trip?"

"Comfortable. It's wonderful that we can see each other before I fly to Canada."

"Rather! Are you still free for lunch today?"

The friends arranged to meet at the Oxford and Cambridge Club. They would have a drink in the bar and then take lunch in the coffee room. Anne was a member of the Club Interallié in Paris and, therefore, had reciprocal rights to visit other clubs all over the globe. She could have stayed there instead of the hotel but had decided to sleep in her favourite hotel before the long flight.

Anne could easily walk the short distance to the Oxford and Cambridge Club in Pall Mall. She passed the guards on duty in identical sentry boxes outside St. James's Palace and crossed the road leading past the Queen's Chapel toward the mall and the park beyond.

She reached the club just as her friend approached from the other direction, having got off a bus at Trafalgar Square. Anne waved, and Sophie, who was wearing a light lemon-coloured raincoat, waved back. The raincoat contrasted nicely with Sophie's dark hair. The two women kissed each other on both cheeks, remarking that the air was a bit chilly. Holding hands they went into the club and saw the young woman at the front desk.

Anne produced her Interallié membership card and letter of introduction, confirmed her luncheon reservation, and then the two friends signed the visitors' book. They were directed to a cloakroom corridor, where they could leave their raincoats. A club official showed them how to release a chain, pass it through a sleeve of the coat, and lock it in place. Coats hanging in this fashion could not be stolen or taken by mistake. A small numbered tab had to be slotted into the right lock to release the chain. They put their tabs into their shoulder bags. Both women were wearing smart suits. Anne's was a light-blue Chanel suit with a knee-length skirt. Sophie wore a dark-blue suit with a skirt that was mid-calf length.

They laughed with glee as they walked up the splendid staircase with its bronze copy of the famous David. They noticed that David was uncircumcised. Large oil paintings, full-length portraits of nobles and monarchs, hung on the walls. A clock with a curious mechanism made them pause to look at it more closely and check their watches by it.

The bar was animated but not crowded. They took a table at a window, and both had a Tio Pepe sherry. Anne took a small bowl of potato chips and another with pretzel sticks. They were too interested in catching up to bother with the selection of daily newspapers available to members and their friends.

"So, what's the Canadian history project?" Sophie asked, taking a sip of her *fino*.

A man with dark silvering hair passed their table to join friends at a table near the fireplace. He wore a smartly cut hand-tailored houndstooth suit, a white shirt, and a tie with alternating dark and light-blue stripes. Holding two whisky glasses, he stopped and spoke to them.

"Excuse me, ladies, but you are perfect for the club. You are, I take it, one from Oxford and the other from that university with which we share the club?"

They looked up at him and laughed.

"You are quite wrong in that assumption, sir," Sophie replied. Anne took a sip of her drink and nodded.

"How so?"

"We are both French, and we did not study at Oxford or Cambridge."

"Well, one of you is wearing the Oxford dark blue, the other a Cambridge light blue."

"Correct," Anne said, laughing, "but that was sheer chance. We did not arrange that as a plan for this visit. I am a member of an affiliated club in Paris."

"The Travellers?"

"No. The Interallié."

"Well, I am charmed to meet you lovely French ladies. Alas, I must join my friends."

He left.

"In France, would a person talk to complete strangers like that?" Sophie asked.

"I doubt it. But to get back to our conversation and your question..."Anne explained her ideas and her planned agenda.

"That's an interesting idea, Anne. And it needs investigating—it certainly needs to be written up."

"I shall start in Vancouver where I'll contact a man called Graham Curtis, a professor in one of the universities there."

"Ah, tell me about this Graham."

"Well, he's a widower. Younger than us. And I'm meeting him for lunch before we both fly to Vancouver."

"Aha. That sounds promising. Where's the lunch?"

"Not here. Simpson's, in the Strand."

They both laughed. Neither woman was married. From time to time they met men who took an interest in them and whom they found to be congenial. However, marriage was only a remote possibility. Both had work to do, and both liked their independence. They wanted a circle of friends. Neither wanted the obligations owed to a husband or, worse still, to a husband's family.

Lunch in the Coffee Room was formal. The room had gilded columns, enormous windows, and many tables. The walls were adorned with huge portraits of the great, whose names, lives, and deeds many of the diners had forgotten.

The beginning of the meal was a matter of penmanship. Forms had to be completed by writing down the dishes ordered and their cost. Then papers had to be signed. That way there could be no dispute about what was ordered or its cost. The two Frenchwomen found this quaint, but it seemed an excellent precaution, since they had grown up in a form-filling, paperwork country.

The man in the houndstooth suit raised his glass of red wine to them when they caught sight of him with his companions at the large oval table in the middle of the room. The two women raised their water glasses in return. They were drinking Scottish Highland Spring mineral water.

Their soups arrived. They found the clam chowder excellent. Then they took roast beef from the massive trolley that was wheeled around. The puffy, crusty Yorkshire pudding was a must. They took French mild mustard rather than the English hot mustard. With their meal they tried a carafe of the club claret and found it entirely acceptable, more than merely drinkable. Dessert was from a selection on another trolley. They both chose English trifle, something they rarely ate. The sherry in it was a delightful touch, but it was heavier than the French baba au rhum. They were pleased with the lunch and decided to take their coffee in the Drawing Room, where they sank into capacious chairs near the windows overlooking Pall Mall. The gold, green, and white décor was elegant and classic. It was ornate but avoided the overcharged ornamentation of some of the reception rooms found in French châteaux and town mansions.

Sophie had to leave soon for a lecture she was giving. Both women were delighted they had been able to catch up with each other's news.

Anne decided to go to the club's library. It was extensive and well stocked with handsomely bound volumes, new and ancient. She scanned eagerly the table displaying newly published books. There were armchairs and desks with club writing and notepaper. Ladders were available for reaching the top shelves of the floor-to-ceiling bookcases. In the silent room, a solitary man was busy writing. Anne wanted to get to work herself. Time was ticking by all too fast. She had to get back to her hotel and prepare for the rest of her London visit before her flight to Vancouver. First, she would scan the club's library catalogue to see whether there were books relevant to settlers in Canada. On her return to

London from Canada, she would try to get a room in the club rather than her usual hotel. The club was comparable to a town mansion with a large domestic staff with all the facilities one needed as a traveller, a scholar, or just a club raconteur. Hotels were not like that.

Should she call Graham? They had exchanged their hotel telephone numbers once their bookings were fixed. *Oh, let him dangle for a while.* She would call the next day to remind him of their luncheon date. Meanwhile, the club's library catalogue had to be inspected. London in early June with a new project and an admirer kept at arm's length, what could be better?

10

SOLIHULL was thinking about that French agent, so quick, so lovely. The Frenchwomen at the club had reminded him of his encounter with that agent, skilled in water combat, whom he called his "frog lady." Could she be seconded to his forces or, better still, recruited fulltime for the UK? Not really, he realized. She would not desert M. Martin and the French. Unofficial as well as official cooperation when needed was clearly the best route to go. The French would still be paying her, and there would be no great toll on the British budget for any such temporary member of his team. Solihull wanted to see her again. He had to maintain his cordial relationship with M. Martin in Paris. Perhaps at some future opportunity he could take her under his wing for a bit of a fling. He smiled and then got back to work. *Get serious*, he thought.

∗∗∗

Anne de Crevennes had gone to an exhibition of work by Babu in the Galerie du XVIieme toward the end of the previous November. She saw him as being in the satirical tradition of Daumier, Hogarth, James Gillray, and George Cruickshank. Then she went to the Avenue Mozart to have lunch in the Mozart Brasserie with some friends before catching the Eurostar to London.

They sat in a corner at a table near the bookshelf. It was an enjoyable lunch with her friends Michelle, Françoise, and Béatrice. Anne told them of women and families mentioned in the French archives who had migrated to Canada. She had leads she could follow in London and Canada. They were all in favour of her project.

She left for London, where she went to the library at the House of Lords. She read Queen Victoria's British North America Act and found some letters written by younger daughters of nobility. The daughters had married and gone to Canada or found suitable relatives there. They were writing home to parents. It was researcher's gold! It would be worth pursuing. And so it had blossomed into a voyage for wherever the project led her. She had also looked at the death warrant of Charles I, signed by Oliver Cromwell and a crowd of followers. She appreciated London's secrets and special charm. She felt fortunate in knowing Paris so well and something of the great neighbour across the Channel.

Now, the following June, she was back with her developing project and en route to Canada. And she was lunching with a Canadian scholar at Simpson's on the Strand. It was exciting.

When she arrived, Graham was already at the table. He had a booth for two. Seeing her approach, he sprang to his feet. She offered her cheek, and Graham kissed her. Once. They both smiled as they sat facing each other, Anne smiling at the prospect of Canada with her new idea and the archival research.

Graham was also smiling at Anne, pleased to be with her once more. He recalled her splendid hospitality in France a little earlier in the year, just after Paul and Mary's wedding. They had talked about their academic projects. Graham was planning a short book, if possible, on literary theory revisited. Anne explained her research, which would take her from Victoria, British Columbia, across the country to the east coast and then back to Montreal.

Anne noticed that Graham was wearing a summer jacket, no tie, and a checked shirt. He seemed less formal than Europeans. His journalist friend Paul might well have worn a tie to such a rendezvous.

"When's your flight tomorrow?" Anne asked.

"Late morning, but I have to be at Gatwick by nine. I'll head off early just in case the train is late or held up."

"Good idea. I'll get to Vancouver a couple of days later. I have things to do. So, I'll phone you."

"Now you know you're welcome to stay in my house as long as you need. It's not a mansion, but you would be comfortable."

"That's sweet of you, Graham, but I have my routines, and I prefer a hotel. I can be a law unto myself. Do you still say that in English?"

"Sometimes, I guess. Well, whatever suits. But at least I could cook for you lunch or dinner chez-moi?"

"That's a treat I cannot refuse, mon cher. I shall be visiting Victoria for the archives almost as soon as I arrive. Perhaps when I return to Vancouver, we can do that?"

"Your wish is my command. I can barbecue some big prawns and some steak. We have some drinkable wines now, from Kelowna and Kamloops."

"So, that's settled. Kamloops! Quel drôle de nom!"

"Yes, droll. It has some excellent vineyards all the same."

"Good. I look forward to tasting some of that wine. Now what are you going to be working on this summer? You'll be teaching again in September, yes?"

"Yes. A seminar, a second-year class, and graduate students. Well, when I get home, I'll be preparing my classes for the fall. I'm also writing about the theories that are so fashionable and which seem to impinge little on the main literary texts in the canon. If there *is* a canon!"

"But you are a professor of literature, yes? Why do you concern yourself with theories that have little to do with literature and more to do with French and other Marxisms?"

"The universities are full-steam ahead with 'theory,' so you have to keep up with it. I hope my book will deal it something of a death blow!"

"These fashions come and go, mon cher. In France the sharpest minds have moved on. Translation studies grow, and there are jobs in Brussels! Theory, mon ami, it will right itself."

"How so? Can anything 'write' itself? Sorry about a pun Barthes might have made."

She laughed. "If the author is dead, as we are now told, then anything goes. No, I meant it will find its place in some lower berth of the intellect, below decks shall we say? When Sartre died, so did the French literary dictatorship."

"I just hope to hurry 'theory' along a little until its death rattle here." He raised his fingers and made "scare quotes," as many North Americans did when talking, especially if they were from the west coast.

They left it at that.

∗∗∗

Bruno was still in Paris but knew from a group that was hunting Kim that he had to be in London very soon. She was in England. They were certain. He was carefully sharpening his favourite knife. Was he a compulsive neurotic? He asked himself that question frequently enough and guessed he was. He had to admit it. It was a special knife though. He had used it to excruciating effect on Westlake. The blubber on that obese body had been repulsive. The existence of two British agents, Momo and his Moroccan wife, had been useful information for his Arab contacts. But the married couple had quickly left their local mosque. For Bruno that confirmed what Westlake had revealed before the heart attack had killed him during the torture session. And now Bruno had some indication that Kim was in England. She might still be there. If so, they would have a nice little reunion. He could tell her of a safe house he knew in Brixton. If one of the British people he had trained could get her on the run, it was likely that she might come calling at the safe house. All he had to do was send the right people to get her on the move and back to London. She was on leave till the last week in July. She must be captured and made "useful." She must never return to Paris alive.

Bruno felt a fierce shame rush to his cheeks. *Do I love her? Perhaps.* His emotional life was a mystery. He had never fully understood it himself. Why did his calm suddenly give way to a seething rage? That rage was a weakness, which he saw clearly enough when he was in a calmer mood. It could lead to impulsive behaviour that revealed his hand. It could even get him killed.

From his apartment above the bistro, using his small yet powerful binoculars, he watched people outside the café. Having seen enough, he put the binoculars back in their leather case.

The waiter's call had come to relieve his boredom. He'd be there but at 16:45 to check out the scene. He decided to sharpen his knife yet again. Was he a neurotic or simply a meticulous survivor? His own ambiguous behaviour was something he relied upon instinctively. It had helped him survive. Did anyone truly understand himself? His Muslim paymaster was not interested in understanding Bruno. It was payment by results, with expenses. Bruno was frugal. He had made excellent investments in his properties. The London safe house had been renovated inside for all necessities, especially soundproofing.

Agent Kim had to be found. The blond woman with the American man was probably a US spook on some mission in liaison with the British. He should have them followed. Or maybe the blonde would, God willing, lead him most of the way to Kim. But why would the Americans want to find Kim? That was Control's project. Yes, maybe the blonde was on some other mission. If he could get the blonde as well as Kim back to the safe house, one way or another, he would have a major catch and would discover answers to these questions. The Iraqi would be delighted and generous. Bruno thought he could recruit some more sex-hungry youths in Britain. Would he offer them the American blonde? Or maybe she was French. All in good time. It was in the hands of a higher power. Life was always a mystery. In fact, his job was a mystery. Why did he do it? Why was he unfaithful to both masters? He had no answer to his own mystery, his own *métier*. Yet he held some of the secrets of both sides. He liked that.

11

THE coffee shop at ground level was quite crowded. That was fortunate. From inside Bruno had a good view of the escalator going to the boarding areas of the Eurostar trains. He had a couple of newspapers, *Le Monde Diplomatique* and *Le Figaro*, that kept him from being recognized by people walking in the concourse to the escalator.

At 17:00 by the station clock, Miranda arrived. She believed in being early. Brinksmanship was a special technique for special situations. She scanned the faces of other passengers in the concourse as she headed for the escalator. The ground-floor café was crowded.

She decided to go straight up to the Eurostar area to get a soft drink. There was no sign of Bruno so far, though a man in the café had been reading a newspaper.

As she went up the escalator, she glanced back at him. He had been watching her, but he raised the newspaper again. It was Bruno. *My goodness, is Bruno slipping? Or did he want me to see him? Well now, the game's afoot!*

She went through the check-in and passport controls. Then she could relax and watch to see if Bruno came up to catch the same train. If he was following her, did he know she was also one of Control's agents? If so, how?

She had booked first class. She had one small bag on wheels with a matching handbag. In her luggage were no obvious weapons, but she had a ballpoint pen of a common enough make—filled with an expensive poisonous ink. One stroke of it stung like acid. It was enough to distract an opponent. A vigorous jab injected enough poison to fell an opponent however bigor strong. Stupor and sleep were the result. A second jab meant death within seconds.

"Now don't go writing any poison pen letters," the "ops man" who had explained the weapon before handing it to her had said. "This ink's expensive." He laughed at his own joke.

In her bag Miranda carried a crossword puzzle book (level five) obtainable from French newsagents. She had each puzzle partially completed in ballpoint. She could seem to be trying to complete a puzzle on any page, if need be. There was no sign of Bruno yet.

Once aboard the train, Miranda settled down quickly. Bruno would be in the crowds getting into a second-class car.

The train left promptly at the curiously minute-conscious time. Why not five or ten past? The banlieue or outskirts of greater Paris were soon left behind, and the French landscape slid silently past. *Aerolians* stood in orderly groups, their huge propellers turning languidly in the evening wind. At 19:25 she would be in St. Pancras station. She ate a light meal on the train.

***

Bruno was in an aisle seat next to an Asian girl—Japanese? Korean? She preferred her smartphone messages and game apps to any scenery.

Bruno drifted into a light sleep. He woke up just as the train emerged from the tunnel into southern England. He wondered how many, since he had last heard on the grapevine, proven killers or potential recruits had managed to get into Britain from the rabble of illegal immigrants camping out at Calais and anywhere else the French administration could lodge them. He smiled at the naivety of European humanitarians. There were too many people in the world. War was not killing them fast enough. And in France and elsewhere the do-gooders were saying life was precious! Even if only one or two extremists were getting into Britain per week, it would soon add up to a wonderful and effective number of recruits each year. How slack Europe was, convinced of the charms of its democracies! Democracy! A Greek invention, and where were the Greeks now? Way behind the Emirates, for example. China was a great nation and yet was no democracy. Degeneration was the name of the path the democracies were on. The path of all who followed America, known to itself as the greatest nation on Earth, was the path of degenerates. No discipline in schools. Wall Street a crook's paradise. The British still yearning to be big players. The volatile French and the orderly Germans trying to have Europe as their empire, and America thinking it was the world's great teacher and policeman. It was sickening. The Governor of New York claimed they had the best of the world's police forces in that state. Pathetic. The Twin Towers strike had caned them. The lesson they all needed now was morality, the discipline of the great religion, and more punishment. They had to learn the hard lessons of revenge. Revenge offered the only true justice. Christ had it all wrong. But then he was a Jew. What else could one expect from an outcast?

The western idea that racism was wrong also made him smile. Whites were now afraid to be thought racist. That was funny when most racists were brown, not white. There was one God and one master religion. The politically correct would soon learn to be religiously correct, or they would disappear into mass graves.

A few minutes later, Bruno spoke rapid Arabic into his cell phone. At St. Pancras two of his underlings had to identify the blonde from first class with her two small bags. She had shoulder-length hair and was wearing a houndstooth hat.

At that moment, Miranda went to the toilet, pinning her hair into a French pleat. She also turned her hat inside out. It was a pale blue with no pattern. She reversed her raincoat, which was now a perfect match for her hat.

***

Bruno's accomplices missed the woman passenger completely. Miranda went into a café opposite the egress from the trains. There she watched the tall, gaunt spy emerge in the crowd of second-class passengers. He carried only a black briefcase. Bruno looked around and marched towards the exit for passengers needing taxis. Two young men waiting near a small food shop followed him. They were Middle Eastern in appearance, youths in black jeans. They both had fleecy grey jackets with hoods.

They are his pawns, Miranda thought.

She took the tube to Piccadilly and then changed to the Central Line. She would find a bed-and-breakfast place and then go for a light meal before turning in for the night. She was sure nobody had followed her. She was also sure that Bruno would be carrying a gun supplied by his young Muslim recruits.

The next morning Miranda could have gone to the Colindale newspaper library for opening time. Instead she took an early tube back to St. Pancras and walked to the British Library, where part of the collection was now kept. She showed the library card she had received by mail in Paris and then found the St. Bees local press in the catalogue and ordered the last two weeks' papers. While waiting for the assistant to bring them, she walked into the corridor and found a quiet nook where she contacted Control.

"All's well?" he asked.

"Two people were meant to greet me, but they bungled it. Our friend must be giving them a hard time."

Control chuckled. "So, the target was aware of you yet all three missed you. What are you doing now?"

"Just reading the local press. I'll keep you posted."

"Crosswords can be fun. Get back on our friend's tail."

Miranda spent the rest of the day and an hour the next morning at the library's new premises learning about St. Bees. The local rag was small beer, so she also looked at a larger newspaper for the area. St. Bees was a popular holiday village on the Cumbrian coast. An arts festival was planned for that weekend. Perhaps Kim would be among the spectators. One never knew. Taking up Harry's tip, she should get to Cumberland. Faster by train or car? No. She would go to Bristol by coach.

She checked out of the bed-and-breakfast place wearing a grey skirt with a red blouse, the blue raincoat and a black woollen hat covering most of her blond hair. She wore her comfortable but stylish shoes. Someone would surely notice them if she kept wearing them too often. She had not followed Bruno. Let him be unaware of her for a while. She wanted to get to Kim before Bruno. After all, she knew where to go, and Bruno did not.

Later that morning she reached Victoria coach station. She bought a ticket for a coach leaving for Bristol at 14:30. Perfect.

As she took her place, a man loading luggage watched her. He went to one side and took out a phone.

"A young woman wearing the shoes you described got on the 14:30 to Bristol."

"Good."

The man closed his phone and pocketed it.

Miranda settled back into her window seat. In Bristol she would go to Temple Meads to find suitable trains to St. Bees, probably for the following day. She hoped that once out of Cromwell Road and onto the motorways her bus would make good time. She'd be in Bristol with enough time to check for any "tails" and buy a good meal before going to her hotel. If Bruno turned up, she would improvise.

The hotel was small and central and she would be able to get a good night's sleep. All went according to her plan. She was even able to get a bite to eat at a restaurant called the Cow Shed. It served good French food. She had fish with one glass of chardonnay from Louis Latour. She felt in a holiday mood, but she could not help keeping an eye out for any suspicious behaviour or unwanted attention. Nothing. She returned to the hotel and slept soundly. She'd be down to breakfast at 7:30 a.m.

***

As Alissa and Brian made love, exploring and discovering each other sometimes slowly, sometimes hastily, taking and giving all to each other for this, their first time together, they heard from outside the occasional cries of birds and the bleating of mountain sheep. Their own passionate cries were part of the same great world of nature. If their cries and shouts and laughter could be heard outside the little cottage, they would be hurled about on the wind and lost in thenorthern landscape, gleaming after a sun shower.

"Alissa, are you ready for a mug of tea—or maybe a glass of wine?"

"Let's just stay here and snuggle for a while. Then let's go for a walk and have some wine. What do you say?" She remembered a line from Yeats: "she bade me take life easy..." Was that it? Could she do the same?

"Fine by me," Brian said and kissed the nape of her neck.

When they went outside, a stiff breeze assaulted them. They didn't care. June weather up there could be changeable. She was certain Brian's sheep art on the hillside would be a great success. It was a surprising and yet *local* show, although the basic idea had come from an Egyptian dancing girl, as Brian had explained to her.

"What are you doing in school?" Brian asked.

"We're reading a Molière comedy in the sixth form, but it's mainly language and songs lower down the school." She made no mention of Arabic. "What about you?"

"Plenty of practice at perspective, composition, and talking about Mannerism. I don't plan to take any students out of doors to sketch or attempt watercolours at the moment. So, we won't worry about what the barometer's doing this month!"

"I guess the barometer will go up and down, come what may, like lovers in bed!"

Brian looked at her, a little surprised, and with a twinkle in his eyes. This woman was a real treasure. "Do you want to go back to the cottage?"

"How did you guess?"

Farther away and not in any way noticeable, a coloured man, code name Ali, watched them through a pair of powerful binoculars as they went back inside the cottage.

"Naughty, naughty," he murmured. He took a satellite phone from his windbreaker's chest pocket. "Solihull. Harry, if Uncle Sam is listening in, I've done it. She's in a cottage near St. Bees."

"You're certain?" Solihull replied.

"Is New York a great city?" Ali asked for the benefit of any US agent.

"It could well be," Solihull said before hanging up.

12

BRUNO was also in Bristol. He thought this blond woman might leave by coach again or by train. But which? He had arrived at Temple Meads by train. When he arrived at the coach terminus, the passengers from the London coach had already dispersed. He decided to walk into town and find a suitable place to eat. Then he would find a small hotel or bed-and-breakfast place. It was supposedly the beginning of summer, but he was wearing his long raincoat.

At the top of Park Street, he wandered into a restaurant on the corner of Berkeley Square. It was trendy but also busy. Just what he wanted. He got a small table deep inside, but he saw people stopping near the door to read the menu.

He looked up from eating the soup of the day when he saw the blond girl. What luck! There she was, outside, glancing at the menu, and then walking into the little square wearing her distinctive shoes. Silly girl. He got up and looked out the doorway just in time to see her go into the hotel a few yards into the square. He went back to his soup. Lentils. Good for the health. God is great. Was she American? He was thinking of the blonde, not God.

In London he had made someone check up on membership in the Oxbridge Club. Yes, Alissa Partridge, MA, was certainly a member, amid the bishops, lawyers, businessmen, sheiks, and assorted others. While eating knuckle of lamb with mashed potatoes, green peas, and mint jelly, Bruno relished the thought of being able to follow the blonde, perhaps to Kim, wherever she might be. If he could get them both securely installed in his London safe house, he would have a wonderful time probing them both, discovering their secrets. His associates could also be rewarded with the delights of these women, one coloured and one white. His underlings would be eager to please him even more in future operations.

He ate the caramel skin of his crème brulée, sliding pieces of it onto his fork. As he savoured the soft but firm and yet creamy custard, he thought of the two women soon to be in his power. He had the beginnings of an erection. *Concentrate, plan, succeed*, he told himself.

He was calm again. He would find a place to stay the night. He would plan ahead before he went to sleep. He would have a call at 6:00 a.m. and would ensure the blonde was followed by a young man, a fairly recent addition to his network. But he would follow them both as well.

Bruno found an excellent bed-and-breakfast place on a road that led from Cotham Hill to White Ladies Road. It was in a late-Victorian terrace of three-storeyed houses with spacious rooms.

From his room on the top floor, he called London. Afterwards he remembered some words from a psalm asserting the power of Israel's version of God:". . . he shall crush kings on the day of his wrath. He shall judge nations and heap up the dead; he will crush the rulers of the whole earth."

Yes, that's our agenda now, and we shall be more successful than Israel ever was. Reciting such thoughts to himself, he was soon asleep.

***

Brian's sheep art on the hillside had been wellplanned. He said he was sure his bit of the action would be effective and surprise many spectators. Alissa hoped he would be proved right. They drove to St. Bees in a happy mood. Would it all go according to Brian's plan? If not, any errant sheep chased by the collies would be amusing anyway. This was, after all, action art; the unexpected added extra zest.

***

Graham was back in Vancouver, and Anne had already gone to Victoria by float plane. Graham envied her that; his trips were always by ferry. Yet that was fun with all the islands they passed with their little bays, sailboats, motor launches, and waterfront homes. Hell, Canada's Pacific coast was a special place to be. And it looked as if they were in for a long, hot summer. But he had to work on his book. He was disappointed that Anne was away. He looked at his watch. He would call Samantha, a recent friend. She'd be home from the hospital now. Graham was restless. He needed company.

"Sam? Hi, this is Graham."

"Graham! You're back in town. Good. How was your flight? Oh, Greg, when will you be back? Oh, okay. That's fine. Sorry. Greg is just going out."

"Yeah, I gathered. Hey, do you fancy a drink? Have you eaten?"

"I have. But why don't we have a drink? Do you know the Manchester Pub on Broadway?"

"I do indeed. When? Shall I pick you up?" Samantha said she would collect Graham half an hour later for their outing. Then he could drink without worrying about the cops, and she would drop him at his home and not the other way 'round.

They were soon ensconced at a corner table. Graham, in summer pants and a short-sleeved green Ralph Lauren shirt, had Glenfiddich on ice. Samantha had a virgin cocktail with a small umbrella and a big red cherry. She realized Graham was looking at her closely. His eyes strayed from his drink to her legs. Her short cream-coloured skirt had ridden up a bit too much. She shifted in her seat and pulled it farther down her lightly bronzed thighs.

"So, are you back in the swing of academic work?"

Graham liked her lipstick as she talked. He also liked her small gold earrings and the fine gold chains around her neck. He liked her as a woman and the mother of a teenager. Greg was a good kid. He reached over and took her ringed fingers in his hand.

"You . . . I think you're special, you know?"

"Graham, we have an agreement. I like my life as it is. I don't want any more . . . attachments. We've already agreed on that." She pulled her hand away and picked up her glass.

"Yes, I know. It's too soon. I guess I'm lonely. It's tough."

Samantha knew that; she also knew Graham had lost his wife not so long ago in a senseless murder. *He should wait before trying to climb into bed with anyone, let alone with me.*

"Do you think I'm trying to get you into bed?"

"It did cross my mind, buddy."

"Buddy . . ."

"I think we should *not* go any further along that trail, Graham."

A voice over a sound system suddenly announced it was trivia night. Pencils and papers would be distributed.

"Let's go after the trivia," Graham suggested. It was fun, but they left after the first round. They did badly on rap performers.

***

The book on theory that he was trying to write was proving that he didn't like theory, preferring the novels, the plays and poems. The doorbell rang. He was delighted to find one of his graduate students on the steps.

"Hello, Camilla, what's up?" She was tall and slim. Her long black hair was twisted into a top knot, which made her seem even taller. Her pale skin was lightly freckled. She smiled, her head bent elegantly to one side, her deep brown eyes alert.

"I've finished my dissertation aftermath of form-filling and all that! It's with the graduate committee secretary."

"Wow! You must come in. Tell me all about it." He led the way into his kitchen. "Coffee? Tea? Or how about white wine, to celebrate?"

"Mmm . . . white wine would be great." Camilla sat on a stool. Her longish skirt was dark green and had a slit at the front. When she put her foot on a rung of the stool, she could casually cross her legs, and the skirt would fall away, revealing a good portion of both thighs. She was wearing green hose. Her white silk blouse was more appropriate for the evening, Graham thought. But he admired her figure. He handed her a glass of chilled chardonnay from the open bottle in the fridge. They clinked glasses.

"To you, Camilla, and to a good dissertation. When is the external examiner arriving?"

"The graduate committee secretary told me he'll be here next week, on Wednesday. The oral's the next day."

"I know. Thursday. I got a notice."

"And I'm, like, going about all calmly, but I'm nervous, like really nervous."

"Nervous, eh?"

Next morning, Graham was in his study working on his notes for the book on a bit. A lot. But you'll be there." She smiled and looked at him with her bright, brown eyes. She touched his arm just above his wrist. His shirtsleeves were pushed up to his elbows. Her nails were silver. He felt the thrill of her fingers on his skin.

"Of course. You'll see. It'll be fine." He noticed she had almost finished her wine. "Another?"

"Oh, what's the time? Noon already? I'd better go and get some lunch."

"Is that a hint? I can give you lunch. Here."

"Really, Graham? Well, could I do my bit by cooking it for us?"

"Yep. It's a deal."

She got down from the stool. "Got an apron?" She looked around the kitchen.

"Here." He held out an apron emblazoned with a red heart, above which was "I" and below which was "Vancouver." She slipped it over her head and tried to tie the strings behind her back. It was the apron he always used. Jacky had been the last woman to use it.

"Let me," Graham said. "There. Done." She turned around, and they were standing face to face, close. She put her arms over his shoulders, and they had to kiss. They stepped away from each other.

"Again, Graham?"

He didn't answer, just kissed her again.

"OhGod, Camilla, what are we doing?"

"Kissing. It felt good. Let's do it again!"

They had a long lovemaking session upstairs. Graham was excited by her clothes and her youthful and, in his view, perfect body. Undressing her charmed away the misery of the last few weeks.

13

CAMILLA'S oral was two days away. She had been feverishly revising everything in her dissertation and going into background ideas. She had done enough. Graham could definitely be counted on to point things in the right direction should she get into difficulties with the external examiner's questions. She lay in bed and, as she drifted into sleep, promised herself that when it was all over, if she had her doctorate in the bag, she would reward Graham with another session in the sack. Lying on her left side, her hair spread out behind her and over her right shoulder, she smiled as she fell into a dreamless sleep.

***

Graham was also asleep, but he was having one of his vivid, unpleasant dreams.

The small examination room in the university's Faculty of Humanities was somehow small and cavernous at the same time. . He saw himself standing on a podium in the centre of the room, wearing only his academic gown. Next to him was a circular bed. Other examiners wearing academic dress sat on tiered benches at one side of the bed. They jotted down notes. Graham's wife, Jacqueline, was lying on the bed, naked and alive. Graham climbed onto the bed and started to make love to her with his cape-like gown covering them both. The other academics took more notes.

Camilla, in full academic dress with mortar board, watched their movements from the other side of the room. Graham lay on his back, and Jacqueline sat astride on him. He looked up at her. She was alive! Then she moved down his body, and he groaned. He looked down at Camilla, her black hair luxuriant and spread out across his abdomen. Then her long black hair on the pillow was the most enchanting frame to her face. He looked down again and saw a face rapidly decomposing. He recoiled and sat on the edge of his bed. He looked at Camilla again in her doctoral robes. Her face was normal. She smiled, but her eyes were closed as if she was asleep.

"Let's have lunch, a naked lunch," Jacky said. "I'll fix it."

She put their kitchen apron on over her naked body and cooked some sausages and mushrooms. Camilla, Graham, and his wife all sat on the huge bed. Graham and Jacqueline were now on opposite sides of the mattress, back to back. Camilla sat beside him. She took up a sausage on the end of her fork and bit the end of it. She turned to him and laughed.

"Don't mind her," Jacky advised.

Graham sat up in bed, gasping for air. The clock radio said it was 4:15 a.m. He remembered his dream as if it had really happened. He also remembered that a few days earlier, Camilla had brought their lunch into that same bedroom on trays. They had sat on the edge of the bed to eat. She also brought up the bottle of chardonnay. They each took another glass. She took the trays to a table near the window.

"Again?" she had asked.

"What do you think, Cam?" he asked promptly.

"I like this kind of oral, professor," she replied.

Graham sighed and then held his head in his hands. He got out of bed and went down to the kitchen, taking some orange juice from the fridge.

"How could I have done it? Am I a selfish swine?" he demanded in the silence of early morning on the edge between night and dawn.

Graham was sure that sex was just what he needed. At this stressful time, Camilla needed him too. Yes, they needed each other. He wanted her youth. He wanted to make love to her with a renewed urgency. To hell with dreams. Jacky—he had jacked her in then. How could he make such a pun? Was he just feeble? He remembered how Camilla had reached her final climax and then suddenly pushed him away. She had knelt, her black hair falling around her face. Her silver-tipped fingers had reached for him. He visualized her long, firm thighs. He had shouted when he felt himself spending again.

After the examination, he had invited Camilla to have a celebration dinner, just the two of them, some weekend soon after she had the usual student party.

Graham finished his orange juice and went back to bed. He could not sleep. He wanted Camilla again. Was it love? Just lust. Just? Unjust lust then. Love? No. Affection? Did Cam love him? She admired him, didn't she? The questions went around in his mind. How could he make love to Camilla after Jacqueline? It had happened. What did love have to do with it? Such things happened. He could not get back to sleep. Professors, he knew rationally, should never sleep with students. He knew he was walking a thin tightrope. Now he was a captive of sorts. He hoped Camilla was not going to be troublesome.

***

Paul and Mary had managed to go up to London for a short break when Mary found herself free of her medical practice on Sunday and the following Monday. It was a well-earned break for her. Though noisy with buses and other traffic, London seemed cleaner than they remembered it on their previous visit, and it was very much alive. A fresh breeze occasionally became a stronger gust that soon calmed down again. It was sunny, and large clouds hung on high, looking like white cotton candy.

They had been to the National Gallery and the National Portrait Gallery. When they emerged it was late afternoon on Sunday. They were on their way back to their hotel, where they looked forward to a rest before going out for dinner. They had made a reservation in an Italian restaurant they both liked in Lion Passage, just off Pall Mall. It was usually quiet and discreet. It was also pricy, but it had excellent dishes, some of them imaginative.

As they walked into their hotel room, Mary was thinking about a slight problem.

"Paul, darling, would it be a good idea for me to change my nameplate and the name of the practice? What do you think? I could become Doctor Mary Wills now instead of Doctor Mary Rao."

"Well, that's true. But it's an established practice. People know it now, and they know you. Wouldn't it just lead to pointless confusion?"

"Maybe, but I like being Mary Wills!"

"I agree because I like you as the lovely Mary Wills, Doctor Rao. And to prove it, I'm going to undress you right away. Sari away!"

"As Mrs. Wills and Doctor Rao, I like being undressed by Paul Wills, husband!"

Soon they were both naked and taking a shower together. After that it was the most natural thing in the world to make love. They lay back, contented and half asleep in the queen-size bed.

"Oh, I'll keep the practice in the name of Doctor Mary Rao."

"Well, you've built it up and weathered the storms, darling. I think it's right, and you're fine as Dr. Mary Rao."

"In private we're okay as Paul and Mary Wills," she murmured close to his ear.

"You think? You're sure?" He wanted her to be comfortable with it.

"Sure."

Paul moved a little, so he could stroke her hair. "We both have professions under our original family names. It could unsettle what we've already achieved to change things at this stage. Besides, it might suit you to be known in some places as Mrs. Mary Wills, Physician, and among your Sutton Coldfield patients as the Doctor Mary Rao they all depend on and can't do without."

Mary lightly punched his arm. She snuggled against him and put her head on his chest. Soon they would freshen up before going to the restaurant. "Yes, you're right," she murmured. She put her hand on his flat stomach and kissed the side of his jaw.

From outside they heard a huge bang and loud screams. The distress of human voices was unmistakeable. Mary leapt up and got dressed while Paul looked out into the chaos of the once-quiet street.

"That must have been a bomb," Mary said. "I must go and do what I can until the ambulances arrive."

The door closed behind her. Paul dressed as fast as he could and then went out into the mayhem. This was breaking news alright. It was material for him as a cereer journalist.

***

Graham was at a table waiting for Camilla. She had warned him that she might be a little late. She had to see her parents off. They were going back home to Calgary. He looked at the wine list and ordered a bottle of Burrowing Owl white. It was an elegant British Columbia wine, difficult to find in the government liquor stores. People snapped it up as soon as it was in stock.

Camilla arrived wearing a white silk blouse and a long string of turquoise beads. Her black slightly flared pants emphasized her height. She wore her hair in a ponytail draped over the front of one shoulder.

Graham stood up. "Good evening Doctor Barber," he said. She kissed him on the cheek and then on the mouth. They sat down, and Camilla took Graham's hands in hers.

"Thank you for all your concern and support. I want to thank you warmly. I really mean it."

Their server appeared and recited the day's specials. She was a woman of about thirty wearing a slim black miniskirt and a black-and-white striped blouse. A burgundy bolero jacket with the name of the establishment embroidered on it in gold thread completed her outfit. She was wearing comfortable flat-heeled shoes that did little for her shapely legs. Graham thought she was sensible as well as elegant. Her blond French pleat was set off by her expertly made up face. She was pretty. She left them to ponder the menu.

When their wine appeared, the wine waiter opened the bottle, offered Graham the cork to sniff, and then poured a little for him to taste. With a nod, Graham approved. The waiter poured the wine and then returned the bottle to its ice bucket.

"To you, Camilla, with my sincere congratulations. Do you like it? It's Burrowing Owl." They clinked glasses.

"It's lovely, Graham. What a treat. I've had it only once before."

"Tell me. When?"

"When I was celebrating with my parents."

"What, getting into grad school and becoming owlish, burrowing into nests of library books?"

Camilla smiled. Then she stuck out the tip of her tongue. Her tongue made him think of her kisses.

"It was when I celebrated my divorce."

This delivered a little shock. Graham had taken her on four years earlier to supervise her dissertation. She had also been in one of his seminars, but he had never looked into her personal file. How was it he knew so little about her, though she had taken him and restored his male sexuality? She had also restored some of his self-confidence. He had always thought of her as a single woman, a research student. Now she was a "good lay," a divorcee. Nothing more?

"I didn't know that. I thought you were single," he remarked as if thinking aloud.

"So I am. And so are you, as a widower. We were not being adulterous the other day. Just adults. It was fun."

Fun . . . She was right. They were consenting adults, and she was not even his student anymore. Graham wanted to take her home and have her all over again.

"Can we go to my place after we've eaten?"

"Yes. You bet. Why not? We could have some not-so-scholarly fun again."

And so it was settled. Graham did not think of his disturbing dream. After dinner they undressed hastily and sank into his big once-marital bed.

Camilla was definitely in charge. She pushed Graham onto his back and kissed him long and hard on the mouth. "That's a thank you, Professor."

When it was over, they lay back, dozed a while, and then she asked in a sleepy, casual voice if any jobs were on the horizon in the department. Graham said he didn't know, but he would talk to the department head and find out. He glanced at the clock radio. It was almost midnight.

She took hold of him. "I want you again. Slow. Make it last."

Graham surprised himself.

"I'm applying for jobs. Will you be a referee for me, Professor?"

"Of course. How could I be blind to all your... *accomplishments*?"

Camilla was a little surprised by his "renewable lust," but she said nothing more about sex. She was thinking of jobs of a different kind. They drifted into sleep.

***

Mary pushed through bystanders and went to people who were lying about with all kinds of injuries. She looked for the worst cases. One man was seemingly asleep but was missing a foot. Blood seeped through his tattered clothes. He was alive. Mary immediately fashioned a tourniquet to stem the blood flow. Approaching ambulance sirens added to the noise around the horror. When she saw some paramedics pushing through the crowd, she waved. One of them ran to her.

"I'm a doctor. I'll help in any way I can."

Paul saw her waving and made his way toward her. He wanted to help to. Help carry the wounded? What? It was a scene of smoke, blood, and the sharp cries and groans and sobbing sounds of wounded people.

14

GRAHAM and Camilla were having a lazy breakfast when, at 10:15, the phone rang. Graham shook his head as if to say it should be ignored. She picked up the phone nonetheless. *Proprietorial*, he thought.

"Hello, Graham?" It was a woman's voice.

"I'll put him on," Camilla replied.

"Yes, Graham Curtis."

"Graham, it's Anne. I'm back from Victoria. I have to work here in Vancouver for a few days before I go east. Calgary and Edmonton, I think."

"How did it go in Victoria?"

"Better than I thought it would. But I've been thinking, I was a bit unfriendly before I left. You offered me accommodation. May I take you up on that? I'll keep out of your way."

"Well ... er ... Anne?"

"If it's not convenient, don't worry. That lady who answered is important to you?"

"No. Well, perhaps. She's celebrating gaining a doctorate under my supervision."

"Lucky woman. Well, we should at least have a few drinks, dinner, lunch, tea, or something before I go."

"Well, yes. How about tonight? Dinner?"

"That sounds good. Where?"

"How about Provence on West Tenth? I'll pick you up this evening at seven-ish if you decide not to stay here with me."

"Perfect another day, but I think I'll be tired when I arrive. Could you offer a simple supper chez-vous? If I am staying with you?"

"Of course. You'll stay at my place. Okay. Let me know when you arrive."

"Yes. You're kind. Did you see yesterday's newspapers?"

"No."

"There's been another bomb outrage in London."

"My God! Don't these people know that religious intolerance is out, and tolerance is in?"

"I think they just like the power and the slaughter. Simple as that. But we can talk later. A bientôt."

"Oui. A bientôt."

Camilla encircled his bath-robed torso with her arms. "Well, Gray-ham," she said, imitating the Anne's pronunciation of his name. "Who was that?"

"Oh, she's a French woman I know. An historian."

"And you'll be giving her dinner tonight?"

"Of course. She wants to stay with me for a few days before heading back east."

"And of course you agreed."

"Camilla, I am not an 'item' with Anne. We're friends and scholars. Besides, she's several years older than me."

"And you're more than several years older than me."

"I."

"What?"

"You say 'I am' not 'me am'! "

Next morning, Graham was in his study working on his notes for the book on.

"Yes, Professor. Methinks you've just proved you're older than . . . I am. Yet we've had sex, I think?"

"What's sex got to do with it? We've had fun, as you once put it. I haven't touched Anne de Crevennes. She's more interested in her research and her life in France than she is in me."

"Well, bully for her. I'll see you in a day or two. Will you be going into the department while she's in Vancouver?"

"Probably. I have things to do. And, yes, Camilla, I'll sound out the head on our hiring plans."

"Oh, well, I'll get ready and see you when we can make it. Together. And you'll be my referee?"

"Sure."

She finished dressing and left.

Good, that was easy, she thought as she walked down the path to the sidewalk.

∗∗∗

Doctor Poynter, a Vancouver psychotherapist, shook hands with Graham and motioned him to a comfortable armchair. The two men looked thoughtful, as if lost in their own private affairs. Poynter asked Graham how he was doing. Graham ran his fingers through his abundant dark hair, cleared his throat, and said he had felt better after seeing his friend, Paul, and being best man when Paul married Mary Rao. He also said he had met a French woman, an independent historian, and they were friends.

"Independent?"

"Yes. It means she's a scholar not working for pay in a university."

"Ah, yes. Are you attracted to her, Graham?"

"Yes, I am. But she's some years older than I, has a good lifestyle in France, and is busy . . . too concerned with her work to be involved with me . . . I mean . . ."

"Sexually?"

"Well, yes. We're just friends."

"Do you miss sexual activity, Graham?"

"I've had some vivid and nasty dreams."

"Do you remember any?" Poynter asked, noticing that Graham had shied away from the question of sex. Was he just not interested, or was he sexually active again? The dreams might be a clue. Was the patient making the outside circumstances of his life internal? Was the internal mess projected outside him to make for an irrational moment or moments in his life?

Graham told Poynter all the details of his dreams that he could remember. Poynter saw at once that the dreams were a result of the sex drive as well as the erotic conscience. Maybe he should write an article, "The Erotic Conscience."

"And this post-doctoral woman . . . is she now significant in your life?"

"She's fun. I don't think at this stage that she's a potential wife."

"Would you ever marry again?"

"I don't know. I should think not."

Both men fell silent. Poynter was not about to speak. He had quickly realized that Graham had certainly been to bed with the postgraduate woman. He was waiting for him to reveal something of his thoughts. He was fairly certain that this grieving widower was not going to be attending the therapy sessions for much longer, even if he, in fact, needed them. Nobody could be certain of what might spark future events or difficulties. Poynter was notjudgmental though. His job was to *understand* as much of his patients' past and present conditions as possible, prescribe any necessary medicine, and lead Graham, if possible, to find his own way out of what seemed to be a mild depression. It was clear that recent sexual experiences had restored some of Graham's self-confidence. Poynter thought that "loins will be loins" just as "lions will be lions." But this sex between teacher and student struck him as unprofessional. Such standards seemed to be slipping. Current comment in private seemed to assume that standards of that sort were "stuffy." The teacher wanted sex, and the student probably wanted something else. This was not a clear case of mutual respect. It was not entirely animal either. Well, nowadays, such things were becoming commonplace. Using people sexually was perhaps already a course in business schools: how to gain influence by getting on and off people.

***

Graham's cell phone throbbed in his jacket pocket. Anne announced that she could be at his place or a restaurant late that afternoon.

"Yes, now do come and stay with me, Anne. I can meet you in town, and we can go to Provence, not far from my place, though if you prefer, as you said earlier, I could take you home with me. I can fix dinner. Something simple. Barbecued prawns, maybe a steak, or maybe chicken with salad and fresh fruit. What do you say?"

Anne promptly agreed and thanked him. She said she had arrived by seaplane and was in town at a big store called the Bay to do some essential shopping. Graham insisted on meeting her downtown. He loved to see the float planes coming and going in a blue sky above the harbour. It was a pity she'd already arrived, and he had missed seeing her little plane land on the water.

In his car on the journey across town, he wondered what had changed Anne's mind about staying with him for a few days, though he didn't ask when he met her outside the Hudson Bay building on West Georgia Street.

"Well, did the research go well in the archive over there?" he inquired as they walked to the car park, Graham carrying her shopping bags while she wheeled her luggage.

"Actually, it did. I found some exciting records of French presence in BC written in diaries and letters but also the spoken French of old survivors who were asked to record their experiences and souvenirs before they forgot them, a polite way of getting them to talk before they passed away into heaven!"

"It's good we have far-sighted librarians and archivists who realize those daily lives were actually part of our history," Graham replied, wondering if this material would be interesting enough to become part of the literary heritage as well. "I mean the history of European and other settlers over here. Everything was so new, although the native peoples hadbeen here for thousands of years."

"True. I also realized another thing I must trace: the culture that the settlers brought with them. England, Ireland, Scotland, Wales, Qing Dynasty China, Sun Yat Sen's China, Japan, America. Ukrainians,Germans,Norwegians, Dutch, Greeks, Italians,and France, from the establishment of a colony and the growth of Francophone places, especially Quebec. They all added to the construction of what there is now. But my concern is the French presence."

"And more recently, you French had Levi-Strauss studying west coast Indians and interesting the scholarly world in his findings and theories. And a French woman became the last wife and widow of our sculptor, Bill Reid. As someone born in Canada, you remind me ofhow mixed our cultures are. People bring their bit of culture with them."

"Oui, c'est vrai," Anne replied, probably because she had started thinking of Levi-Strauss in French.

Graham had cleaned the guest bedroom and bathroom with special care. He had also tidied his master suite to remove any stray signs of recent debauchery. When Anne was upstairs preparing for the evening and an early start the following morningat the City Archives of Vancouver, Graham went to his spacious, recently modernized kitchen to prepare the evening meal.

When Anne entered to see if she might help, Graham gave her a bottle of Louis Latour Pinot Noir and asked if she would pour a couple of glasses. Or she could take an Australian white if she preferred. A bottle was already open in the fridge. They had decided to eat in after all rather than go to a restaurant. Anne needed a bit of relaxation in a cozy house.

So, this is how a Canadian academic lives, she thought, *those who had not inherited much wealth.* She didn't realize that the house and the largish lot were worth more than $2 million. She knew Vancouver was experiencing a real estate boom, but she didn't know precise figures.

"I'll go get some fresh chives from the garden," he said. As soon as he left, the phone rang. Anne picked up the receiver and called out to him. "Phone!"

"Hi, this is Camilla."

"Oh. Graham is in the garden. I'll find him for you. Don't hang up, please."

Anne opened the door. "Graham, there's someone called Camilla on the phone."

Graham came inside and put the chives and scissors on the light-grey granite countertop.

"Hello, is this Cam?"

"Hi, Graham. I guess that was your French friend. I suppose she's staying?"

"Yeah. For a few days of research."

"Well, I won't bother you, but I was wondering if you'd swung by the department. Any news yet?"

"Nothing. I did hear that there's a budget problem though. That's a bad sign."

"Shoot! I wonder if you'd be my main referee and all?"

"Sure. I said I would. No problem. I'm right behind you."

Camilla laughed, but Graham didn't see anything to laugh at.

"I'm serious, and I'm sure you'll get a job. Don't worry."

"All righty. Thanks. I really appreciate your help. I'll see you when you're free."

The evening was a good opportunity for Graham and Anne to relax and chat about life in Canada, life in France, and the problems of terrorism. They were both distressed by the turmoil right across the Middle East and farther afield. They had no real desire for their democracies to join in the barbaric sectarian wars. Anne suddenly felt alive, her weariness gone.

"ISIS must be stopped, but how best do that?" Graham asked.

"Difficult," Anne said. "But these outrages within our country and elsewhere must be stopped—like the Charlie Hebdo massacre and the kosher supermarket affair. Or the London attacks and the one in Ottawa. And all that has happened since. Many such things are nipped in the bud each year before people are murdered. Such as the one I heard about in Victoria. You know our secret services stopped about eighty attacks last year in France. But we have no real information about all that. We do know that France is a major target."

"I am glad you said 'murdered' not 'executed' because terrorists are not carrying out lawful executions. They are simply mass murderers, according to the number of victims. Misuse of language isn't a crime, but it sure doesn't help! Why do journalists use that word so unthinkingly?"

"It might be a way of avoiding the nastiest of facts."

They fell silent. The simple meal had been good with the red wine. Now they were enjoying an after-dinner drink. They looked at their glasses of ice wine from Ontario.

"Graham, I'm tired. Do you mind if I go up? I want to be at the archive as soon as it opens." In fact, she was not really tired. She saw him as a physically attractive man. She reasoned that if she stayed up drinking with him, one thing might lead to another. She felt a certain excitement but knew it was wiser just to go to her room and read.

Graham asked if she wanted water in case she woke in the night. He also showed her that the fridge was stocked with whatever she might need for breakfast, if he was not up in time to prepare it.

When Anne went upstairs, he cleaned up and started the dishwasher. She had obviously wanted to switch off any prolonged thinking about terrorists and the results of their total disregard of other people's lives or rights. Criminals were like that. He felt a sudden spasm of anger at the goons who had shot Jacky. But the terror "brigades" were thousands of miles away from Canada. They had also been a long way from New York's towers. His wife's murderers were here and still alive! He decided to have a scotch before he went up. He hoped he would not have nightmares.

In bed at last, he thought over the session with Dr. Poynter. He remembered he had adroitly avoided the question about sex. Was it shyness? Was it shame for being so eager to have sex so soon after losing Jacqueline? He could not understand himself. Maybe he should confront the question in his next therapy session. Did he need another session? Was he just another academic creep, using his position to get young people between the sheets? Not really, he decided. After all, Camilla was not backward at coming forward! She had been married already, for Christ's sake. She wanted to get ahead. Give head to get ahead. He didn't blame her. He fell asleep thinking of his parents' silver wedding party.

15

MIRANDA had ordered breakfast in her room. She had also inquired as to when the day staff came on duty because she wanted an early start. She had to get all the way to Cumberland.

She showered and was just about to dress when a maid knocked on the door and delivered breakfast on a tray covered with a damask cloth. Miranda ate her toast and a soft-boiled egg, pouring herself a second cup of coffee. She finished dressing and pinned up her hair before donning a dark-brown wig. She went down without delay, paid her bill in cash, and told the front desk clerk that she was off nice and early to Bath before going to Birmingham on business. Then she went to Temple Meads station and bought a ticket to Carlisle. She found that she'd have to change to a local line for Worthington and then take a bus to St. Bees if the local train was not going that far. She figured that Bruno, if he was following her, and she was sure he would try, would be watching the hotel.

She was right. Bruno watched the dark-haired woman go off in a taxi. Where was the blonde? He decided to risk the hotel. He discovered that the new shift staff had checked out several guests already. Bruno told the young receptionist that he was trying to contact a business associate who would be travelling that day. Two had already gone, she said, a man and a woman. She had checked them out herself. Bruno told them his colleague was a woman who was travelling alone. He discovered a woman had just left for Bath. That might be her.

"We have a conference at Bath," Bruno told the receptionist. "I was hoping to travel with her as well by car."

"Oh, she'll be going from Temple Meads, sir, no doubt. She didn't ask for guest parking. She took a taxi."

"Well, thank you for this information and for your attention. I shall doubtless see her at that conference."

"You're welcome, sir. Have a good day."

He gave a little bow before he left. He did not see a man who had listened to his exchange with the receptionist and then got into a car parked farther up the street.

The receptionist thought that, like many visitors to the university, the man asking after the other guests spoke good English. Though next morning, Graham was in his study working on his notes for the book on clearly what wasn't his first language. He was too thin. Did he have a terminal disease? Cancer? Or was it AIDS? She began tidying tourist brochures in a little rack near her counter.

"Solihull. Yes, Ali."

"Bruno is following a woman. I think they'll both be going to St. Bees. Shall I go back there?"

"No, come in. I have something else for you. London spillage."

Bruno went around to the airport bus stop where he had also noticed a taxi stand. A taxi was there, and it was available. He ran to get in before anyone else could take it. Nobody seemed interested. They were patiently awaiting the airport bus, some of them sitting on hefty suitcases. This wasn't the rush for taxis he knew in Paris or London. It was a provincial town, but he liked what he had seen of it. Moreover, the aircraft industry in Bristol might be a good target. It had certainly been a target of the Luftwaffe.

At Temple Meads he scanned the crowd inside the station and the queues for information and at ticket office windows. There was no sign of the woman he was following. Thorough as he was, he did not notice a brown-haired young woman who emerged from the ladies' toilet and then stepped quickly back inside.

Bruno bought a rail pass that was valid for any train leaving Temple Meads. He looked around and saw the brown-haired woman make for the platforms. She looked vaguely familiar. He stepped back among the other travellers when his quarry reached her platform. They waited about three minutes before the train came in. A dense crowd of people was manipulating cases and backpacks of various kinds. He struggled up the step to a second-class carriage but noticed the woman with brown hair and neat appearance as she climbed into first class.

Miranda took out what appeared to be an airline eye cover, settled down in her seat, put the elastic over her head, and fixed the cover over her eyes. If she opened her eyes, however, she could see through it. She would catnap to Carlisle. She had spotted Bruno, tall and somewhat bizarre, and waited for him to get into second class. At any stop before, and at Carlisle itself, she would watch to see if he got out onto the platform. Then she would follow him and any person he might meet.

Back in second class, Bruno took out a national newspaper he had bought. He relished the account of a bomb outrage in London.

***

Graham was in a long hall, like a gallery in a stately home. Someone was throwing a couple of tennis balls at the wall. Both balls were thrown simultaneously using both hands. They always bounced back to be caught expertly by one huge hand grown suddenly bigger. Yet he could see the person responsible for the game.

There was no thudding noise as the balls hit the wall. The player's identity gradually became apparent. It was a woman wearing a tennis outfit, but her feet were bare. Graham walked toward her. She turned to look at him. He didn't know her, but she was smiling. She started juggling the two balls and then added a third. Still smiling, she looked at him rather than at the balls.

"Hello, Professor," she said. "I'm Camilla's mom. I'm sixty-five. I passed away last year."

Graham awoke instantly. His eyes began to adjust to the dim light coming from a gap where his bedroom door was ajar. The soft sound of its opening had probably awakened him. It was then that he saw Anne moving in the dim light. She got into bed with him.

"This is just between friends," she whispered. "I realize I was a bit cruel. But I must work for a day or two more intensively. And then I shall have to leave. So, can we be close just this once? I felt too cruel. I need some tenderness. Do you?"

"Yes. Oh, Anne, yes."

"Just this once. Promise?"

"I promise, madame."

***

Three celibate days later, Graham took Anne to the train station. Calgary was her next destination. Graham advised her to take a day or two in Banff and then go to Lake Louise. She would be amazed by those places. They had seen little of each other since the night she had come to his bed. Before she boarded the train, Graham held her in his arms. She kissed his cheeks three times.

"Keep in touch!" she said.

He waved as the train left. The next stop for him was the department and then the university library. As he walked from his car, he could not help regretting that Samantha had proved "unavailable." Camilla had been different. *From Sam to Cam and, just this once, to Anne.* He pushed this thought away. He had not seen Camilla since the morning of Anne's phone call. He checked his mail in the department office. Nothing of interest. When he went down to the stacks in the undergraduate library, there was Cam.

"Hello, Graham, what are you doing here?"

"I guess the same as you. Profs have a habit, you know. It's called reading. I'm looking for books that could be useful."

"Do you also look for women who could be useful?" she asked with a half-laugh.

"Cam, do you look for profs who could be useful?" He did not even smile.

"I was talking to other grads, and I'm saying, like, it's tough in the humanities. You know our funding is minimal. We're tolerated. It's like business students are the fat cats. Women always get the raw deals in our faculty. We need help."

"You're right," Graham said. "Let's not fight. Anne left for Calgary today."

"Will you be a referee for me when I apply for jobs?"

"Of course, of course. I said I would, didn't I. Don't worry." She was badgering him.

"When we're both done here, we could go get a beer."

"Sure. By the way, are your parents excited and pleased you have a doctorate?"

"They would be, I guess. My dad's back east with a new woman. My mom's dead. She passed away over a year ago."

"Oh, I didn't know." Graham was grave, astounded that his dream had been about somebody he had never known and who had indeed died.

"I'm sorry to hear that. You have my condolences."

He realized he had a recently deceased wife and he had already betrayed her with two women, one much younger than he was and another a little older. A decade older? No. Less? He didn't know. He wondered whether to phone Paul to talk about it. No. He was a little ashamed. Yet he felt powerful. He was a sexual being not a dry, old professor. But if he had seen Camilla's dead mother and Jacqueline in a dream, as if they were still alive, did the dead watch the living? He hoped Jacky could not see him. He needed to get back to Marxist theory, French or otherwise! He felt a sudden surge of anger toward those criminals who had wrecked his marriage.

"Shall we meet in the Manchester pub? It's snug in there when it's raining. A rain belt's moving in."

"Oh... er yes. I can be there at about five this afternoon. Okay?"

"Fine by me. See ya later!"

"I've never had it. I'll stick to beer."

"Never had what?"

"See Ya Later. It's the name of a wine. Saw it in the liquor store."

"Oh yeah. Well, beer at five." Camilla disappeared in search of her tomes.

Camilla... Cam. *Is she just like a camellia to me?* He was unsure. In any event, he was not feeling amorous. He had had enough sex during the past week.

16

BRUNO went to a door, got down onto the platform, and looked around at the disembarking passengers along the train at both of the two stops before Carlisle. Miranda had not done the same. She had seen Bruno's head and noticed a younger man who got off at the stops and then climbed back in before the train resumed its journey. Now she was resting. At Carlisle she had to be careful. Bruno must not realize she was Kim's backup.

She got off at Carlisle and went straight to the exit from the platform and stood in a newspaper shop in the concourse. She found a local newspaper and noticed a booklet about Tomkyn Bridge School. She purchased both. As she positioned herself for a good view of the exit from the platform, a jostling mass of passengers from second class surged toward the narrow exit. Others hung back, unfolding stroller for toddlers. There was the usual noisy crowd, the banging of luggage, and the rattle of wobbly carts. *The echoing of humanity in a station: was it an image of life's journey?* She pushed the thought aside. *Concentrate.*

Bruno emerged with the last trickle of people. He had been looking out for any signs of surveillance. He went into the concourse to find the ticket office. Miranda followed a group laughing and joking among themselves. From a distance she watched Bruno pushing banknotes into the slot below the window between customer and clerk. Miranda didn't realize it, but he was buying tickets for two accomplices. It was a ticket outlet for local trains.

Bruno walked toward the men's toilet. Two youths with hooded jackets followed him in. A minute later they were out again looking at tickets before pocketing them. Four minutes later, Bruno emerged.

Miranda smiled. His two young men were different from the previous ones she had seen. Bruno could call up stooges easily. He must have had a network of them at his disposal. He had to be a big fish. Miranda concluded that Bruno was definitely a traitor.

She went to the same ticket office. When it was her turn, she asked which stations were called at.

"This is the coast train, madam, calling at Maryport, Workington, and Whitehaven. There are some trains to St. Bees. That's the terminus."

"Oh, good. I'll book for Whitehaven."

She decided to mount her train before Bruno, so he and his two young henchmen could think they were in control. Keep close. Then she'd watch out for them at each stop.

It was a good idea. They got off the train at Workington, leaving the station as the train pulled out. Miranda knew then that Kim's hideout in St. Bees was, perhaps, not quite on Bruno's radar. The three terrorists were nevertheless in Cumberland and within striking distance.

Miranda went to Whitehaven. Nobody suspicious seemed to be among the gaggle of schoolchildren and a few middle-aged locals. But then a shop window reflection revealed a young man who had been at the station when she disembarked. She got into a taxi and, after a few minutes, asked the driver to stop outside a hotel.

She went inside and entered a coffee place on one side of the lobby. The young man was no longer following her. She walked quickly to a side street in search of a suitable place to stay, since it was pointless going on to St. Bees at this stage. A spic-and-span Victorian terrace of three-storey houses not far from the hotel had "Bed-and-breakfast" and "Vacancy" notices. The holiday season was not yet in full swing.

After checking in she contemplated her disguise in a long mirror inside the wardrobe door. Not bad. She'd go to St. Bees early the next day. The weather network on TV warned of changeable weather. The next thing was to get something to eat and find out how to get to St. Bees.

Downstairs she asked the neat and lightly made-up lady in charge what time she put out breakfast. The earliest was at 7:00 a.m. That would be perfect. The woman wore a light-blue nylon coat-style overall with a name tag that said "Estelle." Miranda noticed she had no wedding ring but wore silver rings (or platinum?) on her forefinger and the ring finger of her right hand.

"I'm going to explore St. Bees tomorrow and see an old school friend who lives there. What's the best bet for getting there?"

"You could take the local bus. It starts at seven and goes every hour from the train station. It's a lovely little place, St. Bees. There are good walks along the coast," Estelle advised.

"That's handy," Miranda replied. "I canhave breakfast at seven and then catch the eight o'clock or nine o'clock bus."

"It'll take about forty-five minutes, mind," Estelle said. "Depends on how many stops it has to make."

"Well, thanks. I'm off now for a breath of air before I turn in. I came down from Edinburgh to Carlisle and then caught the local train." With that she left in search of somewhere to eat.

A fish-and-chip shop caught her eye. She treated herself to two pieces of battered hake and a healthy scoop of chips. Harry would call them French fries. She smiled. How British she felt, having fish and chips. She had salt and malt vinegar with them. But already she wanted to see Harry again. As soon as she was back in Paris. But for the moment she had to concentrate on staying alive.

A news agent was still open. She bought a local Whitehaven paper and one for St. Bees.

Back in her room, Miranda glanced over the local rags and a Carlisle newspaper and found articles on the St. Bees art festival. There had been a sort of art happening by a St. Bees artist called Quint. The report said it had been a "surprising and wonderfully relevant herding of sheep" made into a "happening" by the sheep having been painted many different colours. Miranda decided to see whether the following day's St. Bees newspaper would have anything useful for locating Kim.

Estelle found a copy of that morning's Whitehaven paper for her. It had an article about the arts festival and a picture of the artist called Quint receiving a token of appreciation from the mayor. It was a small bronze sheep donated by the sheep farmers.

Miranda looked closely at the photograph. In a huddle of people watching to one side was a woman taller than the others in the picture. Her head was turned away from the camera, as if her attention had been distracted. But the part of her face still visible was worth comparing with Miranda'sphoto of Kim. Shelooked from one picture to the other. The woman was Kim alright.

She took out the booklet about Tomkyn Bridge School that she'd bought in Carlisle. As she flicked through it, she found a list of teachers. A Miss Mason was the principal. Under Modern Languages was a Mrs. Chapman and a Miss Alissa Partridge. She'd go to the school and ask for Miss Partridge rather than the married woman.

***

Bruno was of two minds. His first impulse was to find Kim, rape her, and then butcher her in that outlandish place. But no. She must be lured to London. The safe house was wonderfully equipped for visitors. He knew he must become cold, like a snake. He must go back to Paris. Yes. Control must think all was well, and then Bruno would strike with the terrible force of his own vengeance against a country he had come to despise.

17

"**THIS** is Miranda. Have sights still to take in."

"This is Control. Line secure. What do you have?"

"She was definitely in St. Bees, Cumberland, to attend a local arts festival."

"How so?"

"A local journalist took a picture at some arts festival presentation. I noticed a woman nearby had her head partly turned away from the group. It's Kim."

"How careless of her. That's unlike her."

"I'm off to St. Bees on the bus. I'll sniff around. Bruno and two young men are in Workington tonight. I think Bruno's a traitor. They might see the same picture."

"Good buzzing in St. Bees. Check out the artist. Keep clear of Bruno for now if you can. If you can get the two young men arrested, I'll manage the rest from here. You'll need Kim. You should get to her before Bruno does. But don't let him know that, and don't let him corner you. Merci plein. Keep in touch, ma chère."

It was time to go to the bus with her small bag. She might have to stay at the bed-and-breakfast for another night or two. She took one of the books of crossword puzzles and her pen. As she had told Monsieur Martin, it was likely Bruno had seen that press photo and was on the trail. If so, he would surely try to find the artist. If she could get to Kim first, as Control advised, they had a chance of getting Bruno back to Paris alive. Control would be ecstatic. He would think, like Harry, that she and Kim were "awesome." Well, they were. Finding the artist would have to wait. Her hunch was to go to the school. She suspected Kim was posing as Miss Alissa Partridge, a respectable teacher in a respectable girls' school.

In fact, Alissa Partridge, teacher of languages at Tomkyn Bridge School for

Girls, was at the shooting range with six senior students whose parents were paying for them to learn pistol shooting. All were wearing ear protection to deaden the noise as they fired. Alissa taught them the best stance, grip, and firing technique to allow for recoil and the tendency of the pistol to jump up slightly when fired. But most important were the safety procedures and care of the weapon. She had already instructed them on cleaning the pistol, loading, unloading, and safety catch positions. She did not want some silly student fooling around with a lethal weapon.

The girls had witnessed Alissa's expert handling of the gun and openly admired her fast, accurate shooting of the small but lethal weapon. No jokes. No fooling around. Juliet, one of the prefects, was a reliable and rather bright student. She was already doing the best shooting of the bunch. Alissa knew Juliet's family had a country estate, where they did satrap shooting with friends. Alissa could make a crack shot of her. More importantly, it was a good opportunity for Alissa to keep in practice.

After seeing her picture in the local St. Bees paper, even though as part of a crowd, Alissa felt she might need the practice. She had been so pleased with Brian's success in the arts festival that she had noticed too late that she might be in a photograph. She had managed to turn her head, but was that enough? She doubted it. She had been too careless. But she would face any consequences when they arrived. If they did. Perhaps she would have to leave St. Bees earlier than planned. Was she beginning to slip?

***

"This is Bruno. I'm on holiday."

"Line secure," Control replied. "Where? Seen someone?"

"I'm in Cumberland. I'm almost sure our friend is near Workington or Whitehaven. Saw something in a press photo. I'll watch the local papers."

"Well done. Try to pin her down. Tell her she has to get back to Paris. Something big on the menu. Tell her to be in touch with me."

"I'll do that. Oh, have you sent another agent?"

The line was already dead. He decided to start with that question the next time he contacted Control.

He went downstairs to have breakfast in the third-rate hotel he had found. His two followers were in a bed-and-breakfast place one street over. What did

Control mean by something big on the menu in Paris? Had he got wind of the Three Hares operation? No. That plan was so secret that Bruno, as yet, had just a few details yet to discuss.

The waitress arrived to ask if he would have coffee or tea. He decided on coffee but declined the full English breakfast. She took his order for brown toast and plain yogurt.

"Have you a copy of today's paper?"

"Sorry, sir, it arrives about 9:30 most mornings. I do have yesterday's in the meantime." She fetched a slightly crumpled copy.

As she left, she thought her guest had cancer or something. He was too thin. He needed a *proper* breakfast. English, Irish, and Scots breakfasts were the best in the world. Why couldn't these foreigners admit it?

Over breakfast Bruno thought about what to do next as he flicked through the paper with its weddings and deaths listed, its amateurish (as he thought) advertisements, and local squabbles reported from council meetings. Then he saw the brief account of an arts festival. Coloured sheep coming down a hillside. What a useless idea. Art! There was a picture of a crowd watching. Could Kim be in the crowd? He looked again, and yes, there she was! That was Agent Kim. *Ah, Kim, I shall have you soon, ma belle.*

By the time he finished breakfast and a second cup of coffee, the waitress appeared with that morning's paper. It had arrived a little earlier than usual. Bruno smiled at her. She smiled vaguely and went back to the kitchen through a swinging door.

That man is a creep, she thought.

A page in the paper made Bruno pause. It was a follow-up to the arts festival article about the prize given to a local artist. The previous day's photo appeared but in a larger format. In a group of people near the podium was a woman half-turned away from the camera. It was Kim alright! Confirmed! Bruno decided to go to St. Bees. She was certainly near there. He'd soon find out where.

***

Bruno paid cash and used a stolen driver's licence to rent a car. The trip to St. Bees with his two young men passed without incident. It was a fine day with great patches of white cloud in the light-blue sky. The morning sun cast shadows from the trees near the road. The unpolluted air had a slight chill, but as the trio arrived and got out of the car in a municipal car park, they were not cold. It felt good to be alive. God was great.

Now the task was to find out where Agent Kim might be. Was she known to any of the locals? What was her current name? Where could he find her? Bruno explained to his two young men that it was a difficult task. Where would Kim, a French woman, go in St. Bees? Food shops? The post office? The local newspaper? They might inquire after a young woman of colour, tall and comely. One of his recruits to the great cause of carnage and the destruction of other people's human rights suddenly nudged the other young man.

"What is it?" Bruno asked.

"That brown-haired woman I noticed somewhere. She's getting into a taxi."

"Back in the car!" Bruno hissed. "She was on our train. We'll follow the taxi to see where she goes."

18

MIRANDA would soon arrive at Tomkyn Bridge School. She was intrigued by the fact that Kim was a teacher there. What a place to hide when on leave! And who said teaching girls was a holiday? Why work?

As the taxi paused at the school gates, a car passed by and continued along the road. At first she thought it was perhaps going to a farm. A local car probably. But Bruno and two young men were in it. Miranda felt a surge of excitement. *You don't realize what you've taken on, Bruno. I know you've been turned. Time to topple a pawn or two.*

At the impressive front of the building, she got out, paid the driver, and went through the front door. When she announced that she had come to visit Miss Partridge, she was taken by a homely yet smartly dressed woman to the head's office. Miranda told the secretary she was Mireille Martin, a friend of Miss Partridge. After a few minutes, she was able to speak to the head, a woman wearing a little makeup and dressed in an immaculate lightweight tweed.

"Welcome to Tomkyn Bridge School. I'm Miss Mason. And you are Mademoiselle Martin?" The grey-haired, upper-class-looking woman got to her feet and smiled.

"That's right," Miranda said, smiling warmly. "I'd be grateful if I could see Miss Alissa Partridge. She's a friend. She doesn't know I'm here, but since I'm in the neighbourhood I thought I could see her for tea or an early dinner before I go back to Bristol. We were students together."

"Do you teach too?" Miss Mason asked, looking her in the eyes and smiling again.

"No. I work from time to time as a translator for the European Union."

"Well, that should keep you busy. Pity they don't adopt one language as the official one for all documents and discussions. All the translation and interpreting must be quite a costly industry!"

"That's for sure. It keeps me in funds and several thousand like me, I would think."

Miss Mason looked closely at her, thinking this woman could woo the newly appointed Alissa away from the school to work in Brussels. Leading and letting the young flourishwas, to her mind, far better than poring over huge batches of European Union documents in order to translate them. It seemed a singular and solitary occupation.

A bell rang.

"Ah, the end of classes for the morning," Miss Mason explained, rising to her feet. "You should be able to catch Alissa if you stand near the notice board. And if you wish to stay for lunch, she can bring you to the staff dining 'box,' as we call it."

"Well, thank you," Miranda said. "I have to press on this evening, but lunch would be super. Better for me, in fact, than dinner."

The two women shook hands. As Miss Mason walked to the door with her, Miranda noticed that she limped slightly. She also noticed her clothes were beautifully coordinated and probably expensive.

On the notice board in the hallway, Miranda read that Alissa Partridge had organized the badminton round robin. Girls of different ages, all in school uniform, milled about. An older girl wearing a prefect's badge stopped and asked if she could help. At that moment Alissa walked through some swinging doors.

"No, that's fine. There's my friend." The prefect smiled and walked away, thinking that the "Game Bird," as they called Miss Partridge, had a smart, attractive friend.

"Alissa, do you remember me? I'm Mireille Martin from Paris. I knew you in the college debating club when we were at university."

"Oh, yes? I can't say I do. Martin did you say?" Alissa asked.

"Martin. That's my family name. Surely you met my father once? I'm Mireille. I know there are many Martin families in France, but ours is a special one in Paris."

"Of course. Mireille! Let's go to my room, and I'll get ready for lunch. Will you stay?" The two women hugged while schoolgirls milled around, some of them giggling.

***

Alissa closed the door to her room and then looked at Mireille Martin. She was fit and healthy with the skin of a non-smoker who ate a healthy diet. She glowed with health. But her hairstyle was too settled and neat. Was she wearing a wig? Had she undergone chemotherapy? She had never seen this woman before.

"Who are you?" Alissa asked.

"Nomenklatura calls me Miranda. I have a direct line to Monsieur Martin. You are Agent Kim. You are on leave. Here, take my phone." Kim waited and watched her instead. Miranda tapped in four numbers.

"Hello, Miranda. Line secure." It was Martin's voice alright.

"I'm with Kim. Bruno has definitely been turned."

"Noted. Pass Kim to me."

Miranda handed the phone to her new partner.

"Ah, Kim! Something big has come up. We need you back here."

"I'm on leave."

"I know, but we really need you and Miranda. And there's another thing. You're in danger. Miranda can explain."

"I can be back in a week."

"Excellent. I knew we could trust you. Bruno has a difficulty. Miranda will explain that. Be careful, my dear."

There was no demand for an explanation as to why she had not been in touch with Paris while she was away. Control understood her. But he had to be worried about her.

"Miranda, tell me what's happening. It's end of term in a couple of days. Then I'll get back to Paris. So?"

"Control thinks Bruno is working with a terrorist group, perhaps an Islamic one."

"What a bastard! So, what's the plan?"

"Well, Control was not certain, so we had to test Bruno. Control sent me to track you down. He also sent Bruno. If Bruno is a true patriot, we thought you and he would get safely back to Paris. If not, Bruno might try to kill you. But I'm here to back you up. I know now that Bruno is a double agent with

British Muslim recruits. Control accepts my worst fears. We should get back to Paris alive and take our ghoulish traitor with us, preferably alive as well. I'm sure Bruno will try to... detain us, probably in London. Or perhaps in France. When he has wrung us out, he'll kill us. We'll disappear. Forever. Bruno will vanish too. Then he'll return to Europe or even North America with a fresh plan for a killing machine. And Control will have lost three highlytrained agents. Our job is to let Bruno find you. If he tries to make either of us his prisoner, we have to outsmart him, then get him back to Paris for interrogation. If necessary, we can kill him."

"It's risky. Bruno is good, very good. And if we flush him out, who knows what his resources are."

"I think," Miranda said, "that Control could have had Bruno watched and built a case. That's what the Brits did with Philby. Philby—"

"He defected just in time."

"Yes. This way is quicker."

Kim smiled suddenly. "Control must think we're more than a match for Bruno and any minions he may have."

"I think we are! Control wants Bruno back in Paris alive. Killing him would be easier," Miranda replied, removing her wig. "This thing's making my head itch. Ah! That's better." She sighed heavily, puffing out her cheeks. "He has two henchmen. We must get rid of them."

"What's the big thing at home that requires me to cut my leave short?"

"Control didn't say. But he took me for dinner at le Train Bleu."

"Aha!"

Miranda ignored Alissa's exclamation and continued. "I think there might be an attempt on TGV trains and the Gare itself, especially the clock tower."

"I think Bruno will have the answers," Kim replied as she walked into her bathroom and applied some lipstick. She invited Miranda to freshen up and make sure her wig was well fixed on again.

"What were you doing with that arts festival?" Miranda asked. "Do you know the artist responsible for the sheep happening?"

"I do, actually. It was foolish of me to be photographed."

"It led me to you here."

"Well, Bruno can certainly recognize me in that photo."

"The painter... is he... just what he seems?"

"He's a single, handsome teacher who works for the local education authority."

"And nobody else?"

"He's certainly not SIS or SAS."

"Are you two an item?"

"No... you're as bad as Control."

The two young women laughed, checked their makeup, and then went down to have lunch in the dining box. Now Kim knew the dead sheep was not random cruelty. She was not afraid for herself but for Brian.

19

AFTER lunch, since she had an hour free before her next classes, Alissa went back to her room with her "old friend Mireille." They needed to think through the situation.

"Now that we know for sure that Bruno is a traitor, I should let him discover me and be his target," Alissa said. "If he tries to kidnap or even kill me, I need you to act like lightning."

"Absolutely. You can depend on me. In fact, we can just return to London separately but on the same train and let Bruno follow you back to France, where we can arrest him," Miranda offered.

"It might work. If we all go back to Paris quickly with no interference from Bruno, we might lead him to think we have no suspicions. But the more I consider him, the more I worry. He's unpredictable. Let him take me back, but with you unseen and ready to pounce. He'll think he's won. He's volatile, you know. That makes him a dangerously loose cannon. At the same time, it's his great weakness."

"Volatile? That could lead to the unforeseen move that kills us. I'll stay on the look-out but ready to pounce. You're right."

"What's Control's plan for our return to Paris?"

"He didn't mention one. I figure we'll go back by rail and air."

"We should contact Control again and pose the question. He should have a rapid *exeunt* for us all if Bruno is to be taken back alive for interrogation." Alissa was certainly feeling like Agent Kim once more.

Miranda took her special phone, pressed four keys, and put the phone to her ear.

"This is Miranda."

"Control. Secure line. What's new?"

"Kim and I will try to get Bruno back alive. So, how? What's your plan?"

"Talking to Kim about planning, eh?Lead Bruno to London. In five days from now, I will have arranged a helicopter or a light aircraft for you at Stanstead. Report straight to security at the airport. They'll be expecting you, even if you have to bring a coffin with you."

"Good. I'll see you soon."

"I know you'll be careful. Good luck."

***

From his chosen vantage point, Bruno watched a woman with dark-brown hair exit the school and get into a taxi. He decided to trail the taxi. Where was she going, and who was she?

The taxi made for St. Bees. A few minutes later, it was heading for the village's little railway station.

Miranda noticed that the car following her to the station was the same one that had followed her to the school. At the station she bought a ticket for Carlisle, paying cash. Behind her in line was a young man who also bought a ticket for Carlisle. Miranda recognized him as one of the men she had seen hanging around with Bruno.

She left the station and walked to a café called the Copper Kettle. Bruno's second young man followed her, though he walked past the café.

"Sorry, I've changed my mind," Miranda said to the waitress. She went out into the street. The young man was looking at a fruiterer's window. Miranda stood next to him and looked at the fruit and vegetables. Her poison pen pressed into the young man's hand. He collapsed. Miranda rushed into the shop.

"A young man has collapsed. Please call the doctor or the hospital and the police!" The shopkeeper looked at her and then followed her out of the shop. The young man was on the sidewalk.

"Please call someone!" The fruiterer nodded and then rushed back to telephone.

As Miranda walked away, she noticed the shop was called the Melon Cauly.

Soon she reached a small hotel. She asked how much they charged per night and if she could use the telephone. She called an anti-terrorist unit in Carlisle. She told their duty agent she was Miranda from Paris, to confirm with M. Martin, and informed the agent that a young man in St. Bees had collapsed in the street outside a fruiterer and was probably now under medical care, but he and his known associates should be checked. He was a terrorist, probably in training. She also asked if they had a local art teacher, Brian Atkins, on their radar. They told her he was obsessed with painting and helping young students to draw and paint.

Miranda went to the station. The car was still there. She noted its licence number again, just to be sure. She bought some newspapers before she took the train for Carlisle. Bruno's other young man followed suit.

***

Bruno was impatient. One of his followers was on the train for Carlisle with the brown-haired woman. But where was the young trainee who had followed her around St. Bees?

He drove back into the main village. An ambulance was outside a fruiterer's shop. Bruno drove past the shop and stopped farther down the street. The ambulance drove away. He walked back and spoke to a youth who was moving away from the excitement near the shop. The decadent little swine had acid-green hair around his ears and above the nape of his neck. The luxuriant lawn was topped by bright-yellow hair in spiky tufts. Bruno had seen sulphur-crested cockatoos. The lad's beaky nose made him a sort of human, though less lovely, equivalent.

"What was all this about?" Bruno asked. The youth looked at him. Skull-face was tall, thin, and smiling. He was some foreign goon.

"Some young guy collapsed in the street outside the fruit shop. Maybe he was a fruit!" He cackled. It sounded a bit like a parrot.

"Will they take him to hospital now?"

"Yeah. That's what ambulances do, don't they? Where have you been?"

Bruno wanted to cut the arrogant white fool's throat. And then scalp him.

"I'm from Liverpool. Which hospital?"

"How should I know? The nearest."

"Cheers," Bruno said and then went back to the car. He sat until his rage at the youth subsided, and then he drove away. The young acolyte in hospital might recover, but Bruno wanted to be elsewhere when that happened. His trainee's people in Cumbria could deal with him.

He drove to Whitehaven and looked for a bed-and-breakfast place. He was in a small but comfortable room when his cell phone rang.

"Hi. The woman has settled down. She took out a copy of The Times Educational Supplement. She's probably being interviewed for a job in that posh school. I'm in the next compartment. A-Okay!"

"Good. Keep with her. Call me from Carlisle."

Bruno was content. "A" stood for Allah. He would look after them. He would prevail over the infidels, including the Christian scum. Bruno hoped the youth in hospital would die. The young fool might not be able to slip away from the authorities. The local paper might carry the story. He would check as soon as the paper came out. He supposed his young recruits were scared. They lacked the repeated training to give them high-speed reactions. When things happened fast, the speed banished fear. People were only afraid when they were thinking.

***

"Professor Graham Curtis," proclaimed a small white plastic plaque stuck firmly in place above a small rectangle of cork on the wall beside the office door. Notices could be pinned to the cork. A cluster of red-topped pushpins were in the top-right corner. The cork was clear of notices, and Graham's door was open. He had taken to leaving it open whenever he was inside. This was not careless; on the contrary it was a wise and careful precaution against disturbed or malevolent visitors who could testify that a professor had made improper advances while his door was closed.

Every so often somebody walked past, or he heard a sneeze or a cough from somewhere along the corridor. Graham gazed at the mountains. He had a splendid view. Some of the highest peaks, far away, still held the last remnants of snow. The telephone rang. It was a call from his British friend, Paul Wills.

"Hi buddy. How are things in Sutton Coldfield?"

"Hey, you have caller ID."

"Yes, sir. And how are you and Mary?"

"We're fine. Luckily. Just back from a short break in London. A bomb went off. Mary rushed out of the hotel and helped with casualties. Now we'll be staying put until November."

"I don't blame you. How shocking. It was reported in our press. Luckily, we're thousands of miles away from all that."

"I wouldn't bank on it. But what have you been doing, besides correcting essays and seeing students?"

"I've been examining a dissertation and also seeing a bit of Anne de Crevennes, who just left."

"Did she arrive in Canada to see more of you, Graham? I can see you as a bit of a dark horse!"

"She has quite a demanding project for her next book about French women in Canada. So, she did some research and stayed with me a couple of nights. She's headed to Banff, Lake Louise, and Calgary."

"When will she be back in Europe?"

"No idea. She won't know either. It all depends on what she finds."

"Look, I'm calling because Mary and I were wondering if you might get over here again, later this summer?"

Graham thought quickly. This was his oldest friend. Should he tell him? "Hold it. I'll close my office door." He glanced at his watch. Ten in the morning. "Yes, Paul, I'm back. I think I'm getting involved with someone. I feel bad about it."

"You mean you feel disloyal to Jacqueline?"

"That's about it. But this woman is experienced and sexy."

"Samantha?"

"No. Samantha says it's too early for me to let go, and she doesn't want anything more than being friends."

"Well, I can't tell you what to do. But Sam may be right about it being too early. Some widowers have been known to remain celibate for years. Others never remarry."

"Oh, I know. But I've been having nightmarish dreams. And I feel a sort of sexual pressure that needs release."

"Of course, you know yourself and your next partner or would-be partner. If you have any counselling, it might be a blessing. A widower isn't the same as a divorcee. You have more to grieve. But you're single again. You have to get used to that. It's a chance to know yourself more thoroughly. Be careful."

Graham felt suddenly irritated. His just-married friend was trying to make him deny his own sexuality!

"What business is it of yours?" His question was followed by a pause.

"Well, you brought it up. I'm just giving a bit of counsel, that's all. You do what you want."

"I don't need your permission, do I?"

"Look, Graham, I was simply ringing to ask if you might be over here sometime. You'd be welcome to stay. I have to go now."

"I'll let you know. Thanks for the invitation. There's someone at the door," Graham lied, "Gotta go." He hung up.

Paul and Mary would probably have a glass of wine. Then a cozy dinner together. Then bed. Lucky Paul. Why had Graham been so uptight? He didn't know. It was crazy.

Paul had not been able to say anything about Mary's saving a man's life. He supposed the bombs in Europe were no longer front-page news in North America. Now he assumed, as he had hinted to Graham, there would soon be more outrages on the other side of the Atlantic. He was surprised by Graham's sudden mood swing. They were old friends. He hoped Graham would get over to see them soon.

20

ALISSA had finished all her duties for the day. She settled down in her sitting room with a Badoit water and a twist of lemon. She had to think carefully before moving into action. Agent Miranda, masquerading as Mireille Martin, was going to be in Whitehaven and would hire a car. She would call Alissa at the school when they were ready to leave. Before that they had to think out their moves and consult each other. There could be no errors. Bruno was an effective agent. She could master him in unarmed combat, but as a knife man, she figured he had few rivals. This was his metier or mystery, as medieval guilds called it. She knew he was ruthless. If he captured either or both of them, there was little chance of survival. His personal liking for her would count for little. Lust would rule. How to exploit it?

She looked at her desk where, on a small stand, she had placed the ornate eighteenth-century fan her mother had given to her. Whatever she did next, she had to keep that fan with her. She would pack a bag for her trip to Paris, leaving other things at the school for her return the following term. She hoped the big thing in Paris would be over before the end of the summer.

The phone rang, interrupting her thoughts.

"Alissa, it's Mireille. I'm coming back from Carlisle. I've rented a car."

"Good. You had a slight change of plan?"

"Yes. I'll tell you about it when we meet."

"How about the village pub in Ritherdon?"

"I'll find it. See you soon. Bye."

The metallic tone on the line suddenly made Alissa feel lonely, even in the crowded life of the school. *Am I a hunter as well as a fugitive*? As Kim, she knew the answer: she was both. "Hide on Hide."

The shaking of the young man had prompted another disguise. Mirandahad gone to the toilet with her raincoat and a small bag. It was ten minutes until arrival at Carlisle. She removed her makeup, applied a different lipstick, and altered her eye shadow, giving her eyelids a light-green tinge. She exchanged her brown wig for an auburn one with a different hairstyle. Her pantyhose became black net rather than summer bronze. She also changed into black-and-white sneakers and reversed her raincoat. Out of her purse she took a black leather triangle, which she unzipped to make another bag large enough to hold all her other luggage. Miranda repacked her original bag and then put it into the collapsible one, which was long and cylindrical with sturdy handles. She hung her reserve handbag across her body from her left shoulder. That way she could get out her pen with her right hand within seconds.

***

Bruno's phone rang.
"I'm sorry I lost her. I checked but could not see her."
"Come back here. I might need you."
Bruno put the phone away. He could use the boy's muscle but not his brain. He was not a natural as an operator at a higher level. After this operation he could be put on a suicide team. Then he could be useful again—once. The brown-haired woman may have been just a casual visitor to the school, a job applicant or a parent. Perhaps she needed to see her daughter.

Wait a moment. Yes, there had been the shoes connecting the blonde to a brown-haired woman getting on a coach at Victoria. This elusive memory gave Bruno a sudden flash of recognition. Blondie had donned a wig! Simple as that. But into what hiding place had she vanished? Bruno hoped to pin her down if she reappeared. She could be anybody. No, she was definitely an American agent. Yet she might be irrelevant to this operation. She could be British and working with the Americans. This much was definite: as the blonde, she had met with the American from the US embassy in Paris. Unless she turned up again, she could be considered as working on another assignment. Since a majority of assignments now were anti-terrorist, he would eliminate her if he ever saw her again and got the slightest chance. Or had Control put her into the game simply to protect Kim? Yes! That was it. Control wanted him to bring Kim back to France for a "big thing." Control didn't realize his enemies had a bigger thing than ever about to happen in France.

Bruno had to think things through a bit further. If Kim and Blondie returned with him unharmed, all three of them would be considered "safe." If he killed them or held them captive for interrogation under torture, he could not return to Paris but would have to move back to the Middle East. Perhaps it would be best to be a "good agent" by returning Kim and Blondie unharmed and then learn something of the "big thing," so he could leak some, if not all, of its details. If they were attacked by young recruits en route, and Bruno got the two women home unharmed, his stock would be high with Control. He would be able to learn more of Control's plans for defending France, the country that was most under attack at the moment. That's what Philby would do if he were in Bruno's position. Yes! Control would not relax, just overreact to something small, using precious resources, and then Bruno would strike. The "big thing" would look middling when his own attack was unleashed. Havoc! Let loose the dogs of war! Ah, what a good thing he had done some Shakespeare at school!

God was indeed great. But where was Kim? Maybe at that girls' school. That had to be it. He would find a discreet place to observe the school's comings and goings with field glasses. There were hills and moors near the school. He would hike up there.

***

Brian was painting in his cottage. He hoped Alissa might visit again soon. He needed her. He wanted to do an oil painting of her. It could be based on the charcoal sketch, or it could be totally different. He contemplated the canvas he was working on. His agent needed it. She had been delighted with the coloured sheep event. Now she had a number of his oils, some pencil drawings, and a gouache. She also had a silkscreen print of the old Tomkyn Bridge School building. She thought she could sell one to Miss Mason to hang in the school. Others had gone to a dealer. She hoped to sell some to parents of girls at the school. Brian had made thirty prints in the art room at the school where he taught. The equipment there was of good quality. To do such work at home he would need another outbuilding. If sales went well, and his work could be seen in galleries, he might earn enough to build a real studio on his property.

The phone rang.

"Brian, it's Alissa. I was wondering if we might get together. Dinner?"

"Love to. When?"

"I have to go to Paris. Urgent family business. I can travel in two or three days' time. So, how about tomorrow?"

"That's perfect. I could show you what I've been working on. Then we could go out."

"Or I could cook chez-toi? What do you think?"

"Well, if you allow me to provide the food and wine."

"Agreed. Get a shoulder of pork or a sirloin, your choice. Brussels sprouts. Spuds. Those Pembrokeshire ones if they still have any in the shops. They have a good Côtes du Rhone Villages 2012 in the off-licence in Whitehaven."

"I know. I have three bottles up here right now!"

"Perfect. I'll show up around six, if that's good?"

"Brilliant. I look forward to it. I'm sorry you have to dash away. But you'll be back?"

"As soon as I can. See you tomorrow. A bell has gone, and soon a gong will sound!"

"Does your school follow Noel Coward's rule that certain women should be struck regularly like gongs?"

"Certainly not! Bye."

Alissa was grinning as she put down the phone. Then she became quiet. If only she could have a private life. Was it too much to hope for? Was Brian safe up there on the hill? It was quiet and secluded, but she was worried about him. Perhaps she should go up to the cottage after her duties in school and look for anything unusual. Bruno, for example? But he would be silly to undermine a bigger operation just to harm an artist. Bruno was too professional for that, wasn't he?

***

Bruno met Kalim, his remaining young accomplice, with the car, and they found an Indian restaurant. Kalim had brought the pistol Bruno needed. Good. Now for a meal. Both men enjoyed Indian food, and Bruno was glad to be away from the ubiquitous couscous of Paris. They sat in a quiet corner near the wall, where they could talk without being overheard. Only three other tables were occupied. Kalim apologized once again.

"That's the past," Bruno said, "Now we have to plan for today and what will happen next."*War is like a drug,* he thought. *You need another fix.* Peace meant withdrawal symptoms. These young kids had a lot to learn.

Their waiter approached with popadums and dishes of sauces and chutney. Bruno and Kalim both ordered water and an orange juice. Then they placed their food order, and the waiter left.

"Tomorrow we drive to the school. Something must be going on there after that visitor they had." Bruno explained that Kalim must drive beyond the school to drop him off near a field with a footpath leading up across the hillside toward the road at the top. Then Kalim would double back to watch the school. He would note everything and everyone going in or coming out of the premises. Careful observation and preparation were always necessary. He should take notes in his smartphone and take photos of the people whenever possible.

Bruno explained that he would climb up into the moors and watch things with field glasses. Kalim must phone him if he saw anything of a woman in her late twenties and rather lovely. A woman of colour. Naturally, he neglected to tell Kalim that he was hoping to spot a French agent called Kim. If Kalim saw the woman with brown hair or a blonde he must follow to find out where she went and what she did. That was all for today. Tomorrow could be interesting.

***

The next morning, Miranda was looking forward to meeting Kim again. They worked well together. They had a certain complicity, being handsome women with similar training and certainties. They both respected Hervé Martin immensely. Probing Bruno's secret life was a dangerous challenge, but Miranda felt more confident than ever. She wondered where Bruno and his remaining youth had gone. Had they given up on the idea of finding Kim in St. Bees? Bruno was probably more thorough than that. She decided to drive around and try to spot them before she went to lunch at the Ram.

She found Ritherdon on her rental car's GPS. It was an easy drive along the Ridgeway from St. Bees. She didn't need to set out for her meeting before 11:30. With a bit of luck she might trace Bruno or his people before then.

She drove around but had no luck. Then she decided to drive by the school. She approached the gate proclaiming Tomkyn Bridge School and drove straight past. A car was parked on the other side of the road, partly on a grass verge and facing the school. She accelerated but saw the driver as she passed. It was

Bruno's man, who had followed her to Carlisle. Had he seen her? She looked in her rearview mirror. The car had not moved. So, they suspected Kim was in the girls' school.

She decided to go back to St. Bees by a narrow country road, a tarmac-covered lane flanked by hedges. She saw an open gate with a field beyond. Driving into the field, she parked and ran to the gate to close it. She stayed hidden by the hedge and her car. There was silence. Then the birds, no longer disturbed by her sudden appearance, resumed their chirruping conversations. She heard a car approaching. The youth was trickier than she thought. He drove straight past her hiding place, and soon she could not hear his motor. It was the car that she had passed not far from the school. Well, not as tricky as all that.

She ran to the gate, opened it, and drove back past where Bruno's man had been and then past the school. She realized she'd be in Ritherdon at about 11:40. Perfect.

***

Kalim decided to stop the car and report.

"Hello. Can you hear me?"

"I can hear you. What's going on?"

"I was outside the school. Like yesterday. Nothing doing. A car drove past, and a woman driver glanced at me. She had brown hair. So, I turned the car around and followed."

"Did you find out where she was going?"

"There was a small side road I went past, and then I thought I'd stop and go back to that side road. I felt she might have taken it."

"Did she?"

"I went down it, but it led to St. Bees, with a few farmhouses here and there."

"You didn't see her again or the car?"

"No."

"You lost her. We're dealing with a professional. Go back and note comings and goings again at the school."

Bruno hung up and sighed. No discipline anymore. These trainees needed a firm, pitiless, and intelligent commander. Bruno considered himself such but had no desert camp for training the recruits. Well, they were dispensable. They could get the right training and attitudes in North Africa. There they might slaughter scores of people before they themselves died. He took up the field glasses to look across the hillside at the school.

Agent Kim walked out. She went through a gate in the garden wall and was soon hiking up toward him. Bruno wanted to hide and then watch her wherever she went. In fact, she soon changed direction. He was perfectly placed to follow her. He moved slowly and carefully, using slight rises and declivities to conceal himself. Kim was climbing higher. Then he saw the cottage. She was heading for it. This was interesting. She knocked on the door, then looked around. The door opened, and she went inside.

No more than five minutes later, Kim came out of the cottage with a youngish man. Thirty odd? They kissed. Bruno felt a sudden twisting in his gut. His chest was tight with suppressed rage. He breathed deeply. As the man went back indoors, Kim set off up the slope toward a road. He should kill that man, but it could wait. No irrelevances were needed at this stage. Bruno decided to follow Kim, keeping to the side of the cottage, where he was concealed by some bushes and the rise and fall of the land.

On the road he saw her about a hundred yards ahead. He decided to go on the grass behind the hedges that skirted the road. He would follow her unseen.

About twenty minutes later, they came to some scattered buildings, one of which barred his way. He got to the road and quickened his pace. Kim looked back and saw him.

"Kim! What's the hurry?"

She did not look back.

"Kim! It's me, Bruno."

She continued walking but looked back again over her shoulder. Sure enough, he had tracked her down. And she guessed he was holding a knife in the pocket of his long coat. She stopped and waited for him, ready for any move he might make.

"Why are you here? How did you find me?"

"That's not important. Control needs you back in Paris. Something big has come up. He wants me to travel back with you. Just in case."

"Who says I have to go back? Maybe I want to stay away from the job."

"You must come back. Control needs you; he wants you to cut short your leave."

"Who else knows where I am?"

"I don't know. But if I can find you, so can others, people who want to . . . kidnap you . . . kill you."

"Well, that's the story of our lives. But I can't leave until next week. I suppose you'll be in touch with Control. Tell him you've seen me and explained the situation. Please say I'll be back in a few days. You don't know where I'm living, but we'll meet and come back to France together. Will you do that, for old times' sake?"

"Of course. Anything you say, Kim," Bruno replied as he took his hand from his pocket. He didn't need his knife or the pistol Kalim gave him, which he had been holding.

"Okay. Where are you staying?"

"I'm here for today, but I go back to Carlisle tomorrow."

"Later, in a few days then, let's meet at the railway station in Carlisle. Friday at 11:00 a.m.?"

"Good. Agreed. Oh, there's another thing. If somebody else is looking for you, and we get separated and have to fend for ourselves, go to my safe house in London. It's in Brailsford Road, Brixton."

"What number?"

"Not many of those houses display numbers, but mine is the only one with a purple front door and yellow window frames at ground-floor level with white frames on the upstairs windows. The lace curtains are from Brittany. No other houses have such curtains."

"You'd make quite a modern artist, Bruno."

"Didn't you know? I have a special interest in contemporary art—and artists."

They walked away from each other in opposite directions. Bruno had no need to follow her now. He could wait and watch, be a tourist, until Friday. Maybe he'd visit that secluded cottage before they left for what he hoped would be Kim's last trip.

21

KIM felt uneasy about Bruno's last remark. She had to see Brian again. If she did one more operation, perhaps she could officially retire and get back to Tomkyn Bridge School in mid-September. Or if Brian became successful, would he settle for her place in the Loire Valley? *Never plan other people's lives; it seldom works,* she thought as she continued on her way to Ritherdon. But that was exactly what Control wanted her to do in Paris for the rest of her working life! Plan. Make dangerous plans. Have others to carry them out, live or die.

At the pub she found a young, athletic-looking redhead already ensconced at a corner table with a bench seat against the wall. She waved. It was Miranda wearing another wig. Did she have a wig fetish, or was it her main method of surviving the hazards of her job? The two women kissed on each cheek, as if in France. Miranda smiled. Kim frowned but then smiled.

"You want a drink?"

"Same as you. Fizzy water with a twist."

"I'll get it while you scan the menu. I'm having fish and chips," Miranda said as she headed toward the bar.

"I'll have good old fish and chips too," Kim said, enthusiastic again for things English.

When Miranda had placed the order and returned with Kim's drink, she raised an eyebrow.

"He's found you?"

"Yes. He must have followed you. How he knew I'd be up on the road above the fields, I don't know."

"He probably had the school watched, and someone saw you goingup here."

Kim nodded. "Yes. Maybe he saw me going to the cottage on the hill." This thought was worrying. Bruno had said he liked modern art."I've arranged to meet him at Carlisle station on Friday morning at eleven. Then we'll go back to Paris by train."

Miranda was pleased. She had led Bruno to Kim in such a way that he thought he had discovered her himself. Now she would keep on his and Kim's tail and perhaps meet by chance, so he could be tempted to take them both. Or better not. She would be there at all times, keeping a protective eye on Kim, as Control wished. They would bring Bruno in peacefully or under duress— or dead.

She smiled at Kim. "Should I wear this wig?"

"I don't know," Kim replied. "Have they seen you already in the wigs?"

"Certainly in the brown. They might think I'm just a friend visiting the school to see you. Bruno is astute though, so I doubt that. He'll think I am an agent, perhaps British, maybe American."

"Well, you could just be yourself. Blonde."

"You'd recognize me whether or not I used a wig?"

Kim smiled. "I've watched you move, walk. Yes, I'd know you. You could buy a blue or mauve one or become a punk if you want. Another thing is that Bruno gave me the address of a safe house in London in case we're attacked en route. It's in Brixton, Brailsford Road. No number, but it's the only house in the street with a purple front door, yellow window frames downstairs, and white ones for upstairs windows. And it has Breton lace curtains. He says that's unique in Brailsford Road."

"Hmm... A bit like the Marshall Islands flag!"

"If you say so, Miranda. Anyway, remember purple, yellow, and white."

"It sounds as if he expects trouble. But why should he, unless he arranges it to get you to that house instead of Paris? Yes, I think it's his agenda because he's turned, sure as snakes are snakes."

Kim thought Miranda was right. If she went into the house, and Bruno was indeed a double agent, she might never come out alive. But she was eager to see Bruno's safe house. She would just have to wait and be on guard. Maybe she could contact Momo, a British agent she had worked with in Birmingham. But how? She didn't want to go through the authorities. She could contact Harry, a man Control knew at the US embassy in Paris. He could be useful if he came to London. That was only an idea. Harry could be back in the States. No, she'd wait to see what transpired.

Their meals arrived. As they ate, they discussed conditions in Paris, the almost constant demonstrations and strikes, and the huge problem of the unprecedented influx of illegal migrants from the African chaos. The Nice catastrophe illustrated the difficulty of not being able to anticipate everything. Not least of these problems was the concentration of illegals in the Calais area trying to enter England illegally. What about people who applied properly for immigration? What were their chances with all these queue jumpers clogging the system and even demonstrating to demand papers? Miranda thought for a moment.

"Mass migrations have occurred at all the greatest moments of disaster in the history of the human race," she remarked."Of course, this current migration stretches Europe to the limit and beyond much of the time. The patience of host countries, opportunities for employment, checking hundreds of thousands of people, many without papers and others with false papers—all of these have limits."

"It will cost too much to do the job properly," Kim said. "Politicians want action, but they don't like footing the bill! The Americans are getting weary of pulling Europe out of its disorders."

They both knew the problem of infiltration by young terrorists and the older directors of terrorist activities. The job of preventing outrages in Europe was a growth industry but only as far as the limit of funding that governments were prepared to allot to their security forces. Recruitment was a problem. Good agents were rare beings, and they needed rigorous training. They both knew the score.

Kim realized that Control really did need her and that she should give up the search for a quiet single or married life.

"I'm worried about an artist friend," she confided.

"Is that Quint, the sheepsprayer?"

"Yes. He's attractive and a good artist."

Miranda smiled "Aha! Schoolteachers can have fun too then!"

Kim nodded and smiled. *If Bruno's a traitor, and he watched me go to the cottage, I should go back and check that all's well.*

Miranda drove them back toward St. Bees after lunch, but when they reached the stretch of road just above Brian's place, Kim got out and walked down to his cottage. She had to persuade him to go away for a week. By then Bruno would be in London or Paris.

Bruno was lying in a hollow behind a large boulder. He watched Kim enter the cottage after the painter answered his door. Two minutes later she reappeared and made for the path leading down the hill to the girls' school.

Got you. Got you both, Bruno thought. The painter came outside and got into his car. When Bruno heard the car drive off, he ran to the house. He looked at the lock and grinned. He would have a look around before he left.

22

THE sky had clouded over again. A fresh breeze brought a slight chill to the air. Barney, the friendly sheep farmer, noted that Brian had parked his car in the usual place. He would be in. The front door was open. Barney called out for Brian. He heard a low moan. When Barney rushed in, he found Brian sprawled on the floor. A small kitchen knife was stuck into his leg. Barney gasped in horror. "I won't move you. Can you wait for the ambulance?" Brian groaned and nodded.

Barney phoned the hospital immediately. Then he knelt beside Brian, who had lost some blood but had the good sense not to move the knife.

"Don't worry. You'll be fine. We'll get you into surgery."

Brian tried to smile and grunted again. He whispered a few words that Barney could not understand. Barney moved closer to him."Did you see who attacked you?"

"No. Opened door. It was fast . . . staggered back . . . fell here."

***

Brian had a flesh wound but no severed artery and was comfortable after treatment and stitches. He was a lucky man. He telephoned Alissa. She came to visit him bringimng pencils with different grades of lead, which she found in an old jam jar near the sofa in his cottage. Now he would be able to survive the boredom of being in hospital for a few days. She explained that on Friday she had to go to Paris. He begged her to return soon. She said she would be back. She could not know exactly when but soon.

"Keep working, Brian. I'll see if I can arrange for a gallery in Paris to take some of your work."

"Take what you need to show them." He smiled at her. He was still rather pale.

"Do you have photos of your work?"

"Sure. They're on a USB drive in the drawer of the big table. It's got a label: 'My work.'"

"Good. I'll find it and bring it, so you can check I have the right one before I leave for Paris."

"Thanks, Alissa. You are lovely and good and special. I . . ."

"Shh. Get some sleep. I'll be back soon with the USB drive. Did you see who stabbed you?"

"It was so quick. But I saw a sort of long coat. A skull? I'm sorry. I was confused."

"Rest, Brian." She blew him a kiss and left after letting him hug her while sitting up in the hospital bed. She let go of him reluctantly.

So, it had been Bruno. Brian was lucky to be alive. But she would soon be off, taking Bruno with her. She considered the attack as a one-off, another warning perhaps, or maybe Brian had disturbed Bruno, who had been snooping. She still had some crucial things left to do. The sister on duty said Brian would probably be fit to go home in a couple of days. He would have to use a walking stick for a while.

When Alissa got to the cottage, a policeman was inside poking around.

"And who are you, madam?" he asked when he saw her at the door.

"I'm Alissa Partridge, from Tomkyn Bridge School. I heard about the incident I'm a friend of Mr. Atkins."

"I see. Have you seen Mr. Atkins since . . . the incident?"

"Yes, I've just come back from the hospital. He wants me to get him a USB drive that contains photos of his artwork."

"Hmm. Do you know where it is?"

"He told me it was in the drawer of the table there."

"I'll have a look." The policemen soon found it. He glanced around the room again. "There's a laptop. I'll see what's on it. You can wait here." He indicated a chair.

"Thank you, Sergeant."

"Well, there now. Pictures. Paintings, drawings. He looked at the screen and scrolled. "He's done a lot. Course, he's a local art teacher. Bit of a celebrity. Does he have a phone number at the hospital?"

"Yes. I have it. Here. I'll read it from my diary."

Soon the sergeant had Brian on the phone. He identified himself and asked him if he had sent Miss Partridge to get his USB drive. Brian confirmed it and inquired if Alissa was there. The sergeant handed her the phone.

"Hello, Brian? The sergeant checked the USB drive on the laptop. It has your work on it. I'll bring it to you, if that's possible. Do you need your laptop? Okay, I see, just to be sure everything on the drive is safe from any pilferers. I understand."

The sergeant took the phone and wished Brian a speedy recovery before ending the call.

"You can take the drive to him as long as you sign this little chitty for me."

"No problem, Sergeant. And thanks for being so efficient and careful."

"One other thing, miss. Do you have proof of identity?"

Alissa had her passport and driver's licence with her and showed them to him. He made a note of her name and the number and also noted the release of the USB drive to her. She left to go back to the school. She had not mentioned the dead sheep found on the hillside. The farmer would have done that in any case. Nevertheless, she would remind Brian to mention it to the police.

In her rooms at Tomkyn Bridge School, Alissa copied the USB drive onto her laptop and then copied the file onto a USB drive of her own. It could be useful when approaching dealers in Paris. She sat wondering about Bruno, a knife man. Was he sending her a frightening message just to show his power? Likely. He could easily have killed Brian. The police said nothing had been stolen, so far as they knew. Nor had there been any sign of a struggle. In any case she would take the USB drive to Brian and also phone him before leaving for Paris. Did she love him? She certainly felt protective of him.

23

MAGGIE Chan had a free weekend. She had arranged with Jack, Mary Rao's friend, whom she had met—and liked—at Mary's wedding, to go out in his small twin-engine plane for a weekend jaunt. Paul, Mary, and Maggie had all met for the first time when they were students. Jack was the odd one out. He had been a Royal Air Force pilot before leaving military service to set up his small wings-for-hire business in Scotland.

Maggie drove from her medical research laboratory in Edinburgh to the small airfield where Jack had arranged to meet her. She had liked him a lot on two previous occasions when they had met in Edinburgh for quick lunches before she returned to work.

Maggie was a medical doctor who preferred the lab to surgery or general practice. Quite tall, she had the fine bone structure and good looks of some northern Chinese. Her family had been residents of Singapore when the Japanese invaded China. During the war, they managed to survive, but they were distressed that some of the residents had collaborated with the invaders, being involved in a great deal of brutality. Maggie, born when Singapore was reinventing itself after Lee Kwan Yu came to power, was now a modern professional person with a largely western outlook. She wore an elegant tan pantsuit with a rose-pink scarf and casual pink sneakers. Her straight black hair was swept back into a ponytail. Above the nape of her neck, her hair was gathered by an elasticized, braided gold-and-silver ring. Her medical colleagues often approached her for dates. One surgeon had asked her to be his mistress. He said he was going to divorce. Maggie was actually too busy, rather skeptical of such promises, and too wary of her male colleagues to get seriously involved. She liked her independence, her job, and, by European standards, her handsome salary. In some places in Asia, she would have been paid a lot more for the same work and would have paid less tax. But she liked being outside her family's immediate control. Was Jack a dependable man? Would he respect her independence?

It was sunny, and a gentle breeze was blowing. A red-and-white windsock flapped about. She was looking forward to the jaunt. She parked her two-year-old Lexus sport sedan, then walked into the waiting room. It was by no means a luxury lounge, but it offered shelter when the weather was untrustworthy.

A twin-engine plane was approaching. Its pilot made an impeccable landing. No bumps. Steady. When it finished taxiing, Jack climbed out. Was he as steady and dependable as a man, apart from being a pilot? He was older than she, but that was not a worry. Mary had told her that Jack was unmarried. *How had he managed that?* Maggie wondered as she got up to go outside. She looked chic and slim in her casual outfit. Her sneakers had a sparkling finish. She liked a bit of sparkle. She was carrying a small lizard-skin bag, which was also pink, to match her shoes. Jack, in work trousers and an old flying jacket, saw her and waved, quickening his pace. She waved and blew him a kiss. He had rugged, masculine good looks.

"Hello, Maggie! How was your week?" Jack beamed. She was just a few feet from him. He suddenly looked taller than she had thought.

"Oh, much the same routine. Nothing special. And you?" They hugged briefly.

"I got back two days ago. Had to take a couple of businessmen to Sweden."

"Did you stay for a day or so?"

"Two nights, and then they were ready to fly back."

"Do they pay your hotel as well?"

"You bet. We stayed in the same hotel, so I could be found easily if the deal fell through."

"And did it?"

"I shouldn't think so. They were drinking champagne on the flight back!"

They both laughed. Maggie looked into his blue eyes. Once she got used to seeing blue-eyed people as a child, she had grown to like blue eyes and green eyes, though they were rare. A few crinkles around the eyes and a crease in each cheek suggested his age and perhaps some history of laughter and stress. It had been just over a week since they had last met for tea and cakes in a posh hotel near the lab.

"Well, where are we going, Jack?"

"I know a good place for lunch near Crail." Maggie had never been to Crail, so it would be an interesting adventure to visit there.

"Isn't it a small coastal village?"

"Spot on, Doctor. My father flew from there during World War Two. It had an airfield and a camp. Lately, people have been buying property, even pigsties, and converting them into trendy holiday places."

"And the villagers are still there, I hope?"

"Oh, there's good fishing, a lot of farming, and some clean and neat bed-and-breakfast nests for people on holiday. Shall we clamber in?"

"Why not?" Maggie smiled. Here was a man who knew the country well and who could show it off from the air. When she mounted the few steps to get into the aircraft, she smelled new leather. It was like the smell of a new car.

"I had the interior refurbished recently. My passengers like to feel looked after properly with a plane that isn't obviously falling apart!"

"I don't blame them. It's great. Brilliant!" Maggie exclaimed as she sank into a comfortable red leather seat. It matched the aircraft's red-and-white paint job.

"Okay, Maggie, buckle up."

After a brief exchange with the tower, they climbed through the air. Maggie realized at once that a small plane was a different kind of ride from those of the Cathay Pacific or British Airlines jumbo jets she was used to whenever she went back to Hong Kong, Singapore, and other parts of Asia. The fields and hills, banks and braes, and high roads and low roads of one of the most beautiful places on earth passed slowly by, not so far below them it seemed. Although they experienced some sudden jolts from time to time, she felt absolutely safe with Jack as her pilot.

He's unmarried, she mused, *but is he the marrying kind? Why am I suddenly thinking about marriage? Odd. Would he make a good husband? Would my family approve?* She asked Jack if he had automatic pilot on his aircraft. He nodded.

"Well, why not switch it on and sit by me for a chat, telling me what to look at?"

Jack looked at Maggie, a bit surprised. Was this an overture?

"Actually, I'm not putting on autopilot, not even for you!"

"Oh well, later?"

"Certainly. But I'd never be on automatic pilot with you! You give me too much of a lift." He chuckled.

"I get your drift. You're sweet."

"And anyway, it's time to land. We're almost there."

24

IT was a gala evening in Paris. A very lovely young woman named Yasmine had been invited along with some other businesspeople. Just before she left her taxi, Yasmine checked her light makeup, tidied her hair, and retouched her lipstick.

There was a buzz at her table when she entered. As she sat down, a colleague leaned over and told her the boss had heard from the palace. The president might be able to look in later on. He was too busy to stay for the meal. It was a signal honour and almost unheard of. Yasmine had worked on an advertisement for the French president's political party. It had been released in a number of newspapers, and a shorter version had been posted on billboards. The president had gained quite a few more points in popularity polls. In return he was to grace the celebratory dinner given by the agency in the private upper room of a notable restaurant on the Champs Elysées.

Her boss was happy with Yasmine's idea for publicity about the president and his political colleagues. She had worked hard with her team, and it had been good. She was ecstatic; her name card on the table was placed to the left of an empty chair. The card in front of the empty chair informed her that the place was destined for the president of the French Republic. To the right of the president's empty chair sat her boss. Life seemed full of promise. She had a good-paying job and had already scored an important success. She was, she knew, an attractive Algerian with a modern outlook. Her parents were glad she could be independent, holding her own in the *metropole*. She had a work permit. Her father and mother, however, would direct her to a suitable husband; her uncle was to keep a close watch on her activities in her free time. However, now that she was in Paris and working among the French, Yasmine was starting to form her own ideas about her personal future. Her Parisian uncle—half Algerian, half French—was a solid anchor and adviser. The family could depend on him for news from his circle in France. Yet Yasmine already wanted a larger measure of independence.

The main course had just been served when two tall, wary-eyed, and unsmiling men appeared, looking around the room. They nodded. A small tubby man, rather like a provincial civil servant, strutted into the room. He saw the empty seat next to Yasmine, walked quickly to her table, and sat down. He held out his hand to her boss and then turned to her and shook her hand. She had shaken hands with the president of the republic! Then the president shook hands with the others at the table. He stood and looked beyond the table at the assembled company, fingering his tie.

"Ladies and gentlemen, I am very pleased with your efforts on my behalf. It was my popularity that was at stake, not that of my party. Let us look forward to a continuing relationship. Unfortunately, I cannot stay because I have another meeting in a few minutes with the prime minister. Thank you all again. And please excuse me. We'll meet again I hope. Vive la France! Vive la république!"

Everyone was standing. His remarks were met by a round of applause with many voices repeating "Vive la France!" Meanwhile, the president briefly kissed each cheek of the pretty Algerian girl.

"Do you have a business card?" he murmured near her ear.

Yasmine took one out of her clutch bag and handed it to him. The president slipped it into his pocket without looking at it. He turned and waved to the assembled diners as he went out.

In the gleaming black Citroën that whisked him to his next meeting, the president glanced at the card. Ah, yes. Her name was Yasmine Lallouche. His close political colleague, the minister of defence, had mentioned her as a rising star in the publicity business. The president thought she was a delectable young woman.

It was with this perception that their love affair began.

***

"Hello."

Brian spoke into the phone next to his hospital bed. He sat propped up by pillows, with one leg bent at the knee, the injured one stretched out straight and wrapped in dressing. It would be about ten to twelve days before the stitches could be removed. But he'd be home before then.

"Brian, how are you feeling?" He could not mistake that voice, calm and low, never strident.

"Fine, Alissa. I'm living the life of Riley in hospital and will be home in a few days. How are you?"

"I packed a bag and am ready to go and catch a train. Not that I plan to put the train in my bag after I've caught it!"

"I wish I could put myself in the bag in the train with you when you've caught it." Brian liked her playful moments; in fact, he liked everything about her.

"Brian, please don't sell that charcoal sketch you did of me. I'd like to buy it. 'Hide on Hide' has a special space in my rooms at Tomkyn Bridge."

"I'll certainly keep the sketch. Don't worry."

They chatted a bit more, but she would not be pinned down to a specific date for her return to St. Bees. She had to go. The train to Carlisle would not wait for Alissa Partridge, even if it had known she was also Agent Kim.

Alissa caught the train and arrived in Carlisle at 10:40 a.m. She was now firmly back into her role as Kim. There was a meeting point near the displays for arrivals and departures. As she approached, she spotted Bruno coming toward her from a newspaper and book kiosk. Miranda was, it seemed, nowhere in the vicinity. She would get onto whichever train they took.

"Hello, Kim," Bruno said. He was wearing his Australian Driza-Bone coat. Kim thought his grin made him uglier and more sinister than when his face was relaxed. Was he dressed as he had been when he attacked Brian? Was this another measure of his malice?

"Bruno! Hey! Paris next?"

"That's the plan. I have a car. We can drive to London. Then we could relax on the Eurostar."

Kim controlled herself. *If they went by car, how could Miranda be a backup when needed? You're a true bastard, Bruno.*

"Hmm. That's an idea, bel ami, but I'm going by train. It'll be quicker. Getting into London and returning a rented car will take much longer than the train journey. But you do what you like. I'll see you in Paris."

"Oh, you're right. I'll return the car just outside the station, and then I'll be back."

"Good. I'll see you in the ticket office queue. I notice the board says there's a train that leaves at half past eleven. Do you want me to get your ticket?"

"Please!" He was already dashing away to where he had left the car.

He knew she was careful and untrusting. Suddenly, he wanted to teach the bitch a lesson. He changed his plan from the return of good agent Bruno to the abduction and murder of Agent Kim. He lusted after her. Yes, he'd have her.

Kim walked toward the ticket office and saw a young man in a dark suit follow Bruno out of the station as he reached the exit to the forecourt. *Bruno wants to keep me in his sights*, she thought.

In the queue, Miranda was already buying her ticket. She winked at Kim as she stopped near her, ostensibly to inspect her ticket, and told Kim in an undertone to take the express train to London at 11:30. Kim was surprised to see that Miranda had a swathe of blue hair draped over one shoulder. She wore torn jeans, yellow sneakers, and a woven poncho that looked the worse for wear. She disappeared into the milling crowd of travellers, not waiting for a reply.

Kim bought the tickets. She had time to go to the ladies' room before meeting Bruno. When she entered, Miranda was washing her hands. A black-robed woman with head and face almost totally covered had followed Kim. She went to a sink next to Miranda. Then she swung round to face Kim. She was holding a pistol in one hand. Miranda threw water in the woman's eyes. Kim almost simultaneously smashed the woman's hand against the edge of the sinkand took the gun, which clattered into it. The woman yelped and growled as if she were a dog. The two female agents pushed the would-be killer into a stall and slammed her head against the wall. There was a loud crack. Miranda ripped off the black cloth burka covering her face. It was the face of a clean-shaven man, though a bit of black stubble already showed around his chin. Kim twisted the gunman's injured wrist.

"Who sent you?"

The man did not reply. Kim clubbed him with the pistol. The two women sat him on the toilet seat. Miranda spoke French into her phone. She turned to Kim.

"Our people will pick him up from here."

"What about our train?" Kim asked.

"I'll make sure he stays put!"

The two women emerged from the cubicle. Another woman had entered but had not seen anything. She glanced at the two women closing the door of the cubicle from which they emerged. She shrugged and applied some lipstick before going into a cubicle at the end of the row.

Miranda and Kim stayed where they were, adjusting their hair and makeup. They were ready if anyone else came looking for the would-be assassin. Nobody did. Kim had the pistol in her bag. The fingerprints on it and on its ammunition might be useful for tracking isolated "mayhem" people, though Kim thought this would-be killer was connected to the group who had been looking for her in the UK ever since she had escaped the grenade attack in a different ladies' washroom earlier in the year. Miranda should get it to Special Branch in London. Kim put the pistol, wrapped in a paper towel, in Miranda's bag.

"Get it to Scotland Yard."

"You bet." Miranda winked at her. Kim smiled and walked out to meet Bruno. She waved a ticket at him as she approached.

"We have about five minutes before we board the train," he said. "How much do I owe you?"

"We can settle down on the train before we settle up," she replied with a smile.

"I like your sly humour, Kim."

"Good. Let's get onto the right platform to be on the right track."

As they went on their way, Kim looked back at the ladies' room. Two policewomen and a beefy sergeant were outside it already. Bruno was intent on the platform. If he had sent the disguised gunman, he was certainly too professional to give the game away by nervous glances or by asking any questions. Kim decided he had not sent the gunman. She wondered how many groups were on her tail.

A largely unintelligible announcement came over the imperfect sound system, adding to the general noise around the echoing concourse. There was no sign of punkish Miranda, but Kim knew she would not miss the train.

Miranda had changed her appearance again two minutes after Kim left her. She emerged as a smart blonde carrying a rather heavy bag. If Bruno was looking out for her as the blonde in Paris and as she appeared in her passport photo, he would want to pursue her, not realizing he was her quarry, a master of discovered check and an expert in endgames.

She boarded the train at the last minute with some young people lugging guitar cases and settled down with her crossword puzzle book and the pen with which she had lightly pierced the gunman's hand before she left the toilet. She relished the thought of the police, when they contemplated a sleeping Arab man dressed as a woman sporting serious bruises and perched unconscious on a toilet seat in the ladies' restroom. Carlisle certainly had its moments.

25

BRUNO and Kim sat together and read the *Telegraph* and the *Guardian*, exchanging papers. Then they read French paperbacks. Bruno had a biography of François Mitterand, a president of France decades earlier. Mitterand's double life interested Bruno more than his left-wing politics. Kim read a slim volume about Truffaut, the film director. Neither noticed the smart blonde who was in the next compartment studying a book of skeleton crossword puzzles.

During the journey Bruno excused himself to go to the toilet. While there he also made a call to London. He had made up his mind. That artist had organized coloured sheep with collie dogs stalking them, forcing them down the hill and chasing them into a pen. The London recruit he had just called was a collie. Kim would be the sheep stumbling into the pen he had prepared in Brixton. Control would be devastated. After her death, photos of Kim could be sent to the French police. Control needed to be taught a severe lesson.

When they arrived in London, Bruno and Kim took a taxi. The blonde followed them in another taxi. The destination turned out to be St. Pancras.

So, Miranda thought, *they will take the Eurostar, and if they both get safely to Control, he might decide to let Bruno float a little to lead them to other terrorists.* She decided to report to Control when she alighted at St. Pancras.

It was then that she saw a youth in a bulky windbreaker. He had a backpack. She watched him as she phoned.

"All at St. Pancras. All three to take train. But Bruno may yet have a trick or two. He has accomplices here as well."

"The young man who 'collapsed' at the fruiterer is low on the totem pole," Control replied. "The man at Carlisle belongs to yet another group the Brits have been watching. So, they're pleased to have found him again. He had left his last address. But thanks anyway. Good luck, and take care."

"Thanks. Please keep Stanstead option ready in case we need it."

"We shall. Good luck."

Bruno and Kim made for the entrance to the station. Bruno turned his head to his right, where the youth with the backpack was almost level with them. Bruno nodded and then pulled Kim behind the shelter of a niche in the brickwork of the great blocks of the station's wall. The youth disappeared into the station concourse. Miranda went behind a taxi, from which she watched Bruno pin Kim to the wall with his body. There was a terrifying blast from the station concourse. Glass and metal shards went flying, and people inside the concourse screamed. The two agents walked quickly along the road, where the queuing taxis had come to a halt. The tall scarecrow was shouting something, as was his lovely companion. Miranda followed them, dodging people in the crowds still flowing toward the station.

They walked for about ten minutes until they reached a small square in Bloomsbury. Miranda kept well away from the other two, never losing sight of them. A couple of taxis were going around the square, and a bus stopped. The two agents got on the bus. One of the taxis had overtaken the bus. Miranda waved to the driver. He stopped, and she got inside, putting her bag in the spacious gap between her and the two folding seats that faced her. She liked the quaint arrangement of traditional London taxis.

"Hello. Where to, Miss?" He was a pale man in his forties with a bald patch. The pale, shiny skin was surrounded by short dark hair. He wore a fawn-coloured waistcoat over a white shirt with blue stripes. The sirens of police cars and emergency vehicles, fire engines, and ambulances could be heard in the distance.

"Wait a second. There's a bus behind us. Let it go past, and then follow it. I'll let you know when I need to get out."

"Fine. Just watch the meter. I prefer cash,

I wonder what all that siren business is about? Have you heard?"

"Sounds like an emergency at the British Library. I didn't hear anything on the news when I had it on my radio."

The bus went by several stops in Bloomsbury, taking on and letting off passengers. Then Bruno and Kim got off, carrying their bags. They walked a few yards to another bus stop. Miranda asked her driver to turn onto a side street, turn around, and wait. She got out and peeped around the corner at a busy road. A bus marked "Brixton" stopped. Bruno and Kim picked up their bags. Miranda jumped back into the taxi.

"Follow the bus to Brixton," she demanded.

"Right, Miss. Are you a private detective or something?"

Miranda laughed. "No. But I think my friend is getting involved with the wrong man. I want to see where they're going. I think he's after her money."

"Wise. Come to think of it though, it'd be wise to marry someone with a bob or two. But you're right to be discreet. You never know how your friend would react to being followed."

"Yes, I know. I feel a bit funny doing it."

The traffic was quite heavy, but the cab driver was good at changing lanes. When the bus stopped at Tulse Hill near Brailsford Road, Bruno and Kim got out and walked along a side street. Miranda stopped her taxi and paid the fare, giving a good tip. The driver was pleased and, turning on his radio, snaked out into the traffic flow. When Miranda looked down the side street, Bruno and Kim were turning right at a corner.

***

Bruno opened the front door. The house was painted as he had said. They looked both ways along Brailsford Road. Nobody was following them. They heard the shrill cries of children playing at some game in the distance.

"Welcome to my safe house!" Bruno gave a little bow as he let Kim enter the hallway. The three-storey late-Victorian or maybe early Edwardian house had been renovated, and the décor was tasteful, though a little dated. Kim reckoned the house must be worth well over a million pounds.

"This is quite a pad, Bruno. When did you buy it?"

"Actually, an uncle bought it for me twenty years ago for a modest sum. Now I couldn't afford it, not on our pay!"

He led her into a Conran-furnished sitting room. A Bernard Buffet painting of a provincial butcher's shop hung on the wall opposite the window with lace curtains.

"Is that a copy?" Kim asked.

"Certainly not!" Bruno said with distinct pride. "My father bought it from a Left Bank gallery in Paris during the fifties. Buffet was just about affordable then." He walked towards it. "I admire his colouring and sense of form. He makes dead meat attractive!"

"Your father had a good eye," Kim said, thinking that perhaps Bruno had a real interest in art.

"Yes, thanks. He did." He grinned in a friendly way, but his face looked more unfriendly than ever. He had been right to go to his plan B—B for Bruno. He wanted Kim. This was more important than a double bluff, pretending to be clean and then betraying Control yet again later. Yes, he had to take Kim.

"I appreciate your bringing me here after that bombing at St. Pancras. Eurostar service is bound to be interrupted. But we could have taken a flight from Heathrow," Kim said.

"Did you see the young man with the backpack?"

"Not really," Kim replied. "You were pinning me against the wall. I thought you were trying to kiss me!"

"I wish I had. No, that young fool had followed us toward the station. I saw his bulk and a backpack, and then I thought, 'Better safe than sorry,' and pushed us aside at the last minute. He just carried on and, bang! It was just a hunch, but I was right."

"Well, I must thank you for keeping me out of that blast."

"You're welcome. But did you see a taxi following our bus?"

"No. Are you sure?"

"Well, not really. But a taxi also followed our Brixton bus."

"There are hundreds of taxis on London's streets. It would be more amazing if none had been going along the bus route."

Bruno nevertheless looked worried. Then he smiled. "You're probably right. And who could have known where we were? And who could have followed us after the explosion at the station?"

"I didn't notice a taxi on our tail; we're secure here. I didn't see anyone following us into Brailsford Road either," Kim replied, looking unconcerned.

With a shrug Bruno went to a chair, where he had placed his bag. He took out a pistol already equipped with a silencer. "No. Nor did I."

Kim realized in a sickening split second that he had never intended to take the train to France. He could not go through security checks with a pistol. The bombing must have been staged to get her there. Bruno had used a young man's death for his own purposes, not for the greater glory of the prophet or of God.

"Was the boy with the backpack the bomber?"

"He had his instructions. Such young people are expendable. He served my purpose, as you will."

"You're in a bad dream, Bruno. I'm here to wake you up."

"I'm sorry, my darling. But you won't have a dream. You'll have a nightmare. I'll discover everything about you, all your secrets and every square centimetre of your lovely skin. You're beautiful, Kim. But I can alter your appearance slowly and painfully. The thought of it makes me hungry. Our Hervé, in my estimation, wants you all to himself. He'll be disappointed. I'll just pop out for a few necessary things I'll use on you when I'm ready. They intensify the process. Now let's go down to my interrogation room."

26

MIRANDA walked purposefully along Brailsford Road and past the curious paint work and curtains of a three-storey house. So, that was it. She approached a corner in the road and went around it, glancing back at the quiet row of houses. Nobody there. She stopped and waited. *How long should I wait before I enter the lion's den?*

She walked a few paces to the corner and looked back at the commonplace little street. Suddenly, the unmistakeable figure of Bruno, tall and thin, emerged from his garishly painted house. He looked around and then walked off toward Tulse Hill, swinging an empty shopping bag. When he was out of sight, Miranda hurried back to the house and knocked on the door. It opened cautiously, and a young man wearing only shorts and a singlet looked at her.

"I'm here to see your boss," Miranda said.

"You can't come in," he replied with a London accent.

Miranda put her hand on the doorjamb, whereupon he grabbed her wrist to push her away from the door. With her other hand she pricked his wrist with her pen, and he fell backwards into the hallway. A couple of black women with a toddler were coming along from the Tulse Hill end of the street where Bruno had gone. Miranda stepped into the hall and closed the door. She pulled the young man to the end of the hall, stopping outside a tall narrow cupboard door. She opened it. Stairs led down to a cellar or basement. She pushed the youth down the stairs and stepped over his body when she reached the bottom step. She dragged him into a corner of the room and sat him on a couch.

The room was lit by a soft light from small lamps set into the ceiling. It seemed like a waiting room. She spotted a door not far from the stairs. She quietly opened the door and edged into the room. One person was inside: Kim. She lay on her back on a sort of operating table. Her wrists and ankles were secured by leather straps. Her blouse had been undone, revealing her red bra, and her skirt was missing, but she was very much alive.

"Get me out of this!"

Miranda lost no time.

"The room is soundproofed. Bruno likes to hear his victims scream," Kim said. Her other clothes had been neatly arranged on a chair near the table.

"Get your things on," Miranda said. "We'll arrange a little welcome for Bruno. He's gone to the shops."

"Let's give that devil a devil of a big reception! He said he was enjoying the anticipation of raping me until he had had enough. Then he said he'd let his recruits have me. After that he would skin me in certain places."

"The sick bastard!"

"He said Dr. Westlake had talked before he died. He knew he could make me give him even better information."

"Well," Miranda said, "let's get started on a reception party. Let's give Bruno a whopping surprise. First, this young man should sleep on the operating table!"

Now fully dressed, Kim helped Miranda lift the inert youth onto the torturer's bench. They strapped his wrists and ankles.

"How did you knock him out?" Kim asked as they worked. "How long can we ignore him?"

"I jabbed him with my pen. Its ink will keep him harmless for about ten hours." She spoke into her phone. "Dallou," she said, ending the call.

***

Bruno was carrying some vinegar, salt, and a bottle of white spirits in a shopping bag. He had also bought some sandwiches.

As he approached his house, he glanced up and down the road. At the other end of the road, a black youth was bouncing a soccer ball and yelling at another boy hidden by the sharp bend at the corner. Bruno took out his key and entered the hall. The door to the front sitting room was ajar.

"Hello, Bruno. I'm glad you're back." Kim stood near the cellar steps, fully clothed. "Your young man was a great help. He thought I would give him a much better time with active sex instead of all strapped down. And he could have me before even the great Bruno! You should be careful about recruiting overly ambitious and oversexed youths. They're quite dangerous."

BRUNO'S SECRET

Bruno kicked the door shut behind him, dropped the shopping bag, and was reaching for his gun when Miranda stepped out from behind the door to the sitting room. She jabbed her pen into his neck before he knew she was there. He collapsed and lay silent and powerless at her feet.

"Control's team should be here in about fifteen minutes," Miranda said, looking at her watch. "Let's tie up old Bruno, so he'll give no trouble on the journey, even if he manages to wake up."

The two women lost no time.

"I think we might leave the shopping bag and items therein for the Brits."

"Good idea, Kim. It'll make a little gift complete with Bruno's fingerprints and his dozy recruit in the basement, courtesy of the French Republic!"

"Special Branch will be appreciative, I hope," Kim said drily.

They prepared to leave rapidly when the time came.

A heavy-duty utility truck drew up outside. Three men got out and came to the door. One of them banged with his fist. Kim found Bruno's pistol. She held it with a handkerchief and checked to see if it was loaded. It was.

"Password?" Miranda shouted through the door without opening it.

"Dallou!"

Miranda accepted the password she had given when she had made contact with the team fifteen minutes earlier. She opened the door and allowed the three solid-looking men to enter. She spoke rapid French. Two of the men went back to the truck and returned with a plain-looking coffin. Kim put the gun away.

Miranda nodded. "We're taking this lump of shit to Stanstead. There'll be people there who know about the operation."

"Good, let's load up and get on the road to a new abode!" said the man who had usedthe password. Kim smiled. The team did just that, if an inconspicuous part of Stanstead airport could be called an abode.

27

THE special cargo arrived in Normandy from Stanstead. The "deceased" was in a cell awaiting interrogation. He was still unconscious and still in a plain coffin made from regulation heavy cardboard. The house for welcoming "special cargo" did not figure on any map of France, nor indeed of that immediate region of Normandy. Control had arrived from Paris to observe the interrogation and to congratulate Miranda and Kim in person. He was sitting in a great wing chair, facing them across a coffee table. Tea and macarons had been served.

The three were alone in the sitting room of the small private manor, not far from Caen. It had a charming nineteenth-century air in its gold-leaf trimmings, Italian plasterwork on and around the ceiling, and carved oak panelling on the walls. Persian rugs were arranged on the parquet. It had been built in the war-ravaged landscape in 1950 and was equipped with extensive underground rooms for the jobs in hand. There was no sign of officialdom above ground. It was, for all appearances, a private house for a wealthy family. It stood at the end of a farmer's lane. Cows stood in the surrounding fields, but the farmhouse was really a guard house where well-equipped marksmen lived. In the kitchen fridge were some excellent Camembert cheeses in little round boxes.

Control had already told Kim that she should have kept in touch with him, but he also knew the two women had done a special job in unmasking Bruno and bringing him back to France alive.

"The people you sent for the 'cargo' after I called you," Miranda said, "were quick and faultless. We were out of the so-called safe house quicker than a mouse in a cat house! Within ten minutes of their arrival, they did a quick search of the house as well."

Control smiled, nodding appreciatively. "I'm disappointed in Bruno."

"You can say that again, sir, to the nth degree!" Kim laughed. Behind her laughter was immense relief. She had been terrified in the safe house before Miranda's arrival.

Control looked at her with a wonderful sense of relief that she was back in France, alive and safe. She needed some rest. But things were moving fast. He hoped she was tough enough to cope. He saw her as incredibly resilient. He wanted her. He wanted her as his wife. Yes, wife!

"I contacted our British friends as soon as I knew your team had left for Stanstead. The Anglo-Saxons now have the house and are taking it apart. They captured another visitor, a young hopeful recruit from Leeds who, bold as Yorkshire brass, knocked on the door. I think the Brits will keep a reception committee for any other new recruits who might turn up."

"What about the sleeping beauty we left in the cupboard?" Miranda asked.

"Oh, he's in custody. We estimate your activities have probably defused at least three UK terror attacks, maybe more. Congratulations!"

They sipped their tea and sampled the macarons.

Control smiled at Kim. "I'm cutting your leave short, Kim. We really need you for something big. You and Miranda make a wonderful team. You'll prevail. I know it."

"I can't wait to find out more!" Kim said, emphatically ironic.

"Oh, I think you'll be intrigued. As I say, it's rather big!" Control replied.

***

Kim was back in her bedroom on the second floor of the house when the phone rang.

"Ah, Kim?" It was Control.

"I'm here, Hervé. My goodness, it's wonderful to see you again." Control's first name had slipped out. Immediately, she regretted having used it. It was more intimate than necessary. Would he think she was trying to deflect reprimands for having been off his radar?

"My dear, I'm relieved to see you back here alive," he said warmly. "I'm calling you now because our British friends found a rolled paper in the house. It had a French phrase written on the back of a charcoal sketch of a beautiful young woman—a nude. The sketch has a signature: Quint."

"What's the phrase written in French on the back? Did they say?"

"Yes. It was 'Elle est à moi.'"

"Control, please get them to compare fingerprints on the paper with those in the safe house and with Bruno's."

"Good. I'll send Bruno's prints to them right now."

Kim sighed. They already had Bruno's prints on his shopping bags, but the official ones from Paris would confirm the evidence. She was limp and tired beyond tiredness itself. She decided she needed another shower. The shame and filth of being Bruno's victim, although she had been rescued, needed cleansing yet again. His making her undress in front of him and the wide-eyed young recruit, his making her partly dress again, his securing her on the torture bench, his opening of her blouse and stroking her bra before planting a wet kiss on her cleavage, such memories made her shudder. His gloating description of plans for abusing her sexually and then leaving her for further abuse by more young recruits and his plan for torture by flaying before killing her—it all made her suddenly nauseous. It needed another washing away.

Kim was resilient, but she also needed to work out in the gym, get her unarmed combat skills back to their usual operational level, and to talk to her unit's psychologist. She was certain now that Bruno had been in Brian's home. He most likely had seen her visit the cottage. Yes, he had broken in, found the charcoal sketch, and when Brian had entered the studio unexpectedly, Bruno had stabbed him. She thought the fingerprint evidence on the drawing would be the proof. She wondered why Bruno had not killed Brian. Probably he wanted to get away without the area being sealed off by a murder inquiry and a man hunt. Yes. That would be it.

She dried herself and dressed, blow-drying and tidying her hair. She was already intrigued by the big operation Control had spoken about. The thought of this next thing on the agenda helped to dismiss the recent past. It was like being on a battlefield. No time for the recent past. Carry on. Deal with the next objective. She was glad that she and Miranda would be working together. After it was all over, would she be able to get back to St. Bees, Tomkyn Bridge School, and Brian? She was unsure. The immediate future and Bruno's interrogation were the pressing issues. She had to live through Control's "big one" first. She could figure out the rest later. All in good time.

***

"I know my rights. I will remain silent," Bruno said in a sneering, provocative tone and then laughed at his interrogator.

"Yes. I suspect you mean rights you and all other terrorists deny to their-victims," the man sitting opposite him remarked. A man in a white lab coat nodded wisely.

Silence.

"We want some true facts from you, mon enfant."

Bruno smiled. "What is truth, quoth jesting Pilate and would not stay for an answer."

"Well, mon garcon, you are staying here with us as long as we, not you, wish. We can do this in English, French, Arabic, or Russian. Take your pick. You'll talk."

Bruno smiled, then flinched as a needle punctured the left side of the nape of his neck. The man from the lab left the room.

"That's not allowed!"

"Neither is chopping off heads. If your lot do this barbaric stuff, we can relax our strict rules just a little bit and use some twenty-first-century medicine. It's the future, Bruno. It's new! And it's quicker than your sick methods. In ten minutes you'll be singing. You'll be like a nightingale in Berkeley Square. The one in London, not Bristol. Just you wait and see."

"You can't reach my mind," Bruno said. *How did they know about Bristol?*

The interrogator laughed and winked at Bruno. "Oh we've read a lot of medieval texts of every kind. We keep au courant with your thinking, which is five hundred years behind the times. We'll enjoy your mysteries, Bruno, and you'll spill all of them into our recorders. We might even leak some to the press! You'll have to watch your step. Pity you've turned out to be such a coward like young Kalim and the rest of your associates."

"We are all brave warriors for our just cause."

"Au contraire. You all have an uncontrollable fear of the new, of the future. You want to turn the clock back to times when Arabs tried to conquer Europe. They didn't succeed centuries ago, and they won't now. No, mon enfant, you and your associates are 'neophobes.'"

***

Control was with Kim in a secure office under the house.

"Bruno has given us some valuable facts."

"Under duress, no doubt?"

"A matter of opinion, Kim. Oh, and when he was still unconscious on arrival, we inspected his teeth and removed a suicide device."

"Inspecting the teeth of a living death's head is a job for dentists. Thank goodness I never trained in dentistry! So, what's he been doing?" Kim queried.

"We've made arrests and raids on storage lockers and so on. It amounts to thirty known criminals and some new recruits as well as two men we've been trying to find for over a year."

"Which weapons?"

"The usual military arms, including some rocket launchers and some old-fashioned mortars. Boxes of grenades. Quite a lot of Semtex. No bacteria, poison gas, or strontium, thank God."

"Were they all in separate places?"

"Exactly. One of them, however, seems to be a central cache that could supply different groups. I think it was to arm this big operation we've been worrying about. We have some people there to watch out for people who come to pick up weapons. This way we'll arrest more. They might lead us to others."

"We're dealing with several hundred terrorists then?"

"If you include sleepers, we could be trying to track over a thousand."

"It's not what the well-meaning and 'bien pensants' might call 'a handful' then. So, how long will Bruno be in prison?"

"He'll never be in prison, if we can avoid it. A trial would attract press and public. And Bruno doesn't know what he's told us."

"So, do we throw him back on the streets?" Kim asked. "As the Brits did with Dr. Westlake?"

"Ah well," Control said, "perhaps we can put our heads together and come up with a plan."

"We can certainly try. Have we heard any more from London?"

"In effect, yes, we have. I'm about ready to give them the safe house without any more involvement from us. We sprayed all exposed surfaces where there might be fingerprints. Our people went through the entire house. The spray dries in a few seconds into a flexible skin. They peeled off the skin with all prints on it. Now we have all the prints in our database. It makes cross-checking much quicker."

"Does the spray leave any traces?"

"That's the beauty of it, chérie. We have all the prints and no signs of powder, and nobody looking around would know that the prints have been taken. The prints are still on those surfaces. The Anglo-Saxons will have them for their database as well."

"Beautiful."

"Yes. You, Kim, however, are more beautiful. Your prints or 'dabs,' as old cops call them, are beautiful. Seriously though, I need you here for this big coup."

Kim moved over to him and looked into his eyes. They smiled at each other. Control took her hand and held it in his warm hands. Then he kissed the back of her hand.

"Tell me about this big coup," she said, kissing his hands.

"I'm so glad you're safe, Kim."

She smiled. "I'm pretty pleased myself, Hervé."

He took her in his arms. She felt suddenly as if she could weep. But she did not.

Hervé felt suddenly alive instead of world-weary.

28

BRIAN returned from hospital with a slight limp, but he was glad to be home all the same. He tried to get back to work but wanted first to check for himself whether the burglar had stolen anything. He soon realized that his charcoal sketch of Alissa was missing. Had the burglar taken it? If so, why that and nothing else? Was he an old lover who was jealous because Brian had seen her naked in order to draw her? But how would the man have known who the naked woman was? Her face was not depicted.

"Bugger!" he muttered.

His homecoming mood had evaporated. There was no letter or even a postcard from her. It made him restless but not really annoyed. She was busy and had said she would be back soon. He hoped so. He was puzzled by her combination of friendliness, femininity, and mystery. Why did a school mistress suddenly have to take off for a few days without leaving a phone number? No mystery. She was a new friend but nothing more. Yet perhaps she had taken the sketch with her when she went away. Brian hoped so. It would mean she had tender feelings for him. Or was it just that she wanted the sketch? She had to come back. She had a job, after all. If she had the sketch, should he ask her to buy it? His agent would. But he would not let it go commercial.

***

One man in particular had been observed by different agents for just over a year. He was an excessively rich businessman. He seemed at home in Paris and had many contacts at the central mosque, where he went to worship at least twice a week. He also had tea there. Two of his expensive high-powered Italian cars parked in a parking lot had attracted the attention of drug-detection dogs when they had gone close by with their handlers. His Jaguar sedan and his Rolls

Royce had not interested the dogs. Those cars were used either for solitary trips or for occasions when government bigwigs from Europe were passengers. His mansion in Neuilly-sur-Seine was surrounded by high walls and had a courtyard with converted stables large enough to take all the cars. Every person he had met had been photographed and researched. Most were legitimate businessmen from the Middle East and Europe. Two contacts, a man and a woman, were off the radar, for they had no background to check, no family connections, no business, and no names. The next time they made contact with the kingpin suspect, they would have to be followed and thoroughly checked out. Control wanted them badly, but they were no longer in the nefarious loop.

They're abroad, he thought. Would they return through normal channels or by other means? He hoped for the former. Then their photos could be matched with their passports by immigration intelligence officers. They would be able to enter France with no trouble at all, but Control would have their names and more information to build upon. Of course, they would be tailed and observed, *if* he could find the resources and manpower. Something enormous was on the horizon.

There had been messages (phone traffic) suggesting that simultaneous attacks were planned for three big cities. One portion of the chatter had mentioned trains from Paris to Lyon and Paris to Strasbourg. This was normal enough. These cities had never been named again. *That* was a pointer to something. Paris, Lyon, and Strasbourg. They would be the target cities. But what would the terrorists attack? And when? *Soon, oh yes, very soon.* There was no clue as to actual targets. Bruno had not mentioned any of this during the interrogation so far. It had to be followed up.

***

Jack and Maggie occupied separate rooms in a small hotel near Crail. The weather had turned out to be inclement. In fact, it was so bad that Jack was far happier to be on the ground than in the air in a light aircraft. Maggie was even happier to be on terra firma in a cozy hotel. Was Jack as steady as a rock? Suddenly, she stood up at their table in the dining room and stroked the back of Jack's hand with her forefinger.

"Why don't we go to my room?" she murmured.

"Yes, why not?" Jack whispered.

He followed her out of the dining room, and instead of taking the small elevator, Maggie started up the stairs. She was wearing a straight black skirt with a dark-grey silk blouse. Jack admired her figure and her bountiful, shining black hair as she climbed the stairs. This was sudden, unexpected, exciting. *I'm about six or eight years older than her,* he thought. *So, what?* He watched her slim hips and the steady motion of her shapely legs in light-grey stockings as she mounted the stairs.

I want this man. I would like to bear his children. I'll get him to marry me, Maggie thought.

I wonder what the future holds? Would she want an old warhorse like me? Jack asked himself as he reached the top of the stairs.

For the next two hours, they were less in the realm of thought than in the empire of the senses. Afterwards, they lay close together, Maggie's head on Jack's chest. She listened to the steady drumming of his not-so-foreign heart as she drifted into sleep.

29

WHAT *is Bruno's real secret?* Control wondered. The question was still there after all the interrogation sessions. Bruno had answered many questions, giving away many details. The information was a major intelligence coup. Some of it was relevant to the US from the time when Bruno had been there and afterwards. British authorities were greatly interested in leads about the UK terror groups gleaned from Bruno's activities in Britain. Control knew the terrorist problem was not a national one; it was as international and as borderless as the diaspora of Islamists and as ubiquitous as the Internet. It depended on "radicalization," as journalists and others were calling it. Governments wanted programs to counter this radicalization, mostly of young men but sometimes young women. But would the National Security Agency in the US reveal everything they knew about Bruno? He doubted it. Intelligence exchanges were most often partial. Control felt a surge of delight and relief, for he had the details of Bruno's properties in Paris. They were already yielding many more pieces for the intelligence jigsaw puzzle. Yet he knew Bruno still held something they had as yet been unable to find. He would answer questions posed, but they did not know all the questions that should be posed.

***

Bruno lay in a small room. He was sweating. He felt a dull ache behind his left eye. He had recovered, he guessed, from the drug that the infidel dogs had injected into him. He had no memory of their questions or his responses. *There's hope yet*, he thought. He also surmised that they had questioned him about the London house and his torture room. They would have broken his circle of connections in the UK. They would know much more about the death of Westlake, that talented fool. They would have plumbed his US connections. They would know of his Parisian properties. They would be ransacking them right now. They would have questioned him about his money and bank accounts. They would have noted that he was wealthy. But they could not know who paid him all his extra cash. Not even he knew. Furthermore, they could not pose every question that would lead to answers about every link he had. For that they would need the leads to spark the questions. He reasoned that his deepest secret was unknown to Control, just as it was unknown to all his associates in the war against democratic values, Christianity, and equality of the sexes.

He smiled to himself. One of his keenest pleasures was to get young, idealistic, feminist women, preferably blondes, into his power, and when they awoke from drugged slumbers show them explicit films of how he and others had raped them. He liked the slow-motion sequences. Bruno would keep the women for a week or two before packing them off into the Arab world as sex slaves, thus giving him a nice little profit. They would be taught order, discipline, and real sexual stimulation. The school where Kim had taught gave him the brilliant idea of kidnapping some fifth- and sixth-form girls. "Posh" girls. The best looking of them. Many of these would be virgins. But this was not his deepest secret.

His secret of secrets would lead to the biggest strike at western democracy since Hitler and even the Soviets. The wars in the Middle East were creating hordes of refugees heading for the European Union and other democracies across the Atlantic. It was easy to add young fighting men to their numbers. These youngsters, many of them barely trained, had to be organized and armed. First though, Bruno had to be free. He would escape. After that, when he was again under their radar, he would return to the major plan. He had talked about it with a nameless associate in Hastings. Bruno smiled at the rich joke of a terrorist "sleeper" in the town that had once seen the battle that let the invaders into eleventh-century Britain. Then he began to shake with a fury deeper than any anger he had felt before. Revenge was the law of all laws. He would find Kim again and let her live, though terribly maimed and disfigured. He needed a revenge so destructive that it would never be forgotten. Hadn't Hiroshima and Nagasaki been such a revenge?

30

GRAHAM was alone and asleep, moving occasionally in spasms and muttering incoherently. He was dreaming again.

He opened the door to a huge lighthouse on a small island off the Newfoundland coast. He started climbing. There were so many steps in the narrow confines of the spiral staircase. He heard the shrieks of gulls and the steady pounding of his own blood. He stopped to rest. Someone else was climbing ahead and above him. He heard someone climbing the steps below.

He started climbing again. He wanted to see who was ahead of him. He caught a glimpse of a woman's legs and white nurses' shoes. He quickened his pace. Suddenly, the woman stopped, and they met. She was a step above him. She turned. They were face to face. It was Sam Gilmore.

She put the palm of one hand on his face and pushed, but he didn't fall. Someone was close behind him. Just a few steps below.

"I know you, Graham," she whispered from a few inches behind him, "but you can never know me." She laughed with a witch-like cackle. It was a doctoral student. What was her name? He realized for the first time the harsh ugliness of her voice.

She drew closer. He looked back. She was naked. He looked into her eyes, gleaming in the half-light. She held his gaze and slowly put out her tongue. She licked her upper lip, and her tongue became black, slender, and forked, like a snake's.

Graham wanted to run to the top of the stairs. Sam had already gone ahead. He tried to catch up to her. He staggered out a door into a circular room under the great lamp on the roof.

Outside it was night, a wind howling and rain spraying through the open doorway. On one edge of a great four-poster bed, Anne de Crevennes sat naked except for thigh-length light-blue stockings attached to a dark-green garterbelt. She was typing on a laptop that rested on her thighs. She looked up and shrieked at him. "Get away, you silly man! I'm working."

Graham was pushed farther into the room. He turned to see Sam Gilmore dressed as a receptionist.

"You can't have me, Graham. It's a pity for you, my dear man, because I could teach you a lot about love." He watched her clothes fade to reveal the wonderful body of a woman in her late thirties. "I'm interested in reality, integrity, and my son's well-being. You need some lessons."

Graham grasped her right breast, then pulled his hand away, as if he had grasped hot metal. He turned to Anne, who was cupping her breasts in her hands.

"Don't touch!" she shouted.

The graduate student put her arms around him from behind. He realized he was naked too.

"Oh, Graham, you and your, well, you know, disappoint me." He felt a cold tongue lick his ear and then the nape of his neck. The tongue was dry, slender, and forked at the end. The great circular room became an impenetrable darkness. The storm disappeared. He was cold. Cold as a corpse.

"No, no!" Graham shouted as he woke. He was sweating. Could his dreams and thoughts be laid bare before Jackie's spirit? Did she watch everything he did? Hear everything he said? His mouth was dry. He needed a drink. He turned on the light beside his bed. It was 4:30 a.m. He got up, remembering there was no beer left in the fridge. Okay. Gin and tonic would do.

***

Miranda had been debriefed and was back in Paris. Control had told her that she and Kim would meet with him the next morning at 7:30 a.m. It would be a heavy day, but now she was free for an evening. Her American lover, Harry, was meeting her for a quiet dinner in a little place called the Chair on the Ceiling. He would probably try to recruit her again, and she would play hard to get as an agent but would recruit him for high-octane sex with herself, a high-octane woman called Miranda. He did not know her real name. That was Nomenklatura's privilege. Would they ever know each other's real names? She hoped so, one day soon.

Both arrived early and, satisfied they were free of unwanted company, met inside the little restaurant. Their table was in a corner, so they could see the windows and the door to the street, and their backs were protected by brickwork and wooden panelling. They kissed and sat down beside each other, backs to the wall as they held hands under the table.

"Thanks for your info, Harry."

"It worked? Mission accomplished?"

"Copy that!" Miranda replied. They both laughed.

A waiter approached. They agreed they both wanted virgin cocktails. The waiter departed with their order.

"I didn't know you were a virgin, Harry."

"Oh, I have been since my divorce. And you've *always* been one, I guess."

"Absolutely. I want you to take mine tonight."

The waiter reappeared with their cocktails, virgin mojitos.

"Why are we drinking virgin cocktails?" Miranda asked.

"Because we've bought shares in Virgin Airlines?"

"Well, you might have, but I haven't as yet."

"Well, why are we drinking virgins, Miranda?"

"Because making love is better if you're not pickled!" she said, remembering Shakespeare's drunken porter in that Scottish play.

"I'll drink virginally to that!" Harry quipped, taking another sip of his drink.

After dinner, which started with mushroom soup, progressed to duck breast, and finished with rum baba, they went to the hotel they both favoured. Miranda lived in a place she wanted to keep to herself. Harry lived, she guessed, in the American embassy. The hotel was discreet, comfortable, clean, and perfect for amorous liaisons, though it did not have five stars.

Miranda is a five-star woman, Harry thought as they lay naked in each other's arms and began to make love.

***

The interrogators were ready for further sessions with Bruno following the sleep-deprivation gambit. They worked in shifts to keep themselves fresh while Bruno became almost deliriously tired.

"Bruno, mon vieux, we've been watching your pornographic torture films. We've learned a lot about your miserable, obsessive thoughts. You haven't really got a mind. You are a disgusting speck of evil. If you had parents and grandparents, we could show them what you have made of yourself. Pity they're dead. Pity you don't have a wife."

Bruno laughed."You really are naïve people. How much do they pay you nowadays?"

"We think your friends back in the Arab world will disown you when they see these films."

"So?" Bruno yawned loudly, but he wanted to learn as much as possible before his escape. They didn't realize interrogation was a busy two-way street.

His eyelids closed. The one sitting across from him was too talkative. He prodded Bruno to keep him awake. Bruno felt contempt for them, with their petty rules about violence and torture. They used insults. These oafs could not match his knives, patiently sharpened. He yawned again and felt himself being shaken by someone behind him.

"We also learned the identity of one of your blond victims. We followed certain procedures and discovered she was kept in a rich man's house near the Turkish border. Our British friends extracted her. Oh yeah, they also brought the rich guy back with them. He's chatting to us now and hoping he can go back home, after helping with our inquiries. Blondie has told us a lot about your route for sex slaves and the so-called tough guys who get them from A to B, or should that be from Brixton to hell?"

Bruno was silent.

"Well, your Brixton castle was pinning our queen. But one of our chess players took your castle and moved with the queen to checkmate. You lost, Bruno. You lost! You want to sleep, old chap, but what you really need is exercise. It's time for you to go into the gym to have a bare fistfight with a sergeant in our Special Forces. You know the rules, don't you?"

"There are none," Bruno mumbled wearily.

Fifteen minutes later Bruno lay groaning in his cell. His naked body was aching and bruised. He could not sleep. His captors in France had given him a drink of water plus something to deprive him of sleep for another eight hours.

***

In Control's view, watching interrogations was an unpleasant task. Sometimes it was a complete waste of man hours. His disappointment with Bruno, who had once been a competent agent, had set him wondering: should Bruno die in a car accident when being transferred to a prison to await trial? Should he be simply kept incognito for years? Should he be released as Westlake had been? Control had thought the latter might be the best route to go. Certain regulations had to be followed because civil society demanded it. Control did not want to be the lackey of a police state, but he wanted to protect the public from evil. Yes, Bruno could be allowed to go to sleep. In his sleep he could be given the soluble direction indicator (a simple injection) by which they could track him. It was a gem of micro-technology requiring no surgery, which had been a bit of a problem sometimes in the past. No need for a small intervention and telltale stitches. When Bruno was released, it would be easy to track his journey without a team of followers shadowing him all the time. Control thought a new recruit might follow him as valuable experience. Bruno would lose him and then think he was free of observers. How wrong he would be. He would be unable to return to his old haunts. Those premises were now in the hands of forensic teams, who gave the rooms the fingerprint treatment and conducted meticulous searches.

31

YASMINE Lallouche enjoyed her job. Her success with publicity campaigns had resulted in an increase in salary that would get her a little ahead of the tax burden shouldered by all honest French residents and citizens. She was not about to leave her modest apartment in Paris. She was paying off a loan from the bank called BRED.

Late one evening, she prepared to turn in for the night. The salon, with its sofa-bed, Ikea coffee table, and circular dining table, was lit by a lamp on a curved black stem with a large Plexiglas sphere to hide the bulb. The light shed a soft, warm glow. She also had a reading lamp on a side table near her yellow leather armchair. A biography of Steve Jobs lay open on the little table. Yasmine was about to turn on her bedside lamp when the phone rang. She walked the few yards to the hall table.

"Allo?"

"Mademoiselle Yasmine Lallouche?" a male voice asked.

"Yes."

"In fifteen minutes you will have a visitor. Please let him in. You will recognize him if you have an intercom with a screen. If not, please go down to the courtyard to check on him and verify who it is."

"Thank you, monsieur, but why should I? It's late. It could be anybody at this time of night."

"It could be, but it isn't just anybody. You'll see."

"Alright. Fifteen minutes?"

"Yes. And thank you much."

Yasmine put down her phone. The voice was familiar. Had she heard it on television?

Fifteen minutes later she was wondering whether to go down to the courtyard when her buzzer sounded. She looked att he screen and saw a man in dark motorcycling clothes looking into the camera. She could hardly breathe with excitement. It was the president!

My goodness, mon dieu, she thought, *what can he want?*

She pressed the button to unlock the entry to her building and told her distinguished visitor to come to staircase A, fourth floor, and the door to the right when stepping out of the elevator.

A few seconds later, she opened her front door and lookedtoward the elevator. She heard a humming sound as the elevator rose. It stopped with a slight clunk, and the door slid open. The president walked out and came to her. He was alone.

"Come in, Mr. President."

"Thank you. It's good of you to see me at this late hour." She closed the door behind him. His voice was that of the man who had telephoned her only fifteen minutes earlier! She didn't know what to say, so she fell back on the usual formula.

"May I take your coat?"

"Please. Yes, that's better." He was wearing a dark navy-blue suit with a red tie. He cleared his throat and then looked at her as if trying to discover her thoughts. He had a quality of controlled energy. It was a kind of charisma.

"I was impressed when I saw you at the dinner a few nights ago. I have had a lot on my mind each day since then, but I always think of you. I could never forget you. Nobody has affected me like this before!"

Yasmine was as flustered as she was flattered. She knew the popular press stories of a first wife who had left him, of a mistress of many years in his own political party, and of his brief adventure in Belgium.

"Let's sit down. Will you have a drink? I have orange juice, mint tea, coffee, or Canada Dry ginger ale."

"No, just a glass of water." Yasmine left the president sitting on the sofa and went into the galley kitchen. She returned with a glass and a bottle of Badoit water from her fridge.

"Thank you, Yasmine. You see? I remembered. It's a pretty name, but you are unique and more than pretty."

Yasmine scrutinized him and then broke the silence. "You're welcome. But why are you here? Why do you need to see me?" The silence that followed was filled with compressed energy.

He held out his hands, and she moved closer and could not help but take his hands in hers. He pulled her hands gently, and she sat closer beside him on the sofa.

"I need to see you, Yasmine, because, because... oh, it's not a matter of state or politics. It's you. *I need you*. I need to escape that palace and all the problems and the politicians and the official visitors. I need to see *you* and be with you. That's it. So, that's why I have come to see you." He still held one of her hands, his grip tighter.

"Are you sure? I'm nobody. I work. I have a few friends. I'm dull!"

"Look, Yasmine, I have to go now and return to my shackles. I want to visit you again and for longer. But I cannot let you know in advance. I will just telephone and hope you'll be in."

She still felt the electricity between them. She was desperately sorry that he had to go so quickly.

"I'll be in," she said before she could think. She trembled slightly. He leaned forward and kissed her on the cheek. She closed her eyes as a thrill ran through her body. She turned her head toward him and he kissed her lips.

After he left, returning into the Parisian night, she could not sleep. This man was the leader of a great country, and he had chosen her! An Algerian!

It was eight days before he came to see her again. That time they made love. They were in bed for a few hours. He left as quietly as he had arrived. It was 4:00a.m. Yasmine smiled and sighed as she tried to sleep on the side of her bed where he had lain. It was still warm. Would she ever be his wife? She did not know, but she thought not. It was enough to be the mistress of the man who, at the moment, ruled a major western power. She knew he could well be defeated in three years' time if he tried for another mandate in the next presidential election. Perhaps they might think about marriage then. Perhaps not. She was the mistress, and she was happy in that knowledge. It was a secret they shared. A state secret? In any case, it was a secret she would not share with any of her friends or journalist acquaintances or colleagues. They thought she was a loner, under the power of some male in her family who would, in time, select a husband for her. They were wrong. She and the president were accomplices in a secret love. It was exciting. And he was the most fascinating and unpredictable man she had ever met.

***

Dr. Mary Rao, now Mrs. Paul Wills, was enjoying a bubble bath. It was a Saturday, surgery was over, no new babies were about to burst into the world whose wickedness was as yet unknown to them, no new accidents had put any of her patients into hospital, no new terrorist attacks had occurred, at least where she was, and many of her regular patients had gone elsewhere for the holidays. Holiday makers stung by jellyfish or with feet cut by walking on glass that should not be on a beach would be seeing the local doctors and pharmacists. Bliss!

Mary relaxed and closed her eyes. Later, she would dress and make dinner with Paul. They were both content with quiet evenings at home, making the meal and chatting about the week, new projects, or new ideas gleaned from *New Science* magazine or from conversations with friends. A team in Bristol was perfecting a self-healing covering for aircraft wings. It was a product that scabbed over like skin when punctured. It would make commercial and military aircraft safer. A "greenie" friend had told them about wafer-thin solar panels that could make solar energy cheap worldwide and reduce everybody's heating, air-conditioning, and lighting bills to almost zero. Mary had heard a colleague talking about "liquid light." The internet of things was also using new sensor chips that spelled the future and fortunes for investors.

Paul kept a sharp eye on such developments, always looking for an angle that might lead to an article he could publish. Mary was convinced that science and humanitarian projects in democratic societies were the way the world community would flourish. Neither wanted to invest though, because each had enough to support a way of life that was already good. Greed was not their agenda. Terrorists wanting to turn the clock back to barbaric social norms were bound to lose, despite their money and weapons and the vile propaganda they posted wherever they could.

Mary decided to get out of the bath and get dressed. *Long live normal and decent people*, she thought.

Then the telephone rang.

BRUNO'S SECRET

✦✦✦

Bruno would be kept a few more days for final interrogations in light of newly accumulating evidence. He knew nothing of the injection that made his bloodstream into a constant signal for tracking him after his release. He smiled as he answered truthfully all the questions they asked. He smiled because there were things beyond their loop for which there were no questions and, therefore, no answers to be given. He still retained some major secrets.

After his last interrogation, he thought of one such secret: his meeting place in a loge of the Opéra Garnier. While attending a concert or watching a ballet, he would be joined by an accomplice in his network. Instructions were given with no phone record. Associates could get down from Brussels or Strasbourg by train to attend such high-art events in Paris, join him in the loge, and return the same night, if necessary. His money man was a regular visitor to Bruno's loge. Middle Eastern men attending the ballet or a western concert were hardly the kind of radicals working to impose sharia law across Europe.

He smiled at simple-minded idealists who thought people were all kind and nice and chose to ignore small signs of the evil that could so easily be exploited and enjoyed. He smiled as he thought of the well-meaning whites, many of them Christians, who could be rounded up and transferred to mass graves. They would be shocked and surprised as they waited for the bullet or sword before tumbling into a death without any heaven. This had already been the fate of opponents in the Middle East and some parts of Africa. The struggle was costing many, so many, lives of young radicals. All the same, it was almost too easy to undo democratic societies. *All we need*, he mused, *is an elected majority. And the Internet. All we need is time.* History, he reasoned, was with him and his associates.

He saw himself as a great hero whose monument would be set up on some iconic spot, like the site of a demolished Sainte Chapelle. Yet he knew he was ill. His time would run out, but he had a few years yet to deliver the great blow. This enormous coup had to be perfect, and it had to be enacted soon.

Why had Monsieur Martin let him go free? Control (as if he were really in control) had to be hoping that some agent could follow him and monitor any Arab kidnappers. As if he, Bruno, were to have the same fate as that piece of white lard, Dr. Westlake! No, Bruno's instructions were always followed. If arrested by the French and then released "for lack of evidence," he would live as a normal citizen and then rejoin the network when he judged it to be safe. If the French authorities left him without pay or pension, he would set up a small business, such as a shop that repaired bicycles or lawnmowers. In fact, he could see the value of this for his ultimate secret action, the big mystery that only he, as yet, knew. It was a perfect plan. He would need about fifteen operatives. If only half of one percent of the Syrian refugees who had swarmed through Europe were trained and committed terrorists, or eager recruits, he would have far more than he needed.

The interrogators came to the little secure room, breaking his train of thought.

"Well,, Bruno. Feel good to be a free man?" a smooth younger man asked.

"We hope your friends at the mosque will feel pleased to have you back again."

Bruno smiled at them. The older interrogator saw Bruno as almost a living death's head. Was he black energy: a demon, fiend, or devil come from the darkness to plague humanity? No, nothing more than a neurotic killer.

"So, what are your big plans for the future as a free man, Bruno, my lad?"

"You don't know how close you are to defeat, complacent as you are. We are spreading into all the societies worth controlling. We have broken unity in Europe. We are eliminating huge numbers of Christians. We shall win sooner than you think."

The chunky, tough-looking interrogator shrugged."You are a fool who recruits the young to destroy themselves and as many innocents as you can target."

Bruno raised his eyebrows and shook his head, as if he had to explain something to backward pupils in a school."There are no innocents." He sighed.

"What about your plans for ordinary people and moderate Muslims?" the smooth young man asked.

"There are no moderate Muslims."

"Really? How so?"

"There are determined Muslims, more or less strict,like me. And I'm as sharp as a good knife. And there are radicalized Muslims who are deluded and therefore pitiless. And then there are masses of Muslims who are merely passive. They don't march in protest against us. They don't throw terror trainees or veterans out of the mosque. They do not punish them. They don't inform."

"You're lying! There was a big demonstration of Muslims against terror just last week. Oh, you were in a cell. I forgot."

"Many prefer to suppose that all our terrorists are nice young men who would not harm a kitten." Bruno continued his tirade as if nothing they said registered with him. "They are mightily surprised when these nice youths suddenly become killers. They are too scared to speak up or inform on us. Who can blame them? When we have a democratically elected majority in any country, we shall control all the military and declare sharia law without losing any time. The passive ones will follow us out of fear and will secretly rejoice that whites and non-Muslims of whatever colour are no longer in control. In Hitler's Germany after 1933, there was no popular rebellion against the Nazis. People got on with their lives as best they could. The parliamentary minorities will be arrested and executed. We are the heroes. We will avenge the loss of our Spanish empire, the halt we came to in the Balkans, and the retreat from France. We shall mount again beyond Istanbul, and our caliphate will triumph."

"Bruno, my dear young fellow, you are a racist Muslim imperialist bastard. But many of our Muslim friends are not as you wish them to be. You will be disappointed," the older interrogator said. "Another lesson you and your schoolboy recruits have to learn is that you might destroy world heritage treasures, but you cannot build any monument to your cause to equal anything you destroy. Don't forget this: neither Hitler nor the Soviets could destroy the democratic west. You and your followers are certain losers in that campaign. You cannot destroy the spirit of Churchill or de Gaulle. They were real soldiers."

Bruno sneered at them. "I love being what I am. And I love your horror at what will inevitably follow from your welcoming everybody into your country. So noble and so self-destructive. How cozily humane! But it will be the birth of a new empire that will grow rapidly worldwide. Ours will be the last empire, and it will be permanent. It will be the Islamic future of all humanity."

The younger interrogator stood up, grasped Bruno's arms, shook him violently, and then threw him off his chair. Bruno lay on the floor, smiling.

"Such violence! Such temper. I am glad your government respects human rights. Wait till I inform the well-meaning press about this treatment of a French citizen!"

The interrogators pulled Bruno to his feet, sat him down, and then the older one cuffed the back of Bruno's skull-like head.

"Off you go then, lad, back to plotting and failing."

"You'll regret that. So will your families. We'll find them. While they're dying, we'll tell them why. And they will curse you as they breathe their final groans—on camera."

"Great propaganda, Bruno," the younger man said."God knows why you're free. I think the government hopes you'll go off to convert the Chinese and the Russians to your radical ways. Let's get you out of here. You pollute the air . Go to Russia, and revenge your pitiful self on them. And don't forget the Chinese. You mustn't deprive a quarter of humanity of your winning ideas."

***

Mary picked up the phone.

"Hello, Mary? It's Anne. I'm ringing from Canada. How are you settling down to married life?"

"Anne! How good to hear you. We're doing just fine here. Paul has turned out to be a poppet, as my mother says about men she likes."

Anne laughed and repeated the word. She had to remember that one. "Well, do give Paul my best wishes. How's the practice?"

"Oh, coughs and sneezes mainly. People who need to be sent off to eye doctors. People who think they're going deaf but just need their ears de-waxed. But I do have some more serious things and some hospital cases. How's your research trip turning out?"

"Actually, there's more material in the archives than I imagined when I started. I'm in a place called Saskatoon. I can't get over the fact that the campuses here are so well kept, with lovely facilities and hardly any graffiti. Some universities in France are covered in slogans, obscenities, and silly tags. Lamentable. La-men-table. But I saw Graham in Vancouver."

"How is he? Still depressed I suppose, poor lamb?"

"Lamb? Between you and me, I think he might have fallen under the spell of a woman with a shiny new PhD!"

"Really?"

"Yes. I think the lamb might turn out to be a ram!" She laughed.

Mary was taken by surprise but also thought this was an intriguingly funny side to Graham.

"In effect, Mary, when I saw the state he was in, I took pity on him. I wanted to stay in a hotel, but he was so forlorn and wanting to repay my hospitality that I stayed with him as his guest in his house."

"Was the shiny new PhD also there?"

"No telltale signs, if you know what I mean. But I could tell she was not too happy when I turned up. She needn't have worried. I was quick to escape. This research project is a revelation. In fact, I get the impression that I, as a mere independent scholar, am more enthused by it all than Graham is by his own work as a university professor."

"So, tell me, how long is it before you get back to London?"

"I'm not sure. But I'll ring again when I know. Perhaps you and Paul would like to meet me in London? We could have lunch or dinner. Take in an exhibition?"

"That would be lovely if I can get away one weekend. But last time we were there a bomb was detonated in an alley not far from our hotel."

"Oh, my goodness! Yes, I read about that. Horrible. So, you won't go to London again?"

"Of course we shall go to London again. These people want to sow fear, but life must go on as usual. Oh, do you remember my friend Maggie Chan, who was at the wedding?"

"Yes, I do. Wasn't she a lovely Chinese woman?"

"That's right. Well, it seems she's keen on the Scottish pilot, Jack."

"Ooh la la! He was an impressive man. How do you say? A chunk, no hunk." Mary laughed. "Yes. I'd say so, Anne."

"Well, give that poppet husband of yours a hug and kisses from me. I'll phone."

"Oh, do. It was lovely to talk to you, Anne. We'll definitely try to see you in London. Or you could come down to Sutton Coldfield. We'll see how it goes."

"Yes. Au revoir, Mary."

32

GRAHAM sat in front of his computer screen and stared at it with leaden eyes. He had not written a word since he had opened the file. No ideas surfaced. Would he ever be able to finish his paper? He was depressed. He sat there, gloomy and self-pitying.

A flock of crows cawed to each other outside, as if jeering at him. He had a pile of relevant sources (i.e., books) from the university library and notes made some time ago. Yet he felt totally empty. He had no idea how to develop his theme. Every time he lifted his hands and spread his fingers to type, his mind became a jumble of impressions from noises outside the house and a recurring plaint: why me? Then he thought of Anne's warmth and the generous gift she had made of herself. He remembered her mature body and envisaged her face and keenly alert eyes. She could write. She could research. She had a goal. She had energy. She knew who she was. *Know thyself.* Did he know himself? Who was he now? A man who had lost his way? A failure soon to be forty? Forty! *A man's fortieth birthday is indeed a melancholy event.* Who had said that? Life begins at forty. What rot. What life?

He had felt a stirring of more than life when he was having sex with Camilla. Was that it then? Desire? The anticipation of "having" an attractive woman? The act itself? Warm and willing flesh, was that it? A new relationship? What was a relationship? Getting to know the mannerisms and meagre ideas of someone until they became stale? Getting a comfortable feeling of togetherness? Then one day the body would seem ordinary, the act unexciting, the mannerisms irritating, the other's thoughts feeble, boring, their voice a constant irritant. Was that all it was? Was that life?

With Jackie these things didn't apply. He had known happiness then. Now there was a darkened shadow of loss. The guilty pleasure of tasting a younger person's body. But why guilt? He felt a sense of pointlessness. A nagging toothache of the soul, if such a thing existed. What had happened to professional responsibility?

Graham stood up and looked out the window. He could not write his academic book. He had writer's block, as people in the department said when trying to defend their lack of productivity. As a full professor now, he could coast along to retirement. What then? Aye, what then?

"Sod off!" he said to the computer. He decided to go to the department.

Back in his office, Graham settled on his old sofa with a book. The regulation flooring was fashioned from thin tiles of brown carpeting glued to the concrete floor. Cheapo. His desk had its usual messy piles of paper and books. Graham put the book on his chest and closed his eyes. Someone knocked on his door. He groaned and swore under his breath.

"Come in!" He opened his eyes to see his visitor. It was Cam. He sat up.

"I might have a job, Graham!" She was excited and grinning. Graham went to her and gave her a hug. She was wearing a perfume, subtle, a touch of spice and, yes, violets. Sexy!

"Well, let's celebrate!" He walked to the door and turned the lock.

"Now?"

"Now!"

He was already undressing her. She took his head in her hands and kissed his lips. In moments they were naked. Graham put her down on the carpet. Soon he was copulating with a rough urgency.

"Hey, the floor's hard. Let's go to the couch."

"No." He covered her mouth with his and with a frantic series of thrusts achieved his climax. He lay still and silent on top of her.

"Now you can go on the couch," he said.

"And what will you do? You're finished. It'll be a few hours before you can do it again." She started to gather her clothes.

"Yes. I'm finished," he said. "Go and be nice to your new boss."

※※※

Brian was able to walk about in the field and along the Ridgeway to the pub at Ritherdon. He took a walking stick with him but did not rely on it. He was missing Alissa and felt restless. He wondered whether she would telephone.

Perhaps she would be back only for the beginning of term in September. He ached for her and yet could not talk to her or write. He didn't have her email address, telephone number, or postal address. He had a persistent need to see her, a longing for her presence, whether she was silent or talking, and he felt a genuine respect for her. He needed her. He thought she liked him and admired his skill as an artist. He wanted to make love to her again and again. For always? She certainly felt genuine friendship for him, but he wanted more. Perhaps she had left her address with the school; he should try to send her a letter. He felt better and less lonely once he made that decision. That was it. He would get her address.

***

Miss Mason looked across her antique desk at Mr. Brian Atkins. He was the local artist who had a way with sheep. She smiled. "Mr. Atkins, you teach art, I've heard. You're a painter as well it seems. And you exhibit?"

"That's right. One of your teachers, Miss Partridge, bought a painting from me recently. She's gone out of town, I think, and I was wondering if you have a forwarding address."

Brian looked into the headmistress's alert and searching eyes. She was intelligent. Perhaps he or his agent should take a few photos of his work to the school to see whether they might want a local landscape or even a portrait of Miss Mason or the chairman of the board of governors. He decided he would not push for it himself. His agent might be successful. After all, she had to work for her commission! He hated self-promotion. He loved painting.

"I can give you the address of her club in London. They will keep mail for her or forward urgent items." She smiled. "I expect she'll be back within the next two weeks, unless she stays away for the entire summer break."

"Thank you, Miss Mason. That's kind."

He focused on her with his painter's eyes. Her face was angular but seemed softened by age with its slackening skin. She had been a handsome woman. Her hairstyle and those eyes, the determined mouth, they could make a statement of character in a portrait.

"Have you met our art teacher?"

"I did, but it was some time ago."

"She was interested in going to your recent art spectacle but had a nasty cold.

She spent the weekend in bed, poor thing. She's still there now, or I could have steered you to her for a chat. But my secretary will give you the club's address. They will forward your message to Miss Partridge."

Miss Mason stood up. It was a cue. Brian stood, and then the headmistress walked with her slight limp toward the door. Brian realized she might be a good subject for a portrait. She could be painted with the school building behind her or maybe right there, in her study, with its Edwardian interior. Miss Mason opened the door and spoke to her secretary.

"Please give Mr. Atkins the address of the Oxford and Cambridge Club in London."

She turned to Brian and shook hands.

"Thank you, Miss Mason. That's helpful."

She looked at him with a mixture of interest and amusement, a twinkle in her sharp eyes.

***

Bruno walked to a Muslim prayer room. Nobody there knew he had been a French agent. They knew him as a local man who was often absent and probably suffering from a slowly debilitating cancer. He was a lone wolf with no family in France. He was not devout, but he caused no trouble. He was looking for a rental apartment. From what he had told them he had lost his old apartment, the owner having returned from working abroad.

Meanwhile, Control was delighted that his little plan was working perfectly. A new recruit in the French security forces had shadowed Bruno. He had lost him in the corridors of the metro at Châtelet.

Gloating over the mediocrities Control was now hiring, Bruno sauntered along the Avenue de l'Opera, glancing into shop windows. Suddenly, he turned into a side street and struck out toward the rue Molière. By a fairly devious route he reached the Bastille.

The SDI (soluble direction indicator) was working well. His whereabouts could be monitored constantly. Control looked at a small screen on which a large-scale map of Paris showed a small red point at the Bastille. The red dot reached a courtyard. Control tapped a corner of his screen, and the map became a three-dimensional image of the building Bruno entered.

Ignorant of Control's knowledge, Bruno walked through a little gate of iron rails into a small paved lane that led to a yard flanked by squat buildings. The fact that someone had followed him and then lost him amused him. He looked around and, seeing he was alone, walked to a heavy door, looked at the list of names, and then pressed the button to open the courtyard door. He stepped into a square, covered passageway with another courtyard beyond it. Some bushes and ancient stone troughs were overflowing with geraniums.

"So, that's your hideaway, mon ami!" Control murmured. Bruno's street address flashed in a line above the image. How delicious it was. Control chuckled. Then he thought for a long, silent minute.

"Yes,yes,yes," he said. "Now for the big operation."

33

THE CIA had noted as a routine matter the comings and goings of people using the Paris mosques. All of them: people and masques. Harry had urged surveillance of small prayer rooms by discreet watchers, people who fit in with the locals. It had paid off. Bruno had been seen and followed by cyclists and pedestrians to his enclave near the Place de la Bastille. A young man, doubtless a French agent, had followed Bruno but had lost him at Châtelet. There had been curt messages on the cell phone traffic but for the last two days just an ominous silence. Bruno had contacted nobody by phone. Nor had anyone spoken to him. The silence was ominous. It could mean mayhem within a day or two. Therefore, all suspects were watched and tailed. It seemed, however, to be "all quiet on the western front."

Sitting amid a crowd on the steps of the opera building, Harry had seen Bruno cross the road and make for the box office. Was he going to the opera? That would surely corrupt his soul. Mozart? The seraglio piece? Harry nodded to a bearded student type next to him. He followed and joined the queue three people back from Bruno. The "student" had a small "hearingaid" in his right ear, the lobe of which was pierced by an earring. He could hear clearly which performance Bruno was booking. He touched the earring. The information was recorded, and the device sent the recording to the American laboratory that was so dear to Harry's heart. Harry took a taxi to the rue Boissy d'Anglas and then walked to the lab.

***

"Miranda, *ma belle*, it's your one and only, Harry."
"Hey! As they say on American TV."
"Hey. I have new news for you. Let's meet."

"I'll be in a cab and will pick you up from wherever you want."

"Okay. In the rue d'Alger, near the rue de Rivoli, twentyminutes from now?"

"Oui!"

***

Kim placed her palm on a glossy panel and looked into a small round lens above it. She went across the threshold as an armour-plated door slid to one side. It closed after her. Miranda repeated the performance.

"Ah, yes, I need to brief you two!" Control said, looking at a screen on his table in the briefing room. He looked up and smiled briefly. Then he sighed. "There is telephone silence now, so some things will begin to happen soon. We hear from some of our Muslim friends that a rich man has given cash and arms to three groups. One group is in Strasbourg, another in Lyon, and a third, of course, is here. Our guess is they will try for simultaneous actions in all three places. Questions?"

"Can we find this money man and grill him?" Miranda asked.

"I wish we could," Control said. "It's on our agenda if he's still here."

"Do we know any people who could form these groups in the three cities?" Kim inquired.

"I'm glad you asked. In fact, some people in Strasbourg were arrested this morning. It seems they are unable to talk about who is giving orders or planning. We just know what their operation was to be. And their apartments seem to confirm what they are saying. It appears they were to massacre people in Strasbourg Cathedral and destroy whatever they could inside. At the same time, they were to attack the European Parliament there using two vehicles full of explosives. In the resulting chaos, armed killers would shoot their way into the building, killing as many people as possible before blowing themselves up."

"Do we know anything about the Lyon and Paris groups?" Miranda asked.

"Not much," Control admitted, "except that Bruno might meet one of them to spark the operation.

"Did the Strasbourg group have a timetable? When were they going to act?"

"We think it was to have been unleashed tomorrow," Control replied, looking grave.

"The Strasbourg targets suggest they are going for officialdom," Kim said, "secular and Christian. Since it is to be synchronous, could we guess that in Lyon they want to destroy the town hall and another church?"

Control nodded. "Yes. The Hôtel de Ville in Lyon is full of treasures. It's a masterpiece of art and craftsmanship. The chandeliers alone are superb. As for the church, it could be the cathedral. But one telephone call we intercepted said someone was preparing a dinner of three hares."

"Three hares?" Miranda queried.

"Isn't that an Islamic symbol?" Kim asked.

Control nodded vigorously. "Yes, Islamic, Jewish, and Christian—and probably Chinese originally."

Kim laughed. "So, were they really planning a dinner? Hare couscous?"

"One of our analysts says that Notre Dame de Fourvière has a three-hares motif, perhaps in a carving. It certainly appears in an illuminated manuscript."

"And, my dear Hervé," Kim said, "it has a golden statue of the Virgin on one tower and the French Christian Radio antennae on another!"

"Could we prepare to receive the gunmen and the kamikazes in both places?" Miranda asked.

"Hmm. Well, it looks as if those will be the Lyon targets," Control said in a low voice. "But not necessarily. We could have our people inside both buildings as a reception committee, but we need similar arrangements for other likely targets. We must. We will. We'll win."

Control got up and took another look at the screen on his desk. "Now, charging into pedestrians and ramming into a building with a bomb on wheels, like a heavy truck, is a difficult operation to stop. If we're to block off streets, we have to know which ones. And the drivers could damage any street and its pedestrians even if they saw the way had been blocked to the cathedral or the town hall. They could alert their actual assault people for the two buildings to abort."

Both women were quiet for a moment, thinking hard. Kim was the first to break the silence."Can we at least get our reception committees in place, pronto? They must stay put until all hell breaks loose, or the thing will be foiled before it starts."

"Agreed," Control said. "I'll send the order now to my man in Lyon." He pressed a switch and typed rapidly into a keyboard that slid into place in front of him.

"Control, I think similar teams should cover the cathedral and the central mosque." Kim's tone was decisive and firm.

"The mosque?" Control gave her a puzzled look.

"Well, the vast majority of victims of terror tactics are Muslims. They might target them to instil even more fear. People would be unwilling to come forward with information about radical fanatics."

"Or they might be more forthcoming than they are now," Control countered. "But I see your point," he added quickly. "We must get our teams inside the targets without anyone else knowing. I think with the Christian church it's possible."

"Could we drop a team on the roof in the middle of the night?" Miranda asked.

Control shook his head. "Too many lights in Lyon, as in any biggish city. It isn't the middle of the countryside."

He tapped a few more points on a screen and typed. He waited and then tapped the screen again. He smiled nervously at the two women. They were all under pressure.

"Actually, my informants tell me the roof has a small door leading from the building's interior for the purposes of inspecting damage, leaks, and so on. Our people could enter as civilian worshippers and climb to the roof at night, ensure the door can be opened, and lie low in case of action."

He stood and stretched both arms above his head and linked his hands. He swayed a bit from side to side, then relaxed and walked out from behind his desk. He stood still, feet apart, and touched his toes several times before rising slowly. Again the nervous smile.

"Very necessary, ladies. And now for Paris. What's their agenda, I wonder?"

"And are there three masterminds or facilitators—three hares?" Kim posed the question and then relapsed into silence.

Control looked intently at his screen. "Our American friends have sent us a picture of Bruno and the mega-rich middleman from the Middle East. But our British friends say a man from Hastings is making his way to Paris by Eurostar from St. Pancras. He's apparently part Indonesian, part Dutch, and a British citizen now. He attends a mosque. The operation will start tomorrow or at the latest the next day. What are the targets here?"

"Again, church and state!" They all spoke it aloud together. Silence.

Control looked at his screen. "Tomorrow the National Assembly has a vote. Can't rule it out. The Senate isn't doing much except for a lunch. The Hôtel de Ville will be as busy as usual. Notre Dame will be full of tourists. So will the Sainte Chapelle."

"Sacré-Coeur will also be open," Kim suggested, "and if it were to be blown up, it would be seen from all over Paris."

Control looked at the ceiling. "All five must have teams within ready and waiting."

"Chief, can we be part of it?" Miranda asked. "The defence of the buildings?"

"No, I want you and Kim to bring in the three hares, alive if possible. The 'sleeper' from Hastings must be important. The money man obviously is. I want all three under interrogation if at all possible."

Kim knew enough about Control's planning to be confident in his tactics. There might be damage and killing, but it would be kept to a minimum. It would, after all, *be under control.*

Control turned to them both and motioned to his corner with sofa and armchairs. "Let's have a glass of Badoit water."

They sat down, and Control served them their drinks.

"How do we get to the three hares, Hervé?" Kim demanded.

"My bet is that Bruno will lead you to them. There's no telephone communication now. E-mails are quiescent! But we know where Bruno is, and we know wherever he goes. We're tracking him all the time. I think from 16:00 hours you two must follow the instructions we send regarding his movements. That way you can tail him in such a way that he won't see you."

"Arms?"

"You must have pistols with silencers. If you have room, take a stun grenade too. You can also keep a Taser up your sleeve. Ultra-light body armour, girls. Remember, Bruno is a knife man of extraordinary skill—and he's fast. The sleeper from Hastings is an unknown quantity. Miranda must tail him from the Gare du Nord. I don't think he'll go to Lille or Brussels or Strasbourg. We'll arrest him on the platform if he gets off at Strasbourg. They're deliberately cutting it fine for time. Kim, keep the money man in your sights at all times. We'll track Bruno, and I'll give the word when we bring him in. The three hares will meet briefly to compare notes in France until the last moment before their three triumphs."

"They must have an escape planned. I think the money man will have a private jet ready for all three," Miranda surmised.

"Or just for himself." Control smiled. "However, we thinka private jet with four passengers is scheduled to leave tomorrow for Lebanon. The four could be our kingpin, the other two criminals, and a bodyguard."

"When is it leaving?" Kim asked.

"It's scheduled for late afternoon." Control winked at them. "My guess is the boss wants to be clear of French airspace before the outrages. So, I think all will be planned for just before dinner in Strasbourg, Lyon, and here in Paris."

"The people we arrested in Strasbourg have talked more?"

"Only about their operation. They don't know where their money, weapons, orinstructions came from. The people they saw were all masked and gloved. They don't know of any other operations."

Miranda chuckled. "And the three hares will be disappointed when they learn about Strasbourg as a non-event."

"Let's hope we can catch the hares here before they learn anything about Strasbourg," Kim added.

"So, will you stop that late-afternoon flight?" Miranda asked.

"Absolutely. We shall then have far more than we need."

The interrogators came to the little secure room, breaking the Control's train of thought.

"Hello! Even if the three hares or just one of them gets to it, we shall keep that aircraft on the ground. That aircraft will then be a holding cell!" Control smiled, but his eyes were slits with a cold gleam just visible.

34

IF *you can make it work, so much the better. A commission for even just one portrait would be good. If not I will carry on here as usual. I'll do another sketch of you when you get back. Do hurry!*

Oh, I almost forgot: leg nearly back to normal.
Affectionately,
Brian

This brief note to that wonderful woman he had met might help the relationship to progress a little. How life would work out one never knew.

***

Miranda joined Harry in the cab that caught up with her on la rue d'Algers. They drove to Le Nemours, a bistro near the Comédie Française, and ordered hot chocolate.

"Well?"

Harry smiled. "Your skeletal man is going to the opera Bastille to see 'The Escape from the Seraglio' tomorrow evening."

Miranda got up to go and kissed the top of his forehead.

"Gotta go, as they say. See you in three days, I hope."

She walked out and crossed the street to a taxi stand. The cab drove off with her. Harry had gone to the door to watch her. He scratched his head. *This must be the big one*, he thought. He drank all the hot chocolate before returning to the embassy.

Once there he briefed his immediate superior. Something big was about to break. No messages had been monitored among several of their targets during the last few days. If they were communicating at all, it was through personal meetings in the street or behind closed doors. Yet the phrase "three hares" had been heard. Perhaps they were three main players. Harry thought one could be the rich guy he had photographed. The other might be Bruno, the opera guy. But who was the third? Perhaps he would join Bruno at the opera? Yes. Harry decided to have a night at the opera to see who contacted Bruno. He would photograph them together. Maybe all three would meet at the opera, like three of the Marx Brothers. More seriously, were they people who laughed at mayhem? It was useful to watch Bruno and his contacts. Miranda could find it helpful. And if so, she would love him all the more.

***

Yasmine had finished her work for the day. She was about to go down into the Metro when a tall, well-dressed man called her name.

"Your family sent me to contact you, Yasmine. I have to congratulate you on your success. I understand even the president praised your work."

"Who are you?" Yasmine was suspicious of anyone just contacting her in the street.

"I'm a friend of the family. They knew I was coming to Paris and asked me to pass on the message to you personally."

"They could have written. In fact, there might be a letter for me when I get home. But how did you find me?"

"My dear, you are famous ever since that dinner the president attended." He held out a small box wrapped in expensive paper. "It's a little gift, from home."

Yasmine took the box. Who had sent it? "It's kind of you to bring it. Thank you. What is your name? I'll write and let the family know you were here with their gift."

"I am Dr. Mahmoud Petrie. I'm half English, on my father's side. My car is across the street and I could drop you off."

"You're kind, but the metro will be quicker. The traffic is all snarled up along the quais today."

"Well, we'll meet again, I'm sure. Give my regards to the family when you contact them, and mention Mahmoud, won't you?"

Yasmine nodded and then went down into the metro station.

At home she went into her kitchen and unwrapped the little box. It was an elegant, good-quality alarm clock. She inserted the new battery included with it. The clock worked perfectly. She walked into the bedroom and put it on her dressing table, then set it to the present time. She would be able to check the time from her bed when the alarm sounded. She would have to get up to stop it ringing, which meant she could not simply suppress it and doze off again. She had no bedside table, so the clock would have been on the floor anyway. No, it was good where it was clearly visible.

After eating her light supper, Yasmine wrote a letter thanking her family for sending Mahmoud with the little gift. Perfect. She would never travel without it.

It was 2:35 a.m. when the president arrived. Yasmine let him in and give him a drink. After a little while they made love.

The president had needed her. The next few days would be nerve-wracking. His information, which he did not share with Yasmine, was that the next day, or the day after, terrorist attacks of astonishingly destructive force would be attempted. He was frightened for the possible victims, frightened for the security forces who might be killed and injured, perhaps crippled for life, and afraid his popularity would descend to an all-time low. Why couldn't these terrorists be wiped out? Yasmine was brilliant, kind, and loyal—of that he felt sure. Or was she? He pushed the thought away. He had worries and work in equal doses to face the next day and the days after that.

He shuddered as he walked into the chill of night toward his waiting transport. Yes, another security check on her would have to be launched. He would order it.

***

Control cleared his throat noisily, a sign of extreme tension.

"Miranda, my American associates have said our troublesome Bruno will be enjoying the opera tomorrow. What do you make of it?"

Monsieur Martin seemed older than she had thought. His collar was not touching his neck. There was a slight gap. Had he lost weight? She dismissed the thought and concentrated on the present precarious situation.

"They may be correct. I think it would be like Bruno to enjoy the opera, where he'll be watched by our people while something horrible happens elsewhere. He'll have a perfect alibi."

"You mean the attentats will take place during the opera performance?"

"Exactly. It could be the matinee or the evening performance."

"What would you do, if you were Bruno?"

"Well, I'd go to the opera but leave with enough time to get to the private jet and out of French airspace just as the trouble starts."

"How would you get to the airfield?"

"I'd take my escape route, killing anyone following me."

"But how?"

"In an ambulance perhaps. There would be a lot of them screaming around Paris."

Control smiled. He stood and walked over to her and put his hand on her shoulder. She felt a slight tremor.

"How glad I am that you work for us! When would all these strikes in three different cities have been planned? And by whom?"

"The rich Algerian and the Hastings sleeper must have met in person some time ago to work out all details. Possibly as much as six months ago. After all, once they had decided on targets, there would be all the financing and logistics to take care of."

"Absolutely. I have an idea. Like Kim, you should join me in planning!"

"I'd be delighted when I'm older. Thank you for thinking of me."

"Don't go off to the US with your good friend, Harry. Stay here with us."

"Let's get on with stopping these barbaric killers and vandals." Miranda was stunned. How did the old man know about her and Harry?

"Yes, of course. Join Kim in ten minutes to take Bruno and the other hares into custody. Interrogation will give us all the details we need. Then you two can help our commanders in the field, wherever the interrogation reveals the strikes will happen."

"If we can make the arrests quickly enough. I'll be in touch then." She kissed Control on both cheeks. He held her tight for a moment.

"Come back safe and sound, Miranda," he whispered.

"I will." And she was gone, asking herself again, how did old Control know about Harry?

***

Harry was in the back seat of a Mercedes-Benz taxi parked near the restaurant. It was, in reality, a cover vehicle from his embassy. He watched Miranda and another woman fooling around on the steps of the opera building. Then they walked away toward a traffic light and a pedestrian crossing in the opposite direction from the opera entrance. Were they going to join Bruno and his companions later? It had to be an arrest, but when and where?

Harry went to the entrance of a pricy restaurant and looked at a table where Bruno sat with the rich Algerian and another man. Harry blinked, and his high-tech eye photographed them while the recorder picked up the traffic noise behind him and the haphazard clatter and laughter in the restaurant. A hostess took him to a table about ten feet away from the three hares, as he now thought of them. As he walked past them, he heard a snatch of Arabic from Bruno. Now he would be able to record everything they were saying.

Bruno and his two companions knew nothing of Kim and Miranda walking in the crowds passing by outside. Kim took out a small camera. She appeared to be photographing a woman friend on the steps of the opera building. She was, in fact, looking through a special lens made in Austria. Bruno and his friends were quite clear. If anything went wrong with the arrests, at least the police would have an image of their quarry. She walked to the steps to join Miranda.

"I've got pics of our three hares," she announced. "I'll send them to Control right now." She pressed a button. "There."

"We bring them in?" Miranda demanded.

"Yes. Let's spoil their meal and their plans for the opera."

They walked arm in arm into the restaurant. The three hares did not see them, because Bruno was in earnest conversation with his companions. They looked across at a man who had gone to a table not far away.

"Kim, did you see that man going into the restaurant? I know him. He's American."

"Well, if you trust him, let's make the arrests. Call for our plainclothes police backup."

"Miranda, we're hunting three hares."

Miranda listened for a moment, smiled, and then turned to Kim. "Their commander says they'll cover all other exits from the restaurant, just in case."

The two women walked into the restaurant. Bruno looked at them.

"Hello, Bruno," Kim said, "aren't you going to introduce us to your friends?"

"Actually, there's no need," Miranda said. "We know who they are. You're all under arrest. I'm taking you off the chessboard! Sorry to interrupt, but you all have to come with us."

"But the opera..." the Algerian said.

"I've done nothing. I'm not even French," the third man complained.

Taking advantage of their protests, Bruno rushed to Harry and held a knife against the American's face. Harry tried to knock Bruno's arm away and disarm him by twisting his knife hand. He was too slow. The knife left a long cut on Harry's cheek, though it did not find his eye. Harry could not suppress a howl of pain. Bruno had Harry's neck in the crook of his arm and the knife held on the same sliced cheek, but by sheer chance, the pointed blade was near Harry's unmodified eye.

"Drop your gun, Kim, or I'll take out his eye."

Kim put her gun on the floor and kicked it behind her. A plainclothes officer stepped past the gun. Now he was nearer the table.

A shot sounded from behind Miranda. The bullet hit Bruno in the arm. He cursed as he dropped the knife and released Harry, who turned and kicked Bruno's shin. Another howl of pain. Bruno's cries were now the only sound. All the waiters and waitresses were flat on the floor, still and silent. The other diners were also silent. Some watched Bruno. Others looked at the tabletops in front of them. Bruno limped to the stairs leading to the basement washrooms.

Plainclothes officers handcuffed the Algerian and the Hastings sleeper before taking them to a top-of-the-line armour-plated Peugeot among the crush of taxis.

People crowded the square as they made for the opera house. Control and his interrogators would be receiving the two hares in less than ten minutes.

Miranda went to Harry's side, put her arm around him and pressed a table napkin to his cheek. She had already phoned for an ambulance. Kim, having retrieved her gun, cautiously followed Bruno down the stairs to the washrooms. Two of the backup force were hard on her heels.

Kim covered the doors while the two men searched the ladies' and the gentlemen's lavatories. Both were empty. A third door was marked "Private." It was locked. Kim shot the lock, and they pushed into a narrow passageway beneath the restaurant. It was dark. One of the men lit their way with a pocket torch. The musty smell suggested the tunnel was seldom used. It seemed to lead under the Place de la Bastille. Then it curved to the right and came to a dead end. But there was a metal ladder. The torch revealed the ladder, bolted to the brickwork, leading straight up toward street level. A thunderous noise suddenly made them jump. The ground seemed to be shaking as if an earthquake had started. A metro train was rushing to another station not far from the Bastille.

"Thank God it's in another tunnel!" the man with the torch said.

"Thank God it's not a bomb. You first or me?" Kim asked.

"I'll go first, you next, and our colleague to cover our backs."

"Agreed."

The man with the torch climbed up, shining his light ahead and then behind him to help Kim and the man following her.

"We're there," the torch man said. They all emerged onto a narrow ledge along the side of the metro rails. There was another thunderous noise. A great eye came rushing through the dark toward them. The great serpentine monster clattered past, its lighted windows revealing all types of human beings in various postures as they chatted or read or slumped on seats, asleep.

"This is Kim. We've arrested two but Bruno has escaped," she said into her phone. "He's been shot in the arm."

"Don't worry," Control said. "You'll find him at the opera. Get him."

Kim looked at her two companions and smiled. "Back to the restaurant we go. Orders from the boss. The one that got away will be found at the opera. The boss says so!" They all grinned and left for the opera.

In the restaurant all seemed normal. Miranda and Harry had gone, as had the plainclothes officers. Kim realized she needed to use the ladies' room. Better here, she surmised, than in the opera house, where there would be a mighty queue of matrons and daughters. She had just finished when Miranda came in.

"How's Harry?"

Miranda sighed puffing her cheeks out. "He'll survive, thank God. But he'll look like someone from a Hollywood pirate movie."

"There are wondrous plastic surgeons in Paris, Miranda. When the scar fades in about a year, its slight traces will add to his rugged good looks. You'll see!"

The two women hugged each other.

"What now? Did you get Bruno?"

"No, we didn't, but Control says he's gone to the opera. We'll arrest him there."

"No kidding. The cheek of it!" Miranda suddenly cried out. "Idiot! Why mention cheek?"

"Well, let's go and get the swine. Can't wait. I might have known. It's typical;

Bruno likes the unexpected. Only he would think a man on the run should go to ground at the opera! Yet it's about an escape!"

***

Control was outwardly calm but inwardly impatient to fever pitch.

"Kim."

"Control."

"We're in the Seraglio looking for another eunuch. We're starting with the loges big enough for three or more."

"Agreed."

Kim and Miranda moved silently along the dark passage behind the upper level of loges. No sign of Bruno. The music and the singers made a dream-like atmosphere as they descended to the next level and began the search again. Looking across the auditorium from an empty loge, Miranda spotted Bruno leaning forward to watch the onstage action. She crept back to Kim in the corridor.

"He's right across the other side in the first loge to stage left." Kim nodded.

Soon they were standing one on each side of the curtains masking the entrance to the loge. In one superb aria, the diva's highest notes had a clarity and sureness that was sublime. There was no shrill straining but a sense of totally natural power. Then she swooped lower into the range of the normal speaking voice. Her last note was almost a whisper. Tumultuous applause erupted in the auditorium.

July? 1782? Another Constanza? These queries flashed across Kim's mind. She looked at Miranda and nodded. They went through the curtains to find Bruno applauding with the rest of the house. Miranda put a pistol to the back of Bruno's head. "You're coming with us. Get up. Slowly. Keep your hands in front of you where I can see them."

Kim was holding her mother's fan in her right hand. With the other she drew the curtain aside. All three were in the corridor and had reached the stairs leading down to the foyer before the applause died down, and the orchestra continued.

"I wish we could have stayed longer," Bruno said. "I wanted to see how it ended."

Kim had spoken into her phone. When they got outside, an unmarked car pulled up. A man leapt out and opened the back door.

Bruno swung round, knocking Miranda's arm away. A round went off and deflated the rear tire of a nearby taxi. Kim pointed her mother's fan at Bruno's face and snapped it closed as he lunged toward her and Miranda. A puff of what looked like smoke came from the fan and spread around Bruno's eyes and nose. He shrieked as he went down on his knees. The man bundled Bruno into the car by pushing his shoulders, making him yell with pain again because of his flesh wound.

Kim and Miranda got in the back with Bruno. The man got in beside the driver. The taxi driver shook his fist at them. It was just a short drive to Control's interrogation rooms. Bruno was moaning as Miranda spoke.

"We're arriving with the third hare. He's browned off!"

"See you in a few minutes. Jugged hare, n'est-ce pas?"

35

PAUL was in the local library reading a science journal. He also had one about current geology. His new articles would deal with the latest technology in general, and others would deal with recent technology useful to geologists. He also wanted to write about the new ultra-slim, bendable, portable solar panels of different sorts that could supply solar energy to more or less any equipment, large or small, to transport, and to buildings anywhere. Mary had seen the immediate usefulness of such solar panels for medical operations in village hospitals and ramshackle aid stations in remote areas of undeveloped countries. The state of the European economy and the scale of military engagements by European Union states made articles on the state of the economy and the euro as a currency seem topical. He feared that to write about the euro as a failing project required a lifetime study of economics. That was something he lacked. Let others plunge into print as to why the EU wasn't working as its planners and adherents had hoped. But now it was lunchtime. Paul had arranged to go home with Mary for a quick salad and sandwich lunch.

He passed by the stacks of fiction and saw a copy of Dickens's *Barnaby Rudge*. He hadn't read it in years. He must find time again for Dickens.

When he arrived at the surgery, Mary had just finished with her last patient of the day. After lunch she was due to check on patients who had just been admitted to hospital. On the short drive home through light traffic, Mary told Paul that she hoped Anne would visit them when she returned from Canada.

"I'm surprised she stayed with Graham in Vancouver. He was fragile when he was over here."

"Yes. He must be recovering from the loss now," Mary said. "But I think with Anne all would be above board. No hanky-panky."

Paul smiled and looked out of his passenger window as Mary drove.

"He turned out to be well behaved with Mrs. Gilmore, Sam as she's called, but maybe he's feeling the urge again."

"Well," Mary said, "I hope he knows what he's doing, if anything!"

"He should. But professors get into quite a lot of scrapes nowadays."

"Scrapes?"

"You know, graduate student liaisons, wives of other profs, women who move in and won't move out!"

"Not Graham, surely?"

Paul shrugged and smiled as they turned into their parking space. "Oh, anything can happen. Like you, I hope he knows what he's doing!"

Mary stood with him outside the car and hugged him. "Did we know what we were doing, or were we lucky?"

"Both, darling!" he said and kissed her.

They went inside to have their lunch.

That afternoon Mary would be back from the hospital at about five o'clock. Paul decided to stay at home to write up some of his notes. He had also decided to surprise Mary with a freesia plant for the balcony. He was excited because when she returned, they would have a romantic evening and make love.

***

The telephone rang. It was almost five in the afternoon.

"Hello."

"Paul! Thank God I reached you. I hoped you'd be in."

"What's up? You sound a bit stressed."

"I had stomach pains. Went to my doctor. I had tests. It's stomach cancer."

"Oh lord! What kind of treatment?"

"They say I have about six months before I peg out." Graham started to sob.

"Look, do you want visitors? I can drop everything and visit."

"Oh, God. What's the point? 'I am sick, I must die.' That's the deal. We all get there in the end."

"Look, Graham, there are advances every year. New ways of dealing with it."

"That's true, but in my case it's too far gone. It has . . . spread." His voice shook as he held back anger and self-pity.

"Are you in pain?"

"Didn't feel a thing until just last week. Now it's on and off."

"Well, I'm coming to see you. Have they got you on a special diet?"

"Supposedly. Sometimes I eat ice cream. I don't tell them. I'm losing weight. I'll have to go into hospital."

"Look, I'll be in Vancouver in two or three days."

"Not to worry. Not to bother. So, long, pal." Graham hung up.

Paul looked out the window at the front of the house, where Mary had just parked. He went to the door to let her in.

"What's wrong, Paul?" she demanded looking at him attentively.

"Graham just rang to tell me he has a cancer and about six months to live."

"Poor man!"

"He rang to say a last farewell."

"Are you going over there to see him?"

"He doesn't want me to. He said it's pointless. But I think I'll go all the same, if you agree."

Mary hugged him. "You go. He'll be grateful even if he doesn't show it. You might have to cope with anger. If so, try to keep calm."

"Yes, I will. I'll book a flight on the Internet."

The rest of the evening was taken up with preparations for Paul's trip. They made love early the next morning before Paul headed for London and a flight to Vancouver.

✳✳✳

Graham paid $250 for a pistol and $50 for some ammunition. *Cheap at the price*, he thought. He had just read that his wife's killers had been released from jail for good behaviour and in consideration of their harsh childhoods. They were still young. A long prison term would ensure they would be released as hardened men, young enough to do even more damage. According to the press, they were compelled to wear bracelets for tracking their movements, were not allowed to move, and had to report to a special centre every day.

"Pathetic," Graham said to himself. He knew prisons were overcrowded. The governments of whatever party tried to downplay crime as if it were not a growth industry. Building enough prisons would be tangible proof of their failure to control crime.

It was the morning that Paul was due to arrive in Vancouver on a surprise visit. Graham was in his car not far from the office to which the ex-prisoners had to report. He was enraged by his own divine death sentence while two callous young thugs were home free. When would they kill again? Whenever they felt the urge. He was angry with the government. The rule of law was a precious thing, but to deny justice for victims was a quick route back to seventeenth-century revenge culture. The pompous idiots couldn't see that. Bring them to justice. Inadequate justice! No way! *They let these guys out with a slap on the wrist.* He kept repeating the thought in a small, tight loop. Money was the bottom line, not the safety of the community. *Can I do it? You bet!*

He saw one of the killers turn the corner. Graham got out of the car and walked across the road to face him. He recognized him from his court appearance, though now he was in old clothes. Graham shot him in the chest and then stood over him.

"You made a big mistake killing my wife," he growled, then spat in the dying youth's face.

The second killer came running out of the corrections centre followed by another man. Graham turned to face them.

"You bastard!" Graham shouted. He shot the second killer in the chest.

The man from the centre ran back inside. Graham shot each youth in the face just to make sure.

***

Bruno had been injected again. It was a different interrogation room and different interrogators. Control, Kim, and Miranda were watching and listening outside the room.

"Which buildings in Paris are the targets today?"

"Hôtel de Ville and Sacré-Coeur."

"What are the targets in Lyon?"

"Hotel de Ville and that Fougières so-called place of worship."

"Will there be another attack?"

"Yes."

"Where will that be?"

"Strasbourg."

"What are the Strasbourg targets?"

"The European Parliament and the cathedral."

Control winked at Kim and Miranda. Bruno was telling the truth. And he knew nothing about recent arrests in Strasbourg. Good.

"When will the attacks take place?"

"21:30 today."

"The same for all three cities?"

"Yes."

"Could the timing be changed?"

"That depends on circumstances. We could strike tomorrow afternoon if it would mean more dead bodies."

"You mean of your people or do you mean of innocent people?"

"Don't be silly. The more the better."

"Is there another target for that same time?"

"No."

"Who are the three hares?"

"Who knows? It's an old symbol."

"Are you a hare?"

"Yes."

"Who else?"

"The Algerian and a man from Hastings."

"They say hares can see everything going on all around them. They have big eyes. But you three were careless and not vigilant. The king of the hares would be ashamed of you. Who planned all this?"

"Three hares."

"Where did you plan it?"

"In Brighton."

"When?"

"Last December."

Control had already relayed the information and a number of instructions to the Paris and Lyon commanders.

"Kim," he said, "I want you in Paris, and Miranda, you must go by special jet to Lyon right now. You will get a set of orders when you're on the aircraft. Be careful." He kissed her on both cheeks. She embraced Kim and left without a word.

"What are my orders?" Kim was tense and eager to go.

"Go to the Hotel de Ville. Go in the trade entrance. Ask for Colonel

Marchand. He'll give you instructions. Ask for his ID, and speak to him alone, if possible. We can't be too careful." Control looked into Kim's deep-brown eyes. Then he kissed her hand and kissed her on both cheeks. He hugged her. "Come back safe and sound, Kim."

"I will, Hervé." She turned, waving as she went, and was gone.

"Oh God, bring them back alive," Control muttered. He had to get back to work. There was not a minute to lose.

***

Paul always enjoyed arriving at YVR, as locals and others often called it. The sound of a small cascade was comforting after the hiss of the air-conditioned jet cabin. The First Nations sculptures were fascinating and different from the bland artwork in many other airports. Old Bill Reid had shown the way and was an inspiration to the people who had worked for him.

Paul was soon through passport control, and since he had nothing to declare he walked to the green exit carrying just a small cabin bag. He opted for a ride into town on the Skytrain, faster than a taxi. The air was so clean! Sea wind and massive forests ensured it. He got off at Broadway to take an express bus to West Point Grey, the area of Vancouver where Graham lived.

When he knocked on Graham's door, there was no answer. Paul was feeling tired after the long flight. His anticipation of meeting Graham again and perhaps being some comfort to him was uppermost in his mind, but he was also sensible. Graham could be at the university or anywhere. Paul's fatigue began to catch up to him. He walked back to a bus stop, hoping to see Graham's car. No luck. He decided to catch a bus and go to a hotel down on English Bay.

The first thing he did when he was installed in a comfortable room in the Sylvia Hotel was to check the time to see whether he might call Mary. She would be asleep. He would wait until the morning before he went down for breakfast. Then he rang Graham's home phone. Graham used a mobile but still kept a landline.

"Yes?"

It was a man's voice, but it wasn't Graham.

"I wonder if I could speak to Professor Curtis?"

"Who is this?"

"No, who are you? Is Graham there?"

"I'm sorry. He is not. I'm a police officer. I'll need your name, sir."

"Why? What's happened?"

"Professor Curtis died. You are?"

Paul felt his throat go dry. He sat down on the bed. "Sorry. I'm sorry. I'm a friend. I'm Paul Wills. I've just arrived from London. I knew he was ill, but this is so sudden."

"Yes. It's unfortunate. Where are you?"

"I'm in the Sylvia Hotel, down on English Bay."

"Well, sir, we'd like to have an officer ask you about the deceased, eh? We can send someone to your hotel, if that's okay."

"Soon as possible, please. I've had a long flight and feel as if I shall fall asleep soon."

"London, UK. I understand how you're feeling. It's a nine-hour flight, eh?"

"Yes. But when did Graham die? Which hospital?"

"Our officer will explain when he sees you. I have to get back to work at the house. Bye now."

Paul hung up. He decided to go to the bar to mull things over with a drink.

At reception he said a police officer would be arriving to ask for him. He'd be waiting in the bar. After he ordered a scotch and soda and started to flip through a copy of the *Vancouver Sun,* Paul no longer felt so weary. How could a disease be silent, perhaps painless, and then deliver a death blow with such speed?

"Mr. Paul Wills?"

"Yes?" Paul looked up.

A tall young man in plain clothes showed Paul his identification. He was a detective sergeant in the city police force.

"Hello, sir, I'm Sergeant Moody. I know you'll be tired, and this could be a shock, but I'd like to talk about Professor Curtis."

"Please go ahead, Sergeant."

"When did you arrive in Vancouver, sir?"

"This afternoon. BA flight from London, England."

"Not Ontario." Moody thought for a moment. "Do you have your ticket by any chance?"

Paul took out his boarding pass from his top pocket and handed it to the detective.

Moody smiled and then handed it back. "So, did you come here from the airport by taxi?"

"No. I took the Skytrain and then caught a bus and went to Professor Curtis's house. I knew he was ill. That's why I came over here. We're old friends. Were."

"Yes, I see. So, when were you at the house?"

"Oh, about an hour and a half ago, maybe a little longer. When I got here, I phoned Graham's home number to see whether he was in. But it was, as you know, the police."

"Yes. They got there a little after you left, I guess."

"Well, what happened? Did Graham die in hospital?"

"No, sir. He took his own life."

36

IT was 7:30 the next morning when Paul telephoned Mary. She had just got in after her afternoon surgery.

"Paul, darling!"

"Hello, my love. It's bad news. He committed suicide."

"Oh, no! Did you manage to see him?"

"I've asked to see him. The police are dealing with it."

"Hmm. Perhaps he couldn't face the illness. Look, you do what has to be done and then come home. I miss you."

"I miss you too. I'm looking out the window at the sea. Some tankers are anchored out there. Everything is going on as normal. It's strange."

"It's always that way. The world goes on, but we have to cope. It changes us. We get a little older. I love you, Paul. You have breakfast. No hare-brained ideas."

"No. I'll go down to breakfast. I'm staying at the Sylvia Hotel. Maybe you could telephone me just before eleven tonight your time? It'll be about two in the afternoon here. I'll make sure I'm back in my room." He gave her the phone number.

"I've noted that. I'll ring you. Love you."

"Love you too. I realize how lucky I am. Until later. Bye, darling."

"Bye, lover."

Paul listened to the dial tone and then slowly replaced the phone, put on a jacket, and went down for breakfast and to read the newspapers.

He was sipping coffee when he saw that a Professor Graham Curtis had murdered two young men recently released from prison. The brief article confirmed what the police had told him. Graham had not shown outward signs of anger. He had seemed calm.

Was he calm as he put the gun to his temple and pulled the trigger? Paul had no answer for that.

***

Jack and Maggie were definitely lovers now. He marvelled that such a finely intelligent woman should find him worthy of her. He must be eight years her senior? Perhaps. He hadn't asked when she was born. He didn't even know her birthday! They talked about where to go next as they walked along the main street in Crail.

"Have you ever been to Rosslyn church?" Jack asked.

"Even though Rosslyn isn't far from Edinburgh, I've never been. Work just comes to a head and keeps me too busy a lot of the time for jaunts, even day trips," Maggie explained. "I've heard it was being restored," she added.

Jack understood. Most of his clients were just like that. They had to do things on short notice when they could get the time.

"Well, how about it?"

"I'd love to."

"Perfect. We can be there in two shakes of a lamb's tail. Or at least afore the morrow."

Maggie laughed. "I haven't heard anyone say that before."

***

Miranda was met on the tarmac in Lyon by a young, immaculate, dark-skinned sergeant in the French army. Miranda checked his ID. He drove her to the Hôtel deVille, parked in a small discreet courtyard of a nearby building, and escorted her to the colonel in charge of the anti-terrorist operation. Colonel Marchand, a six-footer, slim, and dark, with hair just beginning to show a little grey above his ears, gave her an envelope. Miranda asked to see his ID. He smiled.

"Of course. I'll show mine, if you show me yours!" They checked each other's plasticized ID cards. "Read your instructions, and then give them back to me, Miranda."

"Oui, mon colonel."

He watched her as she read the paper, returned it to the envelope, and handed it back.

"Any questions?"

"No."

"Take the body armour and this bit of hardware."

A soldier stepped forward with her equipment.

"Used it before?"

"Yes." Miranda nodded as she put on the body armour. She checked the Famas assault rifle. It had a modified barrel with telescopic sights. It also had a squat magazine, but it was painted green. The colonel gave her a small red box of ammunition, a similar green one, and a red magazine.

"Our visitors should be here in twenty minutes. We're ready for them. This red ammunition is special. It's so hot it'd cause a fire in hell. Use it on vehicles, not people. People green, vehicles red. Got it?"

"Got it, sir."

"Good. This soldier will take you to your position. You'll be in wireless contact. You are Miranda. I'm Raton Laveur."

The soldier saluted and took Miranda to a balcony overlooking the square in front of the building. He gave her a small earpiece like a clip-on earring. He saluted again and then left.

"This is Raton. Do you hear me?" The voice was clear. There was no crackle or whistle or feedback howl. *Thank God for Dolby sound*, she thought.

"This is Miranda. Yes, I hear you. But where's the micro?"

"On your ear, dear!" She heard him laugh. "When I say, 'aux armes,' you may fire as and when you wish."

"Understood."

The balcony had a clear view of the square and its approach roads. Miranda looked around and saw a perfect spot. She could lie flat, making herself invisible to anyone looking up at the balcony, and she could fire between two of the stone balusters.

She got into position and then checked her sights. There was little wind. She looked through the telescopic sights. The lens altered automatically. In light it was normal. For dark recesses, it switched to night vision.

"Cool," she whispered to herself. Then she fitted her gun with the red magazine. She ejected it and fitted the green one. Perfect. Easy, fast. She put both magazines near the gun and focused her binoculars on the far end of the square.

A woman on a bicycle was approaching. She stopped and dismounted, then looked back over her shoulder. Another cyclist came into view. Another woman.

"Any trucks?" Raton asked.

"Just two female cyclists," Miranda replied. "They looked back as if they're being followed. They're advancing."

Miranda scanned the square again. A cyclist appeared from another side street. Then the three cyclists rode into the square and made for the building's main entrance. They dismounted in front of the steps. Miranda was unable to see them. They were right beneath the balcony. She heard a man's voice speaking Arabic. "Bikes against doors. We'll get around the corner of the steps here against the wall. I'll lead us in."

"Aux armes!" Then there was a triple explosion below her. Debris flew into the square as far as Miranda's field of vision.

Silence. Then three vehicles lumbered into the square and sped toward the building. Miranda put in the red magazine. Focus. Fire.

The lead truck exploded with a huge rush of flame, leaping high. She fired at the other two trucks. All three turned into enormous bonfires as if for some *fête* in the square. The last truck had begun to turn as if to retreat when Miranda's mega bullet connected. Some powerful explosives in the trucks sent it leaping into the air, fragments of white-hot metal flying in all directions.

"Any other approaches?" Raton asked.

"No."

"Stay put."

Miranda scanned the approach roads. Suddenly, a Land Rover came racing across the square toward the building. Miranda fired, and the vehicle became an inferno with one small figure leaping away. The man or woman was on fire, collapsed writhing, and then exploded.

"Well done," Raton said. "Clear up and clear off!"

"Good. I'll come down."

Suddenly, two fire trucks appeared and stopped. Were they genuine?

"Don't shoot the firemen," Raton said. "We invited them."

Miranda delayed picking up her equipment and watched the firemen putting out the fires. It seemed there would be no other attack.

She took her gear down to the colonel. Darkness had almost arrived, but only a few lights were visible in the buildings around the square. Had the residents been herded into basements? Many windows might have been shattered by the blast from the explosions.

Down below was a lot of activity. The colonel was giving orders for the clean-up. A forensics team had already arrived searching for body parts near the doors where the intruders had been shot. The lab technicians and special police would try to identify the "pirates" from any DNA they could find. Meanwhile, the local police prevented the curious and the local press from erupting into the square to see what had happened. A military staff car drove off with the colonel and Miranda.

The colonel spoke into his phone. "Well?" He listened, clenching and unclenching his left hand. "Hmm. Well done. How many casualties? Hmm. See you at base."

He turned to Miranda, who was looking anxiously at him. He sighed. "One dead and three wounded. They've been rushed to hospital, but the cathedral stands. They didn't bring down the Virgin. They didn't get to destroy or damage the aerials either. The big front door will have to be replaced."

They sat for the rest of their short journey in silence, grinning at each other.

37

MAGGIE was delighted with the interior of Rosslyn Chapel. It was so full of carved stonework intricacies that she felt great sympathy for the anonymous masons of medieval times. Chinese homes and curio shops were full of carvings in ivory, jade, agate, and wood, so intricate that their details were dizzying. These stone carvings in the chapel were indeed rough and eroded, yet their clamouring mixture of motifs was almost Chinese. Jack was explaining how the novelist Dan Brown had put the chapel on the tourist map and how it also attracted people with zany theories about Christ, the Knights Templar, ancient Egypt, and Freemasons. Jack mentioned the theory that one of the carvings "proved" that Scots had been to America before Columbus. Maggie was not surprised. She remembered the stories that Chinese had visited North America well before Columbus too. And hadn't Egyptians done it?

As they walked out into the sunlight, shading their eyes, Maggie took up the theme. The carving of that maize or corn (unknown in Europe at the time) was so indistinct it could easily be a wheat sheaf. But she thought it likely that many trips to America and Canada from Europe had been made, though most had failed to return and were unrecorded. People had probably been slaughtered or died of diseases or been shipwrecked and drowned in the merciless Atlantic. She had heard of a North American tribe that used some old Chinese words in its dialect even now.

"Intriguing?" Jack asked.

"Intriguing," Maggie assented. "Skeptical about zany theories?"

"Skeptical," Jack said."Dinner in Edinburgh?"

"Lovely idea," Maggie replied and kissed him.

Hand in hand they walked away, neither skeptical about the other.

In Paris, Kim, the military squad, and police specialists were all in position and ready for anything before 21:30. An officer, codename Rostand, was in charge. Nothing happened at 21:30. Kim glanced at her special combat watch. At 21:35 she wondered if the intel was wrong. Was there mayhem elsewhere? Was the Hôtel de Ville safe? Was the National Assembly the target? Had the terrorists changed direction deliberately? There were no urgent demands that they go to oppose terrorists at different targets. They had to stay put and wait.

She looked down from a window on the front of the ornate building. It overlooked an open space which was transformed into an ice rink in the winter months. People were milling around below, heading for buses, the metro, and taxis. A couple laughed when entering a nearby restaurant. Kim saw four women wearing long black dresses heading for the building's main entrance. They were wearing the forbidden burka, which covered their faces except for their eyes. Their body language spoke determination. This was the start. The traffic jams had probably delayed the attack. Kim had instructions not to fire until the message came through.

"Three female 'pirates' arriving," she said. "Bulky. Have belts? Could be men."

"Merci."

The windows rattled, and glass flew outwards below her. The explosions were deafening. Open mouthed, Kim kept her eyes on the square below. She swallowed. Her right ear had a dull ache. Now that they had been attacked, they could shoot at will.

"More will arrive," Rostand said. "Shoot to kill."

"Oui, mon colonel."

People below were running in every direction away from the town hall, trying to find a place to cower in safety. Two men were running toward the building firing Kalashnikovs. Kim shot each man in quick succession. Both dropped and didn't move.

She used her binoculars to scan the space ahead, part of the crowd still watching, and a sidestreet. A man in a hoodie was kneeling, a rocket launcher on his shoulder. Kim picked up her Famas assault rifle, aimed, and fired. As the man fell backwards, his rocket streaked up over the building. Where it would land was anybody's guess.

Another man in front of a group of people lifted a rocket launcher out of a large black bag. Kim's shot killed him instantly. Four soldiers ran from the building toward the two dead terrorists. They picked up the corpses and their equipment and dragged them into the building.

There was a burst of gunfire from a man with a woman and child. One of the soldiers went down. Kim shot the man. As he fell, she saw that only a part of his head remained. The woman and her screaming child tried to disappear into the metro, but two plainclothes officers blocked her way and led them to a police wagon that was parked on the edge of the square.

To bring up a child in hatred and expose it to death! Scum, Kim thought.

"Okay. A look around," Kim murmured. She made one final sweep with her binoculars. Police everywhere. Crowd under control. Fire brigade doing its work. She gathered her equipment and went to the ground floor.

Most of it looked normal, but the entrance was a smouldering ruin. The debris and fallen masonry made a great dusty swath, some of it still smoking.

Kim looked into the corridor where Rostand was approaching. When he was a yard from her, a security man on Kim's left took out a hunting knife and shouted "God is great!" Rostand crouched, ready for the knife thrust. Kim grabbed the man's wrist, twisted his arm up behind his back, and kicked him just below the kneecap. The howl of pain told her she had dislocated his knee. She had also dislocated his shoulder. She pushed him aside and picked up the knife.

"Take him in," Rostand said. "Thanks, Kim. I couldn't have bettered that myself." He winked and wiped sweat from his face.

"Who is he? How did he get in here?" A corporal bent over the moaning terrorist and checked his ID.

"He's supposed to be a plainclothes policeman, sir."

"Send him to interrogation—before he goes to hospital."

"Sir."

"Mon colonel, how's the soldier who was shot?"

"He died of his wounds."

***

"How's your poetry?" Control asked over the radio.

Rostand stood aside from the clean-up people and his fighting force. "Terrorists dead except for one injured by Kim. He's good for interrogation."

"Damage?"

"What we expected, but curiosity killed quite a few cats nearby. One of my men down."

"Bastards! Anyway, well done."

"Your supergirl Kim just saved my life. Thanks for sending her."

"Good. Well, send her back to me ASAP."

"Will do. Out."

Some sense of order was being established. The damage could have been much worse. Rostand and Control were already thinking about the wounded and disabled. The press would be feigning surprise that terrorists should be so barbaric. They would also blame the authorities for doing too little to stop the menace. Later they might mention civil rights rules that must be observed before fire could be returned. Kim could not have killed the women who blew themselves up. They were just walking toward the building. They could have been stopped and made to remove their burkas if a soldier or policeman had been there. And those who stopped them would also have been blown up. Democratic values, however, still had to be upheld. And whoever had told them to remove the burkas would have died. Sooner or later terrorists would have to realize they could not overthrow advanced societies, even if they could continue to dominate terrified villagers in underdeveloped societies.

"Is the other target secure?" Kim asked.

"Get back to me as soon as you can," Control replied. "And well done. Thank God you're safe."

She realized Hervé did not want to give any details yet. Perhaps the news was grim.

38

PAUL met Jacqueline's parents at the university where Graham, until a few days earlier, had worked. They went to see the chairman of Graham's department to say that a memorial service would be held in a Unitarian chapel in two days' time. The chairman said a notice would go out to the department, so colleagues and students could attend. He had been astonished by Graham's act but could understand it in the circumstances. The chairman imagined Graham's suicide. Gun to temple. Trigger. A fall face forward on the sidewalk. He would miss him as a colleague and friendly face around the department. He hoped Graham didn't even see the sidewalk as he fell toward it and lay still.

Jacqueline's mother had tears in her eyes, and her husband put his arm around her. The impersonal plastic, brushed metal, and wood décor in the newish building seemed comfortless in a largely indifferent world. The universe existed according to the laws of physics and other laws yet to be discovered. This offered little comfort to the casualties of human actions. Stars did not grieve. The moon had no feelings. Humankind knew evil as well as happiness. The skies were indifferent.

Paul went back to the Sylvia and phoned Mary.

"Hi, angel. I have to stay a few extra days. There's a memorial service."

"You must stay. Don't worry. It must be difficult for everyone. How are Jacqueline's parents?"

"Devastated. Graham's revenge has brought everything back to them. I think they felt deeply insulted by the people who decided to let the killers back on the street with bracelets and supervision. But they were not revenge minded."

"Oh my lord. Why can't do-gooders do some good?"

"I think I should write something about sentencing and the correctional services."

"Yes. Do it. Life is too precious to be messed up by bureaucracy."
"People with half-inch methods will mess up any system."
"Half-inch? Haven't heard that before."
"My uncle used to say it. He meant incompetence."
"Well, be competent at the memorial service. I know you will."
"I'll try. Where there's a Wills there's a way."
"I'm glad you're getting back on top, darling."
"Can't wait to get back on top."
"Well, you'll just have to wait, won't you?"
"Yes, darling. See you soon."
"I'll ring you soon. Love you."
"Love you too."

Paul looked at his watch. He would have a drink in his room and prepare some thoughts for the memorial service. Then he would have dinner with Jacqueline's parents, an occasion he did not relish.

***

The Unitarian chapel was a pleasant, modern, mainly wooden building with a highly polished interior. The pews were, in fact, rather comfortable seats. Padded cushions were availablefor people who wished to kneel during prayers or meditations.

Jacqueline's father was introduced by the pastor, who thanked all for being there. Jacqueline's father was greyer and looked much older than he had looked a week earlier. He recalled the happiest days of Jacqueline and her marriage to Graham. He and his wife had been proud of the young couple. He introduced Paul as one of Graham's oldest friends and asked him to say a few words.

Paul went to the lectern and looked at the congregation of university teachers and students, people he had never met. He spoke briefly but, he hoped, in a way Graham would have approved.

"We are here today to say a last farewell to a man who lost his wife in the worst of circumstances. Whatever he did afterwards seems to me a result of another blow or blows. He was gravely ill and told me by phone that he had only a few months to live.

"As many of you will know, Graham had read a great many plays, among them Roman and Elizabethan revenge tragedies. He had also read in translation modern revenge tragedies written by Arab playwrights. I think Graham would never have resorted to revenge if the rule of law in the legal system had not let him down, had not let Jacqueline down, and had not let her parents down. Murderers deserve punishment by prison terms that teach them a necessary lesson and are long enough to keep them from harming ordinary citizens again. Those who are insane need to be treated in secure establishments. When murderers are let loose on a largely innocent public too soon, the rule of law is undermined by officials and thus seems inadequate. Revenge can then seem sweet. Civil society needs strong and purposeful rule because it must also keep us from religious conflicts. If that principle is pushed aside by naïve officials or for want of funding, democratic society is at risk.

"In his preface to Barnaby Rudge, a book Graham knew in some detail, Charles Dickens wrote about the violence of the Gordon Riots in late eighteenth-century England as teaching us a lesson: 'That what we falsely call a religious cry is easily raised by men who have no religion, and who in their daily practice set at nought the commonest principles of right and wrong; that it is begotten of intolerance and persecution; that it is senseless, besotted, inveterate, and unmerciful—all history teaches.' Contemporary societies, now more than ever, know that our best defence is the rule of law, strong and responsible to the innocent as well as the guilty.

"Despite the lessons of history, we still face such killers today among the criminals and terrorists. We must bear the human condition as best we can.

"But now I want to remember the Graham I knew, a buddy who was funny as well as thoughtful. He loved local beer. He loved his good friends. He loved his wife. May God help us to live with love instead of hate!

"Lead me, Lord, in thy righteousness; make thy way plain before my face."

Paul went back to his seat.

The chairman of Graham's department nodded and smiled at Paul and then took his place at the lectern to say that Graham would be missed by colleagues and students alike. He would be difficult to replace.

Life must go on, Paul thought, *and Graham will be replaced by someone junior at a lower salary.*

The ceremony over, people filed out, and some friends stood around chatting before going to their cars. A young woman approached Paul. She was dressed casually but in black for mourning. She wore hardly any makeup, except for a glossy lip rouge.

"Mr. Wills, do you know the nature of Graham's, I mean Professor Curtis's, illness? Was it AIDS?"

"No, it wasn't. It was a terminal cancer."

The young woman gave a profound sigh. "Thank you," she said and walked away to join a group of young adults.

His students, Paul thought. *I wonder why she thought it might be AIDS?* In any event, she seemed relieved.

39

KIM returned after her debriefing to her section HQ and found Control was still there. He had sent for her, and there she was, standing safely in his office. He took her hand, raised it to his lips, and then opened his arms. They hugged.

"Oh, Kim, thank goodness."

Suddenly, she felt her eyes brimming with tears, which trickled down her cheeks. It was the killing that was twisting her stomach. She knew it had to be done if Bruno and his kind were to be defeated and defenceless people saved. Western civilization itself was at stake.

Control led her to a chair and sat opposite her. He handed her a spotless white handkerchief and let her recover her composure.

"Was it Sacré-Coeur?" she asked.

"Yes. It was at 21:30, as Bruno said."

"They were delayed arriving at the town hall because of traffic."

"Yes. Good job the colonel waited instead of aborting. He alerted the Legislative Assembly to expect unwelcome visitors, and then a few minutes later they were able to relax! A drink?" Control hovered near his drinks cupboard, then stooped to reach for a glass.

"Thanks. Yes. I'll have a little kir. Is Miranda alive?"

"Yes. She'll be back from Lyon soon. For you, here and now, my dear, a kir royal!" He brought out a bottle of his favourite champagne, a bottle of Crême de Cassis, and two flutes. He opened the champagne by holding the cork and twisting the bottle's base. There was a small "plop," and then he mixed a little cassis with the champagne. He handed Kim a glass of the sparkling rose-coloured nectar. He took up his own flute and chinked it against hers.

"To us." He smiled at her.

"To us," she replied. Then she laughed, still blinking away tears, adding,. "I know what you're going to say next."

"Really?"

"Yes."

"What's that?"

"To us in Planning!"

Control smiled again and sipped his drink. "To us in Planning. Do you mean it? Will you? After all, you said it first. You formulated the toast before I did!"

"Yes. I'd like to join you in Planning. But I won't become your mistress."

"Kim, you are superb. We can work so well together. You'll see." He stood up again and paced to a fro. The drink was in his left hand while his free hand seemed to be conducting a piece of music running through his mind. "You want marriage? Children?"

"Yes, I do. And I want to go back to having my holiday. You gave me leave, remember?"

"I do!" he replied. "You said it first!"

***

Anne was taking a coffee break outside Toronto's central library, where she had been studying and taking notes. She was distressed to find a brief report in a newspaper regarding the suicide of Professor Graham Curtis of Vancouver. *How could that be?* He had seemed stable enough when she stayed with him. He had been a grateful and pleasurable partner the one time she had slept with him. And now he was dead. It made no sense.

At lunchtime she rang Mary Rao's home number.

"Dr. Rao. Who is it?"

"Oh, Mary, it's Anne. I'm in Toronto. I've just read in the newspaper that Paul's friend, Graham, has committed suicide."

"Yes, it's true. Paul flew over to see him, against Graham's wishes. He arrived in Vancouver to find that the poor man had shot himself."

"Mon dieu! But why? Did he leave a note?"

"I don't know. Paul will be back here soon. He had to attend the memorial service. He said the two men who killed Graham's wife were let out of prison on probation. Graham felt it totally unjust. He shot them and then himself. A terrible business."

"Terrible. Revenge is not good, even if it is understandable. War is often simply revenge or ambition on a massive scale. So, how is Paul? When will he be back?"

"I'm expecting him the day after tomorrow. How was Graham when you saw him? He seemed to be shaken, but he had a visit from a new PhD woman who had been his student. I wondered if there was anything in it, you know?"

"I know what you mean," Anne replied. There was a short silence between them. "He was kind enough to let me stay with him," Anne continued. "I think he wanted to return the hospitality I offered when he was in France."

"Yes. He would want that. So, was he normal again at home?"

"He seemed a bit lost still. I felt terribly sorry for him. I suppose he was trying to make me, what, his partner?"

"Oh dear. Really?"

"Yes. I felt he was a little perdu. I felt he needed some comforting, but I made it clear that I would not have that kind of relationship with him. Poor man. I hope my ultimatum didn't push him to the brink."

"No, don't think that, Anne. You were kind to him but not in any way responsible. He was a tough nut, you know. He had a certain charm, when he wanted to show it. No, he rang us to say he had terminal cancer. The doctors said he had about six months before the end."

"That must have happened after I left."

"I'm sure of it. But once he had that bad news, he acted fast. I don't think he thought much. It was rage. Visceral anger. He must have felt powerless when the killers were let out."

"Ah, well, it's a bad situation."

"Tell me, Anne, how is the research coming along?"

"I'm finding riches. There are more letters and diaries extant than I thought possible. And the Toronto libraries have a good deal that I want to photograph and take home to work on."

"Wonderful. Is there a chance that on your way home we can get together?"

"Why, yes. I'll be in London for a few days. I hope to stay at the Oxford and Cambridge Club, because it's affiliated with my club in Paris. Do you think you could get away to London?"

"Not during the week. But we could if there were a free weekend when you're there. If not you're welcome to stay with us. Do let us know when you'll be heading home."

"Yes, I shall. And perhaps you'll come to see me in France one of these days?"

"Love to, Anne."

"Well, let's hope we'll get together soon. I should let you get on with what you're doing!"

"It was lovely to chat. Take care, Anne. See you soon. Bye now."

Anne put down the phone. So, that was it. A cancer that had gone undetected until too late. Should she have crept into his bed that night? It was impulsive. She thought perhaps it would help him. Or had she just wanted to have a man? A younger man? She didn't know. And now he was dead. She had embraced a dying man without knowing it. He hadn't known it. What impulse had led her to his bedroom that night before she left? Her own loneliness? He had wanted a future with her. That was not to be. Had he lived, a deeper friendship would not have worked. He was too young for her. And he lacked the polish she admired in elegant men in France. Graham was a scholar, but his was a future she had not wanted. And now he had gone where the future did not exist, only an eternal present of light and darkness.

***

Jack and Maggie had eaten a Chinese meal in Edinburgh and were now in bed. After making love again, they were lying huddled together. He had one of her small, warm breasts in his hand. Both felt happy and relaxed.

"Will you marry me? Say yes!"

"Yes, Jack. I'll marry you!"

"When?"

"I have a long-awaited holiday due in September. Can we wait that long?"

"I've waited a long time for you, Maggie. Another few weeks will not matter as long as we can spend time together as often as we can."

"We have to meet often, Jack, because we have to work out the many sensual as well as administrative details. There's logic and scientific reasoning for you! Where shall we live? Who to invite besides family? Where do we go on our honeymoon?"

"Yes. A lot to think about. We'll need a lot of meetings, darling, if scientific experimentation demands it. Oh, Maggie."

"Scotland is the best place for marriage proposals, isn't it?"
"Where did I hear that before? But I'll wager it's true."
"I read it on the back of a book!" she replied.
"Did you now?"
She felt him stirring, some insistent nudging at her hip. She spread her thighs.
"Come on, then, lover, husband to be!"

40

ALL seemed well on la Place du Tertre, with the restaurants doing good business. The Basilica of Sacré-Coeur stood white against the sky. There were so many lights up there that night seemed more like an idea rather than a reality.

At 21:15 two sharpshooters with automatic weapons were on the flat top of the Montmartre water tank. More sharpshooters were on the Grand Dome walkways. The southeast and southwest domes had lookouts posted to scan the people going along the walks around the great church and climbing its steps. The pediment of the Chapel of the Blessed Virgin also had its defenders. The building would close at 22:30, but at 22:00 hours there was a mass.

In the Chapel of St. Michael, a group of young priests and a black nun looked out toward people at prayer. The nun looked up at the Joan of Arc window and then scanned the people wandering around or sitting or kneeling. Any explosives set off in there would be devastating. Four priests, remarkably fit and muscular, checked the bags and backpacks of everyone entering the church.

At precisely 21:32, several loud bangs sounded, followed by a loudspeaker warning people outside to go back into the place or behind the church. The priests and the nun from the side chapel went to join the people looking around. They were soon satisfied that everyone inside the building was a peaceful visitor. The four young priests did not allow anyone to leave and turned away anyone trying to enter.

Outside the church the sirens of approaching ambulances dominated the sounds of voices and the repeated instructions from the loudspeaker.

Four dead bodies with badly damaged heads were being relieved of their explosive jackets. Near them were four sports bags, a Kalashnikov sticking out of one of them. The others were still closed. The colonel in charge was hoping that all might seem normal by 22:00. If not, the Mass could still be celebrated, but only with those who were already in the church. The colonel approached Control's black nun. She looked the part.

"Are you tough, battle worthy?"

"Yes, mon colonel. Control handpicked me for this duty. I should get back when you dismiss me."

"That young man near the front row has been praying non-stop," the colonel said.

"Yes, I noticed. He has no bag or anything bulky."

"Go over and talk to him."

"A vos ordres, mon colonel."

The nun went quietly over to the young man at prayer and sat beside him. "God will forgive you," she said.

He did not move. His eyes were closed, hands clenched. She noticed his knuckles were prominent. He was under some sort of pressure.

"Are you staying for the ten o'clock mass?" she asked.

"Leave me alone. I'm praying." He did not turn his head or open his eyes.

"God will have heard you by now."

"Go away. Nobody can help me. Go away." He had a Slavic accent.

"Where are you from?"

"You French always ask that, as if any background other than French is no good. You must have noticed! Where are you from?"

"I'm sorry. I merely want to help."

"No, you don't. Your god is a fake. Mine is the one and only God."

The youth suddenly gripped her wrists. He was strong and determined. "Get me out of here. I'm taking you with me."

"They'll stop you at the door."

"Not if I have a nun with me."

"They'll still stop you. Come with me. I can get you to the archdeacon. That door over there near the altar. To the side. Get up," she whispered.

The young man stood up. "Put your arm through mine. That's it. I have your wrist. I could break your arm, your wrist, your shoulder. Take your pick."

"We'll go to that door," the nun murmured, "and I'll help you."

He nodded. As they got free of the line of chairs, his grip tightened. The nun was wearing combat boots under her robe. She stamped down hard on the man's instep, shattering a bone. He screamed and released her wrist. Her elbow knocked the breath out of his lungs. As he doubled up, still yelling in pain, she smacked his throat hard with the side of her hand. He was on the stone floor and half choking, half sobbing, surrounded by fit young "priests," all wearing combat boots.

"Forgive him, Father, for he knows not what he does," the nun said as she walked back to the colonel.

"Well done, 'Sister,'" he said. "We'll send him to the centre for interrogation."

"Why didn't he just walk away when they were letting people out?"

"Perhaps he thought there would be a successful second wave."

"Or maybe he wanted to be captured?" Control's black agent, "Sister Sophia," suggested.

"He could have just given himself up. Perhaps he wanted to be arrested, so he would not be under suspicion in some other terror group."

"Next stop the medical unit and then interrogators."

"He's a lucky 'mec,'" the colonel said.

41

BRUNO was still under the influence of the French "truth drug." He smiled at the Frenchmen facing him. "You don't know how close you are to defeat. We're spreading into all the societies worth controlling. We have broken any unity there was in Europe. We're eliminating huge numbers of Christians. We shall win sooner than you think."

"No. You are a fool who recruits the young to destroy themselves and innocents."

"There are no innocents. White people like you are just stupid targets."

"What about ordinary people of any colour and moderate Muslims?"

"There are no moderate Muslims."

"How so?" *He's singing the same old song yet again*, the interrogator thought.

"There are determined Muslims, more or less strict in our faith, like me. There are radicalized Muslims, who are pitiless. There are masses of Muslims who are merely passive. They don't march in protest against us. They don't throw terror trainees or veterans out of the mosque. They do not punish them. They're too scared. When we have a democratically elected majority in any country, we shall control all the military and declare sharia law without losing any time. The passive ones will follow us out of fear and will secretly rejoice that whites are no longer in control. The parliamentary minorities will be arrested and executed."

"We've heard all this before from you, Bruno. It's an old sound system that's broken and can only repeat a few bars. You think if you repeat something it will become true. It won't. You're wrong. Tell us something new. In any event, you're a prisoner facing treason charges. What is the address of the hare from Hastings?"

"I don't know. We are careful."

"What's his name?"

"He never said."

The Frenchman left Bruno alone in the room with his thoughts.

Their human rights legal system will put me on trial, and I'll be out within ten years, given my good conduct. Or, with a little luck, I'll be rescued within a year. And while I'm in prison, I'll create more action units.

A flicker of surprise crossed Bruno's forehead when a Muslim man wearing a prayer cap walked in. He sat in a chair vacated by the previous interrogators.

"Bruno! What a surprise to see you here on the opposite side—of the table. What is your secret of secrets?"

"Brussels and Antwerp will be Muslim in fifteen years' time. Sharia law will be imposed by the democratically elected majority which is, for the moment, a minority."

"And so on." The interrogator laughed.

"And your leaders actually make things easy for us," Bruno continued, ignoring the man's smiling face. "The British Home Office has spent a billion pounds to set up an IT system to track people going in and out of the country. It should have been in place in 2011. They still can't get it right! People can walk in and out at will. Humantrafficking is big business. And our martyrs are among the people crossing the Mickey Mouse borders. A commission wants to remove the Church of England as the official church. All religions are to be equal in a so-called Christian country. When we're in power there will be one religion. *Everyone will convert.* This is why I'm the wolf that is unstoppable. I and my brethren are the future. 'Old Sultan' is my name for moderate Muslims. You are an Old Sultan wearing your little hat! But the majority of Old Sultans will vote for all Muslim candidates, as will white converts and multicultural nincompoops. When a 'rule of law' Muslim government is in power, our brotherhood will take that power, and Old Sultan will keep his head down and submit. We are the future, your children's future. They'll have to behave themselves. Women will have to get back in their rightful subordinate place or be stoned to death."

"I think you should send your message to the National Front party. They'll think it's true."

"You can laugh, but you are so slow to learn. The message has been taken seriously by extreme whites and their supporters, whatever their ethnicities, in France, Germany, Scandinavia, the UK, and the US."

"You've been busy, as busy as a little Arab housewife. By the way, we've knocked out your friends in Strasbourg, Lyon, and Paris."

"You lie."

"What's your next operation?"

"We shall blackmail the president of France."

The interrogator burst out laughing.

"His filmed couplings with his Algerian mistress will be our trump card."

"What will this blackmail do for Islam?"

"Your president will release some of our key players."

"The president practices free love not free terrorism. It's a good old-fashioned Fabian idea. Even the stodgy British socialists believe in free love. H. G. Wells believed in free love—and he was English of late-Victorian and Edwardian vintage. And this is France a century later. Paris is still gay, in essence, even more so than in Wells's day. No, President Champenois can't be shamed about 'illicit' sex. How would you prove it anyway?"

"We have films of the woman's bedroom and their antics. It's just a matter of time!" Bruno laughed.

The interrogator shrugged dismissively. "The press will sell some papers, and the next crisis will make it fade to minor news. A man might be juicier for the press. A woman? Old hat. Charlie Hebdo might do a few vulgar cartoons. What will you do with the girl?"

It was Bruno's turn to laugh. "Your president and his Arab whore will be eliminated after our brothers in the prisons have been released."

"In your rotten dreams, Bruno Who's the girl?"

"I don't know, but I speak truth."

"Oh, we know that for sure, my friend."

The interrogator left the room, locking the door. Control had to be informed of Bruno's deepest secrets. There was no time to lose. In fact, analysts were already reviewing the "Bruno interrogations." The experts would have to search a girl's apartment. But who was she? What did Bruno mean by "a matter of time"? Were things to happen fast or all in good time?

***

Control thought about the new problem he had been landed with at such short notice. In his view there was no point in any of his personnel tracking

President Champenois during the day and evening. They must keep a discreet night watch. The chief would seek this female comfort when? Any weeknight. Especially after a long working day or a return from a journey. But all ways out from the Elysée Palace or Matignon or wherever the president happened to be on any such evening must be covered. Miranda, mistress of disguise, should head the op.

Control picked up his phone. "Get Agent Miranda to report to me ASAP."

Miranda, already debriefed, was still in the building before going to get some sleep. She was summoned—Control wanted to see her. The green light glowed, and she walked into his office. He looked like a worried man. His brow was creased in a sort of frown as he looked up.

"Miranda, come and sit down. What I'm going to tell you is top secret, like everything you hear in this office."

Miranda sat down facing Control.

"But first, I want to congratulate you on your latest achievements. You are superb. And you are, in a real way, a secret weapon."

Miranda smiled, flushed, and mumbled a thank you. *What's coming now?*

Control unfolded the situation. The president was, it seemed, involved with an Arab mistress whom he visited some nights. Knowing his schedules and tasks, Control thought it likely that he left the palace incognito in the early hours after midnight and returned at an ungodly hour before dawn. Miranda must be on watch certain nights of the week, prompted by Control, and find out where President Champenois was going for his assignation. The palace had no information about this affair. It was as if there was nothing to leak. When she had the rendezvous, she must find out with whom and contact Control directly. She understood perfectly. Time was of the essence. But that night she had to go and sleep, the sleep of the just.

***

Mary's phone rang as she opened the door to her home, shopping bags in hand. She put down her bags and hurried to answer it

This is Dr. Rao. How can I—".

"Mary, it's Maggie. You remember I met your old friend Jack at your wedding?"

"Yes, he took a shine to you."

"We're getting married!"

"Oh, Maggie, that is *wonderful*. When did he propose?"

"A couple of days ago. We were on a jaunt. I had some free time. We flew to Crail."

"Brilliant. I always say Scotland is the best place for marriage proposals."

"I think so too. I read it on the back of a book."

"And did you buy the book?"

"No."

"Well, now you must! But when will you get married?"

"We were thinking September because then we both have 'a window of opportunity,' as they say." They both laughed merrily, as if they were schoolgirls or undergrads again.

"Well, that's great news. Don't forget Paul and I are taking our honeymoon in November sometime. So, what great news!"

"I'm glad you approve."

"You have our blessings. I know I can speak for Paul as well."

"How is he?"

"He's in Canada. His friend Graham was ill and is now dead."

"But he was best man at your wedding! He was with Mrs. Gil . . . ?"

"Gilmore. That's right. We called her Sam for Samantha."

"I remember. She had a son. What a shock for Paul and you. So, when will Paul be back?"

"In two or three days. But how's your work at the lab?"

"Microscopic progress!" They both laughed at Maggie's standard way of not going into detail.

"And you, Mary, how's it going?"

"Oh, sniffles and snuffles to keep us in pocket, but I did have a jaundice case and a young patient with diabetes. But she's coping well. And how is my friend, Jack?"

"He's up in the clouds, literally and metaphorically. Very pleased. We are very much in love. And we're marrying here, not in Asia."

"That sounds like an ultimatum to the family!"

"It certainly is! But Mary, I must go. I have a date with my husband to be."

"Well, fabulous news, Maggie. Thanks for ringing. Love you!"

"Love you too. Hugs. Bye."

42

PAUL had settled in for the evening after a day arranging his return flight and trying to work on some of his notes. He had brought his laptop with him as well as a smartphone with an international roaming facility. If an editor or agent called him, he wanted to be able to respond right away. He was tired and probably still had a little jet lag.

As he drifted off to sleep in his hotel room, he suddenly saw himself lying in bed asleep. He was back in Sutton Coldfield and saw Mary arriving at the surgery. He felt great contentment that she was there and getting ready to start her day. Graham was walking toward him dressed as the best man for their wedding.

"*Everything is fine, Paul. Jacqueline is fine. There's always light at the end of the tunnel.*"

Paul repeated the words and, seeing himself asleep in the Sylvia Hotel on English Bay, whispered in his own ear, "Everything is fine. All manner of things will be fine. Mary and her friend Maggie will be fine." He did not see himself now as a separate being within the dream. The situation had simply faded away. He was asleep, but it was a light, untroubled sleep.

He woke up at 6:30 a.m. and made ready for his departure. Then he went down to breakfast. He decided to spread peanut butter on his toast. He hadn't eaten peanut butter for ages.

As he took a bite of the crisp toast and began to chew, he remembered that he had been outside his own body. Was it a case of astral projection? He supposed it was. Perhaps he should try to sell an article about it. He would have to look at specialist journals. He was first and foremost eager to get back to Mary, his wife. Yes, his wife.

Am I a lucky man? Yes, I'm a lucky man.

***

By sheer luck, Miranda was on her first watch when she saw Antoine Champenois, the president of the Republic, walk out of the shadows wearing a crash helmet. His gait was unmistakeable. Yes, there was the political giant wrapped up in the flesh of a short somewhat pudgy man.

She followed his motorcycle on a Vespa scooter, keeping her distance. He stopped, dismounted, tapped in a code, and when a heavy courtyard door swung slowly open, walked calmly in with the motorbike.

Miranda puttered past. She parked down a side street about fifty metres farther on, noting it was 02:45. She walked back, noted the street address, and photographed the plaque with its numbers for entry into the yard. Control's geeks would soon find the entry code and the list of residents. Then she went back home to bed, having filed her information with Control's office.

At 05:30 she was awakened by her phone. It was Control.

"I got your message. Well done. Lucky he moved so soon."

"Do you want me to come in?"

"Yes, and don't bother to shower!"

Miranda went as fast as she could. She was shown into a room dominated by computer screens and by Control, who held out his hands to her.

"You gem! Look at this screen. It shows us residents with names and photographs and the jobs they do, if employed."

Miranda looked at the screen. "That must be his mistress. She's from the Middle East. She's young, pretty, lives alone, and bingo! She's a publicist."

"His ratings went up because of her work," Control remarked, "remember?"

"Indeed I do."

"Interestingly, I saw a message that another security check should be made on this woman. She's the one. Well, when Yasmine Lallouche goes out to work or to shop, she'll be followed, and two agents will go into the premises. She'll never know. She mustn't know."

"Can I be one of the agents who goes in? I might notice something. A 'girlie thing.'"

"As our American friends might say," Control responded. "Well, Miranda, she's from Algeria. See if she has anything to do with this man." He showed her Harry's picture of the rich man with a flashy car.

"Thanks, Control. I will."

BRUNO'S SECRET

***

It was easy to enter Yasmine's apartment. It was on a corner of the *palier* or landing and approached by a short corridor leafing two ways from the elevator. Her front door was just around the corner of the right-hand corridor from the elevator. They would not be seen by the other residents on the floor.

Yasmine had a heavy door with two locks. It took the expert three minutes to enter. Miranda's dark-brown wig went perfectly with a tan jacket over her dark-blue blouse and pants. She wore black sneakers. She followed her anonymous male lock expert, known to Control and now Miranda as Christophe.

They closed the door quietly and stood still, looking around, remembering as much as possible where things were positioned: a small corner table with a cut-glass vase with roses in it, a picture of a desert village with mountains behind it in the distance, a small brass Arab-style lamp hanging from the ceiling.

They went into the sittingroom. One wall was mirrored, thus giving an impression that the room was much bigger than it was. The galley kitchen was divided from it by a low wall, the top of which served as a counter that overhung the dividing wall. Under the overhang were four stools. A three-seater oatmeal-coloured sofa with light-green cushions was in the sitting room. The wooden floor was graced by a Persian rug with a complex design in mainly blue and red. A small table at one end of the sofa had a cigarette lighter and ashtray. An address book was left open on the sofa.

Miranda photographed everything as they worked through the little flat. She also photographed each page in the address book and some business cards that were loose in it. She left it open exactly as she had found it. There were entries in Arabic, French, and English.

The apartment had two bedrooms. One was obviously a guest room. It had a single bed, a cupboard, and some boxes. The bed was unmade, and a yellow duvet was folded up and placed on it in the middle. No pillows!

The small bathroom was painted in white gloss, with a tub and handheld shower. The sink was new and did not match the tub. Miranda wondered if it was a rental or whether Yasmine owned it.

Next to the bathroom was the main bedroom. A queen-size bed projected out from one wall. At the foot and along each side of the bed was a small rectangular mat. Miranda thought they were Afghan tribal mats.

In the wall to the right of the bed was a large window overlooking a courtyard. Spikes ran along the outside ledge, preventing pigeons from perching there. They were probably cooing breathily somewhere else early each morning.

The room had no bedside tables or units because there was not enough space. If Yasmine bought a bedside table, there might just be enough floor space if the bed were moved a little to one side.

Opposite the foot of the bed was another wall, graced by family photos, and a small table and a chair. On the table was a small brass lamp of Middle Eastern design and an expensive looking travelling clock. Miranda's expert, Christophe, walked to it and looked at the bed.

"Oui! If you want to record sights and sounds on the bed, where do you put the device? Up on the ceiling? Nothing visible there. An accomplice at the window? Dicey."

"In the clock?" Miranda asked.

"Voilà, ma belle!" Christophe picked up the clock in his gloved hands. "It's a bit heavier than normal. He took out a magnifier equipped with a powerful light. Then he inspected the clock with great attention. "Hmm...a hare as a logo on the clock face. Interesting."

Miranda grinned. "Bingo!"

Christophe grinned at her. "I'll unscrew the back and take a look."

He took out a kit of jeweller's screwdriver heads, fitted one to a handle, and within a few seconds, the back of the clock was on the table, and he was looking at its workings. "Magnifique! See that?"

Miranda looked over his shoulder. He pointed the screwdriver at a minute metal disc. "That's the device. Now look. Voyez?"

Miranda saw a small red logo of a bounding hare on the clock's face.

"That's translucent. The disc records through this jumping hare whatever and whoever jumps on the bed. We'll take the disc."

"Brilliant. We'll search the cupboards, take our pictures, and leave."

They were soon back in the street, looking as if they might be a couple setting off to work for the day. It was going to be a long one.

43

THE Algerian who had been taken alive faced his interrogators. Lounging in the street and watching Yasmine's apartment block, he had been unable to produce any identity papers to the two agents who arrested him as an illegal immigrant to be processed and either thrown back on the streets or sent across the Mediterranean, if a true identity and country of origin could be established. He had no wounds and needed no medical treatment, but he had been at a crucial site in the ongoing struggle. They assumed he was more important than any ordinary immigrant. They injected him with the "medicinal compound." Interrogators found it "most efficacious in every case." And their suspicions paid off.

"Why were you watching those apartments?"

"I was told to look out for Mademoiselle Yasmine and to see if the president paid her a visit."

"Why should the president visit her?"

"He's her lover and can be blackmailed and then killed."

"When will the president be blackmailed and assassinated?"

"Soon."

"When?"

"I don't know."

"Who knows?"

"The Englishman, Hare."

"The one from Hastings?"

"Yes."

"Where will the president be kidnapped?"

"In Paris."

"Where in Paris?"

"In an apartment."
"Whose apartment?"
"The tenant is Yasmine Lallouche."
"Will she die too?"
"I am sure she will."
"Does Yasmine know you?"
"No."
"Have you met her?"
"Yes."
"How many times?"
"Once."
"Did you give her anything?"
"Only a clock."
"Will it explode?"
"No, of course not."
"We'll see you again."

***

Three interrogators entered the small impersonal room.
"Can you speak French?"
"Of course," the man from Hastings said.
"Where did you learn it?"
"At school."
"You were in a restaurant with two other men when you were arrested. What were you talking about?"
"Our departure from France."
"Well, you've missed your plane. What are your plans for the president of France?"
"Blackmail and death."
"How will he be blackmailed?"
"A film has been taken of his sexual behaviour with an Arab woman. It could appear on the Internet and be released to news networks."
"And if the president simply ignores the blackmail?"
"Then he will be executed without delay."
"When?"

"When he next visits his mistress."
"Well, he might already have finished with her."
"I don't believe you. He's in love with her. She's in love with him."
"How do you know?"
"Recordings will prove it."
"You mean the ones from the clock?"
"Of course."
One of the interrogators stood up and left the room. The questions continued.
"Who planned the attacks in Strasbourg, Lyon, and Paris?"
"I did."
"Who ordered them?"
"I don't know."
"You take orders from unknown people?"
"I took orders from one unknown person."
"How does he send you an order?"
"A brother sits next to me in a café and tells me the order."
"How many times have you received orders?"
"Twice."
"What was the first one?"
"It was an order to live quietly in Hastings and await another order."
"When was that first order given?"
"Two years ago."
"Your next order was to come to France?"
"Yes."
"At that time did you receive an order to plan attacks in France."
"Yes."
"Were you visited by anyone to help you?"
"Yes."
"What is the name of this person?"
"He told me to call him 'Hare.'"
"You were with Hare in the restaurant today?"
"Yes."
"Who is the other man?"
"Hare."
"So, two of the men are called Hare?"

"Yes."
"What did the men call you?"
"Hare."
"Have you ever eaten jugged hare?"
"No."

The remaining two interrogators got up and left the room, locking the door behind them. They laughed as they went down the corridor.

"There's got to be a master hare," one of them muttered, "a giant who sits in safety in some Arab state."

***

Control had read the interrogation reports and one from Miranda about Yasmine's apartment. He looked at the photos Miranda had taken. There was a note on a slip of paper in the address book. It read, "Dr. Mahmoud Petrie is a family friend. Mention him in letter home." He had also looked at the recording from a small disc-like gadget his expert had found in the clock. The clock, the expert had said, was now just an alarm clock—nothing to be alarmed about.

Control's thoughts returned to the erotic recording, if it could be called erotic. "Shocking" was a more accurate word. Clearly it had to be squirreled away well out of the sweaty grasp of journalists, other civil servants, and politicians. Thank goodness they had obtained it before the terrorists could shock the world with it. Its usefulness as a piece of evidence was obvious. Control had a special strongbox in his safe. It was in there now on the little disc, and there it would stay, unless he ever needed it for political leverage. In his job one could never be too careful.

Would he wait until the president's next visit to the attractive publicist? Would agents then intercept would-be assassins outside the apartment as they tried to open the door? That would be noisy. An amateur's solution. No, Yasmine must not be startled, and the assassins would have to follow President Champenois from the palace and see him go into the building. Yet they might decide to kill him en route, perhaps by ramming his motorcycle with a high-powered utility truck or a Range Rover. That would be easier. Why in the apartment? They wanted the story to get out, unstoppable, into the world press. Then they would release edited bits of their recording to the world press. The media would pay handsomely. Then they would have more money with which to seduce the young and naïve. The more he thought about it, the more he thought that was why the president's death must be linked with a young Arab woman who was to be presented simply as his "defenceless, overawed plaything."

In that scenario Yasmine was heartlessly exposed to mortal danger by a politician who knew he was a target as soon as he took office. It was his calculated risk. But to expose a young woman to such a risk, as well as to his irregular sexual demands, was the act of a corrupt westerner. This kind of "infamy," seemingly an epidemic among politicians, was one of the reasons Muslim influence was growing and might, in the end, take over. Control knew he had to make a decision. The blackmailers and assassins had to be caught and killed. There was to be no question of a trial with the legal delays and all the negative publicity. There was to be no involvement with the president himself.

Control poured himself a glass of Margaux (2004) from Chateau Angludet. It was a perfect accompaniment to his platter of cold meat and cold asparagus in a balsamic vinaigrette. It was time to call in Kim and Miranda. They might be able to find a winning refinement for the operation.

44

PAUL rang the bell and then opened the front door. "I'm home!" he called, as Mary entered the hall. They hugged tightly and kissed.

"I'm glad you think of this as your home," she said breathlessly.

"Well, it is, darling. In fact, home is where Mary is. Am I ever relieved to get back!"

"You're relieved to get back! I'm relieved you're back! So, how was it?"

"Difficult. I found he'd sunk into the revenge mentality and then murder before killing himself."

"He must have felt so alone. So difficult. Horrible." She hugged him again. "He was one of your oldest friends from student days, wasn't he?"

"Yes, he was."

"And best man at our wedding."

"I must have been really stressed when I found out what happened because I had a vivid dream or out-of-body experience! I don't really know what it was."

"Really? How strange. Stress can play tricks with us, you know."

"But on the plane, I saw Graham's ghost! I was watching a film about a drum instructor stricter than a sergeant training recruits for the parachute regiment."

"It's a bit of a cult movie now, people tell me, in particular some of the youngsters who see me in the surgery."

"It's a compelling movie, despite its one-track theme. But I looked up from watching it and saw Graham walking down the aisle avoiding knees and elbows."

"Looking as you knew him?"

"Yes, but he had a hole in one temple and a thin line of blood running down one cheek and into the side of his mouth. He still came forward, and it looked as if he suddenly saw me. He smiled, and some of his teeth were blood red. He stood beside me and said something."

"What did he say?"

"I don't know, because his mouth was full of blood. It started running down his chin. Then he vanished, and I was looking at the film about the young drummer and his strict teacher."

"Let's go into the sitting room. I'll get you a glass of grapefruit Pellegrino!"

"You mean a stiff scotch, I hope!"

***

Control pressed a button to let Kim and Miranda into his office. He was not a man to waste time. The current situation demanded swift action.

"Bonsoir! Ladies, interrogations warn us that Champenois and Yasmine Lallouche are on the death list. There is to be blackmail followed by assassination. The blackmail cannot take place. The next step will certainly be an attempt on his life when the president pays Yasmine an early morning or late-night visit. Nobody knows when that will be. Kim, what do you think will happen?"

"I think the killers will be watching for the president's leaving for Yasmine's apartment."

"Correct. As will we. Miranda, what do you think?"

"Agreed, but perhaps they will simply watch Yasmine's place for the president's arrival. There's so much security around the palace. With either scenario, how do we deal with it? He could leave tonight or within the next week. What's his schedule? "

"Good thinking. I've checked with the palace. He's recovering from a cold and will not go out for at least two days."

"Perfect!" Kim said, suddenly excited. "We get a look-alike 'president' to leave the palace tomorrow night and go in his usual way to Yasmine's place. We'll track the look-alike and catch any would-be assassins."

"Brilliant," Miranda said. The two women looked expectantly at Control.

"Yes," he said, rewarding them with his big, approving smile. "Our watchers will keep in the shadows and track anyone who follows our chubby friend. Just in case. If there's any attempt to kill our man while he's en route for Yasmine, it must be stopped. If he reaches her door, he must go in. The assassins will follow him in a little later. Our people will follow them after three or four minutes to cut off their retreat."

"Where do we come in?" Miranda asked. "I've been in the flat, and I know the layout. I'd like to be in there waiting for them."

"Me too," Kim begged.

"Do you know something? You two should be in Planning with me!"

"That's what I thought we were doing already," Kim said drily. Control and Miranda smiled and nodded.

Their boss was serious again in a flash. "You can both go in. Better to be there before Yasmine gets in from work. Make yourselves at home there in mid-afternoon in case she knocks off early. And keep awake in case she has dinner out before getting home late."

"Don't worry, Control, we'll take naps in turn until Yasmine gets home, and we'll be wide awake when the look-alike knocks on the door."

"If there's resistance and anyone gets injured or killed, I want these murderers dead. But, if possible, with no injuries to you two or the 'president.' Try to bring the terrorists in alive for interrogation."

"And Yasmine?" Kim asked.

"She must come in, and then she might have to go into a protection program. If she's alive."

"Tomorrow night's the night then."

"Good luck. Come back alive. We'll have dinner at La Tour d'Argent, my treat."

"Never fear," Miranda said. "We'll be back alright!"

***

Hervé Martin sat looking up at a ceiling light. Then he closed his eyes. *I really must go to bed*, he thought. Then he began to ruminate further: what if the killers were alerted as soon as the look-alike president left the palace incognito? What if killers entered the building immediately to kill Yasmine? Would Kim and Miranda be injured or killed? No, they would more likely capture, wound, or kill the assassins. Or when the look-alike arrived a few minutes later, there could be, perhaps, three dead women and two clever killers waiting for him, and they might kill him straight away. In such a scenario, the killers would probably video the killings for later broadcasts. The bodies would either be left on the premises or transported elsewhere. How long before they left after the president's arrival? Ten to fifteen minutes, if they were practised enough.

It would seem the president was a thoroughly depraved man abusing power like any dictator. And all this would be on the Internet. It would be worse than blackmail. Yes. Why to God had he sent two of his best women agents? He had men as well. And what about the Champenois look-alike? He had to be removed from the scene. If the horror of Internet exposure occurred, Control would let the press know that terrorists had murdered a perfectly ordinary, if energetic, sexist playboy. Unfortunately for him, the assassins had thought quite wrongly that he was President Antoine Champenois! It was a tall order but the best plan under the constraint of necessity for fast action. There was so little time in which to get things done. And the official presidential look-alikes were wellpaid and usually had something mundane, even banal, as a duty.

Control phoned Kim.

"Yes?"

"You and Miranda must be careful entering the apartment. The killers might already be in there."

"Understood. Super careful."

"Good. Bring out the look-alike alive or injured. Contact after crisis point. ASAP."

"Understood."

45

SAMANTHA Gilmore had just returned home from work when her teenage son, Greg, rushed in with the news of terrorist attacks in France. She was shocked by the account she read in the *Globe and Mail*. She had had even more of a shock a few days before, when she had read in a Vancouver newspaper of Graham Curtis's murder of his wife's killers and his immediate suicide. At the hospital the gossip revealed that Graham had been diagnosed with terminal cancer. Poor wretch. Life had dealt him a terrible hand. She remembered him with some affection. He had been good to Greg when they had all gone to Europe. At the same time, she felt she had been absolutely right to keep him at arm's length. For her own reasons, she preferred to avoid another sexual relationship for the time being. In any case, he was looking for some new sexual encounter too soon after his wife's funeral. Were men ruled too promptly by their "organ"? But could she have been friendlier and saved him from his fate? Could any of Graham's friends or colleagues have saved him? There was no answer.

She learned from a friend on the campus where Graham had worked that a memorial service was to take place at short notice because his friend from England had to get back home as soon as possible. She had not attended, nor did she regret her decision. It would have been an opportunity to say hello to Paul, but she hardly knew him. She would not get over to Europe again soon to see him and his wife Mary. No. She preferred to get on with looking after Greg in a comfortable celibate lifestyle. Vancouver was a wonderful city. Her job, now that she was out of her old boss's clutches, was ticking over nicely. Life, in short, was good. The time to consider change was probably when Greg went to university or college, especially if he had to go to another province.

"Greg," she called, "have you got homework?"

"I'm in the middle of doing it!" he called from his bedroom. "No interruptions, puh-leez!"

Why did kids have these crazy words? Awesome! Why? She shrugged and took off her shoes. That was better. She walked across her kitchen's tile floor and opened the fridge. She poured herself a healthy fruit cocktail and sat down with the *Metro*, a free newspaper she had picked up on her way home.

Someone had let a leopard free, and it was roaming through the woods and a small town in BC's interior. Officials were trying, unsuccessfully as yet, to catch it. Justin Trudeau had made another speech. He was still popular after over a year in office. But criticisms were beginning to surface. She remembered when he was running for office. The opposition had said he was not ready. Now his supporters were saying "Justin time!" She wondered how long it would be before the public tired of him more vocally. She had no idea. She had voted for his party member in Vancouver.

Suddenly, she remembered a sixty-year-old Asian patient who had been in the hospital during the election. She had asked him if he was going to vote. He nodded. "They're always the same dogs. They wear different collars, that's all." It might be true in Asia, but was it true everywhere, even in Canada? Her thoughts were interrupted by a shout from Greg.

"Mom? What's for dinner?"

***

Having made all the arrangements for Tomkyn Bridge School to backpedal smoothly during the summer holidays, Miss Mason had decided to revisit Cyprus for a little holiday. As a youngster she had been there when her father was an army officer during the crisis, when the EOKA terrorists (or freedom fighters) wanted the British out. Luckily, he had been posted elsewhere before he or his family suffered any harm.

Miss Mason had been a brilliant student at Cambridge, had gone into the Foreign Office, and had served abroad. In the Soviet Union she had been driving a car that was crossing the border into Finland. Suddenly, a Soviet border guard rushed from the telephone, having been alerted that a person was being smuggled out in the car. It had to be stopped.

When the car was almost at the Finnish checkpoint, he fired at the tires.

The car swerved, and Miss Mason had tried to control it, managing to cross the "Finnish line," as she referred to it afterwards.

As the car spun over the line, a bullet went through her door and smashed into her leg near the knee. She smiled as she remembered the trip to safety rather than the pain. The hospital had been good. Her leg, however, had never gone back to normal, which explained her limp and her scar, which was like a large dimple. Her mother had pleaded with her to take up teaching. She had done so. Now she was a headmistress heading back to Cyprus with happy memories of the island, its lovely beaches, and its charming Greek Cypriot villages.

Perhaps she would visit the Turkish part as well. There had been angry tensions between the Christian Greek Cypriots and the Turks, almost leading to war. But now there was relative calm. The Greeks still harked back to Turkish expansionism, conquest, and rule. And now Turkey wanted to be in the European Union! Why had the Turks been allowed to keep a bit of Cyprus when the European empires had been cut back and people had maintained Britain should creep away from the Falklands and leave it to the Argentinean junta? Ah well, Mrs. Thatcher had listened to the Falkland Islanders, who did not want to be taken over by a dictatorship, many of whose citizens "disappeared."

As she packed for her holiday, she thought of her beautiful languages teacher, Alissa Partridge. How was her holiday working out? Was she abroad, or had she stayed in England? She liked the young woman, who was intelligent, well-mannered, and seemed good at her job. She hoped Alissa would return to teach but feared that her departure was definite. She was popular with the girls. When the parents visited the school, Alissa would be just as popular with the pupils' fathers.

Good. She checked her list. Everything she needed was packed, so she was ready for an early start in the morning.

***

Kim and Miranda met for breakfast on the day of their operation with the look-alike. After collecting the equipment they needed, such as secure phones and their preferred pistols, they each checked their personal survival weapons. Kim had her mother's fan, loaded with the powder that could blind an assailant, even one as vigilant as Bruno. Miranda had the crossword pen that she had so elegantly used to stun him.

Miranda's official weapon was a 9mm SAMAS G1. She liked the fact that it had a fifteen-cartridge magazine. It also suited her in terms of weight. It felt right when she used it on the pistol range. Kim agreed. It suited her too. Although it was a copy of the Beretta 92, they preferred it to the Italian pistol. With each carrying a spare magazine, the two agents had sixty shots between them. They hoped they would never need to use all those rounds, but it was comforting to know they had enough for a prolonged firefight.

Just in case they were disarmed, each carried a concealed Glock G 26. They hoped they would not have to fall back on the second gun. Miranda was an excellent shot, and Kim was an elite shooter. Both were, as their instructors had remarked to each other, exceedingly fast young women!

They took their separate ways to Yasmine's nearest metro stop. They looked like tired workers dragging themselves to some boring menial task in a small business or factory. They carried battered, well-worn shopping bags. Other passengers would have been surprised to see the contents. Their eyes seemed to be closed most of the journey.

When they disembarked from different trains, they left the station with the crowd. They arrived at the building mid-morning, satisfied no one had followed them. Even so, they waited a few minutes before they each buzzed in through the courtyard door. Someone would be watching. They must seem ordinary and dumpy. They certainly looked like that. They were, one would think, cleaning ladies.

Once inside the building, Miranda led the way to Yasmine's door. The corridor was empty. Everyone was at work, it seemed. Kim put a stethoscope-like instrument in her ears and placed it against the door and then a longish wall. She shook her head.

Miranda took out two special keys that the "expert" had made since their first entry. She opened the door's two locks carefully and silently. No movement. No sound. The two women went in, closing the door as silently as possible behind them. There was a slight click as it locked.

They stood still. The place had no feeling of a presence. It was empty; they were sure. Still, they kept still and listened. They took out their SAMAS G 1 pistols and moved through the entire apartment, looking in every closet. No one was there.

Kim looked in the fridge while Miranda opened cupboards and doors under the counter. Kim noticed that Yasmine had a shoulder of lamb, a couple of steaks, a litre of milk, vegetables in the fruit and vegetable drawers, and a large pitcher of fruit and vegetable health drink. Miranda found half a baguette and a cut sandwich loaf in the bread drawer below the counter. Other drawers contained cooking utensils. On the countertop was a two-spout coffee machine for capsules, favoured perhaps by Monsieur George Clooney.

"Well, I guess we have a lazy afternoon until she comes home," Miranda observed.

"Yes," Kim replied, "but if her phone rings, we pick up without saying anything. We'll try to find who is calling first."

"Agreed."

46

YASMINE was at the Gare Montparnasse with a notice proclaiming "Arnaud Rivière." He was a top business executive with whom the publicity firm hoped to do business. Yasmine was at the barrier five minutes before the 16:35 train was due to arrive. Suddenly, a young man wearing a short light raincoat over a dark-grey suit approached her and held out his hand.

"Bonjour, Mademoiselle Lallouche. I'm ArnaudRivière."

"Oh, you're here early."

"Correct. I was able to catch an earlier train, so I could look around in the infamous tower. Let's get a taxi?"

"Of course," Yasmine said. A Mercedes-Benz taxi came to them in the forecourt of the station. Yasmine gave her firm's address to the driver. He smiled.

"Oui, Madame."

Soon they were speeding along the big circular highway that coils around Paris.

"We could have gone directly down the Boulevard Montparnasse."

"Yes, but we're going somewhere else." The young "executive" showed her a pistol he took from his pocket.

***

Arnaud Rivière's train arrived at the Gare Montparnasse one minute late. The young executive walked to the barrier and waited to see if anyone from the firm he was visiting would contact him. Nobody appeared with a notice, a smile, or a firm handshake.

After ten minutes he phoned the publicity firm. He was assured that Yasmine Lallouche had instructions to meet him and bring him to the firm's premises and then take him a little later to the Sofitel at Bercy. Rivière decided to wait another five minutes and then take a cab to the hotel.

This he did and checked into the suite prepared for him. He was unpacking when the phone rang. The publicity firm's manager assumed since he had not come to their premises, that he must have gone to the hotel. He trusted that the suite was satisfactory. Affirmative. Had he seen Yasmine? Negative. They would see him as arranged in the morning. A car would pick him up at 9:00 a.m.

This Yasmine, the visitor thought, was unreliable. Yet she had certainly improved the French president's ratings. He prepared for a quiet dinner in the hotel or maybe at a restaurant nearby. In the morning, he supposed Yasmine would either avoid him or come to him with abject apologies. He would assess her and the firm with his usual business acumen.

***

"Subject has not arrived," Kim said. "News?"

"Sit tight," Control replied. "Wait for big fish to swim by."

Miranda was looking in the fridge. She was getting hungry.

"Yasmine may come in with a big bag of groceries. Maybe she's planning a party for some colleagues tomorrow evening," Kim suggested.

The two agents decided that however boring their watch, they had to sit tight. Miranda actually did some of her skeleton crossword. Kim started to read the memoirs of General David Richards. Skimming through its pages and the index, she realized the general had met many politicians and leaders from a variety of countries. The new president of France, M. Antoine Champenois, did not figure in the book. The general had retired. The president was just forty-three this year. *Everything changes; that's what history teaches*, Kim thought. But human nature was slower to change than technology.

"Why not make steak and purée! It's time for a meal. We must be in top shape for this operation, n'est-ce pas?"

"Bad Miranda." Kim laughed. "We can't disturb a possible crime scene."

"Okay. You imagine peeling the spuds, and I'll imagine I'm cooking, as long as you imagine making a purée and washing the dishes after the meal," Miranda said jauntily.

"Deal."

The telephone rang. Miranda picked up the receiver, pressed the switch for speaker, and waited. An anxious voice, male, launched into a torrent of questions.

"Yasmine? What's happening? Why didn't you meet M. Rivière at la Gare Montparnasse? Are you ill? Why didn't you call us?"

"I'm sorry. It's a neighbour here. Yasmine had an accident. I gather she's in hospital. What time should she have been at the station?"

"Mon dieu! Is she badly hurt? She was to meet the 16:35 train and bring our prospective client here."

"I don't know which hospital she went to, Monsieur, but she or they will call you. I'm sorry I have to go now. Bon courage!"

She replaced the receiver and looked at Kim, who was already phoning Control's secure line.

47

AT 01:30 the president's look-alike left the Elysée Palace on a dark-grey motor scooter. As he approached Yasmine's street, a black-windowed Range Rover, generously muddy, especially on its licence plates, slowed down and nudged the scooter. The "president" fell sprawling and rolled into the gutter.

The Range Rover stopped, and two men emerged. One clubbed their quarry, and then they pushed him into the back of the vehicle, which raced off with one of the men and his victim. The other man picked up the scooter and then disappeared into a maze of old Parisian streets before abandoning the scooter near a black Volvo sedan. He got into the back of the Volvo, and it drove off.

***

Control's watchers reported the unexpected kidnapping of the look-alike. It was fast, and they had been unable to stop the vehicle involved. Control needed to think and quickly. He called Kim and Miranda.

"Abort."

"Understood."

Kim and Miranda left Yasmine's apartment exactly as they found it, except for listening bugs in the sitting room, the bedroom, and the bathroom. Any telephone calls would be monitored.

The two agents left the building looking like cleaning ladies. They were watched by two men wearing hoodies. The men waited for thirty minutes in the shadowy courtyard not far away and then went to Yasmine's apartment.

They searched to ensure it was empty. In the bedroom they found the clock and opened it. They found no concealed device. They put the clock into a small backpack. They looked in all the cupboards and the drawers, finding a diary, an address book, and a bank book. They put these items into the backpack. They did not speak, but their movements were heard.

When they opened the front door, they were arrested by two men carrying sub-machine guns. Twenty minutes later they were in an interrogation room. They refused to say anything apart from claiming their human rights had been abused, and they wanted their lawyer. They were given their choice of warm drinks: coffee or hot chocolate. Once they had taken a few sips, they were sound asleep.

Just before they were due to regain consciousness, an agent came into the room and injected each man with the truth drug. Then they were put into separate rooms.

In the first interrogation room, the following was recorded.

"You left the apartment to go where?" one interrogator asked.

"I was going to Créteil. To the house."

"Please write the address on this paper."

The interrogator looked at the paper once the man was finished. "Is this the correct address?"

"It is."

"Where did you leave your vehicle?"

"Le Square Sarah Bernhardt."

"Make and plate number?"

The same routine was followed in the second interrogation room. When compared a few minutes afterwards, the answers matched. The interrogators compared notes outside the rooms. Control, who was to be up all night, said that much was satisfactory except for the kidnappings.

"We'll pay a little visit to Créteil," he concluded. "No time to lose."

***

An old light-blue Toyota Corolla drove past the address in Créteil. It was a fine detached house with a view of the lake. It was half-timbered, like some English mock Tudor houses in stock broker neighbourhoods. Or perhaps it took its inspiration from Normandy. What mattered to Miranda was what and who were indoors.

All the shutters were closed, as if its owners were away or it was someone's holiday home. While Miranda drove past the house, her passenger took photographs of it simply by looking at it. He also looked at a newly cleaned black Range Rover parked in the street near the house's driveway. Her passenger's name was Harry. The owner of the house was seldom there but was known to his associates by one name: Abassi. His chauffeur in Paris was inside the house. He was known as Abdel Kadir. Harry had been attached to the operation because the Americans already had Abassi under observation whenever he travelled. Miranda was pleased that Harry was in on this. Control was happy for some American help, as long as it was understood that they were on French soil, and the French were in charge. For his part, Harry was quite content with the arrangement. He felt that, if need be, he could protect Miranda. No bastard was going to hurt her.

"Nothing doing outside, but we must disable that Range Rover and anything tucked away in the garage."

"Copy that," Harry said. "I guess Control's team will want in soon. The sooner the better."

Miranda smiled. "Certain, jeune homme."

Harry never knew whether her calling him "young man" was a compliment or a put-down. He shrugged. It didn't matter. He had made love to this remarkable woman, and he was not going to lose her. In fact, he wanted to take her back to the good old US of A.

"We've found a bird's nest," Miranda said. "You know where we are?"

"Indeed we do," Control replied. "Well done."

"Nests are protected, so we'll give this a miss."

"Absolutely. We want the eggs. Will send boys who climb trees."

"Thanks. We'll wait at the RV."

Control moved on to the next thing he had to do: check for a report on readiness with his colleague who commanded the Special Forces for the operation.

48

THE house at Créteil was beautifully decorated and furnished, except for the top floor, the entirety of which was a sophisticated communications centre. From there the daily business of smuggling people, arms, and money across frontiers was commanded. It also produced recruitment videos for young jihadists.

Another room in the house had no décor at all. It was an all-purpose soundproofed room for interrogation using varied barbaric levels of torture. Yasmine had been in that room since her abduction the previous afternoon.

Suddenly, the door opened to admit a man who looked like the president of France. It was 3:00 a.m. Yasmine knew this fact because she still had her watch. She knew another fact: the man who had just been pushed into the room was *not* the president. He looked at her and then approached her.

"Hello—you okay?" he asked as he wiped sweat from his brow.

"No, I'm not okay," she replied, "in fact I'm angry, and I'm afraid."

"Yes. I can understand that. How long have you been here?"

"Since about 5:40 yesterday afternoon."

"Have they questioned you?"

"No. But they took my bag and phone."

"I expect they'll wait for the morning, until some bigwig has had breakfast."

"Who are you?" The president's double put his finger to his lips.

"The less we say, the better, Yasmine, my dear." He came close to her. "I'm the president," he murmured in her ear, "and you're my beautiful mistress. It's our one chance for getting out of here alive." He looked at her and smiled. Then he took her hands in his. "Let's hug."

At that moment they heard the muffled thunder of an explosion in another part of the house. It was followed by the crackle of small-arms fire and shouts from various directions. Someone banged on the door. The president's double pulled Yasmine to one side of the door. They heard a loud bang, and then the door flew open. Two people wearing body armour, leg protection, and helmets with night-vision goggles leaped to either side of the door, pointing their submachine guns in rapid arcs from side to side. One of the men spoke into a microphone attached to his helmet:

"Belmondo. We have two birds in a nest."

He smiled and gave a thumbs-up to his partner and then to the two hostages huddled together.

"Understood, Belmondo, sir. We'll get them home."

The house was full of the sounds of men moving around as they cleared and searched each room. Irate shouting erupted from somewhere above.

"Where's Abassi? Where's his chauffeur?"

***

"The less Yasmine knows about this, the better," Control said to the debriefing agents, a man and a woman.

The woman went into Yasmine's room in the "nursing home." The room had a single bed with a colourful duvet, a side table and lamp of Swedish design, a comfortable oatmeal-shade couch with cushions, and a capacious armchair. Yasmine was lying fully clothed on the bed. She had found it impossible to sleep. *Why had she been kidnapped? Who was the man who looked like Antoine?*

"Hello, Yasmine. You're safe now. We shall get you home as soon as we are able. I'm Josiane. How did you get to Créteil?"

"I was at the Gare Montparnasse to meet a man we were hoping to get as a client. I was to meet him and take him to our office and then to a hotel in Bercy."

"That was when?" Josiane asked with an encouraging smile.

"Oh, it was the 16:35 train. That is, yesterday. I arrived five minutes or so early, and a man claiming to be our visitor approached me, and we took a taxi together. I thought we were going to Bercy."

"Why didn't you stop the taxi?"

"The driver was a crook, and the man I met took out a gun."

"That was a dirty trick," Josiane said. "And then you were driven straight to the house?"

"Yes. I was taken down some stairs to a horrible concrete room with no windows."

"That's where we found you. But who was the man with you?'

"I don't know. He told me to pretend he was the president. He said it was our only chance to get out alive."

"What time did he arrive in that nasty room?"

"It was the middle of the night. About three a.m."

"How long were you both there together before we rescued you?"

"Maybe tenminutes, or fifteen. It was still three something at night. Maybe fifteen after he arrived. When will I be able to go back to work and go home?"

"You must be in shock, Yasmine. We could say you were taken ill and had to be rushed to hospital."

"That would help. But I could simply tell my boss what happened. He would understand."

"Well, I think we must keep to the hospital story for the time being. To say anything else could be dangerous for you. And it sounds unlikely. Would your boss believe you? I doubt it. Can you describe the man who kidnapped you and the taxi driver?"

"I'll try."

"I have some photos here. See if you recognize anyone."

49

"**DR.** Rao to Nurses' Station Four, please." The message came over the system as Mary stepped out of the elevator.

She hurried along the fourth-floor corridor to the nurses' station, where the ward sister was at her desk.

"Hello, Sister, I'm Dr. Rao. Anything wrong?"

"Sorry to interrupt your normal rounds, but yes. Mr. Baxter was recovering well, and suddenly he had to go down to theatre again."

"Do you know the problem?"

"I'll know when they send him back from the recoroom. But the surgeon is a lung man."

Mary thought about the Baxters. They'd had a new baby recently, and Ted had returned for good from his posting abroad. All was going well, and then he suddenly started coughing blood. Mary thought he should be in hospital for observation and a possible operation. She had thought the right drugs could perhaps take care of the problem. Obviously not.

"The diagnosis was some unspecified lung disease."

"When is he due back in the ward?"

"I think in an hour. Shall I have you paged?"

"Please. I have two other patients to check on. After that I'll go down to the cafeteria. No point in leaving and then coming back."

"Good, Doctor, I'll see you later then."

Mary was worried, but she had every confidence in the lung specialist and his team. Mrs. Baxter would be on her way back to the hospital. Mary could imagine how frantic she would be. She was a good mother and was relieved when Ted had returned to England for good.

After seeing her other patients, Mary went down to the snack bar for a pot of tea. She also bought a newspaper. Three terrorist outrages had been counteracted in Strasbourg, Lyon, and Paris. But there had been some civilian casualties. Mary was surprised that there had been two targets in each city. She was annoyed by the information that in each city a Christian church with wonderful religious art, statuary, and carvings had been targets. She was angry as she thought of the barbaric fanatics trying to destroy democratic societies, to deny the efforts to repair abuses of racial and colonial origin and succeeding in taking over villages and towns in order to oppose modern law with the imposition of a merciless sharia regime. As an Anglo-Indian, Mary knew about the racism of some English people. She also knew of the racism and xenophobia in India and other Asian cultures. She imagined the Middle East also had its fair share of racists, apart from those among the Muslim fanatics. The idea that all people should be Muslims flew in the face of modern diversity. But then in some parts of the African continent, slavery still persisted. Human slaves were worth less than a camel. Societies needed the best talents from their people, whatever their background, working to solve the pressing problems. There was no going back.

"Dr. Rao to Nurses' Station Four, please."

***

Abdul Mejid, known to certain associates as Abassi (the Lion), was walking with a boxer dog on a stout leash along a street in Créteil. He was followed by his chauffeur, Abdel Kadir. The two men had been in Paris and had returned to Créteil for dinner. After a delicious *tagine* and a good deal of planning and checking business transactions, Mejid had decided to walk the dog with his chauffer bodyguard. A security officer had not seen them re-enter the house. Neither Mejid nor his chauffeur was in the house when it was raided. Nobody had seen them leave. The two men were in the Lion's favourite late-night place sipping mint tea. Abdel Kadir was the faithful servant, ready to defend the Lion with his life.

When the late-night brasserie closed, the manager told them the house had just been raided. They could stay on the premises if they wished. The Lion and his keeper preferred to be just two men walking their dog in the streets toward another refuge, an apartment a few blocks away. They were well out of range of the raid on the luxurious house Mejid owned. In fact, as he walked, Mejid was contemplating the best way to get back to Morocco. Or should he stay in

France, benefitting from the luxurious estate down near Montpellier? But how safe was that? He was disappointed that he had changed the plan at the last minute. The three hares had tried and failed. He had instinctively thought that changing the plan for the president's major "embarrassment" would throw the French authorities into chaos. Some of his underlings had clearly made errors. There would have to be a settling of accounts with any of them who survived the swoop by the French authorities. He decided to get some sleep in the safe apartment and think over the problems when he was fresh.

At that moment in a quiet side street near the apartment block, a blue Toyota Corolla slowed to a crawl, and a window slid down on the passenger side. Mejid slowed a little and looked with a faint smile at Harry. Abdel already had a pistol in his hand inside a coat pocket. Harry eyed and photographed the Lion. Harry had learned of his activities when he had served briefly in Iraq. He thought the Lion was lucky to have missed the raid on his mansion.

The car stopped. "Excuse me, monsieur," Harry asked, "do you need a ride?"

"Well, I doubt whether you and your lady friend want to have two men and a boxer in your car! We like the calm of the night."

"Oh, I just thought we'd offer you all a ride," Harry said, looking across at Abdel, whose hand was still in his pocket.

"Actually, we were going to the metro or the RER to take the earliest train to Paris."

"When do you count on being there?" Miranda asked, leaning across Harry.

"We were going to have breakfast at the Place de la Bastille and then call on my old aunt in la rue de la Roquette."

"We're heading for Paris. At this unholy hour, we could get you there almost as fast as the metro. We can drop you at the Bastille. No problem."

"Well, in that case we accept. Thank you so much. You don't mind my dog, Ali, in the back?"

"A boxer called Ali is welcome anytime," Harry said. "Hop in." They appreciated Harry's quick wit.

"My Ali's never lost a fight," Mejid said as he clambered in behind Miranda, leaning forward a little to take in the scent of her hair. *This blonde has great possibilities*, he thought. Ali curled up in the middle of the back seat between Mejid and Kadir. The dog was used to automobiles, though all three passengers were used to luxury automobiles. This ride would be a novelty for them.

Miranda signalled and moved out from the curb. Should she head to Paris as promised or go straight back to Mejid's mansion? The latter: that was where quick arrests could be made.

After a couple of minutes, Kadir felt uneasy. This was not the direct route for the Paris road. They were getting too near to the mansion.

"This isn't the way to Paris, Madame," Kadir said.

"I'm taking a shortcut," Miranda replied without looking back.

Mejid nodded to Kadir.

"Attack!" Kadir said. The boxer leapt into action, biting the nape of Harry's neck. Kadir removed his hand from his pocket. "Down, Ali." The dog relaxed his grip, blood seeping from the tooth marks. Harry had not uttered a sound, but he had a pistol in his hand. Kadir pressed the muzzle of his pistol to the back of Harry's head.

"Drop your gun, white man. That's it, down by your feet."

"My dear, please change course for Paris. It would be a shame to set Ali onto you. You are outgunned and have bitten off a little too much to chew, shall we say?" Mejid chuckled.

Miranda changed course. Mejid handed Harry a handkerchief. "Here. Hold this to the back of your neck," he advised. "We don't want blood over madame's chic little car."

***

Samantha and Greg, had just finished playing a computer game. Greg had won.

"Hot chocolate?"

"You bet, Mom. Muffins?

"Okay, but I'll have just a little of yours, Greg."

"Oh no! I knew it."

"No arguing. Put one in the microwave. It's better warmed up."

They set about getting their snack. The phone rang.

"Hi there," Greg said. He listened. "Oh, I remember. We chatted at the wedding." Greg liked the caller's English accent. She was a pretty Chinese woman friend of Mary's. He had wished he was older and could date her. Was that adolescent lust? He guessed so.

"I'll tell her. Mom, it's for you. It's Maggie."

"Hi, Maggie, how have you been? . . . Yeah. It seems ages since were all at

Lichfield . . . Hey, that's great news. Jack, the pilot? My goodness. He was a great guy . . . Still is! Yeah." Sam laughed. "Yes, you may call me Sam . . . The invitation? . . . Well, that's great. Samantha Gilmore on the invitation. . . And Greg? Wonderful. Just Greg, not Gregory, and yes we'll certainly try to come. I've never been to Edinburgh. Oh, could we? You mean the one in the Dan Brown book? Fantastic . . . Yes, I understand . . . And congratulations to you both. Bye now. Bye, Maggie."

"Mom, what was all that about Dan Brown?"

"Well, since you were listening, Maggie's invited us both to her wedding in Edinburgh. She's marrying the pilot."

"Jack."

"Yes, and she says the chapel Dan Brown featured in his novel is not far away. It's a tourist attraction. What do you think? Shall we go?"

"Great, Mom."

"I know I'm a great mom. Do you want to go?"

Greg gave a gleeful laugh. "Course I do. It's awesome!"

"Well, we'd better start a few jobs, so we can pay the airfare."

"I could try for a part-time job?"

"Yes, you could. But it mustn't affect your schoolwork."

50

THEY skirted the lake on a narrow road leading toward the major road to Paris. On the other side of the lake, lights were flashing in the early morning light. Miranda realized the investigation of the mansion was still in progress. She accelerated gradually, and then Mejid put a hand on her shoulder.

"Slow down. You're speeding."

Miranda stamped on the accelerator and twisted the car violently toward the lake, throwing the passengers, including the dog, off balance. The Toyota bumped across the grass verge, the pedestrian pathway, another slim grass slope, before taking a leap into the lake. It took only a few seconds.

She pressed the button to lower the front windows, but the rest of the car was locked. Murky water surrounded the car as it sank into a deep trough in the mud. Miranda expected a bullet in the back of her head, but at least two dangerous men would die. Water rushed into the car through the front windows. The boxer was barking, its snub nose and jaws just above water level as it balanced precariously on Mejid's back. He was slumped forward and unconscious. His head had banged against the steel pillar between the doors on the side of the car.

Miranda and Harry unsnapped their seatbelts as the car sank further, filling rapidly with water. As the two agents tried to get through their windows, Kadir groped for Harry's leg. Harry kicked him in the face and heard the man's nose crack. Harry was free of the car. Mejid, unconscious and not moving, had his head turned to one side, his cheek resting against the back of Miranda's seat. Miranda held her breath as she took a pen from a small compartment near the gearshift. She scrawled a mark across Kadir's forehead and then Mejid's. She pushed herself out the car window and swam for the surface. The boxer slipped out through Harry's window.

Harry swam to the lake's edge and climbed onto the bank as Miranda swam toward him. The boxer, doing a doggy paddle, its nose just above water, was slower. Harry helped Miranda onto the bank, where they both jumped up and down, shivering. The boxer was still swimming toward them. They laughed with relief at the sight of the once-fearsome dog.

"We bit off more than we could chew, Harry."

"Yeah, and so did the mutt. And our nasty duo got in deeper than they expected."

"Now we get them out?"

"No, Miranda. Let them die. Baby, it's cold out here!"

But she was already wading away toward the car's trunk, which was just sticking out of the water. Harry followed.

Miranda reached into the car and turned the ignition key. She pressed the unlock tab, and the back door nearest the surface unlocked. Harry yanked it open, and within a few minutes they had both terrorists lying on the bank and were trying to resuscitate them.

Majid spit out water and began to breathe. Harry searched him for weapons and found nothing. Kadir was unresponsive at first, but then he coughed, and muddy water trickled from his mouth. They kept working to restore normal breathing. Harry searched Kadir and found a long knife in a sheath strapped to his left leg. His gun, like Harry's, was still somewhere in the car.

"They'll sleep for about eight hours," Miranda said.

"How do you know?"

"I know many things, excellency. It is written! MashaAllah!" She hugged Harry. They were both shivering. Their phones didn't work.

"Run along the path until you find a house and a phone," Harry suggested. "It'll warm you up."

"Okay, Harry. Hey! Where's that dog?"

"We'd better both go," Harry said.

"No. Maybe I'll stay here," Miranda said. "We want these two horrors to be interrogated. The dog won't attack me, or I'll scratch his nose!"

"Well, why don't I jog in search of a phone? Bye now."

And off he ran, the terrorist's handkerchief wrapped around his neck.

51

IMMACULATE in her white lab coat, Mary reached the nurses' station. The ward sister, Helen McCrae, as her badge proclaimed, looked up from her paperwork.

"You can see the surgeon now, Doctor Rao. Mr. Baxter is in recovery, rather groggy still." She went back to her papers.

Everywhere now there are papers to complete . So much for the paperless office or hospital or business or civil service, Mary thought. She saw the surgeon walking purposefully toward her. He held out his hand.

"Dr. Rao? I'm Professor Higgs. They called me in because it was unclear what was destroying one of Mr. Baxter's lungs. I took out a suspect portion"

"I see, Professor," Mary responded anxiously as they shook hands."And do you know now?"

"Afraid not. We're awaiting the lab report. I suspect nothing until we know." He looked disturbed by something, as if he could not reveal what it might be.

"I appreciate your seeing me. I expect Mrs. Baxter is on her way. She'll be here when he gets back from recovery."

"Good. Well, I'll be in touch when I know something."

Still looking a bit unsettled by something unexpected, he turned and walked away. Mary had to go too. She told the ward sister she'd look in later.

***

Nellie Baxter had arrived and was sitting by the bed in a room with two beds, separated by a curtain. She had been there a good half hour when her husband, Ted, was wheeled in and transferred to one of the beds. Nellie watched him lying with eyes closed, head propped on pillows. Despite his recent time working in the Middle East, he was pale.

A nurse looked at the chart at the foot of his bed. He was still on a drip. Nellie looked out the window. A pigeon had alighted on the sill outside. She heard a crow on a tree in the hospital garden. She turned back at the bed. Ted's eyes were open. Nellie smiled at her man. He returned her smile and then closed his eyes. She took his hand and held the back of her other hand on his pale forehead. Then she touched his arm. He was back. They had not lost him. She had not lost him. The family was still there. *There must be a god somewhere,* she thought. *Thank you, God.*

She sat back on the simple regulation chair near his bed. Ted opened his eyes again. "That's my Nellie. I love you; you know that." He spoke slowly in a voice that was just above a whisper. He sounded so weak. Nellie smiled.

"I know, Ted. I know, love. Tomorrow I'll bring the kids." The nurse had said the surgeon would be up later to check on him. Nellie would stay to see if there was more she should know.

About an hour later, the surgeon looked in.

"Hello, Mrs. Baxter. How is he doing?"

"You tell me, Doctor. He's tired and a bit groggy."

"Well, I have good news, though we had to remove a bit of lung. But it's now certain: there's no sign of cancer. He'll make a good recovery."

Nellie felt released from the great fear that had been hanging over her. She flushed and smiled and wept suddenly. "Oh thank you, Doctor. Thank you."

"Now when he gets back home, you have to be strict. No smoking—ever! And no alcohol for at least two weeks. Then you can celebrate. In moderation."

"He likes his pint of bitter, mind."

"And he can have his pint of bitter. In moderation, after two weeks." He turned to go. "I'll look in again tomorrow," he said over his shoulder.

***

The next day Mary went to Ted's ward to see her other patients, one of whom was going home that afternoon.

"Nelly and the kids will be here soon, Ted. She's got them from school, and they won't be long. How are you feeling?"

"Groggy, but I'm alright, Doctor. No pain. A bit stiff."

"Well, it's been a success. The surgeon will come by later on I expect to see how you are."

"He looked in this morning. I'm glad I'm still here!"

"Yes, and I bet Nelly is too. They shouldn't be long." She saw a nurse signalling her. "I have to go now, but I'll drop by tomorrow. Nelly knows she can call me if need be." She waved and went back to the ward sister.

"Dr. Rao, could you go to Professor Higgs now? He wants to talk to you."

Mary looked at her watch. "Yes. Where's his office?" The sister gave her directions, and a few minutes later, Mary was sitting across from the professor at his desk.

"Here's a copy of the report. I've highlighted the thing that puzzles me."

Mary was relieved to see there was no cancer. The highlighted section said that some corrosive condition may have been started by an unidentified substance, perhaps something Mr. Baxter inhaled.

"Toxic fumes of some sort, Professor?"

"Exactly. But what?"

"He's recently been in the Middle East."

The professor bunched his cheeks in a wry grimace and sighed. "What kind of work did he do there?"

"Something to do with construction for the oil industry I believe."

"Well, we know there's no cancer. He should make a good recovery. He should stay away from all industrial dust though. Enough said, eh?"

"Yes. If I notice any other developments, should I let you know directly?"

"Most certainly. No delay. I'll respond straight away. You have other patients to see, I would imagine?"

"Yes. One apart from Ted Baxter. Thanks for seeing me." They rose and shook hands. Mary left.

Professor Higgs picked up his phone. "Arnold? I have something odd for you. You'll get a morsel of lung and a lab report. I sent it yesterday. Should be with you. It could be something nasty being developed by those bastards in the Middle East. On the other hand, it could just be simple industrial spin-off. I don't know."

"I'll get back to you in two shakes of a scalpel, Charles."

***

Jack was in heaven. He couldn't believe his luck at the prospect of marrying Maggie. Her dark hair looked wonderfully sleek on the white pillow. She fit beautifully into the slight hollow between his chest and shoulder. His right hand felt so warm on her small breast. She was a passionate woman. She was also a brilliant professional woman. She wanted his children. She wanted him and didn't mind that he was almost a decade older than she was.

Maggie knew her parents would accept the match, after some persuasion. They were not *particularly* racist, but like most people around the world, they valued their own culture above others. They wanted marriages within their own culture, if possible. As a scientist, Maggie was already in a universal culture of sorts, so how could they stop her marrying this Scot? That he was a pilot was a plus. Perhaps he would fly for Singapore Airlines.

Maggie stirred and then woke up. She turned her head and looked at Jack. She loved his blue eyes as much as he loved her shining dark eyes.

"What are you thinking?" she asked.

"I was thinking how wonderful it will be for me to marry you."

She smiled and kissed his cheek. "It will be wonderful for both of us, Jack, and so we must plan our wedding. Edinburgh? St. Andrews?"

"Aberdeen, Gretna Green?"

"Anywhere in Scotland. Then my family, or at least some of them, will have to come for a holiday to attend the wedding."

"We were thinking of September, yes?"

"Yes. That's when I can get away from the lab."

"Where shall we go for our honeymoon?"

"Villefranche-sur-Mer," she said with no hesitation.

"Never been there, but we can easily fly down to the south of France. Isn't Monaco nearby?"

"Yes. And we can go to Genoa, Rome, Florence, Venice, Ravenna, and Sorrento!"

"What about Pisa and Assisi?" he asked. "I have a soft spot for Saint Francis."

"So do I."

"And Padua," Jack continued, "so we can ask Saint Antony to help us find whatever we lose."

"I've found the man I never want to lose."

"Oh? And who's that?"

"You, my one and only pilot!" She kissed his cheek and then whispered in his ear. "Again?"

52

THE commander of the Special Forces looked at Miranda, a pretty young woman fresh from a hot shower. She was wearing a thick blanket and holding hands with the American spook who told them he was called Harry. He too was wrapped in a blanket. A first-aid bandage was on the back of his neck. He'd also had an injection just in case the boxer or the muddy lake water carried some nasty infection.

"So, how did you get these two bits of scum to go to sleep after you got them out of the water?"

"The crash shook them up and banged their heads," Miranda said. "We revived them to ensure they'd be ready for interrogation. Then they lost consciousness. And they should be awake in about three hours."

"Yes, but you didn't answer my question."

"Ah, well, that's because it's a state secret. My boss might have the authority to reveal it if you must mention it in your report. But they were too weak and cold to do anything but sleep after we 'de-laked' them."

Belmondo smiled and nodded. That secret could escape his report, and he would not mention little marks on their foreheads that looked as if someone used indelible ink on them. Why drag a secret into the light for political people to mull over? *She's a smart woman*, he thought. *Wish I could get under the blanket with her.* The American seemed to have gotten the girl. Yet again.

Harry looked at him and smiled. He had guessed at Belmondo's thoughts and taken several mugshots for the record back at the embassy.

"Is this conversation off or on the record?" Harry asked.

"Well, you can be debriefed now by your own people. We can arrange transport back to Paris."

"I have a question for you," Miranda said. "Have you found any juicy docs here?" She had hit the nail on the head. The mansion's office and computers were intelligence riches.

"We certainly have. Control will be delighted, and so will my boss."

"Thanks for all your help, Belmondo," Miranda replied. "We should get back to Paris now. I hope we meet again."

"I hope so too, Miranda."

He got up from the ornate chair in the even more ornate salon and walked over to her. She stood up to be kissed on both cheeks. As he kissed her, the blanket slipped a little, revealing an agreeable glimpse of her breasts.

"Give my regards to Control. Can't wait for the next joint committee meeting!"

"Well, I hope I'm in on it," Miranda replied. "By the way, have you seen a boxer dog?"

"Oh yes, one came running into the melee in the garden and leaped at one of my men. He shot it."

"What a shame!" Harry said.

***

Debriefings for Miranda and Kim were over. The president's look-alike had been given special leave. He went to Malaga to stay with friends, an English couple who had just retired. He had met them at the Travellers Club in Paris some years before, and they had met since in Paris and in London.

The French thanked Harry for his part in assisting Miranda in the matter of bringing in the Lion and his chauffeur. After his debriefing at the US embassy, his colleague in the laboratory congratulated him on having kept an eye on things. Then Harry came down with a bad cold. He was in his pyjamas and nursing a hot grog when the phone rang.

"Hi... Miranda?"

"C'est moi," she murmured. Harry loved hearing her voice.

"I've come down with a bad cold."

"You poor thing. But I'm not surprised. My throat tells me I'm teetering on the brink of one. I'm dosed up on vitamin C. How's your neck?"

"Stiff but not infected. It seems to be healing. I've had a few stitches. I can't see it without using mirrors. But I have a good nurse here. She's from Chicago. She's black."

"And pretty?"

"Yeah, a real looker. She's efficient and gentle when she dresses my wound."

"Sounds wonderful to be wounded in the line of duty. But when can we meet? I have some leave. How about you?"

"I'm good for sick leave starting tomorrow."

"I think you need some TLC."

"Sure do. Funny how we think the same things."

"Let me know where and when we can meet. It'll be fun. We can see Paris as if we're there together as lovers on holiday!"

"Well, we will be, won't we? We'll keep under the radar for a while."

"Absolutely. Call me. I have to go. Kisses. Thank God you're okay."

"I'm okay. Have fun. But not too much fun! Stay away from Belmondo. Save some for me."

"Course I will. Looking forward to our holiday tryst. Take care, lover."

53

"**BRIAN?** It's Alissa. How are you?"

"Wonderful! Alissa, you're a model model. Where are you? Are you back? I wrote to you care of the O and C Club in London."

"Next time I pop in I'll get your letter. I should be there tomorrow."

"I'm on summer break, so I shall be painting. Will you be coming back here soon?"

"I should be back for a few days on Wednesday. Pub lunch?"

"Yes. That'll be good. And I'll show you what I'm doing in the studio."

"How did you know to write to the club, by the way?"

"Oh, I went to Tomkyn Bridge School. Miss Mason said I might be able to reach you through the club."

"Yes, I've been moving around. Well, see you soon."

"Can't wait."

"I'll phone when I get back."

Kim put the phone down. She liked Brian, but Hervé was a more compelling man. She needed a little distance from both. Thank the Lord she still had some leave. Hervé had been a wonderful host to her and Miranda in the Tour d'Argent. Working with him in Planning would be a treat. With Brian she felt good, but could she live with him? Could she work as a schoolteacher for years to come? No. Children of her own? She had to make serious decisions about her own life. Putting herself in danger as an agent in the field was no life for a mother, whether that mother was a wife or a mistress. She didn't want to mull things over and over again in the same groove. She needed a good workout at the gym.

***

Bruno was almost blind. He silently cursed Kim, who had sprayed powder in his face. He would have to kill her when he was free again. The authorities thought they could transfer him to a prison to await trial. He knew they were angry that there had to be a trial. He would play the French press for suckers. *Le Figaro* would, of course, be hostile, and *Le Parisien* would be alarmed that such treachery could remain undetected for so long. The rest would emphasize all the discrimination and racism that he had to contend with. No wonder he had turned. Colonial guilt would be another tune they would play. However, all that would not take place. The contingency plan would work. How could it fail? He didn't know if all three hares would be transferred together, but he guessed they would be sent separately. That's what he would do if he were Control. But they might just be lucky and all go in the same wagon.

In fact, Bruno was surprised. He was transferred that day in an unmarked police car. There was a driver, a man in the front seat, and Bruno, with a man on each side of him in the back. A motorcyclist followed. On the ring road, the famous Périph, their motorcyclist would spend some time behind them and then roar past to lead the way.

The motorcyclist was leading as they took the exit near Saint-Mandé. The light on the small exit road changed to red as the motorbike went around the corner. He would wait for them.

Two beggars approached the car, one on each side. Instead of holding out their hands, they used spring-loaded devices to punch through the bulletproof glass. They dropped their tools and ducked out of sight. Two gunmen behind them shot the driver and guards with automatic pistols. They pulled Bruno out of the car and took him with them, running with the first two rescuers past the traffic light, which was still red. As they made for a car, waiting farther away, they shot the motorcyclist, who had heard the commotion around the corner. The gunshot that killed him was the last thing he heard. Speeding away to the Bois de Vincennes, the rescuers and Bruno were soon outside Paris. They changed to two separate cars and drove by a circuitous route to Saint-Denis.

They had a safe house there in a quiet street near the Centre for Heart Research. Bruno had seen little, but he had heard the wonderful rattle of gunfire and the last groans of the dying men. That was his music. He grinned as he realized how well it had all been planned. He hoped he could meet the mastermind behind the operation. He hoped the necessary informant inside the French special police had been able to walk away or remain undiscovered. He hoped he could get his hands on one of their pistols, for he had not seen that model before. Bruno congratulated his rescuers. God wasgreat. All had gone well because it was God's will.

A church bell tolled a street or so away. Damned Christians!In the new world order, they would have to convert or be executed. Executed!Yes, Kim had tobe executed too. She was so beautiful and so dangerous. He regretted that she was such a decadent bitch. She would have to be brought to him, so he could kill her in person. Death by a thousand cuts? Perhaps. It was something to live for, this revenge.

54

TED Baxter had been in hospital for five days. Mary understood that his wound was healing nicely. Professor Higgs thought he would thrive at home if he were able to relax and convalesce. Mary had told him *not* to go painting the house or repairing the roof or giving the car a thorough servicing. He could do some washing up, a bit of cooking, and keep off the alcohol until the following week. Moderation. The golden mean. There were no smokers in the family, thank goodness. Mary could keep an eye on him; she did not want to go on any trips out of town for the next few days. Paul was working steadily and had just sold a couple of pieces.

Liz, Mary's receptionist, had blossomed lately. She was still bubbly and full of fun. In fact, she was obviously getting exactly what she needed from her relationship with her "delicious" policeman, Dave. Mary wondered whether marriage was in the offing. She expected it was. She was right.

The next day, Liz turned up for work with a beautiful engagement ring. It had been made in the 1920s in Birmingham's Jewellery Quarter. It had been Dave's grandmother's engagement ring and handed down after her death to Dave's mother. Dave was her only child. His mother liked Liz. She could have the ring if she wanted it. Liz was delighted. Mary thought it was something special: a gold ring with three small emeralds on each side of a central diamond. Mary reckoned the diamond might be one carat or perhaps one and a half. What really counted, in Mary's opinion, was the beauty of the craftsmanship and the ring's family history.

"It's beautiful, Liz. I'm so pleased for you. And I think Dave will make a wonderful husband. You two must come around for a celebration. I'll make a special curry dinner."

"That's lovely. We'd both love that."

The first patient arrived. Mary disappeared into her office. She settled her things for the day and then pushed a button. Liz saw the green light go on. She sent in the first patient of the day.

***

Brian was still moving about the cottage with a slight limp. His spirits were on a high from Alissa's call. She would be back soon. He was painting again and revelling in the change to a much more vigorous sense of space, design, and colour. It crossed his mind that if he had been out, her voice would have been recorded. Then he would have been able to replay her message again and again. No. The immediacy of her voice was sensational. Was he in love? *What is love?* Brian asked himself. He could not frame a definition in words. It was painful to be apart from her. He did know that he wanted her there in the studio. He wanted to paint her. Could he start that when she arrived and finish it with her still there? The here and now rather the here and soon to arrive! When would she slip away again? In fact, her school holidays were a little longer than those of the state schools.

His thoughts of Alissa were suddenly interrupted by another thought: there were still one or two things he had to finish at school before he could retreat completely. He could drive there and try to finish up, so his summer painting plans would have no unwanted interruptions. But what if she rang while he was out? Unlikely—but then, if she left a message, he would play it and savour it. Oh, Alissa, what was it about her, apart from her stunning physical beauty?

As he locked up the cottage and made for the car, he saw quite clearly that she was a *force*. She had a strength and a purpose he knew nothing about. But he was intuitive enough to feel the sheer strength of her personality. He knew she had a real presence. She was still a mystery to him. Would he ever be allowed to know her fully? Could people ever know each other completely? He doubted it. However, portraits could capture the mysterious force of presences. As he drove up onto the road, he knew he would try to snatch in paint some of that Alissa he barely knew. In studying her as he painted her portrait in the studio, he thought he would see into her essential being, a look about the eyes being its signal. Then he remembered she did not want him to paint or even draw her face. Why not? The question nagged at him. It would not go away.

BRUNO'S SECRET

***

Paul and Mary had both worked hard all day. Mary had told him Liz's news.

"Us, Maggie and Jack, Liz and Dave! Everybody's getting married!" Paul observed.

Mary wondered if Paul's mystery woman, the lovely Kalitza, was also getting married. She didn't voice that thought. Paul had not crossed her mysterious path again, nor had he spoken about her.

"Paul, my darling," she said, looking at him, "getting married is what the majority of people do in most cultures whatever their sexual orientation."

"You're right. It's a good old standby for magazine articles. Who's with whom? Who has cheated? Who has divorced? Who's the new woman? 'A Modern Marriage' might be an article I could sell."

They finished their little glasses of *fino* sherry and then ate a simple, leisurely meal of Paul's wonderful mushroom soup followed by Black Forest ham with salad. They did not bother with dessert. They contented themselves with decaffeinated coffee. With this they settled down to fixing dates for their November honeymoon.

Paul thought they should book early, if dates for Mary's locum could be firmed up and depended upon. Tourists would be pouring into Goa in November. They had decided to stay in a big American-style beach resort: a Hilton or Sheraton. Then each day they would explore some different aspect of Goa. They would certainly want to walk around old Goa and visit the great basilica, built at about the time that *Hamlet* was being played in Shakespeare's London. They also wanted to visit the former Portuguese governor's mansion. Then there were Portuguese forts. A guidebook assured its readers that at least one of them was now an excellent restaurant. Mary wanted to go into the forest to an old pre-Portuguese fortress she had read about. It was a Moghul relic she would love to explore. Paul wondered if old hippies were still living and smoking weed in Goa. Mary said it was a distinct possibility, especially if the hippies had a bit of cash and did not need to work.

In one of their travel guides was a photograph of a long track between cultivated fields. On the track was a man and an old elephant. On the facing page was a closeup of the great head, made up with intricate patterns of coloured chalk on the cheeks and enormous ears. Worshippers of Ganesh, the elephant-headed god, could still be found there. Mary was always intrigued by the strange ways in which human beings imagined the world of the spirit.

"Is there a world of the spirit or spirits, Paul?"

"Certainly. The distillers call it Scotland." Mary threw a cushion at him.

"I wonder how Jack and Maggie are doing. Have you heard anything else from them?" Paul asked.

"No. But I wonder if they're living together yet or searching for a different place. You know, one convenient for them both, from a work point of view."

"I bet they're getting together when they can, given their jobs, either at Jack's or Maggie's."

"I expect you're right." Mary smiled as she remembered the last time she had visited Maggie and stayed a few nights in her house. She had also spent a couple of nights in a village inn not far from Jack's place. Jack had been close but never attempted to make the relationship physical. They were just old friends, and it was comfortable that way, as if he were her older brother.

55

THE "treasures" taken from the house in Créteil were in the hands of the analysts. Control looked at the first reports. Abdul Mejid was an extremely naughty boy, a smart naughty boy but not cunning enough to have no records of his terror networks in France, Belgium, Germany, and the UK. Arrests would have to follow with no time to lose. His arrogance, coupled with a belief in the laxness of the French, had made him careless.

What a pity he and some others would have to go to trial, Control surmised. There would be the inevitable cries from the sentimental conspiracy theorists of injustices by a so-called socialist French police state that was really a fascist police state. Then there would be months of legal arguments, followed by the erratic ways of the judges. Then there would be prison time to serve in establishments where the library and other facilities could provide opportunities for new networks to be set up.

Control sighed and ran his fingers through his greying hair. With what they had in documents, disks, and film from Mejid's house, they had no real need for his interrogation. *Pity he hadn't been left to drown with his chauffeur.* Control put the thought aside. He dealt in realities not regrets. One reality he still wanted to face was the search by Moroccan authorities of Mejid's property back across the Straights of Gibraltar. He was awaiting a return call from his Moroccan counterpart. After the Lion had served whatever time he was given in a French jail, the Moroccans would, in all probability, want him back to stand trial there. He would not be made into a national hero, like some of the late Colonel Khaddaffi's henchmen. Control resolved his thoughts by referring to the poet Yeats' idea that savage gods would arrive and have their cycle of history. But he had also prayed that civilization might not sink.

His door light blinked. He pressed a trusty button, and Miranda entered.

She looked tired, but her face was as fine as always. She needed to do something with her hair. She needed some time to do that. She deserved a little R & R. But there was the awful matter of Bruno to deal with.

"Ah, Miranda, take a seat over here, and let's talk about Bruno."

"Thanks, monsieur. What about Bruno?" She took out a tissue and blew her nose.

"While you've been resting and recovering, Bruno has escaped. His police escort was betrayed. So, we have to find him before he finds you and Kim. He will certainly try to eliminate you both."

"He's good at his trade, isn't he?" Miranda saw her boss's tired face as if for the first time. He carried a heavy weight on his shoulders. Each innocent death lost by the wanton savagery of these criminals weighed on him, as did each betrayal by those who should know better. It weighed on his agents too, as she knew well. Bush had said it was war. Hollande had said it was war. The Brits had always known it was war. Perhaps the sentimentalists among the public would believe it at last. The security forces and the military people had known it was war, even before the Twin Towers outrage. It had been war in Northern Ireland, but that was largely resolved. Yet there were always the few who needed to vent anger through horrific violence. Civilization was a fragile condition. Indeed, civilization was also recent in western democracies, and if they were not careful, the savage gods would return with a vengeance. Control knew all this, and she knew he regretted the fact that things were as they were.

"You will have to be careful, Miranda. You must go away for a few days to a good health spa. Shall we say Normandy?"

"Yes, let's say Normandy: one, two, three . . ." Then both said "Normandy" together and laughed. It was idiotic, but they needed the release.

"You must give your wonderful hair a luxury session in a good salon. You can bill it to expenses. You might get some of your expenses paid!"

"What about Bruno?"

"Kim will be in danger too. We think we can locate Bruno wherever he goes, thanks to a bit of nanotechnology." Control was thinking of the soluble "chip" that had worked well for them so far. But its life was limited. It was small and gradually dissolved into the bloodstream until it was undetectable. He cleared his throat. "You must get away in disguise as fast as possible. Not the same as when you were tracking Bruno in England. Be someone he has never seen before."

"A vos ordres, Patron. When must I report back?"

"Next Thursday. Contact me before that only in an emergency. If I get edgy, it's because I know Bruno's compulsion for treachery." Bruno was a type of evil.

***

Maggie was driving to Jack's place in the country. It was a small house, an original cottage set in a generous amount of land. As her Lexus stopped in the short driveway, Jack opened the front door. He stepped outside and, beaming, opened his arms wide. Maggie switched off the engine and got out. They hugged and kissed.

"Welcome! That's a lovely perfume, Maggie!"

"Coco. You like it?"

He took her hand in his and led her to the open door. "It suits you. Elegant but funloving!"

"Have you been reading advertisements for perfumes?" she asked, looking up at him.

"No. I've been reading a guidebook to the South of France."

"Come on! Really? Already?"

"Why not? Now come into my cottage. It's said that Burns, the poet-farmer, once stayed here for a night or two."

"Really? He was quite the lover, wasn't he?"

"Aye, he was, as well as being married and having children."

"And are you a man who follows in his footsteps, Jack?" Maggie looked serious.

"No, lassie. Since we've been close and on the way to getting married, nobody will get between us. I'm yours, even though there's a tale in our family that we are descended from one of Robbie's illegitimate children!"

"Well, don't tell my parents!"

"Do *you* mind?" he asked anxiously.

"Not a bit. Maybe you'll become a pilot-poet. Or maybe one of our children will."

He grinned, shaking his head, and took her hand again, leading her indoors.

They stood in a room that extended the width of the cottage. A large open fireplace was at one end of the room. A sofa and two comfortable armchairs covered in a light-blue fabric stood near the fireplace. The windows on either side of the door had small tables standing under them. A cordless telephone sat on the table to the right of the door, nearer the fireplace end of the room. The other half of the room had a sturdy dining table with four matching chairs. The low ceiling had the original dark beams. The walls, windowsills, and doors were all painted off-white, the plaster work with an eggshell finish, the woodwork with gloss. The lighting came from a series of angled halogen lamps on the ceiling and a modern standard lamp near the sofa. A deep-blue vase on the dining table was bursting with a generous bunch of light orange South African lilies.

"This is charming, Jack," Maggie observed, looking around with delight. "I expected a bachelor pad, all untidy."

"In my job I have to keep things tidy and in good condition. If not, I mightn't survive!"

She kissed him and led him toward the fireplace. "Where does that door lead?" she asked, pointing to the back of the room. It was a swinging door, and they walked through to a kitchen area to the right with a staircase and a cupboard to the left. The kitchen, modern and shiny, had a large window overlooking the back garden. A solid-looking back door led to the garden from the small vestibule between the kitchen and staircase.

"Here, let me take your coat."

Maggie slipped out of her lightly quilted car coat. She was wearing dark-blue pants with a white silk blouse. Jack opened the cupboard to reveal a number of coats and some empty hangers. He realized he was wearing dark-blue pants with a white shirt open at the neck. They looked at each other and laughed.

"Snap!" Maggie said.

"Well, shall we explore upstairs?"

Maggie slipped off her flat driving shoes and went ahead up a narrow staircase. At the top she gasped with joy.

The entire upper storey was a long room whose windows looked out to the back and front gardens and the trees beyond. To the right was an open fireplace, furnished with logs. A large brass bucket contained more logs. Jack's queen-size bed was covered by a bright claret-coloured bedspread that looked rich next to the pine headboard. Matching curtains hung from the windows. On either side of the bed were small pine tables on which were some books and another cordless telephone. The floor was made of gleaming bare boards that looked at least a hundred years old. Spread across the floor were Persian rugs with deep-red and Oxford-blue tones. A chest and a wardrobe stood against the walls. The wall to the left was made of thick frosted glass. A door formed a quarter segment of the wall.

Jack opened the door, and Maggie peered into the bathroom. It had a free-standing tub of sleek modern design, a large square sink, and a walk-in shower in the corner. The lavatory was sleek and obviously designed to complete the set. Everything was white except for the tiles that covered the entire floor, including the shower. They were large, about a foot square, with a shiny light-brown glaze. The generous towel rail was draped with fluffy white towels. Above the sink, and stretching from the shower right into the corner near the bath taps was a mirror. A white seat doubled as a small cupboard. The walls and woodwork were painted white, as was the ceiling. There were no beams. Expensive track lights at various angles could be controlled from the door and the headboard. On the wall just outside the bathroom's glass door were switches for the bathroom lights and fan. Jack switched on the fan and opened the door. The fan was powerful and not at all noisy. Maggie entered the bathroom and then turned to face him.

"When did you have all this done?"

"Last year. I've never had a steamed-up bathroom since."

"Did local workmen do it, or did you get people from Edinburgh?"

"Did most of it myself. I planned the entire renovation, bought all the fixtures, and did the painting and electricity. Local builders remodelled the walls and windows; plumbers did all the waterworks and pipes." He smiled and looked with a certain pride at his handiwork.

"Wow. You have an eye for design, and you're an electrician. My fiancé is a whizz."

"He's also a bit of a chef. Let's go and eat!"

"Haggis?"

"No chance, my love, it isn't Burns Night, and it isn't New Year's Eve. I don't touch the stuff otherwise."

They went down into the kitchen, where Jack poured them each a glass of Chardonnay by Louis Latour.

"To you, Maggie. You are my precious pearl."

"To you Jack. My pilot always!"

∗∗∗

Miranda and Harry arranged to meet at the station for a coffee before their train was due to leave. From there they would both go to a spa in Normandy.

Luxury, Miranda thought, before the inevitable confrontation with Bruno. *Why was he so valuable to the jihadists?* His cover had been blown. He was in hiding. What was his special quality that fascinated them so? Or would they suspect him of betraying them to the French? Would they figure he was still loyal to the French Republic? They would be wondering what had led the security forces to the mansion owned by Abdul Mejid, the Lion. Had Bruno broken under interrogation? That was a possibility the jihadists would have to consider. Yet Bruno had commanded enough clout to be sprung. Perhaps he was from a powerful family that nobody in the service had discovered. Connections of that sort could be complex and devious. *He must be killed*. Miranda shook her head as if to shake that thought away.

"Hey!" Harry said. He had come across to her table from the door as soon as he saw her. She looked like a tired old schoolteacher or minor civil servant. The disguise was good. But she was carrying the bag they had said would be the "identifier." He looked like a tired businessman carrying a briefcase as well as a small travelling bag. She smiled and motioned for him to join her. They could have been strangers or just recent acquaintances. Harry wore a blue-and-white striped scarf that concealed the wound on the back of his neck. He sat down as a waiter appeared. Both ordered coffee and croissants.

"I'm looking forward to the rest. I'll laze away the days."

"Same here," she replied. "But I'll need a little leisurely exercise."

"Oh, I'm all for that."

They ate their coffee and croissants in a contented silence but kept their wary eyes alert. The train was on time. They sat across the aisle from each other in the same car. Nobody suspicious had followed them to the train, and nobody followed them to the spa near Caen. They were safe for a few days, just a few hours from Paris.

56

BRUNO was in the safe house at Saint-Denis. There was no sign of any suspicion about his allegiances. He and his companions did not evoke any interest in the neighbourhood. Almost everyone was coloured. One or two old white people lived a few roads away in another block. Young white families tended to avoid the area. It was a dreary little hideaway. He would not stay long.

Parisians and other French people from the provinces went there only to visit the tombs of French kings. St. Denis also had a modern theatre and a celebrated centre for heart medicine. Yet there was crime, and the schools were not academic. The champagne socialists and the eager business school followers of the Republican party preferred to inhabit the chic areas of the right and left banks in Paris. People talked leftist sentiments but lived in the Latin Quarter of Paris and sent their children to the famous *lycée*, Henri Quatre. Another possibility was to pay, if one had enough money, for a private school education.

By contrast, the tramway ride from the market in Saint-Denis was usually free, because the trams were crowded with passengers in traditional dress from a variety of developing nations. People were so packed together most of the time that it was difficult to move and well-nigh impossible to process a ticket at the machine. In fact, it would have been wise for the municipality to make the tramway officially free. It would be some small recompense for those compelled to live in the vice-ridden suburb.

Only a firm government willing to have the army sweep the neighbourhoods with weapon and drug searches could clean up the area. Politicians were unwilling to do so. If the elected were unwilling to act, little could save the area from the gangs and drugs.

Two blocks away from Bruno's little haven, a seemingly old Renault saloon rolled to a stop and parked in a reserved space for invalids. Two young

Frenchmen of African origin left the car, smart leather bags slung over their shoulders. As they walked, from time to time they looked at their watches.

They entered Bruno's street. A red spot appeared on each watch face. When they were at his apartment block, the red spot turned green. The men walked past without pause.

"So, our man is in Résidence Royal. It looks nothing like Versailles to my mind," one said, and they both grinned. They continued around a corner and passed through a short street until they were back at the car. They relayed their findings to Control's section and then drove back to central Paris. They had confirmed what had showed up already on Control's electronic map of St. Denis.

While they were stuck in a traffic jam, Control issued orders for a raid on Résidence Royal in that back street of St. Denis. Things would have to move fast because Bruno was too experienced to stay there for more than a day or two.

At 4:00 a.m. the next morning, the raid took place. There was gunfire from within the apartment as well as from the windows when the door was knocked down. All five shooters were killed. Luckily, nobody set off any explosives. Unluckily, Bruno was not there. His implant was still active, but the signal was weak. He seemed to be near the marketplace when the signal faded and stopped. Bruno could be anywhere, no doubt armed with a pistol and a knife. He might also be carrying grenades.

Control was worried. A sports bag could contain a Kalashnikov. Bruno was capable of any kind of mayhem or insidious and brutal villainy. Another pressing worry was the fact that someone had known that Bruno was leaving the detention centre for transfer and which route to follow. There had been a major leak. That had to be resolved immediately. Control picked up one of his phones to inquire about progress on the matter.

***

Abdul Mejid sat in a small utilitarian room confronted across an equally utilitarian government-issue desk by what he thought was a minor official of the security forces. In fact, he was facing a top analyst with direct access to the Minister of the Interior.

"Well, well, well, Abdul. MashaAllah."

"No. Allah has not willed it," Mejid retorted.

"Oh, I think he did. Your house is an Ali Baba's cave of intel treasures. We're going to arrest many a minion now. We shall be busy. You will just be twiddling your thumbs."

"Aren't you going to interrogate me? What tortures have you got left over from your days in Algeria?"

"No, Abdul, we don't need to interrogate you. Your faithful chauffeur betrayed you, chattering away. We don't torture people. We leave that to your people in the Middle East. No, we figure that two hundred arrests will keep us going until Christmas and the New Year. Then we'll need another swoop, I suppose."

"I'm not speaking until my trial."

"Trial? How much would your trial cost the French state? Have you a rough idea?"

"It will last many weeks. I have good lawyers. Influence in high places."

"But not in heaven, it seems. You don't understand, do you? Abdul Mejid, you have lost your soul."

"Infidel! What do you know about the soul?"

"I know what war does. It kills bodies, but it also kills souls. Those who survive the slaughter find themselves without souls. Sorry, monsieur, but you've lost your god and your soul."

"You are an irreligious idiot."

"Even so, I have the power to keep you locked up without trial for many a year because we must investigate in the minutest detail all the hundreds of documents we have seized, as well as the films, the disks, and the computers. You'll keep us busy for many, many years. We have to probe you about all these details. And you know what? You might die by accident before you get to a trial. There'll be no luxuries for you. No media attention. Just relentless lonely nights after gruelling days of endless questions. You won't be able to joke about slaughter with the three hares again. But then a lion doesn't really respect a mere hare. So, you see, unlike you, we idiotic functionaries of a corrupt democracy will be living good lives, with plenty of work. I might even go on holiday—with people I love—to Morocco. I could send you a postcard. Oh, I almost forgot. You'll be moved to an even nastier place tomorrow. I must be off. I've arranged to meet an attractive friend of mine for an intimate dinner. But no chance of another rendezvous gallant for you ever."

Mejid remained silent. The faithful one who had leaked the removal details of one of the hares could also arrange his escape tomorrow! *Insha Allah!*

Allah, however, was not willing. The dispatcher in charge of transfers had been closely watched. The phone he used had been lifted, modified, and replaced. When he phoned to arrange armed interception the next day to rescue Mejid at a good place en route, Control heard it all. He arranged for a vehicle containing the soulless Mejid to take a different route the following day. An identical vehicle containing armed agents took the supposed route, approached a false "Road Closed" sign, and stopped. The agents leapt out and arrested the would-be rescuers before they could even put down their false stop signs and get out their weapons. In this way Control had cleaned up nicely. But Bruno was still on the loose. Kim had been warned. She was coming to see him the following day. He dreaded the meeting.

57

ANNE was in the British Airways business-class lounge at the airport. She was flying to London, having finished her research in Atlantic Canada, having tied up a few loose ends in Quebec made a final roundup in Ontario's splendid archives. She'd also had time to visit the museum out in the countryside that held a fine collection of paintings by the Group of Seven. Now she was tired. She was browsing through *The Times* while sipping a grapefruit juice. She was looking forward to getting back to London. Her laptop and back-up storage contained enough materials from her research to keep her writing and getting ahead with her draft of a book on French ladies living away from Quebec during the early years of Canada. She realized it would soon be the 200th anniversary of Quebec, but she would not be able to write her book and get it published in that anniversary year. Before going back to France though, she wanted a few days in the Oxbridge Club and to see Paul and Mary. If they could not get to London, she might pop up to Birmingham by a fast train. After that she would take the Eurostar back to Paris. There was a Matisse cut-outs exhibition she wanted to see. After all, when he was very old, and she was too young to appreciate the occasion, she had been introduced to the old artist at his house in Venice.

Her flight was on time, comfortable, and she even managed forty winks before landing.

She took a taxi to the club in Pall Mall. Once settled into a recently refurbished single room, she partly unpacked, freshened up, and placed a pair of pants in the splendid Corby trouser press. Fifteen minutes would do the trick. Then she phoned Sophie. There was a message saying she was out of town for a week. Undaunted, she picked up the phone again.

"Hello, is that Paul? It's Anne . . . Yes, I'm back in London. Can we get together within the next few days? . . . Ah. Yes, I understand. Yes, I can get down to Birmingham for a couple of nights . . . I understand. A patient in hospital. Yes, she has to be available to check on him and see the surgeon . . . No, no. Please find me a hotel room nearby. Oh good. See you on Wednesday? . . . You'll meet me at the station . . . How kind. Yes. Yes. I'll email you the time I'll arrive. So, how's your work going? More publications in the works. That's good . . . Well, I have a lot to keep me busy when I return to France . . . Yes, to both of you. Hugs. Bye-bye."

Anne put down the phone, feeling pleased. She would dine in the club and get an early night. But first she'd have a glass of quite drinkable club champagne in the bar. She was looking forward to seeing Paul and Mary again. It seemed so long since they had last met.

***

"Kim! Thanks for coming to see me. I know you're on leave." Control held out his arms. Kim crossed the room, and they hugged. Then Control took her hand and pressed his lips to it.

"But?" She looked at her boss keenly. He seemed a little older. He had probably not had much sleep recently, yet he was full of an intense concentration of energy that made his eyes gleam with the steady force of an animal in the wild.

"My dear, I know you will be off to relax, but I wanted to warn you that Bruno escaped. His implant is no longer functioning. We lost track of him. He could be anywhere. He'll want to kill you. So, watch out."

"Yes, I will. What about Miranda?"

"Yes. He'll want her as well." Control sighed. He pushed his hair back with both hands.

"I'm off to St. Bees today. I'll try to ensure I'm not followed."

"Will you stay long?"

"I hope to be back in France next week. The Loire and then a little place called Charlas."

"I know it. Charming. Well, amuse-toi bien."

"Oh, I'll amuse myself alright. If I see Bruno, I'll give him your regards before I put him out of harm's way."

"God. Oh, Kim, be extra careful. But you know him and his nasty ways. I hope that gives you an advantage."

"Thanks for warning me, Hervé."

He has been so wise. Could I marry him? Yes. Yes, I could.

Control went back to his desk but stood and held out his arms again. They hugged. Kim kissed him on the lips. Their eyes locked for a moment that seemed like a charge of energy coming from the unknown depths of their beings. Control kissed her on the mouth.

"Come back soon!" His voice was strangely throaty, as if he were struggling with his emotions.

"Yes. I'll be back soon."

She turned and was gone.

Control put his head in his hands. God, he was tired. His eyes were closed, but in the darkness he saw Kim's beautiful face. She was smiling.

***

Mary was home talking with Paul about what they might do when Anne came to visit. A good curry at home was certainly on the agenda. Maybe Anne would enjoy a visit to the Birmingham art gallery. It had paintings by pre-Raphaelites. They could saunter along to a wine bar on a barge on the canal later on. Or they could take a trip on Saturday or Sunday to Stratford-upon-Avon. It was something they anticipated with great pleasure. Suddenly, Paul had an idea.

"Mary! Why don't you call Maggie or Jack and ask them if they're free to come down to see us?"

"What a good idea, darling. I'll do that right now." She picked up the phone. Maggie was not in. Mary left a message asking her to call back. Then she dialled Jack's number.

"Hello. This is the private local airline that comes up trumps." Jack's voice was unmistakeable. Mary chuckled at his buoyant mood.

"Hi, Jack. It's Mary. Sorry, I didn't mean 'hijack,' as in 'hijack a light aircraft.'"

"Well, lassie, I'm pleased to hear that. Do you want to speak to Maggie?"

She detected a clear note of pride in his voice. *He wants me to know she's there with him and ready for bed.* "Well, if she's there, yes. But I'm calling because Paul and I are entertaining Anne—you remember her, of course?"

"Certainly."

"She'll be with us for a couple of nights and staying in a local hotel while she's here. We wondered if you and Maggie might fly down and join us."

"I think I'd be free. But talk to Maggie. She's sitting on my knee!" Laughter at both ends of the line.

"Hello, Mary. I wasn't on his knee, but, oh my goodness, I am now." More laughter.

"Well, that's good. Anne will be with us this weekend. Might you and Jack be free to fly down here? Sorry it's such short notice. You can both stay with us. Anne will be in a hotel."

"Why, that's great. Are you sure? Jack's nodding at me. I'll check my diary. Call you back in a minute or two."

"I'll hang on and chat to Jack when you dismount from his knee and search for your handbag!"

And so it was. They were both free to come down to Sutton Coldfield. They were all pleased. Mary would cook a superb curry for ten, just in case. Any leftovers she would freeze for another meal. She thought of inviting Liz, her receptionist, and her handsome policeman, Dave. But perhaps not. She'd decide on impulse.

58

ANNE was in the club bar when a man who had spoken to her and her friend Sophie on a previous occasion approached her table. He was carrying a glass.

"Good evening. Do you mind if I join you? I believe I saw you here with a friend some weeks ago."

"Yes, that's right. I remember. Please, sit down."

"Drink? Club champagne?"

"Thank you. That would be good. But who are you?"

He held out his hand. "I'm Colonel Voysey." His navy blazer and grey slacks were classic smart casual attire. His white shirt was a good backing for his club tie of dark- and light-blue silk. As she shook his hand, Anne noticed he was wearing the somewhat bulky club cufflinks.

"My name is Anne Crevennes. I'm just back from Canada."

"Oh, Quebec?" he asked and then turned and ordered her champagne.

"I've been there but no, I'm French."

"Oh yes, I remember. Whereabouts in France?" He took a sip of his scotch.

"I live mostly in the Midi. And you, Colonel?" Anne wondered if he had been in Afghanistan. He was tanned. She finished the last of an excellent gin and tonic as the colonel fetched her champagne from the bar.

"I'm from Bournemouth originally," he said, placing her champagne glass on the table, "but I have to go where the army sends me. When in London though, I always try to get some time in at the club." He swirled the ice in his drink.

"I agree. I'm not a member, but my club in France has reciprocal rights. I prefer the Oxbridge to other London clubs I've visited."

Anne sat back and studied him. He was obviously fit and strong, and he had an easy confidence. Perhaps he had fought in battles. Or perhaps now he had a desk job. Dinner together? She could ask him about the terror campaign being forged mainly in France among the European countries. How old was he?

"I remember! I think last time I met you, the Interallié was your club in Paris."

"That's true. You have a good memory, Colonel."

"How could I forget, having met you here in this bar?" He smiled. Anne looked at him with an air that was both shrewd and amused.

"I don't want to intrude on your evening," he remarked, "but why don't we dine together? Or are you meeting someone?"

"No. If you're going to dine here, let's dine together."

"Splendid." He looked at her glass. It was half empty. "Do you want another?" He picked up his empty glass.

"No thanks. But go ahead if you want another drink. We can chat. Do call me Anne."

He looked at the small amount of melting ice in his glass. "Hmm. Anne, let's go into the Coffee Room and have dinner. I'm Alex."

As they left the bar and made for the Coffee Room, they glanced at the stairs that led up from the entrance. At the reception desk, a strikingly beautiful young woman who might have been in her mid to late twenties was checking in. She was a light-brown colour. Her long black hair was in a single plait hanging over one shoulder.

The colonel did a double-take and then quickly turned to look at the dinner menu posted at the entrance to the Coffee Room.

"What a beautiful young woman checking in downstairs," Anne remarked.

"Yes, indeed. They weren't like that when I was at Oxford. Ah, I see there's a roast beef trolley."

They went in and took a table for two placed against a wall under a huge portrait of a distinguished person from the Victorian age. A waiter appeared with menus, wine lists, and the slip one had to fill in and sign with any order for a meal or drink. Anne took a ballpoint pen out of her bag.

"Oh, let me do it," Colonel Voysey urged.

"That's kind but no. We French are experts at paperwork. It's in our culture! But let's go Dutch." The colonel smiled and held up his hands as if she were holding a pistol.

As they occupied themselves with the culinary paperwork, the beautiful young woman walked in and took a table for one farther down the room. She looked across at Anne and Colonel Voysey, did a double-take, and then hastily searched in her bag for a pen.

"Wine? Could we share a carafe?" Anne asked.

"Yes, let's. I'm having beef after the soup of the day. You?"

"The same. When I'm in rosbifland, I always have roast beef, at least once. Let's have club claret. I found it good for the price last time I had it."

And so the meal progressed. The colonel confirmed what Anne already knew: the British and French armed forces did a certain number of training exercises together and were serious about cooperation in the struggle against terrorists. The antagonism between France and England was largely a journalists' game now, sparking abusive remarks among the ignoramus clients in some of the English pubs and French cafés and bars.

Alex assured Anne that Muslim terrorists were the real enemies of all European countries and of North America. He found it appalling that young people born into democracies should convert and become radicals raging for blood. Anne thought that most of these militant converts didn't realize what they were letting themselves in for. The politicians, as usual, were slow to react, counting the political implications as more important than immediate action. Alex did not comment on this. He nodded, as if thinking over her remarks.

The young beauty left before they did. They had passed on dessert, but both had a post-prandial port.

"Nightcap, Anne?"

"It's good of you to ask. But no. Are you here tomorrow, Alex?"

"'Fraid I have meetings all day, but unless something pressing crops up, perhaps, er... we might dine together again?"

"I'd love that."

"So, goodnight, Anne. Sleep well. I'll have a brandy before I turn in." They left the Coffee Room together.

"Goodnight, Alex. Perhaps tomorrow then. I'll be in the bar about seven." She went to the elevator.

Alex went into the bar and saw the fabulous young "frog lady" sitting alone at the table where Anne had been sitting.

He ordered a sparkling water and took it over to her table.

"May I join you?"

"Yes, do, it's good to see you again." Kim looked up at him.

Oh god, she's a knockout. I wonder? He let the thought hang in his mind. He looked at the portrait of Clement Attlee hanging on the wall above the bartender's head. *How could that man look so commonplace and this woman look so perfect?*

"It's lovely to see you again. You're as brave and accomplished as you are beautiful. Another drink?"

"No thanks, I have to turn in soon. I must leave quite early."

"Call me Alex," the colonel said. "Are you a member of the club?"

"Actually, I am. I was at Cambridge. Call me Alissa."

Suddenly, she reached across and took his hand. "You were wonderful to work with. I was afraid all the logistics might have glitches."

"Well, we were lucky. I think you're brilliant. In fact, I've thought about 'Kim' quite a bit. I was hoping for another joint op."

"I think we are all relieved that nothing that big is going down right now." He nodded.

"I hear you've had the big bag of rotten eggs over the Channel."

She nodded. She wanted to see him as a man, a person. He was an intrepid and professional operative, but he was also an attractive man. *Who was the woman he had dined with?*

"Do you want to chat a bit more, Alex? I mean elsewhere."

"That would be good."

"Tell me your room number. I'll be there in fifteen minutes."

She got up and left. He stood as she left and then sat to finish his drink. He looked at his watch. *What an evening. I'm not a lonely old sod. After all, a chat with this incredible woman will be a gift from the gods. What if there's more?*

He left some of the fizzy water and went quickly to his room. *Be prepared!* Perhaps old Baden-Powell was a great scout who knew a thing or two.

***

Anne was already in bed. She had read the booklet about what was on in London. Tomorrow she would take her time enjoying the city and some of its many attractions. She was nearly asleep. *Perhaps she should have invited him to . . . well, there was dinner with him tomorrow . . . perhaps a brief encounter . . .* Anne fell asleep.

Not so Alissa. She had prepared, using some of her favourite Guerlain perfume. She walked along the slightly creaking corridor, went up three steps, along a short corridor, down six steps, and found the room with the number that Solihull, a.k.a. Alex, had given her. She tapped on his door. It opened almost immediately.

"Come in. I'm glad you could make it." He closed the door after her. The room had a double bed.

"Do you always book a double room when you're here alone, Solihull?" she asked using the code name he had used when they had worked together against terrorists in Birmingham. He chuckled. He liked her calling him that.

"Actually, no. The club is pretty full, and when I checked in, they'd run out of singles, so they gave me a double at the single room price."

"The gods smile on you." She walked into his arms. He held her close, feeling her body fit next to his so willingly. They kissed with chaste little kisses and then with eager abandon. Soon they had undressed each other and lay together on the bed.

"I've been under pressure in Paris. I . . . well, I need you, even if it's just this once."

"I've needed you ever since we worked together, Alissa." He was a handsome man, probably about forty. She noticed a scar on his left arm near the shoulder.

"Are you married?"

He shook his head. "I was once. The divorce came through ten years ago. Youthful mistake. What about you?"

She climbed on top of him, knees on either side of his ribs, and kissed his forehead. "Never married. Therefore, never divorced. Have you got condoms?"

"Under the pillow on your left."

"You're ready for action."

"Yes. Oh, yes."

They made love with an assurance that gave them both a great deal of pleasure. They didn't speak. They both needed the immense relief.

Afterwards they lay holding each other and kissing.

"How did you get that scar?"

"I was silly," he said ruefully. "I put my arm up to show my men to move forward. I put it up too high or for too long and was hit by an enemy bullet. Luckily, it missed the bone and major blood vessels. A little flesh wound, that's all."

"Well, that was bad luck. Pity I wasn't there to kiss it better. But here we are, and I have a better idea." They explored each other tenderly.

"I've never made love to a woman as beautiful as you, Alissa. I shall never forget this night, even if we never meet again."

"I shall never forget it either, Alex. You're a handsome brute, you Solihull man!" she laughed. "That sounded funny, calling you by that code name."

"Well, I know you only as Agent Kim."

"For tonight I'm Kalitza. Shall I try to 'decrypt' you again?"

"Yes, I have to leave early tomorrow. So, I can't see you at breakfast. Yes, I want you again."

They made love, taking longer this time. That didn't bother them at all.

Alissa Partridge, schoolteacher and French secret agent, codenamed Kim and on rare occasions Kalitza, went back to her room at three in the morning. She lay in her single bed and gave a big yawn. She sighed, thinking of Hervé, and wondered if he were with a woman in Paris. She smiled, dismissing the thought, and fell into a deep, dreamless sleep.

Alexander Voysey, a British colonel, codename Solihull, in his double bed, was asleep, deeply contented. He murmured "Alissa" once, then in a sleepy voice, "Kalitza," as he went willingly to the brink of contented sleep.

59

CONTROL had just received a brilliant lightweight device from R&D that was harmless in ignorant hands but lethal when used by an agent who knew its secret. It was something for Kim when she returned to Paris.

Control pressed a panel in the mahogany-clad wall behind his desk. The panel slid aside to reveal a matte grey metal door. It was a Solon Company safe, a one-off from the Paris firm prized for its expertise. Control's father had bought a safe from that family business. Control's safe was not only difficult to open but even more difficult to remove from its concrete surround. In addition, Control's room was bomb and earthquake proof. Its secrets were too sensitive to be lost.

Control spun the sunken dial in the centre of the safe's door to a combination only he knew. A small portion of the edge of the door slid aside, revealing a keyhole similar to the kind used in a bank's safety deposit boxes. Control inserted his slender ten-centimetre-long key into the keyhole and turned it clockwise twice. The door swung open silently. Control placed the new gadget for Kim's use in the safe and closed it. He went back to his desk to continue looking through some top-secret reports.

His phone rang at noon, 11:00 a.m. in London. He hastily pressed his secure line button.

"This is Solihull. She's in great shape."

"Many thanks, mon ami."

"Our minder saw no followers or pirates anywhere near her. She took an express to Carlyle."

"Anything else?"

"I had dinner with a French woman I met in the O and C Club. I saw our girl dining alone in the club yesterday evening."

"Aha. You alerted your people as we arranged?"

"Absolutely."

"Who's this other French woman?"

"Anne Crevennes. We researched her. She's actually *de* Crevennes."

"Ah, a distinguished historian from one of our noble families. She's okay. Clean."

"Kosher in fact."

"Oui. Merci, mon ami."

"De rien. Out."

Control smiled. Good old Solihull. Kim was fine. However, her problems would return as soon as she got back to Paris. She might well need his new box of tricks, as would Miranda. He'd get another of the gadgets sent up.

***

Mary was back home and had just gone through her personal mail. A flyer promoted an American supermarket product. Paul scanned the evening paper. The silence was broken by the phone.

"Jello!I mean hello," Mary said. "Sorry, I was thinking of something else."

"Hello, Mary," Anne said, laughing. "It's me. Just ringing to say I catch the train for Birmingham tomorrow morning. Then I'll catch one to Sutton Coldfield."

"Look, Paul has to be in Birmingham tomorrow. Will you get into New Street?"

"That's it."

The two friends arranged for Paul to meet Anne at New Street station and drive her to the hotel they had booked for her not far from them in Sutton Coldfield. Paul was looking forward to seeing Anne again.

"So, what's good in London just now?"

"I saw a splendid exhibition of Turner and, of course, I've spent time in the British Library. I have a reader's card."

"Where are you staying?"

"At the O and C Club in Pall Mall. It's so convenient, central, and I love it."

"Are you seeing a play tonight?"

"No. In fact, I'm joining a British colonel for dinner."

"Sounds clubissimo to me!"

"Absolutely. I had dinner with him last night, and we got along so well, we decided to repeat the experience."

"Parfait, Anne. You must tell us everything tomorrow."

"D'accord. I will. I must go to prepare for the evening."

"Well, now!" Mary announced, as she went over to tell the latest to Paul. "Anne is breaking out of her academic mould, it seems."

At precisely that moment, Anne walked to the Corby trouser press and took from it her beautifully tailored dark-blue pants. She had a light-blue silk blouse. She slipped into it, covering the snug cream-coloured bra that enclosed and lifted her delightful breasts. Her only jewellery would be small diamond clip earrings and her diamond solitaire set in white gold, apart from the small signet ring bearing her family crest.

She looked in the long mirror inside the closet door, slipped on some navy-blue shoes, put on rose-bleu lipstick, and sprayed a little perfume. She smiled at herself, her head tilted slightly to one side. *I'll do*, she thought. She collected her bag and room key and made for the elevator. She was looking forward to a flute of club champagne.

Colonel Voysey, tanned, fit, and smartly dressed in a houndstooth suit with a light-blue shirt and his regimental tie, was already in the bar at a table for two. He had no drink but was reading a copy of the *Guardian* fitted to a long wooden handle. As Anne walked in, he spotted her and was on his feet, smiling broadly.

"Anne, you look wonderful," he said, taking her hand to somewhere near his lips but not actually kissing it. "A drink? Let me."

"Thank you, mon colonel, I'll have a club champagne."

"Excellent. I'll have the same." He motioned her to a chair at the table and went off to the bar. He soon returned with their flutes of golden sparkles with mounting bubbles.

"To the club and its wonderful French visitors!"

Anne wondered at his use of the plural. *Ah, his military friends perhaps. Or did he remember her with her friend?*

They chatted for about half an hour and then decamped to the Coffee Room for dinner. It was busier than it had been the previous night. The club table in the centre of the room was almost full. Again they went Dutch, filling in the culinary clerking caper. Alex ordered a dozen Scottish oysters and followed them up with Dover sole off the bone. Anne thought it a perfect choice and ordered almost the same, though : she ordered only six oysters and preferred hers cooked. The colonel bought a half bottle of a delicious Chablis, which they shared. They passed again on dessert and this time on port as well. Anne came from a long line of warrior nobles serving kings in the *ancien régime*. She was as courageous as any of her ancestors. She felt comfortable with this modern military man.

"Are you married, Alex?" She looked into his pale blue eyes.

"No. I divorced years ago. I was pig-headed enough to marry too young. You?"

"Unmarried. But I'd like you to come to my room." She smiled and made a slight kissing motion with her lips.

"Wonderful. I'd be delighted. But are you in one of those single rooms with a monk-like bed?"

"Yes. But I have a Corby trouser press."

"Now that's standard issue. Why don't you come to my double room? When I booked they had run out of singles."

"Lucky man. What number?"

He told her.

"I'll be there in twenty minutes," she said, looking at her watch. It was 9:00p.m. "Let's have an early night!" With that she got up, and the colonel followed her out of the room. Nobody paid any attention to them. The other diners were all deep in conversation, either serious or hilarious.

As she walked to Alex's room, Anne felt a stirring of sexual desire she had not felt for a long time; she was delighted to see the double bed. Alex was already in a bathrobe. They kissed, and he undressed her slowly, kissing her shoulders and arms as he did.

"Anne, you are a beautiful woman, and you have a marvellous tan. All over."

"I have a place in the south of France. My balcony and my private pool are perfect for sunning oneself. But your stomach and er . . . elsewhere . . . are white where you wear a bathing trunk."

"Trunks," Alex said. Anne reached for his white flesh. Their lovemaking lasted for a couple of blissful hours. They got to know each other in great detail, and each liked what they learned. Anne explained that she had to catch an early train to see some friends in Sutton Coldfield. She gave him her card. Alex, still naked, took a card from his wallet, telling her that anything sent to the address would reach him quickly. Phoning would not work. His phone number was not on the card. They arranged that when he had a leave, she would love to see him in France. Anne dressed to go back to her own room.

"Could we sunbathe there together? Naked?"

"Certainly," Anne said, "But only in warm weather." She kissed him once more on the lips, on his nose, and then elsewhere. The door closed quietly, and she was gone.

Solihull, known in the club and to Anne as Colonel Alexander Voysey, went to the shower. He liked Anne a lot. She was a total adult with a scholar's instinct for hunting out the truth. It was similar to his own hunter's instinct. Yes, he must see her again. Neither had pressured the other. Alissa was more beautiful physically and fit, but she was a young woman still and self-willed. A killer, yes. Well, he was too. Yet as he put on his pyjama trousers, he remembered the warm tenderness of Anne's breasts as he held them and kissed the nape of her neck. Her tan was natural and attractive. She was the woman he had to see again. Soon. He must check on his leave entitlement. How old or young was she? They were most likely about the same age.

60

"**JACK,** I can get away on Friday for that weekend trip to Mary's. What are your commitments? Still free?" Maggie was on her cell phone. Jack scanned the large sheet on the office wall. It was a monthly schedule of private flights booked usually by businesspeople. There was nothing as yet for the weekend. They always had to confirm things in case there had been last-minute changes for Maggie or Jack.

"Maggie, darling, all seems good. I'll check the meteo and, barring filthy weather, we can fly down. If the weather's too dicey for small planes, we'll go by train."

As things worked out, they were able to fly and then rent a car. On thinking over the accommodation situation, Maggie and Jack decided to book in at the Royal on High Street. It seemed the logical and most convenient thing to do. Anne had come to the same decision. Both friends had phoned Mary to say where they were staying. Mary decided not to say the three of them would be in the same hotel. Let them have the fun of a nice surprise. Paul would collect Anne while Maggie and Jack would hire a car. Mary was actually relieved not to have houseguests because she didn't know if she'd be needed for an emergency. Such an eventuality couldn't be ruled out. It happened from time to time.

On Friday, when Paul was helping Anne with her bag, they saw Maggie and Jack at the reception desk. Paul put his finger to his lips, so Anne and he could wait behind the other two as they filled in a form and got their room key.

"Good morning, sir. I won't be a second." The receptionist had looked up and seen Paul standing behind Maggie. Jack and Maggie looked behind them and burst out laughing.

"Well, fancy meeting you two here!" Paul said.

"It's a small world," Anne replied. "We were hoping we wouldn't be noticed!"

Maggie took the room key from the receptionist and turned to her friends. "We *had* heard that Sutton Coldfield was the sexiest little town in Britain, but we didn't expect this!" They all laughed and chatted merrily. Then Anne checked in, showing her French passport, just in case.

"Anne, can you join us for lunch?" Jack asked. She nodded, smiling. He turned to Paul. "Can you and Mary join us too?"

"I'll call Liz to find out what's on Mary's agenda today. Should be okay though." Paul walked away to near the large window and took out his cell phone.

Mary said she could join them at 1:00p.m. Delighted, they booked a table for five for lunch and chatted a little longer before the guests went to settle into their rooms. Paul went home to do a bit more preparation on the side dishes for the big curry Mary had already prepared for the evening meal.

The lunch at the Royal turned out to be animated and at times hilarious. But Mary and Maggie were also able to exchange bits of medical news. Maggie was intrigued and a little concerned when she heard about the lung problem Mary's patient had. Anne told them about her rounds of the galleries in London. She even mentioned that she had met a rather gallant English colonel in the club. Paul asked about her Canadian research. She revealed that she had covered a lot of ground, making enough progress to have some material to write up already.

"I was sorry to hear the bad news about Graham," she said quietly to Paul as they were all leaving the table.

He nodded. "It's sad. But I can understand his anger. For me though, the rule of law is better than revenge."

"I agree, Paul. However, I think that if people like those murderers aren't punished sufficiently for brutal crimes, the authorities are, in effect, encouraging acts of revenge."

Paul nodded. "And that weakens the entire idea of the rule of law."

"True. It's a matter of balance to achieve justice. As an historian I know how recent the rights are that we now depend upon. They can easily be lost. I felt so sorry for Graham when I last saw him."

"Yes. He was a good friend when we were young. But when Jackie was murdered, he just went to pieces. He wasn't the same Graham I once knew."

Anne looked down. "Oh, I left my bag under the table," she said, walking over to retrieve it.

BRUNO'S SECRET

✳✳✳

Alissa was back at Tomkyn Bridge School and had settled into her rooms. Miss Mason, she had discovered, was on holiday. She took a bath and as she was drying herself wondered if Brian might be free for dinner or lunch the next day. She dressed in black linen summer pants with a light rose-coloured loose-knit sweater. Going to her desk, she phoned Brian. He was pleased to hear she was back. She heard it in his voice as well as his words.

"I was wondering about dinner together tonight," Brian said. "Are you free?"

"Certainly. Can we go into St. Bees?"

"Of course." He was eager to please. "I can pick you up at the school and deliver you back."

"Brilliant, as my sixth-formers say."

"Awesome, as my students say. I'll reserve a table. What time shall I come to the school?"

They settled on seven o'clock. Alissa calculated that, with luck, she could be in bed at about ten or eleven. She'd sleep in a bit the next morning.

Elated by her return, Brian was five minutes early, but Alissa was ready. She had walked down to the main gate in the mild evening air.

Later on, in the snug little area at a corner of the restaurant, Brian reached across and took hold of Alissa's hand. She didn't withdraw it straight away. Yet she envisaged Solihull looking into her eyes as they made love. As she looked at Brian, she wondered what life with him might be like. Too quiet and settled perhaps. He had to paint. She spotted a fleck of yellow paint on one of his fingernails. It reminded her of the smell of freshly mixed oil paint in his studio. She was not in love. She withdrew her hand, and they both arranged the white dinner napkins over their knees.

"So, what takes you away again so soon, Alissa?"

"Well, spending one's days and nights with the girls of Tomkyn Bridge is a lot of work. To spend all my holidays here as well would be a form of masochism!"

"We could do a lot of trips around here and to the lakes. We could nip up to Scotland."

"Yes, we could, but you would have to paint. It's during the school holidays that you can forge ahead. Besides, I have things I want to do with family and friends."

"Let's look at the menu. Since I'm driving, I'll just have one glass of wine. I have more at home if we want a drink later at my place."

It was a rather stiff, almost inhibited start to the evening. She answered Brian's questions about her family with little fictions. It was part of her training. Brian had an agenda for later on, but she was tired. She was looking forward to bed, a deep sleep without a partner. She realized that since she had been tracked there by Bruno, she could be tracked and watched again. But she had noticed nothing unusual. In any case, she would be back in London soon and then Paris. She and Hervé were hoping to recapture Bruno and smash any cells he might have had time to set up since his escape. She felt sure Bruno would be hiding somewhere in the greater Paris area. She felt suddenly close to Hervé. She wanted to be near him again in Paris. She had enjoyed her time with Solihull. She had no real urgency for an adventure with Brian, but Hervé was a magnet for her.

"I want to show you something," Brian said, interrupting her thoughts. "We could go to my place for a noggin."

"Brian, I've had a long journey. Let's meet again tomorrow. I can hike up to your cottage and see what you've been painting or drawing. I can buy us lunch."

"Oh, well, let's play it that way then," he replied with a small, quick smile.

Throughout the meal, their conversation was somewhat stilted. She was tired, and he seemed a bit hurt that she did not want to rush to the studio to see his latest work.

"How's your leg, Brian? I noticed you have a slight limp."

"Ha. I wondered when you were going to get 'round to that! In fact, I don't think about it anymore. My doctor thinks my limp will disappear in a few more weeks."

"That's good news. I wonder if the culprit might get arrested."

"I doubt that. The 'plod' around here don't seem concerned about small burglaries, especially art theft! In fact, when I realized he'd taken that sketch, I wondered if at last I was being taken seriously as an artist." He smiled ruefully.

After the meal, Brian attempted once again to persuade Alissa to go to his place instead of straight back to the school.

"No, Brian. If you want to show me some of your latest work, I can arrive sometime after eleven and give you lunch."

When they arrived at the school, he obviously wanted a kiss. She kissed his cheek, then opened her door and got out. She waved. As Brian drove away, Alissa recalled her night with Solihull. It had been a wonderful release for them both. However, it had been a one-night stand. Her real future was with Control. She thought of him now as *her Hervé*.

***

Thanks to another small prayer room frequented by a radicalized youth, Bruno had found yet another hiding place. Although he could show no clear photo of Kim to his people, he had described her carefully. No trace of her. Bruno decided it was worth watching out for Eurostar passengers at the Gare du Nord. He wanted to be there to see for himself if she came loping along from first class, probably on those strong legs that had once clamped on his neck during a training workout. He would have to be in a wheelchair with an armed attendant wheeling him along. Yes, a young man dressed as a woman. Perhaps he should also dress as a woman. But he would be old. An old woman who was anything but an old woman! Bruno smiled grimly. "Her" robes and a thick rug could conceal considerable firepower and a trusty knife. Agent Kim must be eliminated. This was the way. But he could not welcome every Eurostar train for the next few weeks! He would also deal with that American and his blond bit on the side. He would take a satisfying personal revenge, for Kim had almost blinded him. Now one eye was almost sightless. Yet if he went to any hospital for treatment, he would be putting himself in danger. He was still hoping for a visit from a Muslim doctor who could be trusted. He had to see Kim again, when she would be, of course, dying. He had to see that before his own sight failed.

A savage rage took hold of him, and he tasted bile at the back of his throat, but he swallowed. He kept his anger locked inside. A rapid clenching and unclenching of his fists was the only sign of what he was feeling. A fanatic, he was as cunning as he was tenacious, as tenacious as he was ruthless, and so single-minded now as to be, well, mad. His mood swings were as pronounced as Hitler's. Luckily for Control, he lacked that dictator's "clarity of vision," as "Quex" Sinclair had put it in his description of Hitler. Bruno also lacked Hitler's military resources and highly organized terror.

61

ALISSA knocked on the cottage door. She heard some sheep bleating in the distance. It was a cloudy day, but there was little wind and no rain. She had enjoyed her fast hike up from the school.

"Come in! It's open!"

She went in to find Brian painting at an easel. He looked 'round at her. She detected the faint smell of oil paint.

"Your burglary and knife attack don't seem to have made you more security conscious, Brian."

"Well, I think nobody will want to burgle this workshop and attack me again. They probably realized my work won't make them rich." He sighed as he put down his brush.

"What's that you're doing?" Alissa, thinking as Agent Kim, was alarmed.

"Oh, I'm painting your portrait from memory."

"But I said no pictures of my face!" It was a mistake to have met a painter who was now obsessed with her and able to paint her from memory.

"Yes, on a nude sketch. But this is just a portrait."

"You don't have my permission. You must alter it or scrape it off." She sounded sharp and impatient.

"What? Why?" he asked, incredulous.

"Because I say so. It's my face, isn't it?"

"But I'm a painter. I need to paint it, Alissa."

"Yes, but it's my face, and I have a greater right to it and to my privacy."

"You're cruel. Why?" he snapped. "I need to paint you."

"No, Brian. Not me. Hire a model. Get a commission to paint famous people or, failing that, the mayor of St. Bees." Her last words had been unfair. It was a put-down for an artist with Brian's talent.

"Please, Alissa."

"I'm not going to allow my portrait to be made. Let me see you scrape and paint over or dissolve it. Whatever you have to do."

He shrugged, uttered a heavy sigh, and did what she had ordered. Alissa thanked him and then left. He came to the door and waved as she walked away. She did not glance back.

I'm walking out of his life, she thought. *Why did I ever get involved*?

She went back to her rooms at the school and started to read. But her problem and her future came back. Her one-night stand with Solihull had been a wonderful release. But that was it. She had wanted him just that once. No more. Could she make a real life with someone, like Hervé behind the cruel deceptions of a continuing war? She abandoned the book, a Pierre Loti novel she was preparing for the September term. Life back in Paris working with Control was pulling her away from her life as a teacher. The small community had been a refuge, but it had also been a danger. *If you want to hide, hide in a huge city*, she thought. It was a truism. But it was so. She decided to pack up all her personal things and return to Paris. If she decided to stay in France, she would send in a letter of resignation to Miss Mason.

***

Bruno could not comb Paris for Kim or the blonde with the American because there was obviously an alert and people trying to recapture him. Meanwhile, he was free to lie low and set about making efficient terrorists out of the more than four thousand radicalized French Muslims. Bruno realized they had much to learn, and he had much to teach them. All the same, he wanted to settle accounts with the two troublesome women. Disguised as an old man in a wheelchair pushed by young men or women, he could still go to places where the women or the American could be found. The American would be around the American embassy or going down to see the British. The streets around and connecting the two embassies would be a good start. Mornings between nine and eleven might produce results. *Lucky numbers*, he thought, chuckling to himself. He would need a woman who would be the wife pushing his chair. A son and daughter would also be useful. They could follow the American to see where he went and whether he met the blond woman.

After six days of this procedure, Bruno struck it lucky.

"That man in front of us who just came out of Hermès is the one I'm looking for. He's dangerous."

"The one in the light-grey suit?" Bruno's "son" asked.

"Yes. I need you and your 'sister' to follow him. See where he goes, and then find a discreet place to keep him in sight if you can, but you must phone me to tell me where he is. Call me papa. Don't mention the man. Just tell me where you are."

The two young people hugged the woman, their '*maman*,' and then followed the American, taking opposite sides of the road. They kept their distance.

Forty minutes later a cell phone rang under Bruno's blanket. The woman took it and answered."Allo! Oui." She listened and then handed the phone to Bruno. "The children are in a restaurant called Le Nevers."

"Where's our friend?" Bruno demanded. He listened attentively."Well, buy me three tickets too. Let me know if you can get them for the same night as our friend." He closed the phone."Push me to La Comédie Française," he said to his 'wife.'

About fifteen minutes later the phone rang again. This time the 'daughter' informed Bruno that the American had joined the queue for a performance that night. At the box office she had managed to get three tickets: two regular seats and a *strapontin* or fold-up seat next to them.

"Where's your brother?" Bruno asked.

"Oh, he's gone off with our friend. He'll be in touch."

"Good," Bruno said. "Try to catch them up." He closed the phone."Push me to the Louvre," he ordered, and the woman gladly obeyed. He seemed to be in a good mood, even though his eyes were so bad that he had to wear sunglasses all the time.

Bruno hoped the American was taking his blonde to the play. Now he needed to decide how best to assassinate them. Inside the theatre or outside? Before, during, or after the play?

***

Maggie looked at some of the books in Jack's sitting room bookcase. They were back from their trip to see Mary and Paul. It had been fun to see Anne again, fresh back from Canada.

"Jack, this looks interesting. It's an old guidebook to Scotland."

"That'll be Black's guide. It's been in my family since one of them bought it, before the First World War!"

"It has good illustrations of the scenery."

"Maggie, you've just uncovered a grand part of my little plan for us."

"What plan?" she asked, all curiosity and hope.

"What do you think about looking into Black for a route or several routes across the country?"

"Fun."

"Even more fun if we fly along those routes and see what has remained the same and what has developed since."

"Oh, yes. When can we do that?" Maggie was eager to start.

They decided to check on their free time and pencil in days when such trips might be possible. Jack was enthusiastic about it and promised to consult meteo forecasts and reports for their getaway days. Maggie felt again that marrying a pilot who ran a small business was a stroke of luck.

Jack took her in his arms. "You're very precious to me," he whispered.

"I feel the same," she said, kissing him. "We get on so well together."

"I think we should marry," Jack replied.

Mary grinned. "I *know* we should marry."

"What a good job I proposed, and you accepted." Jack smiled. "In my diary I have a list of things to do. Top of the list is 'Propose marriage to Maggie.' I ticked it the day after I proposed."

"How efficient. I have a to-do list as well. It has an item called 'accept repeated proposals of marriage'!"

"Hey, how did you know I was going to propose again?"

"A woman always knows, Jack. Anyway, I didn't add your name. It was open. Someone else could easily have proposed."

Jack laughed. "Well, Maggie, what a good job I got in first. I bet there's a queue out there."

"I wouldn't say that, darling, but there are one or two work prospects in white lab coats. I wouldn't bet on them though because they tend to have a slight scent of chemical products!"

"Come here, Maggie angel. You're wearing Coco by Chanel. What else are you wearing?"

"You'll have to find that out for yourself."

BRUNO'S SECRET

***

Harry left the US embassy and walked toward the Place de la Concorde. He skirted the Crillon and the old Admiralty HQ to walk along the rue de Rivoli. He looked in shop windows, stopped as if intrigued by something, and made to cross the street to go into the Tuileries gardens. Then he changed his mind and slipped down a side street on his left. He would make his way in a leisurely fashion to the Palais Royal and the theatre. He had arranged to meet Miranda in Le Nevers, a bistro he knew well.

In the doorway of an empty shop awaiting a new tenant with new hopes for success, Harry stopped, looked around, and put his secure phone to his lips.

"Hunting Gold," he said. There was a click.

"Panther. I hear you," came the reply.

"I see something we can bank on. We can sell a lot of product."

"You're hunting gold as always!"

"Got it. See you around." Harry closed the line and pocketed his phone.

It had taken him, as a man known in the criminal network as 'Hunting Gold,' almost a year to set up an operation for supplying small arms and varying amounts of explosives to a number of people in Paris and Marseilles. Another American agent known to the criminal clients as Panther worked with him. Panther was from a family of Iraqi immigrants. He and Harry would meet later near the embassy to make the necessary arrangements. The arms deal was a simple lure. When buyers came out of the woodwork, they could be arrested.

Harry had noticed the wheelchair and Bruno's assistants. He knew he had been followed when he bought his tickets for the play. And there was the old man in the wheelchair again. He obviously liked the great courtyards of the Louvre. Harry followed.

Soon they emerged from the Napoleon courtyard into the road alongside, Harry hanging back in the shadows of the grand entrance with its "N" mounted above in stone. There was a line of taxis, but Bruno and his followers waited. After a few minutes, a black Ford wagon drew up. Its sliding door opened. A steel shelf slid out and lowered for the wheelchair.

Someone inside the van asked, "Where's the old woman?" Bruno shook his head and said "Change of plan. Behold, old man!"

Harry sidled across the sidewalk to the queue of taxis and walked to the driver's side of a cab. He reached the first in the line and got into the rear seat.

Nobody but the cab driver had noticed him. He sat back and wrote down the licence plate on the black Ford van some yards ahead.

"Wait a minute, I just want to check my cash," Harry said, pulling out a billfold. The van was signalling to pull out."Oh, no problem," Harry said. "Just follow the Ford van ahead of us. I have to do business with the man in the wheelchair."

The driver nodded. "American?" he asked. "I notice you have just a bit of an accent."

"Yes, once upon a time. Now I suppose I'm more French than anything else. Where are you from?"

"I was born in France, but my parents are from Egypt originally."

Their conversation started to explore the wonders of ancient Egypt and then the holidays the driver and his family took every two years back in their old village, where they still had a few relatives.

The van ahead of them turned into a side street not far from the Gare Montparnasse. It entered a one-way street and stopped in a parking space outside a building. There were no other gaps in the rows of parked cars.

"Go on ahead," Harry said."I'll walk back to them when I've made a call. Women, you know?" They both grinned.

Harry paid, and the taxi disappeared. When he got to the corner of the street, Bruno and his party were going into a modern-looking apartment block. Harry blinked at the street's name plate. He crossed the road to the opposite corner and looked back at the building, which could be Bruno's new hideout for a few days. He blinked and then went down another street. There was a small cluster of shops at the end and a café on the corner at the far end. Harry walked on and blinked at the café. Turning into a larger street, he noticed a taxi stand. A couple of cabs were waiting. A woman with a miniature poodle arrived just before him and took the first cab. Harry took the second one.

"Comédie Française," he said.

A few minutes later as he walked into the Nevers bistro, he saw Miranda looking at her watch.

"Hey!" he said as he sat down beside her.

"Hey," she replied. "You're late. Where have you been?"

"I had a stroke of luck. I saw Bruno and his gremlins. I have the address of his latest hidey-hole."

328

"Wow! You're not late. You're not sheepish. In fact, you're bright-eyed and bushy-tailed. Give me the address, and I'll phone Control. In fact, I'd call you Prince Harry if there wasn't one already."

"You can call me Prince Harry anytime you like, babe, if that turns you on!"

A waiter approached to ask if Harry wanted anything, but Miranda paid him for her cappuccino, and they left.

Once outside she relayed Bruno's latest address to Control. Then she took Harry's arm and suggested they find a good place where they could share information of an intimate kind for the mutual benefit of their countries.

62

CONTROL was delighted to learn Bruno's latest address. The building near the Gare Montparnasse was now under surveillance. A tracking device had also been placed under the Ford van. Harry and Panther were putting out feelers for people wanting powerful explosives and military weapons in a hurry. Control hoped the Americans could arrange to be in the bidding to sell when the call came. They would ask far too much and so lose the bid, but they would know exactly what the terrorists wanted to buy. From this information it would be possible to deduce what kind of operation was being planned. Miranda was an extremely useful operative when it came to cooperation with Uncle Sam's people under the radar in Paris.

"Well, Miranda, what's your latest?" Control asked as he sipped his coffee. Miranda put her cup down rather carefully. He always used expensive china for his coffee.

"Since we know where Bruno is for the next few days, I suggest we tap *all* phone lines from his building. There's a café nearby. It's called L'Estaminet de Tonton."

Control said nothing. Both were thinking ahead, like chess players. "Could we watch from there and as soon as we know Bruno is inside his pad, raid and arrest?"

"Oh yes, yet risky. We need him without a firestorm, if possible. But I think we'll win this one. Trust me!" She looked at him. He was so cultivated. He had beautiful casual clothes and impeccable formal ones. He was cunning with charming manners, a deadly opponent of terrorists. He was, after all, Control!

"I think you should contact your good man, Harry, isn't it?" Control continued. "Keep me informed, ma chère, of what can be done."

"I shall, of course. I'll keep closely in touch." They both stood up. Work to be done; they had toget on with it.

"I want you back alive, Miranda. Be extra cautious. Bruno is a devious swine. I'll keep you informed when we find anything from little birds twittering around." He hugged her. She left the inner sanctum without looking back.

Control sat behind his desk. He tapped a pencil on the surface of his leather-framed blotter. He needed Kim again. He had given her too generous a leave. But then he had a special place for her in his feelings. His soul? His heart? Did he love her? Yes. *What is love? What does it mean?* Control asked himself. He knew one thing and shared it with Shakespeare: love is now, "not hereafter." His phone rang. It was Kim.

"I'm in London. I have a strange feeling I should be in Paris."

"You're right. Come."

There is, yes, a soul as well as a mind, Control thought against his will. *There's a god, but he doesn't have an infallible prophet. We serve his will whether we know it or not. Kim and I will prevail! God will help us even if we don't really believe in him.*

He got up and poured himself another cup of coffee. *If we wait a little longer, our net might bring in Bruno and some other big fish.* It was dicey to wait longer, but the right timing could bring in another shark.

63

BRUNO was being wheeled through the Tuileries from the Place de la Concorde. He was silent as he tried to plan for the next week or so. He let his thoughts run over a variety of possibilities. Finally, he considered that from wherever she was hiding, Kim would return to Paris via London on the Eurostar train. But at what hour and on which day?

He decided it was better to watch the area around the old headquarters they had used when working for Control. It was a mansion not far from the Louvre. It was known to them as "Private Dancers." She would definitely go there when she was back. Why waste time at the Gare du Nord patrolled by young soldiers? No. Kim would be sure to check in at the mansion, supposedly a company of sorts.

Bruno sneered with contempt as he whispered the name "Private Dancers" to himself. Yes, Kim would go in and out of there. She often arrived early in the morning on Tuesday, Wednesday, and Friday. There would be few pedestrians on the street then. She could notice suspicious people on those mornings. Mondays and Thursdays were usually 10:00 a.m. days. An ice cream parlour was on the street leading to the mansion. Bruno would be in there with the wheelchair and his "family" on Mondays and Thursdays. The van would be nearby for a quick getaway. He would have to think about the method. Disable and kidnap or a quick kill? The latter was the surer and faster method. He also had to deal with the American and his blond mistress.

Since his resources were limited, Bruno decided on the quick kill for all three of them. Weapon? Silenced pistol, knife, or what? Noise had to be avoided. A father was walking with his son and dog. The boy would be about ten. He carried rather proudly a plastic bow and a small quiver with four plastic arrows. *That's it*, Bruno thought. *I'll have a crossbow with some steel bolts. Silent, fast, lethal.* It would be excellent for killing the American and his blonde that evening near the theatre.

"Kim, you need my cupid's dart," he muttered, clenching and unclenching his hands. His eyes were running. He took out a clean Egyptian cotton handkerchief from under his blanket, removed his sunglasses, and dabbed his eyes. Could he see enough to shoot a bullet or acrossbow bolt? He smiled. One eye was functioning well enough.

"My cupid's dart," he repeated. He would send a man to buy a small crossbow. It could easily be concealed under his blanket in the wheelchair until Kim arrived at the scene of her death. And Control? *That self-satisfied functionary will be heartbroken, if he has a heart.*

He glanced at his watch. He had a meeting with an Iraqi to talk about arms and explosives. They had toget back to the van. Bruno knew what he wanted them for. He could raise enough money from the sleepers who were money men. It all depended on the man called the Lion. He would repay Bruno for the materials needed. His plan demanded five automatic weapons with ammunition. He also needed plenty of Semtex with some fuses. Some hand grenades could also be useful. Nobody but Bruno knew his plan. He would tell his recruits at the last minute. He looked at his watch. He saw the van parked where it should be. Now for the Iraqi whom an associate had contacted in a friendly bistro.

***

Kim loved the bustle of the port, the lines of the ferry boat, the cries of gulls, and the sea air. It was a fine day, and the crossing to France would be a good time to think over the future. The ship's loud blast as it left harbour and edged into deeper water was strangely moving. *Sad farewells with handkerchiefs waving.*

No, not for me, she thought as she walked between the rows of seats. Perhaps she would have a coffee and a bite to eat in the snack bar. No. She could visualize Control, her Hervé, welcoming her back and pushing her straight into another job. Could they live together as man and wife? Could they have children? And could they keep planning together to save their country and the diverse, democratic republican country they both loved? Could she survive marriage, let alone combat against savage fanatics? She knew she could not survive life with Brian on a windswept hill. When children came along, she would probably have to give up teaching for several months, if not years. Years! The bleating of sheep would be ever present, as would the smell of paint. And there would be life with a talented artist who had never been to prison, never murdered anyone, never taken drugs, and never cut off his own ear. Journalists would not be interested in his talent. They wanted sensation. Outrage. They wanted a new movement of some sort led by ascallywag of a painter. Their interest was not the artist but some bizarre concept or social phenomenon thatconnected with the artwork.

Kim realized she still needed a degree of danger and adventure. She liked the uncertainty when she had to face a new and unknown person. She liked the excitement of not knowing how dangerous a new adversary might be. She liked the precision of planning and the mounting excitement of the trap, like a well-oiled mechanism, as it snapped shut on its prey. Their prey. And she enjoyed grim satisfaction when the field agents and later the interrogators outsmarted people who thoughtthey were powerful and superior because they could kill unarmed people who just wanted to live a life. There were no excuses for such arrogant killers.

She remembered her night with Solihull in the London club. He was a professional soldier of high quality. Both of them had needed the release and pleasures of that night. He was a good lover, but they both knew it was a one-off, not a preliminary bout leading to more and a settled routine. She preferred her Hervé, even though they had never made love.

She decided to go to an orchestral concert when she was in Paris. There she would see and hear skilled musicians working together to produce great works of the musical imagination. It was moving and a joy to see how many human beings could work together for harmony rather than destruction. This was intelligence, emotional sanity. *Sometimes music outsmarts murder,* she thought. She could open her senses to the music. She could share its emotion, its passion.

***

"Bonjour, mon frère,"Bruno's associate said, then introduced the Iraqi to Bruno.

"Your name?" Bruno demanded, looking intently at the stranger. They were at the same level, the man sitting at a table and Bruno in his wheelchair.

"Names are unnecessary. I am the Iraqi,and you, monsieur, are the Frenchman. Anything else could make things easier for people we want to avoid."

"Agreed," Bruno declared, holding out his hand. The two men shook.

"What do you need?"

"Can you supply military weapons? Let's say Kalashnikovs with ample ammunition."

"How many?"

"Five?"

"That's no problem. If you need more in a month or so, that will not be a problem either. Anything else?"

"Semtex and fuses as well as, say, a dozen hand grenades."

"I can deliver it to a safe place in two days. A rocket launcher, handheld?"

"Not necessary just now. How much Semtex can you supply?"

"That depends on what you can afford."

They settled on enough explosive to bring down a big, solid building. They haggled over the price just a little because that was the way their culture did business. The Iraqi pointed out that fuses would be necessary and would be an extra expense. Bruno was delighted with the outcome. He had ample funds among the brothers.

"Where do I deliver it?" the Iraqi inquired.

"My associate will contact you in two days with a venue. He'll meet you on the avenue Daumesnil where it joins the Place Félix Eboué. He will drive a Ford van and lead you to a safe place where we can take the material without being interrupted. He'll be with a bodyguard just in case."

"I shall be with a bodyguard too. We can't be too careful." The Iraqi smiled and stood up.

The two men shook hands. The Iraqi sat down again to finish his coffee. Bruno left the bistro. Now he had to perfect his plan. It was simple. The best plans always were.

Back in the Ford van, Bruno beckoned to another young man who had waited on a rear seat. "Follow the Iraqi. I want to know all you can discover about him in the next two days. Don't lose him." The young man nodded, smiled, and got out of the van on the traffic side, where he could not be seen from the bistro. He crossed the road and disappeared.

I can rely on that young man, Bruno thought. *But the Iraqi?* He decided he needed another quote on arms.

***

The Iraqi left the bistro a few minutes later. By a circuitous route he went to an apartment block near the rue Mozart not far from the metro station La Muette. Inside the courtyard was a row of separate lock-up garages that a century ago had been for horses and perhaps a carriage. The arms dealer opened a garage door with an electronic key. A few minutes later, he emerged driving a large dark grey Dodge wagon.

Bruno's young man had watched the dealer drive into the courtyard. Now he had an address. He could not see if the Iraqi was driving the Dodge wagon, but he noted the license plate number. Bruno would have the information by word of mouth within half an hour. *No telephone, no listeners, no compromising any plan,* he thought as he made for the metro.

Bruno was delighted. Within two hours of receiving the new information about the Iraqi, Bruno discovered that the man had arrived in Paris about three weeks earlier and was living in an apartment with garage that was rented to middle- to high-income tourists by the week or the month. It would be a convenient way for him to move in and out of France when conducting some of his deals. It was more discreet than staying in a hotel. This struck Bruno as a clever arrangement. If the Iraqi was in the dark-grey Dodge, perhaps he was already on his way to collect Bruno's order. *Ah, Control, you'll get your comeuppance! I'll take you down a peg or two. Or nine. Or eleven. Twin Towers*! Part of his training would be useful in a day or two. How ironic. Bruno felt like laughing out loud. He remained silent, but he was pleased with his plan. *That's one of my mysteries they will see unfolded soon enough.* But he had other tasks to finish first. Get another arms quote and kill the American and his blond companion at or near the Comédie Française.

He was disappointed the next day, however, because his targets didn't appear outside or inside the theatre. Why had they changed their plans? The play had been a colossal waste of time. Why people crowded into seats that were too small and too close together merely to see people emoting on stage struck Bruno as one of the human idiocies he would never understand. Ballet and opera were much more to his taste. Both had orchestral music,and ballet showed off perfect human forms to great advantage. His only regret about probably having to retreat back to the Arab world was that people, especially women, would have to be covered in robes. Yet in private he would be able to disrobe and abuse as many girls as he desired.

He suppressed the thought and turned to plans for the great uses he would find for his "arsenal." The following day he would be contacted again, this time by the Iraqi and another dealer, a Libyan. He decided to arrange for the delivery near, but not too near, the house he had to move into that same day, just in case Control was about to discover his present quarters. If he were discovered before he could take his revenge on as many members of the French population as possible, he would commit suicide in the middle of as many security people as he could lure and muster. He was confident, deep down, that all would go as he planned. He just had to be prepared for all eventualities.

He considered the wheelchair; it could be a wonderful asset when he struck. The seat would contain explosive material. A space for a parcel under the seat was perfect for a parcel of explosives the men could take with them. The chair could be parked anywhere without much trouble. All his main fighter had to do was be helped out of it and then make sure the battle got started. Three would have to force entry and then blow everything up together with as many people as possible. If they could not escape, they would go down shooting policemen. It was a glorious thought. Bruno's plan demanded different transport for himself and his remaining two men to back him up. One of his men had already rented the transport. It could carry a good deal of Semtex. There were some minor purchases to make.

He went over his plan for two different attacks. Then he drilled the men. All were pleased. It was simple, sure to succeed, and a great death-dealer. *The best aspect of it*, Bruno thought, *was its humiliation of Christian France and indeed of France itself.* His men were going to be delighted. They would discover their precise tasks after prayer and purification on the day itself.

64

IN Sutton Coldfield life was back to normal. Paul and Mary's friends had returned home. Paul knew he needed to be in Paris soon for about ten days.

"Darling, I have an idea," he declared.

"I'm delighted to hear that, Paul. Is it something about god particles or the curve of light when affected by gravity or black being the absence of colour?"

"Not quite, Mary. I'll have to spend about ten days in Paris soon. I was wondering if you could get away for a weekend while I'm there. What do you think?"

"Darling, I have an idea. It's not about quantum physics. More complex really," Mary insisted as she bit Paul's earlobe. "Mmm. Not bad," she added.

"Well?"

"I wonder if Anne would come and meet us?"

"That's a point. Why not call her?"

"Yes, I will. I'll check my professional diary."

Mary beamed when she got off the phone. "Anne's keen. We can all meet next weekend. She wants us to have lunch at the Travellers Club near the bottom of the Champs Elysées on Sunday. If we arrive in time on Friday, we can have dinner with her at another club, the Interallié."

"Good heavens!"

"What's up?"

"She's inviting us to two of the best clubs in Paris!"

"That's generous. She really is a genuine friend."

"That's for sure. She says there's a wonderful concert in Notre Dame on Saturday afternoon. There'll be an orchestra, the great organ, the cathedral choir, the Notre Dame children's choir, and a visiting choir from an English school, famous for its music and boys singing treble. Anne says these free concerts are usually crowded, but this one will be packed. We can go in a shorter queue for those who have tickets. We pay what we can afford to the people who take the collection. She'll get tickets for us all." Mary looked through her work diary again. The weekend was certainly clear, but anything could happen.

"That's a real opportunity. Those concerts are quite special. If you want to go as much as I do, why not call her back and ask her to get us two tickets?"

Mary did just that. She also invited Anne to dine with them on the Saturday after the concert, but Anne had to see a publisher for dinner that day. He was interested in the book she was researching and wanted to discuss it with her. When Mary got off the phone, she told Paul she'd try to be finished at the surgery in time to take an early afternoon train on Friday.

***

Harry waited below a lock-up garage behind a mansion near the Bois de Boulogne. When the dark grey van appeared, the garage door rose and locked in its horizontal position. The van lost no time entering. The door descended and locked automatically behind it.

Bright lights turned on. The Iraqi sat in the van as the floor descended to a lower level slowly and steadily, the mechanism shirring slightly.

When it stopped, the Iraqi jumped down from the van and shook hands with Harry. They were in an extensive underground warehouse. Metal racks were loaded with crates and cardboard boxes. A man wearing a royal-blue baseball cap backwards and a dark-blue tracksuit was driving a little forklift among the shelving units. He kept stopping for parcels that sometimes needed the driver and a helper in similar clothing, red rather than blue, to lift them. The man in red also had a clipboard. Each parcel or box loaded was marked on a paper list. The Iraqi and Harry both noted one each, but they used iPads.

"That's it then," Harry said when the van was loaded with parcels. "When does he want it?"

"In a couple of days. What's his target? Any intel on that?"

"No. He's a professional and a goddam cunning one at that. But at least we have an idea of how many gunmen there will be. Where does he want it delivered?"

"No idea yet. I'll let you know."

"Great. But when you deliver, make sure you have a driver following you. When you get the money, walk to your car, which should pull up beside the van, ready for a quick getaway. Hand him the keys to the van. Tell him he can check the merchandise, and if it's all there and just what he ordered, he can give you a thumbs-up, and you'll be on your way. Tell him if he needs more, he can contact you again in the same way."

"Yeah. I'll be careful. I'll have two men in the car with me besides the driver."

"Well, my friend, good luck. If you find out anything about the target let me know pronto."

"You bet." The Iraqi climbed back into the van. Soon he was driving carefully back to his garage near Avenue Mozart.

Harry assumed that Bruno would unleash terror in some spectacular way. He was pleased with the precautions he had taken for the operation.

**

Control looked at Miranda across his desk. He loved her blond hair, now cut in an expensive style, quite short with small flame-like curved tendrils around her forehead and ears. She wore a silver-grey tracksuit as if she had just come from the gym. In fact, she had. She had received a call from Harry to meet him in the street. They had met. Now Control had to know the latest developments before she got back to her workout. Control preferred not to hear from Harry directly unless there was an emergency. This kept the two allies more secure. Both could rely on Miranda, and both could deny all knowledge of what the other was up to.

"I can tell by your charming smile, Miranda, that something intriguing is on our menu."

"Harry says his contact has arranged to deliver to Bruno in two days' time, that large quantity of Semtex, the fuses, the guns, and the ammunition."

"Where will he deliver the material?"

"He doesn't yet know. As soon as the delivery man knows, he'll inform Harry, and Harry will inform me."

"Good. Let's hope Bruno doesn't kill the delivery man, or we may never know where the delivery takes place. There could be a rendezvous and then a change of plan of a treacherous sort."

"Harry says his delivery man is extremely careful."

Control went to his safe and took out a small device. He warned her it was lethal and then showed her how it worked. She might need it to kill someone who would try to kill her. She nodded. "Thanks, I hope I don't have to use it."

"Good. I'll need you to return it after this operation is over. Well, back to the treadmill and the punching bag, Miranda."

After she had gone, Control pondered the dangers of the situation. Bruno's commando or team, as the Brits would call it, would be a total of six or maybe seven, including Bruno. Therefore, the plan would be fairly simple but would deliver a maximum of deaths and injuries. The amount of explosive suggested the destruction of a large building. Five or six men carrying large amounts of explosives and armed with Kalashnikovs would not be practical. Control thought Bruno would get entry to somewhere crowded and then explode the vehicle. Porte de Versailles? The exhibition hall full of visitors on a weekend? Men, women, children. *Keep calm. Anger gets in the way. Clarity.*

A light gleamed. Another visitor.

The door opened, and in walked Kim. Control leapt to his feet.

"I need you," he almost shouted, hugging her. She held him close. *Oh my god, she's so lovely. Did you send her to me just at this moment for a purpose?*

He took her hand and led her to an antique chair: it was a Louis Quinze. Genuine.

"So, what brought you back so soon?"

"Hervé, I realized I was missing you, and Paris and France."

"In that order I hope?"

"Yes." She stood up and kissed him on the lips. He responded. But both knew that they could not go further there. They needed another place, another time.

"There's a crisis, Kim. I need you before you go on leave again."

She sat on her antique chair as before, sitting up straight. "I'm listening."

"Bruno escaped, but the implanted tracking device faded. We are now in contact with him through an intermediary. Our American friends have arranged to sell him arms and Semtex. He's planning an operation, and he has little time. We think he has a commando of six or seven at the most, himself included. He takes delivery of his material tomorrow. His attack will be launched soon after. Perhaps as soon as Saturday or Sunday."

"So, that means we know what material he needs. How do we stop him from using it? Arrests as soon as it's handed over or later? Will Bruno's attack be this coming Saturday or the following week?"

"I think it wise to anticipate this coming weekend as problematic."

"Problematic? But surely you'll arrest him as soon as he takes the delivery of arms from our dealer."

Control looked worried. He cleared his throat. "If we arrest him and his men, who might not all be with him at the handover of weapons, he and maybe one or two recruits will eventually go to trial. That will be messy for us and for the government. There are circumstances I can't reveal. You know what the press can make of security forces."

"Oh yes." Kim frowned. "But once he has weapons, innocents will be killed. Semtex!"

"We shall kill Bruno and his men before they can kill anyone. He must be eliminated. A treason trial would be a nightmare."

Kim looked at Control. How could he be certain of their killing Bruno and his fanatics? How could he be certain that the public would be safe?

"So, you know his plan? You know where he'll strike?"

Control looked down at his desk and start sharpening a pencil. "In effect, no. Unless we have hard facts and we can at least make an educated guess, we just have to find him, follow him, let him prepare to attack, then rush onto the scene and take these terrorists out." Control looked up. He was certainly uncomfortable though not shamefaced.

"Hervé," Kim said, frowning, "that will definitely mean many civilian deaths. He wants to kill as many as possible. It's too risky. I think I know what you're planning or have already planned with our Yankee chums'"

"And what is that?"

"You tell me!"

"You know I'm sworn to secrecy. But can you think of the kind of target Bruno may have in mind?"

"We should consider his career and his special training. He's a notorious knife man. In fact, yes, I remember, he did some water training in the Seine once with me."

"And he has done explosives training. Hence the Semtex. He's an arrogant bastard, if you'll excuse my English."

Silence. Her boss was thinking. Kim smiled. The "old" Control was in his element again, and she was enjoying his company.

"I want to join you in Planning," she said.

"You are already, my angel. That's what we're doing. Haven't you noticed?" They'd had such an exchange before, but it didn't matter. Kim felt good despite the danger.

"What big occasions are scheduled for the weekend?" she asked. "Do you have an *Officiel des Spectacles?*"

"Of course. All good men should have one at hand." Control took the latest *Officiel* out of his top drawer and gave it to her.

"Forget about cinemas," she observed, "there are not big enough audiences. Bruno will want spectacle. He wants the biggest splash of blood he can manage."

"Plays? Ballet? Opera?"

"Given his arrest some time ago, I think he'll avoid those."

"I agree, my wonder woman. What about big trade fairs? Will he hit the Porte de Versailles? Any big concerts anywhere?"

"I think I had better work out in the gym. I can think things through. Shall I get back to you directly if I have a brainwave?"

"Off you go then. But get back to me, brainwave or not. Oh, and take this device." He went to the safe, took out the lethal object, like the one Miranda had now, and explained what it could do. He told her it might save her life.

65

MARY had been lucky: there were no sudden emergencies, no broken limbs, and no aged patients succumbing to summer flu. She and Paul reached the Gare du Nord dead on time. They went straight to his place on the Left Bank to dump their bags and spruce up for the evening with Anne. They took a taxi to the Interallié near the British embassy. But when they got to the rue du Faubourg St. Honoré, the fashionable street was choked with traffic. They didn't want to sit in the cab and be late, so they stopped the driver, paid, and walked a hundred yards to the club's entrance, passing the stationary vehicles pumping noxious fumes into the air.

The club receptionist after some formalities showed them into a beautiful reception room where sofas and chairs awaited visitors. Intricate chandeliers sparkled as if they had just been sprayed with starlight. Enormous vases crafted a century or more ago contained spectacularly elegant flower arrangements. In the room an elderly man reading a magazine. Paul noticed his dark-blue suit was of superior cloth and cut. In his lapel was a slender bit of ribbon, a medal of some sort, perhaps the *Légion d'Honneur*.

Suddenly, there was Anne. She came down the few steps into the room and embraced Mary. Paul kissed Anne on both cheeks, but she managed to make it three rather than two kisses.

"It's lovely to see you again so soon!" Anne exclaimed.

"Yes, it was lucky we could get away. We're really looking forward to the concert too. You look so elegant!" Mary replied.

"Anne, you're ravissante," Paul added.

Anne led them into the main entrance area and then up to the dining room. The friends had a window table with a splendid view of the garden behind the club building. Anne explained that meals were served on the terrace, but it could be rather noisy. People were out there already.

"Would that be from the traffic?" Mary asked.

"The traffic noise doesn't really get that far. I suppose the building screens us from that. No, chers amis, we get noises from the garden of the British residence from time to time. The ambassador has garden parties, and sometimes they have a jazz band. But it's all good fun."

The friends chose their meal from a menu that offered a good number of optionsfor each course. Paul thought the mushroom soup was a masterpiece. They all had the *blanquette de veau*, which was exceptionally good. Paul had never tasted better anywhere in Paris. This did not surprise him because his budget when he had lived in Paris was severely limited. All three resisted the temptations of the desserts, choosing instead the cheese from a sumptuous selection that included white Stilton and a tasty cheddar as well as an assortment of French cheeses made from cow, sheep, and goat milk and ranging from smelly to well-behaved and from soft and creamy to hard. Anne chose a light red wine for the veal and a stronger Burgundy for the cheeses.

After the meal they arranged to meet the next day at NotreDame twenty minutes before the two o'clock start. Anne warned them that the cathedral would be swarming with people. As ticket holders though, their seats were assured. All three were looking forward to being in the ancient building again and seeing the wonder of its stained glass. Anne told them that radicals during the French Revolution had vandalized the building, which had taken over a hundred years to build. The original work had been a collective effort of the citizens of Paris in the eleventh and twelfth centuries. But it was no use telling that to puritanical vandals.

"Not a bit," Paul added, thinking but not voicing his thoughts about what happened to much of England's heritage under Henry VIII, then Cromwell, then Hitler's blitzes on British cities. Such desecration had to be resisted whenever and wherever possible. He remembered reading Dalrymple's *From the Holy Mountain*. Perhaps he could do an article on the recent destruction of world heritage sites by Muslim extremists. He did not voice his thoughts because he was weary of discussions about the wreckage of modern values in a variety of countries. *The history of humankind is a sorry tale,* he thought.

BRUNO'S SECRET

✱✱✱

Bruno let an underling go out to the big van when it drew up not far from the new house. A solid-looking dark-red Peugeot saloon was parked in front of the van. The Iraqi got out of the van with another man who looked like a burly street fighter. The saloon had dark windows, but Bruno did not doubt there were armed bodyguards inside, ready to intervene if necessary. The Iraqi did not take chances. Bruno approved. He could do business with him in the future. He went out to shake hands with the arms dealer.

"You may keep the vehicle. All you asked for is in there."

"Grenades as well?"

"All. You may check. You have the money?"

Bruno nodded to one of his men, who held an attaché case. "My man will give you the money when we have checked the merchandise."

"Naturally. Let's get on with it," the Iraqi replied, taking a quick look around the street. The van driver took Bruno and his arms man into the van's back seat. Everything they wanted was there.

"Give our friend the money," Bruno ordered. His man gave the Iraqi the case.

"I'll need a five percent surcharge," the Iraqi announced.

Bruno had an instantaneous surge of anger so intense that he could not speak. His bodyguards stood silently, wondering what their boss would say. The Iraqi shrugged and gave the money back to the man who had produced it earlier. He looked at the van driver, who got back into the van. The Iraqi went to the Peugeot and got inside. Bruno yelled with rage. He strutted to the Peugeot. The driver's window came down about six inches.

"Everything's not in order? You can't pay my commission?" the Iraqi asked from the front passenger seat.

Bruno was edgy but ice cold. "Are you sure about the van? If we keep it, we'll save a bit of time. How much do you want for it?"

"It's a sweetener. Five per cent more please, and then we can both shake hands and say, 'to our next deal!' You'll be moving soon then? Interesting headlines in the press coming up?"

"Buy *Le Journal du Dimanche*," Bruno's money man said.

"The deal's off!" Bruno shouted.

"Well, au revoir, mon ami. Get the money." The car and the van left at a normal pace.

They are careful people, but they spring surprises, Bruno thought. What now?

He went to the money man and reprimanded him for mentioning the Sunday paper. Now they had to get arms elsewhere. Someone in the prayer rooms?

※※※

Harry was in the laboratory, where a technician located the van's trajectory.

"It's five minutes away from where you waved it on its way to Bruno. The deal's off, as planned."

Another technician handed Harry a paper that had a transcript from the voice recorder. "Thank God for old Dolby," Harry said.

"You betcha," the technician remarked over his shoulder as he walked back to his bank of instruments. Harry followed. A few remarks indicated that Bruno and his helpers were frantically seeking another dealer. The Iraqi had done a great job of sticking a micro device to the briefcase of cash. They were suddenly in touch with a laconic Arab who could supply all they wanted in four hours.

Someone had said it was a mistake. It could not be true. And it was cheaper than the Iraqi's price, even without the extra 5 percent. Bruno was jubilant.

"That man doesn't make errors. He's as careful as I am." *That's my Bruno,* Harry thought.

A phone on a secure line clicked on. There was no code name or call sign. Voice recognition indicated "Iraqi" on a screen near the phone.

"Watch out on Saturday." There was a second click, and the screen turned black again.

Harry had to warn Miranda and Control that the party was on Saturday. There was no time to lose.

66

KIM had showered and dressed. It was mid-afternoon. Her idea that had gone over and over inside her head as she exercised would not go away. She was with Control again.

"Well, what have you been mulling over?" he asked without courteous or mildly flirtatious preliminaries.

"I think they're going to destroy NotreDame."

"Hmm. How?"

"They have the guns and the explosives, some grenades as well."

"Hmm. They'd need a lot of time. How could they get into the cathedral for long enough to plant the Semtex in the best places for a demolition job?"

Control looked at his desk panel and pressed a button. "Miranda!" he exclaimed. "What's new?"

Kim looked up, saw Miranda enter, and the two women smiled at each other.

"My American tells me that the job will be tomorrow, Saturday. They aborted the deal, but Bruno has another source."

"Bruno isn't wasting time," Control said, looking very worried.

"Where?" Kim asked.

"Harry doesn't know," Miranda admitted. "But the American eavesdroppers have heard mention of the Twin Towers. Bruno was laughing about New York."

"Well," Control mused, "There's only one Eiffel Tower. Happily, the Montparnasse monstrosity has no twin."

"It's Notre Dame," Kim said with grim conviction.

"On Saturday afternoon there's a concert, and the cathedral will be packed. Kim's right," Miranda added.

"But how can they plant enough Semtex in there? Security is tight. They do thorough inspections. It can't be in there already."

"That's right. Their delivery was so recent," Miranda observed.

"They don't have to go inside. They can *go under*." As she said it, Kim looked distressed.

"They could just do that," Control said, tapping his pencil on the blotter again.

"You remember when Bruno and I were being 'water babies'?" Kim asked. "That training paid off in Birmingham."

"Since the Birmingham attempt, we have checks on all barges on the Seine approaching Paris or moored here," Control objected.

"There are two tunnels. The Roman excavations lead to the crypt. Gunmen could go in there and blast upwards. Masonry would fall and weaken the building under the twin towers of Notre Dame. Bruno and some others could take Semtex into a waterlogged tunnel that leads from the Seine to beneath the cathedral. Explosives could be placed there. The entire structure could fall in on itself, away from the exterior buttresses."

"Yes... You must be right... That's Bruno thinking, Kim. And it's tomorrow. When this is over, come in here, you two, and I'll take you to dine at La Tour d'Argent. There's only one!"

"We have to finish with Bruno and his men before we get treats!" Miranda shook a finger at him as she said it. They all laughed.

"Quite right!" Control said. "I think Bruno's attack will be near the beginning of the concert. This would put the maximum number of victims inside the cathedral."

"He's striking at the heart of Paris, an icon known throughout the world, a Christian focus for almost a thousand years!" Miranda added.

"Miranda, will you command a group in the Roman tunnel?"

"Of course. A vos ordres, Patron."

"Kim, will you command a group for a nasty game of, shall we say, 'water polo'?"

"Naturellement."

"So, Bruno will attack tomorrow afternoon during the concert, if Kim is right that the target is NotreDame de Paris. I want both teams in place with necessary firepower *inside the tunnels* before Bruno and his pirates attack. How you do it is up to you. Whatever equipment you need will be available within an hour of your demanding it. But *when* you go into the tunnels is my decision.

I want both teams inside the tunnels at about 4:00 a.m. and all quiet by 5:00 a.m. You'll have a long wait. Take a good book and some skeleton crossword puzzles. You might need a pillow or two!" Control permitted himself one of his brief smiles. "Questions?"

"What do we do if Kim is wrong and Bruno attacks somewhere else?" Miranda asked.

Control was ready for this eventuality. "We shall be in contact with special satellite phones. We shall tell you both if the attack starts somewhere else. We shall have helicopters or other vehicles ready to rush you and your teams to the trouble spot. We'll also have special hostage negotiators at the ready for all eventualities. Seconds lost may cost us innocent lives."

"Are our teams for tomorrow on alert?"

"Yes, as we speak, Kim. And equipment will be delivered where you want it and when. No problem. Anything else?" He looked from one to the other.

"I'm glad you see it my way," Kim said, adding, "We won't follow, then, but wait for them."

"Yes. But we'll have people on alert for any moves by Bruno and others. If they are sighted, they will be followed. If they have a different target, we shall try to follow and prevent mayhem."

Control was tense. But they really were a wonderful team. And it was not like work to think things out with such lovely young women. But when he sent them off into the danger zone, he always felt terrified. He would not be able to forgive himself if either were killed or horribly injured. *Kim, come back here and love me*, he thought as the door closed behind them.

67

JACK had a two-day blank in his business calendar. It turned out that Maggie could get away early afternoon on Saturday and would be free until the following Monday morning. They decided to take their first aerial "Black's tour" of Scotland. Poring over Jack's copy of *Black's Picturesque Tourist of Scotland* and using the Victorian map from its rear pocket together with a modern map of Scotland, they decided that with the time at their disposal they would fly across to Greenock, where they would stay on Saturday night. The next morning they would fly over the Grampians and along the Firth of Lorne to Oban. Then they would cut back to Stirling for Sunday night. Jack promised that with an early start on Monday morning, he could get Mary back to work on time.

"Are you quite sure, darling?"

"Of course. I'll get you anywhere on time, including the church."

"Well, just make sure of it," Maggie said, kissing his broad forehead. She was enjoying the little bit of power lovers have over each other.

"I'll make all the arrangements and file the flight plans. Don't worry."

"What if the weather is bad?"

"If it's really stormy with fierce gales, we'll cancel. We don't want to be caught in treacherous weather around the Grampians."

The weather turned out to be sunny, with a couple of showers by day and a little rain during the Sunday night in Stirling. There were no high winds. Their first aerial tour was a delight. The views of the west coast and the Grampians were stunningly beautiful with cloud shadows gliding over the land from time to time.

Flying over Greenock, Jack pointed out the enormous white anchor. "That's a memorial. During the war the Luftwaffe bombed Greenock with about three hundred aircraft. It was a naval base. But a free French ship had some bad luck and sank. That's why the anchor's large stem is made like the cross of Lorraine."

"It's still a lovely town after all that," Maggie said.

They liked everything they did together. Maggie loved the famous city of Oban, destination of many a tourist. The views over Mull and the Clyde from Jack's plane astonished Maggie, who was more used to Malaysian landscapes seen from the ground.

"I knew Scotland had spectacular beauty spots, but seeing them from the air is an extra thrill," Maggie remarked over their evening meal in Stirling. She was delighted by their walk through the heart of the old town. They thought it a good omen for their wedding. *Their wedding!* Maggie thought. They were both professionals and good at their respective callings. They weren't kids rushing into something that needed a lot of life experience. Maggie thought love was the basis, but marriage also required wisdom. She thought of her parents and smiled. She knew from experience that they were wise old birds in their own way.

68

THE sun had come out again over the milling crowds in the spacious area in front of Notre Dame. Anne was standing near the shorter queue of ticket holders waiting to go in for the concert. Paul and Mary spotted her and waved. She smiled and waved to them. As they met and exchanged *bisous* like old friends, Mary realized it had been a wise move to get tickets in advance, even for a free performance. It was probably a privilege for regular supporters of the cathedral and its many activities. The other queue was immense. How could all these people go through security checks at the door and find seats before the concert started?

Inside it was pleasantly warm, unlike some of the chilly, rather musty churches Paul and Mary had known in a number of English parishes. Mary was always impressed by the scale of the massive stone architecture, the number of side chapels, the wood carvings, and above all the sunlit glory of the stained glass. She was taking it all in again, even though she had wandered around before with Paul as a tourist. At the end of a row, Anne chatted withMary, who sat next to her. They both enjoyed the anticipation, the air of expectancy before the performance. There were rustlings of coats and the clacking of someone's shoes over the great stone slabs. People coughed from time to time, and there were echoing noises of distant doors closing.

Paul had no qualms about churches with richly decorated interiors. He realized the Puritans had wanted people to keep their eyes on the ball, so to speak, on God! He also speculated on the need some human beings had to be "holier than thou" in a multitude of politically correct ways. It seemed to Paul that thought control was unfortunately alive and well in democracies as well as autocracies and dictatorships. After many centuries of struggling to reach an adult level of free thought and speech, there were always "clampers" and "dampeners," as Paul called them, who preferred to think that their code, and their code only, was best for everyone else in the world, whatever their race or country.

His thoughts were broken by the sudden impact of the great organ playing a run of notes and an orchestra ahead of them tuning a variety of instruments. The tuning process reminded him of some "modern" musical experiments.

When the choirs in their different robes walked along the nave and then arranged themselves in their ranks behind the orchestra, there was loud applause and the hum of conversation. Many proud people in the audience had children or older family members in the choirs.

The choir members smiled and applauded along with the audience as the orchestra stood, and the conductor walked in. He wore slim black trousers and a silver-grey shirt that looked like silk. It had a collar like that of some Indian or Chinese tunics and full sleeves with tight cuffs about four inches long. Was he a musician or a magician? Paul reckoned that, as a conductor, he was both.

He faced the audience, all smiles, and bowed. The musicians sat down, some inspected their instruments or straightened the music sheets a little on their stands, and the conductor turned to face them. He raised his hands. There was silence. A cough echoed from somewhere in the audience. Silence. The conductor's arms and hands moved, and the music began as if it somehow issued from this one man's gestures. The result was certainly a kind of magic.

***

When Miranda and two men from the security forces entered the excavation tunnel with its Roman brick and stone work early that morning, Harry joined them. The security force people wanted to see his ID. He showed them, and they smiled and nodded. Miranda assured them she could vouch for Harry. They had to settle where they were going to be when the terrorists entered the premises. The public would not be allowed in. It made their job simpler.

Miranda took out what might have been an architectural drawing and spread it out on the remains of a Roman brick structure. They crowded around, shining their lights on it. According to the detailed plan, a door separated a tunnel of the excavated site from the crypt of Notre Dame. Harry suggested they explore the entire site before deciding where to position themselves. They all agreed. This was a "recce" they were all trained to do. All were equipped with strong lights. Harry worked with Miranda, blinking frequently as he looked around.

As they neared the door to the crypt, Miranda stopped and alerted the two specialists from the Special Forces.

"Look!" She pointed. On top of a Roman column and near the vaulted roof was a sandy-coloured "stone." One man linked his hands together, so the other could get a step up.

"It's a lump of Semtex," the Special Forces man said.

"So, they've been here even before us to prepare," his companion replied.

"They could still be here," Miranda added in a whisper. "Is there a fuse?"

The Special Forces man shook his head. Negative.

"I think we proceed," Harry whispered. "We haven't heard anything to suggest they're here."

Miranda nodded. "We continue, guns ready."

Harry stole alongside Miranda, blinking. Now they were all looking for another bomb. They found four more crucial placings of Semtex but no terrorists. There was no Semtex anywhere near the opening into an area of the crypt. *What did it mean?* Miranda wondered. She looked at her plan again and marked on it where Semtex had been placed.

"Someone knew what was what with explosives," one Special Forces man said. The other grinned and nodded.

Bruno did this, Miranda thought.

"When they come back, probably during the concert, all they have to do is plant the fuses and leave," Harry remarked.

Miranda used her secure line to Control:

"We're in a rabbit hole."

"So, what's hopping there?"

"Marauders expected. A hare on the loose was here and left before we arrived."

"That hare won't be there. Prepare!"

He didn't waste words and rhymed into the bargain, Miranda thought, smiling. So, had Bruno been caught? They would find out soon enough.

"Why is the door to the crypt not plastered with explosives?" Harry asked. He went on to answer his own question. "They're going to open it when they get here today. They have a method of entry. Someone inside the crypt?"

"One of us must stay here, and if the door opens, nab the person who does it," Miranda said. "They'll plant more Semtex and fuses inside the crypt, timed to go off with all the other fuses. If they had gone in there earlier as well, someone going to the crypt could have discovered it all this morning. They'll come back soon. The plaza and the cathedral will all come tumbling down if we don't get these devils first." Everyone else agreed.

"Okay. Let's get into position between the entrance and the first place they planted the explosive," Miranda said as she started to move. It was an order.

"Shall I cover the door to the crypt?" Harry asked.

"Affirmative," Miranda said. They had to wait and relax until the concert was ready to start. That would be when the pirates arrived. Control had arranged that a notice outside would inform the public that on Friday and over the weekend there was no admittance because another archaeological survey would be starting the following Monday. That way a firefight with terrorists would not involve civilian casualties.

"Lights out and wait. Act as agreed." Miranda's voice echoed along the tunnel, followed by silence.

69

MIRANDA alerted her team that the concert was about to begin. The door opened with a clatter. Afternoon light, along with the noises of the crowds in the square and the nearby traffic, flooded in. Silhouetted against the daylight was a bulky figure pushing a wheelchair. Three other bulky forms followed. They closed the door behind them and switched on the lights.

From her hiding place, Miranda saw that the wheelchair seemed to have a pile of blankets in it. A pair of hands threw the top blanket aside. Beneath it was a sizeable quantity of plastic explosive. Hands lifted it in portions to give to three other people.

"Here are fuses."

"Now!" Miranda shouted. Harry and the two Special Forces men, all wearing balaclavas, leaped out of hiding, weapons at the ready. Miranda was alone. Harry was ready at the crypt door and did not move. The man with the wheelchair pushed it at Miranda, who was down in the main passageway.

"They're reaching for suicide buttons!" Harry shouted. Rapid gunfire felled all four with wounds to the head. The man who had led them in was flat on his back. He moaned slightly. Miranda rolled him onto his stomach and tied his hands with a couple of zap straps. Miranda and the Special Forces men checked the other three for signs of life. All three were dead.

"Crypt?" Miranda queried.

"Not a sound," Harry said.

"Well, perhaps this one will live to be interrogated," Miranda said.

"Or maybe he'll croak on the way to hospital," one Special Forces soldiers said to the other.

"Four bunnies down," Miranda said into her phone. "One might stew."

"Another miracle," Control replied. "Notre Dame has had two today as well as a concert."

***

Kim and her team were well prepared when they got themselves as comfortable as they could manage in the ice-cold waterway leading from the Seine to the base of Notre Dame. A medieval stone ledge outside the small but solid door led into the building. Kim and two agents known to her only as Nemo and Loti prepared for their long wait by putting upright an old door brought to their ledge to protect them. Small holes had been drilled in it, so they could spot any intruders approaching their position along the waterway from the Seine. Kim looked at her military-grade Rolex Oyster. It was 05:30. They were ready.

None of them knew what to expect, except that swimmers or a crowded inflatable dinghy would approach in the darkness. It might have a powerful light. If so, the door would be exposed but not the three agents behind it or the powerful light they could switch on to dazzle the marauders. Kim guessed that Bruno and his men might tow all the explosive material behind them in another dinghy. Their guns and hand grenades would probably be at hand in their boat. If they were trying to demolish the cathedral during the concert, they would have to arrive at about 1:30 p.m., should they risk arriving during the day. But Bruno was careful. Kim figured he and his team might arrive at any time in the early morning and wait before going through the door to plant Semtex and sow mayhem. He would break down the door, place his explosives, stun any stray priests down below, and set the Semtex to explode with the other batch in the Roman excavation tunnel during the concert. She told Nemo and Loti that there could be action any time or after 13:00.

"Good," Nemo said. "Then we can get the bastards and debrief."

"Then it's hot chocolate and croissants for me!" Loti remarked with a grin.

They got into their black wetsuits without further comment. Each had anautomatic machine pistol athand on the ledge as well as two spearguns each. Kim said they would use goggles, flippers, and oxygen only if needed. She had already briefed Nemo and Loti about Bruno, who always came up with the unexpected and was also an expert knife man.

"Try to get him before he's within arms' reach," she reminded them. "He's tall and thin. Too thin. He's a snake."

"Venomous, by the sound of it," Nemo said, chuckling.

"Well, we're a welcoming committee he won't be expecting," Kim said in a low voice. "Okay, guys, now we listen. Only necessary whispers."

They had been shown a photograph of Bruno that Kim had courtesy of Control. None of them knew that Bruno now had a beard. Kim passed them the photo again.

At 13:05 a splashing noise came along the tunnel from the Seine. A light flashed briefly in the dark and then lit up the tunnel near the river. The splashing got louder. The "welcoming committee" could see nothing but the light. They had to hold fire and wait, trigger fingers itchy.

Kim tapped each man. In the light coming around their door they saw her make an "A" sign. Plan A was to collapse the door by pushing it down in front of them. They would use spear guns to sink the boats, if they were inflatables, and they would shoot to kill the terrorists, who might be wearing explosive vests.

The light was bright. Someone spoke an Arabic name. A boat was right up to the ledge. Kim nodded and switched on their own lamp and crouched while her two men pushed the door down. There was a yell from the boat and a huge splash. Man overboard! Another was moaning beneath the door. The lamp on the lead boat was out. Kim saw a second boat with a hooded figure sitting in it. Both boats were inflatable. She shot and pierced the second boat containing the hooded man, who had to be Bruno. He was sitting while grasping something. A crossbow! Kim flattened herself, her pistol at the ready.

Loti crouched to fire his spear into the leading inflatable. He gasped suddenly and fell. A metal bolt from Bruno's crossbow had gone straight through his chest, its serrated point protruding to the right of his spine.

As Loti coughed blood, Bruno reloaded the crossbow. But his inflatable boat was sinking. His roar of frustration and anger echoed around the tunnel.

Nemo shot at Bruno with his speargun. Kim heard the sudden whoosh of the spear, and Bruno screamed as it tore through his right shoulder near the collarbone. The tunnel echoed with pain and frustration. The water lapped calmly near the ledge where Kim was still invisible to Bruno.

"We'll get you all!" Bruno shouted, still defiant. He groaned but didn't try to remove the spear.

Kim saw the man under the door move to get away from it. He was wearing an explosive vest. His head emerged at the side of the door. Kim squeezed off three quick shots, blowing his head apart. The man in the water was floundering around. Nemo turned to Kim.

"I'll take the man overboard," he whispered. "He might be a suicide guy."

Both slipped into the water. The floundering man was suddenly still. As Kim struck out for Bruno's sinking craft, she was armed only with a diver's knife strapped to the wetsuit and Control's lethal device secured on the inside of her left wrist. She had to reach Bruno, who was trying to go backwards in the boat, which was filling with water. The crossbow was too difficult for him to use because of his shoulder.

Bruno saw a dark shape swimming toward him. *That's Kim*, he thought, *if it's now, then so beit.*

He grabbed a knife with his right hand, yelling with pain. He bit his lip and took the knife in his left hand. In the light spreading over the murky water, he saw her about three yards away. He set the knife down and threw the crossbow at her head. Then he picked up his knife again.

Kim swung to one side, and the crossbow missed her by a few inches. She pushed the collapsing inflatable boat, heavy with water, to one side of the tunnel. *Why?*

Bruno lunged at her, his left arm swinging, and the knife sliced toward Kim's neck. But she was gone.

Under the boat, Kim slit the bottom of the dinghy with her commando knife. She surfaced behind Bruno, who was clambering into the water, and got an arm around his throat.

Lethal thigh strike, Bruno thought and swung his left hand down, but her legs were thrashing under water, and she hardly felt the steel cutting her wetsuit to reach her thigh. She was intent on the kill.

She clapped her left wrist with its lethal device against Bruno's neck and was rewarded with the cracking sound of breaking bone. Blood spouted from his neck, and his head lolled in the water, attached to his body only by skin.

Nemo approached with a wet, unconscious, prisoner in the boat. He had expertly disabled the young fool's suicide vest, even though it was thoroughly soaked. He hoped the wounded terrorist would live long enough for questioning in an interrogation room.

"Let's get these corpses cleared away, Kim."

"Oh, poor Loti. I never expected Bruno to use a crossbow."

"Well, how could we know what he would do?"

"Did you get Control?"

"Yes. Like you he thought they might attack early. Miranda is reporting all's well at the Roman tunnel."

"I bet the people attacking the other tunnel arrived hoping to find it full of tourists," Kim remarked.

"Agreed. Well. . . Debrief. Hey, your thigh's bleeding! Tourniquet." They went back to their landing. It was another half hour before they were brought back. At the base. Kim was sent straight to the infirmary and dosed up with antibiotics. She asked them for hot chocolate.

***

Control walked into the infirmary. Kim had been lucky. The cut was through her skin and the edge of a muscle but not the major blood vessel that Bruno had tried to sever. She was stitched and dosed on painkiller through a drip.

Control approached her bed. She smiled at him and raised her arm. He took her hand in his, then leaned over and kissed her forehead. "You've been in the wars, but thank God you're back here and safe." He squeezed her hand.

"Kiss my lips, Hervé," she said in a low voice, not quite a whisper. Their lips met.

"He had a crossbow. I. . . poor Loti."

"You couldn't have anticipated that. Nobody could."

"Bruno's dead. Your little device saved my life."

"Yes, my one love, my Kim. Oh, yes, he was too dangerous to bring in again. A trial would have . . . been exploited by their propagandists. You did well. You had to defend yourself. Remember, he was the best knife man we've had."

"How's Miranda?"

"It seems she did well. She and her crew are coming in. The pirates were late or early. It's not yet clear. We'll get all that in the debriefing room."

"Help me sit up!"

Control did as he was told.

"Now hold me, hold me close," she said.

Once again, Control obeyed. Kim could not stop her tears. Hervé wanted to marry her. His eyes were dry. He was still "operational." There were things he still had to do.

70

"**WHAT** a magnificent concert! Thanks so much for thinking of bringing us here, Anne."

"You're welcome. It's lovely to share things like this with friends." Anne linked arms with Mary outside the cathedral as they walked along with the rest of the crowd filtering outside. It was still daylight, and it seemed bright after the interior of Notre Dame.

"Shall we walk along the Seine?" Paul asked. They all agreed.

"Pity the Roman ruins are closed for more work by the experts. You could have visited them now or tomorrow," Anne remarked as they gazed at the river, flowing as it had done for so many centuries around the island that was now a tourist hub.

"I'd love to see those, Paul. You did promise me. Well, we'll be back!" Mary said.

As they walked along the river, a breeze blew her sari, making it suddenly cling to her and yet billow a little at the skirt. She was lovely, professional, and knowledgeable. And she was his wife. Paul realized again how much he loved her.

"There's a fascinating exhibition across the river, near Jussieu," Anne said. "I might be able to take it in before I leave for the south. It's at the Institut du Monde Arabe."

"Pity I don't have time for it. I have to be back for Monday surgery," Mary commented. "You might be able to get to it, Paul."

"True. Depends on how the work goes. If I do get to see it, I'll bring you a catalogue. When does it end, Anne? Do you know?"

"I think it runs to the beginning of September."

"How about stopping for a drink together before we go our separate ways?" Paul suggested.

"I mustn't," Anne said."I have to be alert when I meet my publisher."

"Your name isn't Dylan Thomas then?" Paul asked.

"No, it isn't," Anne replied, "but I'll imitate Nana when we're in the Travellers for lunch tomorrow. In fact, I have to leave you now. Here's a taxi." She waved it down."See you at 12:30?"They waved as she left.

"Let's walk for a while along the Seine," Mary said. It was a mild, sunny Saturday afternoon with evening approaching. The sky promised a lovely sunset, and when it was darker, the Eiffel Tower would sparkle like a giant firework on the hour.

They decided to have dinner in a brasserie with a view of Eiffel's masterpiece and ensure they would be watching it at 10:00p.m. *Life is good for young professional people in love, enjoying a good relationship, and able to enjoy the numerous cultural events the civilized world has to offer*, Mary thought. She laughed silently at herself and her goody-goody middle-class guidebook thoughts. Then she thought that she wanted children, despite the horrors reported on TV and in the newspapers.

"How many children do you want?" Paul asked.

"Why do you ask that out of the blue?"

"I don't know," he replied."It just popped into my head."

"Well, I was thinking of it myself. But not in terms of numbers. Do you have any ideas on that?"

"Not really. Let's go back and spruce ourselves up and then wander out into Saint-Germain des Prés. We can haggle over the number of children in a little place I know over on that side of the river but with a good view of the tower."

"Do you mean your usual, near the apartment?"

"How did you guess? You must have read my mind. No, in fact I know a place where we can watch the tower scintillate," he said. They kissed before strolling on, hand in hand.

***

Kim had been debriefed and had a painkiller-induced siesta. Miranda also completed her debriefing. *More like "degriefing,"* she thought. She had also attended the interrogation of the survivor of the raid on the tunnels leading to the crypt of Notre Dame. The young man had been knocked unconscious by a bullet whizzing across his scalp. He was bandaged and awake but had a relentless headache. With the Lion and his three hares out of the equation, Bruno, now a thoroughly dead hare, had recruited rapidly from a number of willing youths. The only one still alive was indignant that his suicide belt had not worked, even though he had activated it.

"Oh, these things happen," his interrogator said, smiling. "While you are in prison, you can try writing an epic poem called "Paradise Delayed.""

"What were the hand grenades for?" Miranda asked.

"If anyone tried to follow us in, we'd have rolled one or two outside."

"Where was Bruno before you received instructions for this suicide mission?" the interrogator asked.

"Don't know. He said he had business elsewhere. It was suicide as a last resort. We planned to plant the explosives and then row away."

"Really? What business did Bruno have? Girls? Recruiting? Travelling to the Middle East?"

"Don't know. Asking leaders to tell more than you need to know isn't a good idea." The young man was sweating. He kept wiping his forehead with the back of one hand. He winced from time to time.

"No freedom of information or human rights for you people, eh? Until you're caught, that is."

"I asked for a lawyer."

"Oh, he'll be here soon after the regulation waiting period, I should think. Do you have French nationality as well as Algerian?"

"Yes. I want my civil rights."

"Oh, of course. Our president has said we are at war with you terrorists. He's taken a leaf out of Bush's book!"

"So, get me a lawyer."

"And you are a traitor to the French Republic. During the First and Second World Wars, traitors were executed. But we in the West live in more enlightened times. You'll be tried here and imprisoned. I want you expelled from France, so you can go back to Algeria with your tail between your legs. They'll also arrest you for terrorism. But at least you'll be at home, whatever your sentence, and whatever your prison conditions. That'll be a comfort. Adieu."

The young man could control himself no longer. He wept, full of self-pity. He was not really a "hard man."

※※※

Control was with Kim, who looked refreshed, and Miranda, who appeared dogtired.

"Cognac? Coca-Cola? Grapefruit Pellegrino?"

The two women shook their heads.

"What about our special dinner with you?" Kim asked.

"I'm really looking forward to it," Miranda added.

"Good. We have a table for four next Wednesday."

"That was miraculously quick," Miranda said, full of admiration for Control's ability to pull strings. "I hear the Tour d'Argent often has a six-week waiting list, even though it's lost a star or even two."

"Longer to wait for a reservation in tourist season," Kim said. "But Control can work miracles, even with the Japanese booking everything in sight."

"Especially when I have you two at my side," Hervé replied, laughing.

"But who is guest number four? Not an expert on terrorism?" Miranda inquired with an inquisitive raising of one eyebrow. She stifled a yawn.

"You could say that. It's a friend of mine. You call him Harry."

Miranda was suddenly wide awake. She got up and took hold of Control's hands, kissing them both. "You wonderful, cunning, kind old fox."

"Thanks. But not so old—I'm a bit of a young teddy bear as well. Let's all go home. Don't forget, Wednesday at 7:30 p.m."

71

PAUL and Mary arrived at the bottom end of the Champs-Elysées by taxi. The Grand Palais and the Petit Palais with their exhibitions loomed above them to the left. Behind them to the right was the president's Elysée Palace. But they were looking at the magnificent wrought-iron and gilded railings curving around the corner. Then Paul stopped near a restaurant extending onto the sidewalk. A narrow driveway led alongside the restaurant to a mansion standing back discreetly from the road.

"Come on, we're here," Paul said, leading Mary down the pathway to the carpeted steps. Paul pushed open the front door, and they entered the club, some of whose members were spies or had been spies. Inside the hallway was a reception counter and a long rack for coats. Paul told the man at reception that they were guests of Anne de Crevennes.

"Yes, sir. Shall I take your coats?" Paul and Mary were wearing light raincoats. The man gave Paul a cloakroom ticket.

"Go to the bar, sir, around there. Madame la Marquise is expecting you."

Paul thanked him, and they went to find the bar.

"Anne!" Mary exclaimed. They kissed. Mary felt a real warmth between them. Already they were firm friends. Paul and Anne kissed on both cheeks.

Anne indicated a table and chairs. They all sat down. "I suggest we have a drink, an apero before lunch in the club."

Over their drinks and nibbles, they chatted about the Saturday concert in Notre Dame but then moved on quickly to hear Anne's comments on the history of the extraordinary mansion, dating from the mid nineteenth century.

"I usually drop in here when I'm in Paris," Anne said. "A few years ago, I attended a lively talk about the owner, La Païva. Michael Wilcox, I think the oldest extant member of the club at the time, gave us a tour and brought to life the epoch when Esther Lachmann, a fascinating and seductive woman of modest Polish origin, paid for the construction of the house. She had married a rich Portuguese nobleman, Païva. Hence, she became La Païva. Later she married a Prussian nobleman, also extremely rich. As you can imagine, Franco-Prussian relations being at the time 'tenuous,' they had to rush off to Silesia, where La Païva died. It's a real 'rags to riches' story of an ingenious courtesan."

"She certainly kept the richest and most lecherous men in the Parisian society of the day under her spell," Paul added, nodding vigorously.

"You seem to approve!" Mary exclaimed.

"Well, er, yes, in the context of her times, you know." They all laughed.

"Her bathtub had three taps," Anne said, winking at Mary. "What on earth would they be for, Paul?"

"Hot and cold water for the two anyway."

"And number three?" Anne prompted.

"Ass's milk?"

"I rather think so. But it could be changed at will to dispense champagne."

"Paul, I think we want a tub like that in Sutton Coldfield," Mary said.

"I've got one in Eden Roc," Anne added, laughing. "You must come to visit. I can offer goat's milk, but if you want champagne, you'll have to pay for it."

At lunch they chatted some more about La Païva and about her house with its yellow onyx staircase and wonderful ceiling. Afterwards, Anne showed them the silver bath with three taps.

"She also had a yellow onyx bath," Anne said.

As they were leaving, after a lunch of fennel soup, roast pork, and a baba au rhum, Mary said she was going to look up the house and its brilliant Polish courtesan on the Internet.

"That would be a good follow-up for the visit," Anne said. The doorman reminded Anne that she should sign them in. He gave her a pen and a large visitors' book.

"We'll keep in touch," Anne said afterwards.

Mary and Paul turned at the foot of the steps to wave. "Au revoir!" Paul said. Anne and Mary blew kisses.

✱✱✱

Jack had arranged to see Maggie at her place. He had been away for two days making short business flights for wealthy entrepreneurs. He found car trips easy enough after flying. He adapted smoothly from one mode of transport to the other but, like many statisticians, considered the roads more dangerous than the air. When he arrived, Maggie was preparing the table in front of her sofa for a light evening meal. On the kitchen counter was a letter written in Chinese characters. They hugged, and then Maggie went to the fridge.

"What'll you have to drink?"

"Thanks, Maggie love, a beer please."

"I've had a letter from back home," she remarked with a humorous twitch of her lips. "You can read it if you like."

"It'd take me ten years to master just half of those characters! What does it say?"

"My parents want me to marry in Singapore."

"What about your marrying a white man? Have they recovered yet?"

"Just about. They'll be welcoming enough when they meet you. But they really wanted me to marry another Singapore Chinese."

"That narrows your choice. Don't they think about that?"

"They don't even realize their attitude is racist. They probably think of a white as a colonel drinking gin and tonic and calling Chinese waiters by snapping his fingers.'Chop chop' and so on. They would deny that and say it was just a matter of culture."

Jack looked at Maggie as if studying her face and her fleeting expression of worry."I expect they want you and a husband rooted in Singapore. It's prosperous. Taxes are reasonable rather than punitive. And they would be close to their grandchildren."

"That's about it, lover, but what do you think about having the wedding there?"

"Maggie, darling, we live here and have friends here. I'd prefer a wedding in Scotland. What about you?"

"Yes, I agree. Let's marry here. But I have an idea. Actually, it's what Lee Kwan Yew did. We could marry here and then go to Singapore and marry there. The Lee Kwan Yew solution! My parents would foot the bill, as is our custom."

"Two weddings? Why not? Let's have a simple wedding here for us and a few close friends and then fly to Singapore!"

"Good. We can marry over there, and that will give them some 'face.' They can decide on the scale of it. It can be a two-dress or a three- or four-dress wedding. So, I would start off in a white dress and then change dresses to other colours—red or yellow, for example. In any case, I know my dad will insist on a fourteen-course banquet."

"Including a wee haggis?"

"There's no such thing as a 'wee' haggis, Jack. I've been here long enough to know that! But you'll have to wear full Scottish dress. I'll get Dad and Mom to hire a piper. You'll have to practice your dancing, Scottish and ballroom."

"Oh, what have I let myself in for? Maggie, you're enjoying this, aren't you? A wee bit?"

"Actually, I'm warming to it. But the real wedding for us will be here with our friends, especially Mary and Paul."

"Agreed. I'll get my best man up to speed. He's a commercial pilot too, but he works for British Airways. That's why you haven't met him yet."

"You mean Joe Fraser?"

"That's the guy. I'm sure you'll like him. He hasn't been around much since we became... an item, as they say. Long-haul flights to New Zealand."

"Perhaps we can juggle our wedding date a bit, so he can be there."

"Yep. After all, he's got to be there. I'll call or email him and give him a choice of dates."

"Good. I think I'll have a glass of wine. You? Oh, a beer? Let's fix a date or two or three before you contact him."

72

CONTROL was in a morgue near the canal at the Bastille, where many a corpse hauled out of the Seine or the canal were brought. An attendant and a doctor showed Control into the cold, sterile, functional room. Bruno's corpse was on a gurney and covered by a green sheet. The attendant pulled back the sheet to reveal the head. Control was a little surprised by the calm repose of Bruno's face. He saw the livid mark and torn flesh that signalled a broken neck. He wondered suddenly what he would do if the eyes suddenly opened. Then he got a grip on himself.

What evil had possessed this man, who had at first done excellent work for the Republic? It was certainly evil. The thought of Westlake's agonizing death made Control shiver, despite a career that had forged his iron nerve. And how many others had Bruno killed? How many discontented youths had he recruited? How many had he seduced into the murderous work of trying to deny history and social progress? Yes, regression was always at work. Bruno had come to embody it.

They had learned some of Bruno's secrets, penetrated his mystery to some extent. Mystery or enigma. Why prefer evil to good, murder to harmony, war to peace? Was evil simply the drive toward power over others? Absolute power? History taught that "absolute power corrupts absolutely," but Bruno's mystery, meaning *métier* or trade, what had that been?

Control looked at the face again. Bruno's trade had been torture using knives. Yes, that was Bruno's brand of evil. There was no devil—just human evil. That was our condition at its lowest level. It was Bruno's only trademark. And he had stabbed Kim.

"Yes, that was my man," Control said, feeling suddenly older than his years, and then he left. He could not fully understand Bruno. That twisted,

Janus-faced being, with its unfathomable core, was the last intimate secret. No interrogation or psychotherapy could reveal it.

***

Kim's thigh was healing well. She was back in her apartment, though still limping slightly. The stitches would soon be snipped and removed, but she would have a fairly long scar. She was irritated that Bruno had managed to wound her and noticed the irony that Bruno had also stabbed Brian, a harmless artist and teacher, in the leg, just as he had stabbed her. Bruno had been well trained in the death cut to the major artery in the thigh. He had been jealous of Brian's friendship with her and so had to hurt him slightly to show her that she would never be free of the danger he could impose. They had sparred in the gym, worked out together, been on special courses together from time to time. But there had always been something silently sinister about him. She had once thought it was simply an effect of his unusual appearance. Now she realized that perhaps she had sensed his duplicity without any firm evidence of it. His disgusting plans for her death horrified her and then made her exhale with relief that she had finally killed him. She sighed and then shivered involuntarily. She felt no regret. It was an immense relief to have killed Bruno. After all, it was war.

Over the last few weeks, Bruno's treachery had been proven in bizarre ways. She was deeply glad to be alive and not gurgling her own life away, swallowing and choking on blood, the image of his deathly face grinning down at her—triumphant. *Thank God I got him before he got me.* Now she had to evade whoever it was who might be watching her, perhaps some new recruits following Bruno's last commands. It was possible, but unlikely, that a watcher or watchers did not know her face. They would almost certainly have been shown the indistinct press photograph. Bruno had loved mysteries and was as secretive as he was deadly. But he would surely have pointed her out in some way to his underlings. Kim was also secretive and dangerous, but she was careful too, so she decided she must change her hairstyle and her overall look.

When she left the apartment allocated to her as a government employee of her rank, she got on a bus that had stopped to take in passengers. When it moved away, only one person had mounted after her: a dumpy black woman carrying a shopping bag. Was she going home from an evening shift or going to a night shift? One could never be sure. The homeliest people could be effective agents.

After two stops Kim got off the bus. The woman did not follow. Kim moved along with a group of laughing young people, all wearing hats in the shape of rugby balls and speaking Italian. She went down into the metro station and took a train to Vincennes.

She re-emerged into the bustle of the streets. She was looking for a busy restaurant, of which there were many. She passed a few tables clustered near the door of one, went to the counter, and ordered a mixed salad followed by scampi in a light batter. The bartender nodded. A young woman, dressed like a maid from an Italian movie, led her to an interior table with a view of the door to the washrooms. Kim ordered a small bottle of Pellegrino to drink while waiting for her food.

She knew Control was as obsessed with his work as was her painter, Brian or Quint. But she could readily share Hervé's work; both had a scrupulous attention to detail. It was different from what life would be with Quint. She could work with her boss in Planning. Control was a man who knew the dirty devices of the world but had kept, she was sure, an integrity to do with being human, not a machine. She knew he loved her. She also knew he would want her in his, or her, bed, and as soon as possible. She admitted that she wanted *her Hervé* but as a husband, not as a casual lover. "Love, O love, O careless love." Yes. They would marry, and then they'd be together in Planning.

After her solitary meal, she walked to Saint-Mandé, where she had a modest apartment on rue du Parc. No man had ever visited her there. It had an oblong entry that led into a large salon. The salon looked onto a garden with a high wall. A patio was outside her sliding double-glazed and toughened window, so she could have a coffee and read outdoors at a small table. Rambling roses grew up the garden's main wall. In the centre of the lawn was a stone pedestal with a bowl and a small jet of water that climbed and fell in perpetual motion when she activated the pump. She liked the tinkle of water as she read or did a crossword puzzle.

From the salon a door led to a large bedroom with an en suite bathroom, the plumbing being modern Italian. Her queen size bed was covered by a spotless white duvet. An oblong chest sat at the foot of the bed, as long as the bed was wide. In it she kept pillows and another duvet. The room also had a dressing table with a stool. It was part of the built-in closet that hugged one wall. Along one side of the bed was a sliding window with access to the garden that surrounded the building.

The second bedroom was equipped with another queen-size bed, a dressing table and stool, and a large built-in closet along one wall. The window looked out onto a pathway with a line of rhododendrons on the far side.

Kim's kitchen was an almost perfect square, a sink with a window above it on one wall and the necessary appliances along the opposite wall. A small table with three chairs stoodnear a blank wall.

Kim poured herself a glass of Sancerre that was nicely but not too severely chilled. She turned on her TV. There was the usual grim news from Syria. The report was broken by a string of advertisements with images of laughing, friendly people enjoying great products in garden suburbs or streets in London, New York, and elsewhere. "Nice" people were everywhere with healthy children. Life seemed to be a fun-filled frolic. Then the screen displayed the ruined cities, jihadists waving weapons as they stood in the backs of trucks. Could she say, "Forgive them, Father, for they know not what they do"? *No*, she thought. *We and they know well what they are doing. We must preserve the decency of people's lives.*

Civilized societies with people living contented lives had come and gone, even if they knew little or nothing about other parts of the world. *We have to protect ourselves and our need to live unmolested.* What Control and his counterparts, like Solihull, and their officers were doing was *essential work*. Bruno was dead. Evil was not.

She turned off the television. She needed to rest. But her picture, "Hide on Hide" was there in a discreet frame that set off the vivacity of the picture. It should hang on the long wall in the bedroom. This was her hideaway, wasn't it? That settled it.

She took out her beautifully bound and illustrated copy of Rice's *Byzantine Painting: The Last Phase*. Byzantium, Constantinople, Istanbul. Change always happened, destruction or the simple decay of beauty. She wanted to marry her boss in early autumn, she decided.

Suddenly, a memory from her Cambridge days came to her, a scrap of verse from W. B. Yeats. "Autumn has come again/a leaf glides into the mud/on Nineveh's crown." Something like that. Yeats's haiku? The fall of civilizations in three lines. It was a comfort to her that scholars, working patiently over decades, could preserve what had almost been lost Yes, here it was: *The Golden Headed Angel of Novgorod*. Kim read for half an hour and then sank into sleep and temporary oblivion.

***

Control, Kim, Miranda, and Harry all arrived at La Tour d'Argent from different places at the agreed time. None had been followed! Kim, wearing a long shiny grey quilted coat and shod in dark-blue boots, had come by bus. Miranda, in a short black coat, and Harry in a dark-blue coat, had shared a taxi. Control had been dropped off from a beat-up Volvo. It did not look as if were equipped with armour plating and bulletproof glass. Its normal progress through the evening traffic gave no hint of the powerful Porsche engine specially fitted under the hood.

"Are we all here? Yes. Well, let's eat, drink, and be merry," Control proposed.

I can't argue with that, Harry thought.

They were ushered to a discreet table to the side, where they were not exposed to a window, though they still had a good view of Notre Dame and a safety-first view of the door. Before they sat, they all looked at the window that framed the ancient cathedral. The men held the chairs for the women to take their seats. Notre Dame was basking in the evening sunlight. It was the ancient icon of Paris. *It was still there.*

Control wore a light-grey suit with a Bordeaux-red handkerchief in the top pocket. Both men wore crisp white shirts with thin blue lines running from the collar down. There was no unsightly bulge to show that slim shoulder holsters were discreet nests for their pistols.

Miranda's blond hair was cut beautifully into an elfin cap with wisps curling around her forehead and temples. She wore a spectacular light-blue dress with wreaths of olive-green feathers at the hem. Her blue shoes had stiletto heels. In her blue clutch purse of the softest leather she carried a pen, which was a life saving asset. She had written death sentences with that pen when, out of dire necessity, she had no alternative.

Kim shed her quilted coat to reveal tight black trousers and a loose, baggy-sleeved blouse in silver-grey silk. It gave her the look of a Cossack dancer. Her ankle-length boots had short heels and a pattern made of silvery studs. In her silver leather evening bag was her mother's fan. It was loaded. Their true roles in the defence of freedom were not apparent to any onlookersor to any of the waiters. The latter were aware, however, that the Frenchman in the party was a VIP. The proof was the two beautiful women in the party! The American spoke good French, but any of the experienced waiters, used to American clients, could pick up a slight accent. He was American alright. The two women were a *garçon's* dream come true. The waiters were going to enjoy the evening.

The Frenchman ordered a bottle of Dom Perignon champagne for the *aperitif*. The waiters imagined that the tip (apart from the obligatory one) would be as lavish.

"Mes amis," Hervé said, "I propose a toast to a job so brilliantly done that even I am staggered." They all drank the toast. "To NotreDame, our beloved old woman of Paris," he continued before they all resumed their seats. They raised their glasses again.

"Mes amis," Harry said, "long live Miranda, long live Kim, and long live Hervé!" Harry raised his glass and drank, as did the others.

"Well," Hervé said, "I drink to you three musketeers!"

Miranda and Kim looked at each other. Then in unison they raised their glasses in unison. "We drink to the best men we've met in a long line of men!"

"Hey, you rehearsed that!" Harry accused.

Miranda shrugged. "I guess so."

"Not at all," Kim said.

Their meal was a fine example of French cuisine. Hervé suggested for their food glasses of wine whose qualities made a good match. Itwas truly worth the trouble, creating marriage of food and wine.

The evening passed quickly with a lot of humour as a necessary release after the tensions of the past few days. Through the window the view of NotreDame had changed. The sky had darkened, and now the building that was the heart of Paris stood bathed in light from its strategically placed lamps. *Yes, yes, she's still there*, Hervé thought.

There was a pause in the conversation as they all looked at the splendour of the old stones, the twin towers, the flying buttresses. "Kim," Hervé said without any preamble, "will you marry me?"

Nobody spoke. They all looked at Kim. She smiled,a radiance about her finely moulded features. "Yes, Hervé, yes, of course I will. I thought you'd never ask! It's a secure line I hope!" A burst of laughter erupted from the unlikely merrymakers.

Harry clapped his hands, and Miranda followed suit. Everyone was smiling. Harry raised his glass. "To a truly great couple."

"To a truly great couple," Miranda echoed.

"Thank you," Kim said, "you're invited to the wedding. Will you be there?"

"You bet," Harry said. "We'll be there."

"How do you know I shall be free on the happy day?" Miranda asked.

"Because we're an item, remember?"

"Well . . ." Before she could say anything else, Harry popped the question.

"Miranda, princess, will you marry me?"

"Harry, you're really a poppet. How could I refuse? Of course I'll marry you."

"So," Kim said, "that's all settled then." Harry and Miranda held hands across the table.

"A minute, a minute," Hervé said. "What are the implications of this happy moment?"

"Are you going to lose Miranda to old Uncle Sam?" Harry asked rhetorically. "No, sir! I'm going to retire. Right here in gay Paris. How about that?"

"Miranda?" Kim looked at her across the table. "You're not applying to join the CIA or some other organization of which there is no public knowledge, are you?"

"Not now. Harry has seen the light. He knew he was really a European, didn't you?"

"Yes, ma'am."

"Will you sing for us, even in the rain, Harry?"

"I guess I will. I'll have to." They all laughed.

"What about these weddings?" Kim asked. "When?"

"How about September?" Miranda paused, looking from one to the other around the table. They all nodded, smiling.

"Darling Kim, will you be my bridesmaid?"

"Yes. That would be an honour. Will you be mine?"

"Absolutely, if we marry the same day. One in the morning, the other in the afternoon."

"It's settled then," Kim said.

"Date?" The women looking expectantly at the two men.

"You choose, Hervé," Harry said.

"All right. Second Saturday in September, InshaAllah!" Hervé said.

"God is willing," Harry said.

"MashaAllah!" Kim said.

"How do you know God has willed it, Kim?" Harry asked.

"Women know these things, Harry."

"They do." Miranda smiled and took hold of Kim's hand.

"Well, well, well. That's all settled then. Dessert? Pink champagne?"

"Thank you, Hervé," Harry replied. "We thought you'd never ask!"

They all laughed. Life was good. *Carpe diem*, Kim thought. She looked at the window. Notre Dame was bathed in light.

Harry glanced at the window, following Kim's eyes. He blinked. *There's light from below. Strange. There's a light, totally different, from above.* Harry pointed to the window and the others all looked.

"That light from above, what's that?" Harry asked.

"Moonlight," Miranda replied.

"You're right. It happens on a number of nights per year," Kim explained. "I think it's a good omen."

They all nodded and smiled. They didn't think of Kim as superstitious. She wasn't. She was optimistic.

73

KIM was shown into Miss Mason's office at Tomkyn Bridge School.

"Ah, Alissa, my dear, come in and sit down over here on my sofa. You're limping a little." Miss Mason watched her intently. "And you have something to tell me."

"I'll get straight to the point, Miss Mason. I can't come back to teach here in September. I shall have to resign my post. I'm sorry to disappoint you."

Miss Mason smiled. She had the summer to advertise. She could fill the post by mid-September. "You've been injured. Mountain climbing?"

"Water sports," Alissa replied.

"Is the limp permanent, like mine?"

"The physiotherapist says that if I continue the exercises, the muscles will readjust, and I should be walking normally again."

"That's a relief. But why this sudden decision to leave?"

"Actually, I'm getting married. To a Frenchman. I've known him for a few years."

"Wonderful. So, you'll be living there?"

"Yes. It's wonderful."

"I wish you all the happiness in the world." She looked out the window, tears in her eyes. She dabbed them with a tissue.

"You lost someone precious?"

"Yes. Years ago. Sometimes I feel he's still near me."

"Perhaps he is. We don't know everything."

Miss Mason smiled. "Quantum physics holds many more surprises, I think. But you must go and make the most of your marriage and life in France."

They stood up.

"Miss Mason, did you once do secret work for the government?"

There was a pause. The two women looked at each other. Miss Mason smiled. "I did. It was when I lost him. I was wounded differently. Twice. A bullet in the leg and a terrible loss in my heart. I've limped ever since, and my heart still aches. I work for the young now, and it helps." She smiled. "Come here." They hugged.

"Go on, Alissa. Go and get married! I think I can guess the work you'll be doing. The young need a better world. Go, with my blessings!"

Has she been keeping an eye on me for Solihull or someone? Kim had no answers for this question.

***

Kim could shed her Alissa Partridge role for the time being. She decided to go straight to the station. She did not want a clinging goodbye from Brian. He was best occupied painting and letting his agent make him successful. Kim believed in his talent enough to be confident of his eventual success. She wished him luck. Fame in the arts often depended on doses of good luck in addition to good work. She realized it was also true of her own line of work and many others. But what was luck?

From St. Bees she travelled to London to stay a night in the club before taking the train to Paris. She wanted to see Hervé as soon as she returned to Paris and ask if he might be free for a day or two in Avignon. They would be able to relax and discuss the wedding. She thought of that date in September. It would be the fourteenth. It would be fine and possibly quite hot in Paris as autumn approached.

In London she decided to join the club table for dinner. She had taken a glass of dry, cold *fino* sherry in the bar. When she went into the Coffee Room for dinner, only two other members were at the large oval table. One was an old man with a bald head fringed with sparse grey hair, similar to a monk's tonsure. The other man she knew as Solihull.

"May I join you?" Kim asked with her wonderful smile. She didn't realize it, but she had never looked so beautiful.

"Please do, my dear," the old member replied. "You are?"

"Alissa, Alissa Partridge. And you, sir?"

"Oh, call me Theo. Everybody else does."

"I'm Colonel Voysey," the fit-looking man said. "Do sit here. But you're limping."

The colonel, Kim thought of him still as Solihull, got up and held a chair for her beside him. She sat down and looked quickly around the room.

"Thank you, Colonel. An accident. Water sports. But it will be fine, according to my physiotherapist." She smiled again.

"Dashed water sports can be dangerous I'm told." He winked at her.

"Did you know," the older member asked, "that Sir Walter Raleigh landed in White Rock, British Columbia, and traded with the local tribe?"

"British Columbia is in Canada, isn't it? I mean, it's not some small portion of South America. Am I right?"

Alissa supressed a laugh and put her hand on Solihull's arm. "Absolutely right, Voysey. It's always gratifying to find that the ancient universities are still teaching you youngsters a thing or two."

"I've heard," Kim offered, "that British Columbia covers a land mass as big as Europe. Is it true?"

"Oh dear, yes. Absolutely. When I was young, I met Commander Campbell."

"Wasn't he on a radio program called 'The Brains Trust'?" Colonel Voysey asked.

"Yes, indeed. He told me that British Columbia's coast was a sailor's paradise."

"By all accounts it still is," the colonel said.

Alissa occupied herself with the obligatory paperwork for ordering her meal.

"Ah, the good old culinary clerking," Voysey remarked.

Theo regaled himself by sparking off several different topics for conversation, their links known only to himself. Kim admired Solihull's good humour. Their meal passed in this way accompanied by a bottle of club claret ordered and paid for by Solihull. Somehow, she couldn't think of him as Colonel Voysey. *Is that his real name?* she wondered.

Theo announced that he must toddle off to bed for an early night. He kissed Kim's hand before he left, his old eyes twinkling.

"So, we seem to meet fortuitously in London. Can we make a habit of it?" the colonel asked.

"Not the kind of habit you might wish for, mon colonel," Alissa said. "I'm one of the walking wounded, remember?"

Solihull sighed. "I'm rather taken with another French woman, so that's just as well."

"Aha. Did you meet her in the UK or in France?"

"In here, as a matter of fact."

"Intriguing. What does she do? Is she a spy?" They both laughed.

"In point of fact," Solihull said, "she spies on the past. She's an historian."

"What's her name?"

"I couldn't reveal that. But we keep in touch."

"You mean it might be indiscreet?" Kim laughed. "You English!"

74

IT was mid-September. Paul and Mary had arrived to attend Maggie's wedding. Samantha Gilmore and Greg had arrived from Vancouver, and neither seemed to be suffering overmuch from jetlag. Anne had also been invited. Jack's best man, Joe, had been a perfect and stalwart support for Jack and for Maggie.

Unknown to these civilian friends, on that same September day, Kim and Hervé and Miranda and Harry were married in the mayor's office of the second *arrondissement*. The mayor had insisted on marrying both couples on the same morning. The four of them had thus reserved a private room for a traditional champagne luncheon followed by dancing at Les Noces de Jeanette, an unpretentious restaurant not far from the Opéra-Comique. Their guests were a mixture of French and American friends. They started the festivities at 12:30 p.m. They had finished eating and were dancing to favourite music when a messenger arrived.

Hervé spoke to him. The messenger saluted and left. Control gathered Kim, Miranda, and Harry together while the music and dancing continued.

"There's been an explosion at a hospital in the UK. I've given the order for a highest alert on all people entering from the UK. It might already be too late. Or they might just lie low over there. One never knows."

"That's for sure," Harry remarked.

"We'll continue with our few days of honeymoon. Let's start now!" Control said.

"Damn right," Harry replied. "All's quiet here. But for how long? Actually, our boys say there's no suspicious babble just now!"

"Well, let's slip away and leave our guests to dance blissfully until the manageress closes the room to them!"

They slipped away and Hervé and Harry settled the bill between them.

The two newly married couples hugged and then went their different ways in chauffeur-driven cars.

***

"Oh my goodness," Mary said. "I have to go to Walsall straight away. A news flash on TV said there's been an attack on a Walsall hospital." She and Paul were with Anne, accompanied by Jack's best man, Joe. Jack and Maggie had already flown away for their honeymoon in France.

"I have a patient in there." Mary was already making for the elevator to go pack.

"Paul, find out from Mary the name and, if possible, the ward of her patient."

Following Joe's suggestion, Paul caught Mary before the lift arrived.

Joe was already on the phone. He had a connection to Walsall. "Mary! Here," he said as he handed her the phone, "ask if your patient is a casualty. Do you know the ward?"

Mary nodded gratefully. "Dr. Rao here. You have one of my patients. Here are the details . . ."

When she returned to the others, she sat down. "My patient's ward was not affected; he's fine. They attacked a different wing. Quite a number of children were killed though." Her eyes filled with tears. Anne put her arm around her. Paul held her hand. "I must get back," Mary said.

"I can get you all down there first thing tomorrow morning," Joe offered. "I'll fly you down."

"Really?" Anne queried.

"Yes. Piece of cake." And so it was.

***

The outrage merited headlines across the world in a huge number of countries. Leaders of some Muslim communities condemned the cowardly attack. The bereaved parents were left to their grief, but some spoke out on television and in the press. Two terrorists had been wearing suicide belts to add to the mayhem. One member of this "commando," as French news journalists called it, had been captured alive and was helping the police with their enquiries. A semi-detached house in a road off Soho Road had been cordoned off and searched. A rocket launcher and some other military equipment had been discovered there.

With help from Solihull, Momo had been working around the clock. He already had technicians working on the laptops and some mobile phones found in the house. Following his promotion, Momo had now become, ironically enough, Hockley and was involved in directing operations and analyzing and assessing transcripts when he thought it necessary for him to do so. He listened to recordings himself at times if he thought it wise. He figured that when listening he might detect a nuance or tone lost in the transcripts of a conversation. He also assisted with the interrogation of the captured man. More arrests would follow based on what had been found in the house.

Solihull had been summoned to London for top-level meetings. He decided to stay at the Oxford and Cambridge Club, as usual, for a couple of nights.

After an exhausting day, he was settled in the bar contemplating a goodly measure of a single-malt scotch. He was also remembering the largely unhelpful interrogation of the deluded young man arrested as he left the scene of the hospital bombing in Walsall. They had been able to identify the conspirators' favourite café. He supposed that might lead to further arrests. And then Anne entered the bar.

She looked around and saw him. He waved. Smiling, she approached his table. He jumped up. "Please join me, Anne. What are you going to drink?"

She kissed him on both cheeks. "A club champagne, please."

Moments later, he returned with her flute. "We must stop meeting like this, or the bartender will begin to talk."

"Don't worry, Colonel. I imagine this has already reached the Squash Bar and the Blomfield Room!" He liked her sense of humour. He had loved her that last time. Would it happen again? He felt a glow of contentment. This woman affected him like no other.

"Are you dining here tonight?" she asked.

"I was going to. Will you join me?"

"I'd be glad to. I'm going to France early tomorrow morning."

"What time are you leaving?"

"Before seven, I'm afraid." Anne shrugged. "I have to get down to my house by TGV the same day."

"Ah, the South of France?"

"Yes, Eden Roc. I've been in Scotland for a wedding, and now I have to get organized and back to work. Do you know Eden Roc?"

"Afraid not. I once went to the Bai des Anges. Rather touristy with traffic jams in the season, I expect."

Exactly. It's a nightmare at certain times."

"It's a lovely name though I remember thinking when I first heard of it."

"The entire area is packed with interest. When do you get leave? You could come down and stay for a while after this latest outrage has been sorted out. I have plenty of room."

"That's a wonderful idea. Thanks for the invitation." They looked steadily at each other. It was a moment from which there was no turning back, no shrugging it off. They knew they had a real depth of feeling for each other. Was it love? He supposed it was. They were not hungry for food but for each other. There was so little time.

Soon they were in bed together.

"I'm thinking of retiring instead of staying on in the service."

"What will you do then?" Anne asked, her head on his chest.

"I think I'll spend some time thinking about it. It would will be a new stage in my life. It needs requires careful thought."

"Yes, you're right. You should do something you enjoy. Why don't you come to stay with me while you think about it?"

"I'd love that, Anne. Are you sure? You are persistent."

She lay on her back. "Of course. I don't issue such invitations to all and sundry. Only special friends. And you are special."

He held her tight. Then she turned on her side. He realized she was asleep. He felt the sudden rightness of their relationship. It had happened so quickly, and yet it seemed as if they had always known each other. How was that possible? There was no answer except the knowledge that it *was* possible and that it was *right*.

Anne left him at 5:00a.m. to prepare for her long journey home. Before she left, she gave him her card with a cell phone number written by hand.

"I'll phone you," he said.

75

"**THAT** was almost a secret wedding," Maggie said.

"Aye. You were a perfect bride. And it was good to see those close friends." Maggie and Jack were lying in a king-size bed after making love.

"We could get lost in this bed," Maggie observed.

"But we'd certainly find ourselves again."

"It's funny that we'll go through an opposite kind of marriage soon in Singapore."

"Aye. We'll have to have another honeymoon as well."

"Of course. We have to get away from them as soon as we can, even if they are my family."

"And where do Singapore people go for honeymoons? Is there a favourite spot?"

"Not really. They're usually able to go almost anywhere. Nowadays, quite a lot of them, I've heard, go to resorts in China."

"How about Goa? Mary and Paul were thinking of that."

"Or we could simply come back here and resume what we're here for!"

"You're a witch, Maggie. I was thinking along those lines too."

***

Mary entered the dining room, where Paul was sitting at the table jotting down some ideas on a notepad.

"That was Samantha. Graham knew her before..."

"I remember. She and Greg are safely back home?"

"Yes, and guess what? She's thinking of bringing Greg to Europe this December. She thinks he should have a European Christmas with time in France and Germany as well as in London."

"Good idea. We could perhaps see them one day?"

"Well, why not? And Paul, my angel, I'm pregnant!"

"What? How do you know?"

"I'm a doctor, remember?"

"And I'm a nig-nog. Hey, I'll be a dad!"

"And I'll be a mom!"

He held her and kissed her. It felt so good. They would have their own family.

"How did it happen? Amazing!"

"Well, you ought to know that by now, darling!" Mary said, laughing.

As the sun went down, Paul drove them both (or the three of them) to Cannock Chase. He parked facing the setting sun.

"I think it's all this marriage business that did it. Jack and Maggie. Us. Maybe others all over the world. All this marriage business, that's it!"

"Well, it's certainly us wot did it, Paul. Give Maggie and Jack a chance. They're still on their honeymoon."

"What's that got to do with it? We haven't even had one yet!"

"Actually, I've been thinking, darling. Goa. I don't want to fly there in November. I think it best to be in Europe while I'm pregnant."

"I'm sure you're right. We can go somewhere easy, like Cornwall, the Channel Islands, or France for two weeks, if you can arrange it."

"That sounds good. I can get a lovely rest." Mary smiled.

She knows all about pregnancy without having had her own baby. Now she'll learn more. First-hand. Would they have more children? He was lost in the wonder of it all.

"Look, Paul! The sky!"

The sunset was a vast show of colour. Some wispy black clouds were giving way to colours. A poem, "Love at Dusk," hovered at the back of his mind: "We who know so little/though once we knew so much/discover wisdom/in love's lightest touch." Yes that was it.

Unknown to Paul and Mary, Jack and Maggie were also watching the setting sun. So was Anne as she sat in the garden at Eden Roc and spoke to her colonel, who had arrived on a three-day leave. They were holding hands.

"It's good you asked," Anne said, "but I want to remain unmarried. We can be together whenever we can arrange it. When you retire we can be together most of the time. We'll be constant lovers but not married."

Her colonel could but follow her orders. He smiled and nodded.

The sunset began to fade as it changed.

In other parts of France, Hervé Martin and Kim and Harry and Miranda were also watching the sunset. Both couples had glasses of chilled wine from Sancerre. It was a coincidence, but both couples knew their white wine.

All of them, with their different lives and beings, were astonished by the beauty of the darkening sky tinged with delicate pink and yellow.

"This is our only earth," Mary said. "We must preserve it; it's wonderful. The beauty of it all! Life, it's everywhere! Even on Cannock Chase!"

Paul took her hand in his and raised it to his lips. The colours were already changing, slipping away, letting night prevail for the few hours before a new day arrived, bringing surprises, hopes, and disasters.

One such disaster was a hostage-taking in the hotel where Harry and Miranda were staying.

About the Author

Andrew Parkin has worked as a butcher, a delivery boy on a bike, a Russian Linguist in the Royal Air Force and a teacher in schools and universities. He has lived in England, Scotland, Germany, France, Australia, Hong Kong, and Canada. Arriving in Canada in 1970 he became a Canadian citizen after almost four years of residence in Vancouver, BC. His published books are mainly about drama, though he has published nine books of his original poetry and a previous novel, Private Dancers or Responsible Women. This novel showed how female agents working for security forces respond to terrorist attacks.

Bruno's Secret tracks the fate of double agents such as the Cambridge Arabist Dr Westlake and Bruno himself. Andrew is now revising a third anti-terrorist novel to complete the trilogy.

CPSIA information can be obtained
at www.ICGtesting.com
Printed in the USA
BVHW081912020720
582423BV00006B/50/J